Position of Trust

A. M. GRAY

Copyright © 2014 A. M. Gray
All rights reserved.
ISBN: 1499755708
ISBN-13: 978-1499755701

DEDICATION

For Joanne, Georgia and Emily. You renew
my purpose every day.

And to my parents, who persevered with the
fidgety little boy who hated reading.

Acknowledgements:

Cover illustration by Ethan McLean
(ethanmclean@btinternet.com).
Origami rose design by Valerie Vann.

Thanks to Susan Feldstein of *The Feldstein Agency*
(susan@thefeldsteinagency.co.uk) for her judicious editing.

Thanks also to my own English teachers, Jack Dalzell, Prudence
Bates and Michael Andrews, whose enthusiasm for literature
proved infectious.

Disclaimer:

This is a work of fiction. All names, characters, places, and
incidents are either products of the author's imagination or are
used fictitiously. No reference to any real persons is intended or
should be inferred.

1

CONTENTS

Chapter One

Few things ruin the reputation of a distinguished grammar school quite like a sex scandal. But that was not the only malpractice at the time; it was just the one reported in the newspapers. Enough time has passed now for me to tell the rest of the truth – or my version of it.

When I first met Samuel J. Baxter I thought him a pompous fool. He had just been appointed the headmaster of Chancery Grammar in the summer of 1975 and I was one of four secretaries in the school's General Office. From the beginning, his attitude, as much as his lack of social grace, irritated me.

A personable man, with some measure of humility, would have introduced himself to the staff in his new place of work. The awkwardness of that repelled Mr Baxter. No doubt, it would have diminished the aura of authority he wished to generate. That would not do. Instead, he withdrew to his office and issued name badges to all administrative staff. We knew who he was, naturally. Now, he could discover who we were, without taxing introductions or having to remember our names. For two weeks we wore adhesive labels, written on in black felt-tip. One week before the beginning of the new term, we were promoted to plastic badges, engraved with name and function: 'Rose Maylie Administrative Assistant'.

The word 'secretary' was much too prosaic and offered too few opportunities for alliteration. Mr Baxter – as he was very fond of saying – had been an English teacher. 'Secretarial Skivvy' would have demonstrated his attitude accurately but 'Administrative Assistant' fulfilled Mr Baxter's sense of grandeur.

My first conversation with Mr Baxter ensured he would have no difficulty remembering my name. Two days before the beginning of the new academic year, he wafted into the General Office with the pomp of a high priest. His black, academic gown billowed around him. We, the office girls, were almost half-way through our lunch cycle. Dorothy Giles (Administrative Assistant) and I were on the late lunch rota and waiting for our colleagues to return. We expected to be relieved at any moment and were chatting about matters unrelated to our work.

After a moment, when his presence had not been acknowledged, Baxter's complexion darkened into a frown.

I could see him but I wanted to finish what I was saying first.

"And on top of that he cleared out the bank account," I said to Dorothy.

"Oh Lord, Rose, that's terrible," Dorothy said, a hand over her mouth in shock.

Baxter paused and affected a smile. This left the upper and lower parts of his face in contrast.

The headmaster had not chosen a good moment to be making his late introduction. Men were my least favourite mammal at that time. I only tolerated his intrusion as he knew no better.

His greeting was toned and measured perfectly; its clarity and articulation were balanced and weighed. He extended his hand to me. "I need this typed."

For a moment I had believed he would descend from his cloud to introduce himself – a courtesy three weeks overdue. At first, I had not seen the letter he offered. I thought he intended to shake hands. But Baxter could not communicate as though we were living on the same plane, let alone make physical contact. That would be unclean.

The handwritten letter he held may as well have been his dirty underwear. I am sure the disgust registered on my face.

I held his gaze for a moment and noticed his unfinished, lumpy brow and nose. He looked like a rugby player – one of those neckless types. I nodded, as if to concede, then looked past the headmaster, to Dorothy. "Dorothy, I believe the headmaster has his own *secretary.*"

Little Dorothy had remained frozen in shock from my last revelation, hand on mouth. At the mention of her name, her eyes widened in horror.

"This must go out before the last post," Baxter said to me. He reasserted his resolve by jolting the letter down a level, closer to my reach. His cloud swelled and darkened for the approaching storm.

4

I continued, regardless. "I believe, *Dorothy*, that the last post is three o'clock. A skilled secretary like Mrs Bedford, *the headmaster's secretary*, should have no trouble in typing a short letter and mailing it between the end of her lunch and last post."

Dorothy's eyelids peeled back to their limit. She froze, hoping to blend into the office background. Doubtless, she feared I would drag her into the career void towards which I was hurtling myself.

Baxter leaned forward, reading the badge pinned to my bosom. "Perhaps, *Mrs Maylie*, as I am headmaster here and responsible for the running of the school, I can best decide who should type my letter," he rumbled. "Especially in the absence of my personal secretary or the office manager."

Behind him, through the door, came Betty Trent (Administrative Assistant). Her return ended the early lunch shift. I confess to feeling some relief at seeing her. I could compose a dignified retreat without losing face.

Baxter's malevolent brows were more than a little imposing. I had the feeling of being swept into the funnel of a tornado. It was both terrifying and exhilarating. Betty's arrival would cushion my landing as I tumbled back to earth.

"And I do *not*," Baxter continued, "Need some impertinent secretary –"

"Administrative Assistant," I interrupted, indicating my badge.

"– to be deliberately awkward when I present her with a matter of urgency." A speck of saliva launched itself from his lower lip and was lost on my desk. The clouds around him foamed and thundered. It had begun to rain.

I lifted my coat and handbag from the wall peg behind me.

"Betty, if you get a minute, I trust you'll be able to type a short letter for the headmaster. Apparently it's urgent." I heard the insolence in my own voice and was shocked. I had always been such a tractable young woman but Baxter's attitude had stirred defiance in me.

Betty nodded slowly, assessing the situation. She paused at the door a moment before carefully sliding across the office to her desk, avoiding sudden movements. "I'd be glad to type it, Rose," she said and set a shopping bag down. "Just after I defuse this bomb."

Betty had a gift for making us laugh. She had provided us with hundreds of witticisms over the last few years. Frequently, we would find ourselves cackling into our mugs at break-time. When required, Betty took it upon herself to clear the air and free the office of the tensions that women, working together, inevitably generate.

This time, however, it did not work.

The storm god was outraged by my challenge to his mastery. Betty's quip was evidence that she had joined the rebellion. Her comment drew his baleful glare.

He strode three paces to her. With each of his steps she withered. Then, he snapped the letter down to her desktop and hammered it with his fist. "At once!" he growled and gusted from the office, crackling with malice.

In the airless silence left behind, we all stared at the letter on Betty's desk as if it were the ticking bomb of her joke.

After a long pause, Betty whispered, "Rose, what have you done?"

After another pause, I said, "I think I made my point." The defiance in my voice was betrayed by my shaking hands. I duly folded these across my chest.

"And your point is that you'd rather not be working here?" she said, "He doesn't strike me as the sort of man who considers other people's points, Rose."

"I don't care! I've had enough of men and their egos. I'm going out to lunch now. Dorothy, are you coming?"

Betty and I looked to Dorothy, still at her desk, in the same attitude of shock. She had been in that pose long enough to petrify in position.

Admittedly, Baxter had no idea of how ill-timed his interruption had been. I had been telling Dorothy the sorry progress of my failed marriage, when he had interrupted. My defiance did not spring from a distaste for our new headmaster. I was simply going through a misandric phase in response to Harry's betrayals. No man could have prospered in those conditions. Had Mahatma Gandhi, wearing only his nappy, kneeled in broken glass before me, I would have snarled at him too.

6

Before my husband had deserted me, I had been under the impression we were both trying to make our marriage work. It was hardly ever the case with Harry that he could just tell me something. His furtive nature meant I often had to find things out for myself. In his eyes, if I could not find something out for myself, I did not deserve to know it. And so, commonplace events would take on a new significance. A casual phone call to his place of work, Bardell and Spenlow Solicitors, was one such occurrence.

"Harry Maylie?" the receptionist's voice tilted with surprise. "Mr Maylie hasn't worked here for several months."

"There must be some mistake, my dear." I tried patronage and patience. "How long have *you* been working there? Are you new to the firm? Mr Maylie is one of the solicitors."

"I've been working here ten years and, I assure you, Mr Maylie is no longer a solicitor with this firm. Would you like to speak to Mr Spenlow? I believe he has taken on Mr Maylie's cases."

"Yes, that will do," I said.

"May I ask who is calling?"

"Mrs Rose Maylie. Harry's wife."

"Oh!" Awkward pause. "I'll put you through to Mr Spenlow right away."

At times of extreme pressure, I admit, I can be easily confused. Old Mr Spenlow was explaining with great sympathy why Harry had been fired.

"My dear, I know this must be difficult for you, but Harry was found to be taking inappropriate short-cuts to his work."

My mind had clouded over. Harry had been fired as a solicitor. Harry had been leaving the house in his usual routine for the last three months and had said nothing of this.

"These short-cuts were illegal," Mr Spenlow continued. "And, as much as we all liked Harry, the firm had to protect itself. We had to report him to The Law Society. In response, they disbarred him." Spenlow's voice creaked like the leather of old books. It had litigated harsh truth for over thirty-five years.

I could not fully understand. "Short-cuts? How could he have taken short-cuts? Harry always gets the train." Overwhelmed with shock, my brain had shut down.

7

Mr Spenlow deserved credit for his gentlemanly professionalism. After a short pause, he continued. "Mrs Maylie, I do apologise. I don't think I made myself clear. Harry had been taking short-cuts *in* his work – he was settling claims before they had gone to court. Several clients complained that they had not received proper compensation as a result of Harry's..." He searched for a euphemism.

"Laziness," I concluded for him.

"I was going to say 'expedience', but 'laziness' will do just fine."

The remainder of the conversation was padded with sympathetic platitudes.

After I had put the phone down, I sat in a crushed heap. I remained there, beside the phone, until Harry came home for dinner.

When I thought about it, Harry's life had been characterised by short-cuts. Rather than work at his cases and see them through to their rightful conclusions, he had disposed of them as soon as possible. The same could be said of his personal relationships. Rather than work at his marriage, when the newness had worn off, he would philander with younger women until he got bored or caught. When I became aware of these affairs, rather than start afresh with a new woman, and all the effort of breaking her in, he would return to me, wringing with remorse. Fool that I was, I had always taken him back – twice already, in only five years of marriage.

Fool that I was, I felt sorry for him, when he cried in my lap that evening. I made the excuses for him: he had been too ashamed to tell me the truth. He had done it to spare me the worry. The trouble was, I had always made excuses for Harry – to the point where he never had to make them himself. All he had to do was look sorry and I would churn with sympathy for him. It was easier than facing the truth.

While I consoled him, one question hung in the air. I tried, but I could not ignore it. "What have you been doing all day if you weren't at work, Harry?"

Then came his blinking panic.

Most of the time, Harry was an accomplished liar. His speciality was The Prefabricated Yarn. Given an appropriate time for composition, he could weave a convincing cover story like a master bard. When it came to specifics, he had a remarkable eye for detail. However, Harry's weak spot was The Spontaneous Excuse.

And so, my question caught him completely off guard. His face twitched like he had a ferret in his trousers.

"At the library," he blubbered, "Mostly – after the job centre, of course." He fumbled with the answer like a bar of soap. "I feel terrible for letting you down, Rose," he said, changing the topic. "I didn't know how to tell you. I'll get some kind of job. Anything."

He must have known it was one of his poorer performances, for then came the tears.

As I cradled his head in my lap I felt something was amiss. But, as I frequently did, I ignored my instinct and said nothing. A mist descend over my suspicions. The man I still loved, in spite of his flaws, had been afraid of disappointing me. He needed me to be supportive. He promised we would overcome this. He would do anything. He had said so.

If someone could lend me a time machine, I would travel back and slap myself.

Harry never did get round to finding another job – not while he was living with me, anyway. For three months I took an evening job as a waitress to meet the mortgage payments. Harry was always wringing his hands with regret but never lifting them to do any work. He considered it all beneath him. Drive a van? Beneath him. Work in the same restaurant as me? He had a law degree, after all, so that was beneath him too.

While I was working a fifty-eight hour week, Harry had plenty of time to plan his exit. Thankfully, his new girlfriend had a well-furnished apartment or I am sure he would have cleaned out our house as well as the bank account.

Over those last three months it had become increasingly apparent to me that there was some unspeakable impediment between Harry and me. I had thought it was his guilt at losing his job, or even his shame at having to be supported by his wife. No. How naïve of me not to know my man, even after five years. If Harry felt any concern, it was the fear of discovery.

I left work early that afternoon for some reason that is now irrelevant. Arriving home, I had driven in through the open gateway as usual. I was surprised to see a new sports car in our driveway. I parked behind it, blocking it in. My old, hatchback banger looked ridiculous by comparison to the sports car's sculpted lines.

I shuffled through mental images of Harry's friends. One of them was probably calling to show off his new car. The car was empty, so they had to be inside.

Then Harry emerged from the house, carrying two suitcases. He froze when he saw me. I am sure he soiled himself. Suddenly, I perceived with remarkable clarity: he was at his tricks again. But this time he was leaving.

He had borrowed the car from his tart to clear out his belongings. She had been prudent enough not to accompany him, at least, or he had fabricated a reason to do this alone. She may not even have been aware of my existence.

As I walked up my driveway, staring at Harry, I considered my options. Some women would have made a display, but I have never been one for histrionics. Nothing could be gained by crying, cursing or hammering the life out of him with a wheel brace.

He remained wide-eyed and frozen in place. In the time it took me to walk to the front door, I decided that my life would be better without him. I would hear no more lies and allow him no more access.

"Rose," he juddered.

"Give me your keys before you go."

"I'm not going. I'm taking some old clothes to the charity shop." He flushed and smiled tightly.

We both looked at the new sports car. It was a Mercedes of some sort. I reconsidered the wheel brace option for both Harry and the car. "If you want me to move my car so you can leave, give me your house keys – and the spares for my car." I was surprised by the resolve in my own voice.

"But Rose," he began.

"Now!"

He conceded and dropped a case to reach into his pocket.

I noted the suitcases. We had bought these for our honeymoon, and packed them with freshly laundered hopes. Now they were crammed with his filthy betrayals.

I took the keys and avoided his sulky look.

10

"Keep the cases. You may be needing them sooner than you think." With that as my Parthian shot, I returned to my car, reversed it out of the drive and let him go free.

Of course, after that, I fell apart in remarkable fashion.

Two days later, I received a bank statement indicating Harry had cleared our joint account. Thereafter, Baxter had confronted me. On him, I had affixed Harry's face.

My encounter with the headmaster had exhausted me, physically and emotionally. I dreaded work the next day and could think of a hundred reasons to call in sick. The new day was sure to bring more anguish with it, if not from Baxter, then from Harry.

Apart from that, I had serious financial concerns. My salary alone was insufficient to meet the mortgage payments. If I planned to continue eating, there was no option but to sell the house. While I was at it, I would divorce the bastard.

Chapter Two

The next morning, I could not turn my mind to work. Instead, I deformed four paper clips into a rough likeness of the Eiffel Tower. The typing and administration laid out before me would have been enough to occupy my mind, but laziness seemed more appropriate.

I suspected the office door would thunder open with Baxter wielding my letter of dismissal and P45. The headmaster would conclude the apocalypse that Harry had begun. Under this threat, it was much better that I recreate architectural feats in miniature.

My logic was flawless.

As I began work on the Golden Gate Bridge, Joan Spenser, the office manager, brought the kettle to the boil. With only seconds between them, the kettle clicked off and the 11:05 a.m. break-time bell rang.

Joan – or "Mother", as Betty called her – was a marvel. Over the years she had honed an intuition for kettle-craft. Someone less gifted might have used scientific methods to measure the necessary water for four mugs and timed it to the boil. Joan used maternal wisdom alone. The kettle would always precede the bell. For it to boil after the bell would be a waste of her girls' circle time.

I looked at the ceiling reflected in my coffee mug. In my self-absorption, I was late to notice Joan draw her seat unusually close to mine. She had been in the headmaster's office for the last half hour. Now she would tell me my fate.

"Our Mr Baxter was asking about you." Joan leaned in, speaking to me alone.

I had no response to that. I could only wait.

"'Does this woman have a history of insubordination?' he was asking." She frowned to capture the gravity of Baxter's words. "Of course, I spoke up for you." She patted me on the arm, and removed the rogue lint from my sleeve. "I hope you don't mind, but I had to tell him a little about what you've been through recently. I kept it to a minimum, mind." She looked through large windowed glasses, searching for my consent.

I had cried myself weak the previous night. In the morning, waking to a house full of emptiness, I promised to bury my grief

12

inside. Only pride dammed back the swelling waters. But, as Joan cooed to me, I knew they would lap over the edge, if my composure faltered.

I took a breath for steadiness.

"I have every faith in you, Joan," I said. "I know you wouldn't feed one of your girls to that wolf." My bottom lip quivered a little – the traitor.

Joan had noticed it.

"You're quite right." She bobbed in agreement, plumping her feathers. "One of *my* girls." She stroked my forearm as though I had a kitten up my sleeve.

This unexpected tenderness brought with it two flood warnings: the first, that I might dissolve in a puddle of tears; the other, that Joan's grooming would spill my coffee.

"I told him you were my best girl." She whispered this, and we both cast a quick look at Betty and Dorothy to ensure they had not heard this. They were gabbling away and oblivious to us. "You watch that one," she said. "He's a bully. You embarrassed him publicly. I'll bet he's waiting to get something on you. The whole time I was talking to him I knew – I could sense – that he was more concerned with his reputation than anything else. You damaged his reputation, you see. He's a proud man. Insecure too – as men of power can be. You watch out for him, pet. He's a wolf, all right." Joan returned my arm and sat back in her chair. She confirmed our alliance with a nod that shook the grey bun balanced on her head.

As long as Joan Spenser was running the office, she would do her best to limit my exposure to Baxter.

When I had served my first day in that office two years before, she had shown me every kindness – along with the switchboard, typewriters and copying machines peculiar to life in a school. After a week, my adoption into her family was made official when she presented me with my own mug and a place on the cake rota.

I had been a secretary in various accountants' offices for the previous ten years, but a school ran on an entirely different scheme. While I was more than competent at office administration, I knew as much about how a school office operated as I did about car maintenance.

13

To my eyes, the General Office looked like it was stuck in the 1940s. The desks were made in the old style, using as much of the tree as possible. They were built to defy the Hun and doubled as air-raid shelters. The clack of old typewriters rattled like gunfire. Heavy, drab curtains absorbed every sound exchanged between drab walls.

When I had started at the Grammar School, I was twenty-eight, married three years and a recent migrant to the town of Chancery. This was the fresh start Harry and I had needed, after fleeing his last infidelity.

Joan's thoughtfulness eased the transition for me. If I had ever wanted a second mother, Joan would have been it. She had three daughters of her own, not far from my own age, but she still had surplus compassion for "Her girls" at work. She was one of those few people who expected loved ones to take her for granted. For Joan, it was proof they relied on her.

A natural lull had occurred in Betty and Dorothy's conversation and they turned to us. "Cake?" Betty asked. "A special one for Rose. I baked it last night." She presented me with the opened tin.

Inside, eight slender, Swiss rolls were bundled together. Each one was wrapped in tan icing. From her mix, Betty had fashioned a clock face, two wires – red and blue – and the letters "TNT".

I understood the reference immediately but could only manage a smile.

The real laughter broke out when Betty offered me pliers instead of a cake knife.

"Very good, Betty," I said. Her kindness brought another flood warning. My look of gratitude told her it was appreciated, though.

"I'd thought of making it in the shape of a naked man," she quipped.

Joan sat up a little.

"And we all know where you'd make your first cut," Betty continued.

Dorothy gasped and covered her mouth.

"Elizabeth, behave," Joan said. Her grey bun almost dislodged itself, but she was pinching in a smile.

"Yes, Mother," Betty said, not sorry in the least.

14

Eventually, the conversation turned round to Dorothy. Betty was always nosing for truffles of gossip. She broadcast her own business freely and expected us to do the same. Dorothy, on the other hand, was extremely guarded about her personal affairs. I respected her privacy, but this secrecy only made Betty more determined. What information could be so sensitive that it had to remain confidential?

"Come on, Dorothy," Betty said, "Are you and William hooking up or not?"

"I'm not sure what you mean by 'hooking up', Betty." Dorothy's suppressed smile contradicted this. She was rarely the centre of attention.

The "William" in question belonged to the Physics Department but was on loan for evenings and weekends. William and Dorothy had arrived together in his car for Spring Concert and they had been seen together on other a few occasions outside school. Rumour even had it – among those who could be bothered – they had actually been holding hands. Fascinating.

Dorothy affected not to be thrilled by the attention she was now getting. She was a sliver of a girl: even approaching thirty, she looked so young that she would have had difficulty getting into a bar. Her little girl's body was undernourished to the point of fragility, and her skin was like rice paper. Neither had she overcome the girlish tendencies for secrecy, shyness and shock.

In spite of all this, she was being pursued by William Butler. Physically, he was her antithesis: bearish and potent. He had missed out on an international rugby career because of a problem with his knees, but he ruled over county matches like a barbarian king. Had he been inclined, he could have scooped Dorothy up in a knotty arm and run for the mountains. William and Dorothy could be an adequate match – if he could tolerate her ridiculous reserve. Eventually, a woman may emerge from the body of that famished child.

As fond as I was of Dorothy, I could feel only contempt for her at that moment. Her disapproval of Betty's question made me sneer. Dorothy had a promising relationship ahead of her, tracks disappearing into the distance. I had nothing.

"Are you a couple?", Betty said, biting into a stick of TNT.
"I think so."

"Does he think so?"

"As far as I know."

"Have you talked about it, then?"

"Yes, Betty, we have." Dorothy said, indicating the interrogation should end there.

"Did he ask you out first in school, or did you bump into him somewhere else?" Ignoring the tone of the previous reply, Betty made one last lunge for information.

Dorothy looked to me. It was a clear appeal for assistance. I paused a second or two, then interrupted. As it happened, the bell and I both came to her rescue.

"Betty, leave the poor girl alone. You'll be getting out the thumbscrews next."

"Umm", said Betty, biting another stick of cake. "I'll beat the soles of her feet."

"That's lovely cake, Betty. The rolls are so fluffy," Joan said and redirected the conversation to Betty's Advanced Patisserie evening classes.

The moment was lost. Dorothy mouthed her thanks as we withdrew to our desks. I felt no solidarity with her but I smiled anyway.

Very few had been trusted with the secret of Dorothy's first date with William Butler: her first date with any man, in fact. I was one of those chosen. With an exaggerated sense of its importance, Dorothy had emphasised the need for confidentiality. Secrets were important things that people wanted to know. To make something a secret, she thought, made it important. Important things happened only to special people. Such were the workings of her childish mind.

The truth was colourless. Sympathetic mutual friends – a married couple – had organised a blind date for Dorothy and William. How the pair had laughed when they recognised each other from school. The evening had begun with a meal at the couple's house and extended into a few bottles of wine. Dorothy confessed to me that she was "Slightly tiddly". I am sure this helped. William had drunk enough to confuse embarrassment with enjoyment. Since then, he had paid Dorothy a number of return visits.

The rest was a mystery, even to me. I was preoccupied with my own concerns and knew she would confide in me further only if it suited her.

It was not only in the General Office that Samuel J Baxter had been demonstrating his social grace. The new term was just a week old when my good friend, John Souseman, paid our office a visit. He had called to run worksheets on the Banda machine and lingered to discuss our new headmaster.

Although predominantly a Biologist, Dr John Souseman fashioned himself on Albert Einstein. John's features were not so bulbous – he had a beak for a nose and thin lips – but his mousy hair had been styled by high voltages. His students joked that he washed with formaldehyde, so yellow were his hands and face. His favourite chemicals were actually nicotine and single malt whisky. These were much better as preservatives, John said: they consumed his body but preserved his sanity.

John Souseman was one of two men, the other being my father, exempt from my vow of misandry. I always had kind words for him. He was a sensitive soul, hiding behind cynical humour. Once a promising young medical doctor, some mishap had led him into biology teaching. He agonised over being a bachelor at thirty-nine. Although his relaxed attitude to personal grooming did not help. But he was a thoughtful spirit – a crusty gentleman. We had adopted each other as siblings not long after I had started at Chancery Grammar.

When John started to relate his first personal encounter with Baxter, it was not difficult to predict the course of his narrative.

Baxter had been conducting a grand tour of all departments, loitering outside classrooms and eavesdropping on the proceedings within. This was rumoured to be part of his scheme to blacklist underachieving teachers. Stalinist purges would follow, driving out the undesirables. The rumour appeared to fit Baxter's character profile thus far. It had a ring of truth to it. That is why I had invented it. My faith in my own foresight was justified by John's first meeting with the headmaster.

Now John dragged a chair to my desk to tell me all about it. Very soon, the other girls joined his audience.

17

"Period four ended. My fifth form lads left – unnaturally quiet on their way out. It's usually a stampede. That told me someone big was out there." John nodded and acknowledged his growing audience. "I knew he was there, lurking in the corridor. I'd heard Baxter was doing his rounds."

"He's been patrolling like this every day," I added to the truth.

"Knew he'd get to me sooner or later." John shrugged. "I'm not worried. My results speak for themselves." He puffed out his chest and thumbed some nasal hair back inside. "In strolled Baxter. Closed the door when he came in. Always a bad sign." He nodded after each statement. "He drifted around the walls. Looked at work displays. But he wasn't there to see the classroom. He'd timed it carefully. Didn't come while I had class. Came during my free period." John paused for effect.

"He came during your smoke break, more like," Betty said.

John winked at her.

"I sat at my desk and waited. It was a power game to see who'd speak first. The one who's more uncomfortable gives in. Baxter was there at least three minutes before he spoke. Long time to wait. I did some marking. Really busting for a fag, though." John laughed.

"That must be a record: over forty minutes without one," Betty said.

John was a gifted mimic and reproduced Baxter's sonorous tone. "'This work is remarkably detailed. I'm glad to see you have the boys' work displayed. If there is one thing I learnt in my fifteen years of teaching, it is that excellence should be celebrated.'"

John spoke in his own voice again. "Profound! That wisdom has changed my life. Excellence should be celebrated! Didn't know that. I used to punish boys for being excellent." He shook his head. "Cleaners know more about teaching than that fool. It's as well he's out of the classroom."

"Did he ask to join your Einstein Society?" Betty said.

John wheezed with laughter.

"I need a good woman to look after me, Betty. Do you have any friends left?" he said.

"I don't dislike any woman that much. I'll send my gardener round, though – he can give you another trim."

18

Beside me, Joan's mouth drew tight.

"Anyway," John sniffed, "Baxter was pacing round. I was marking papers." He rubbed his hands together. "I could have gone to the store for a smoke. But he wouldn't have stood for that." John's eyes widened for emphasis. "I've done some research on him. Dave Handel – old pal of mine – works in St. Ethan's, Baxter's last school. Dave said Baxter's a self-righteous git. Complete teetotaller. Loves to be religious. Just for show," John said, looking to Joan. "Religion's fine by me. As long as you don't wear it like a suit. But, in my opinion, a man who doesn't drink will never fulfil his true potential "

Joan shook her head with exasperation and John continued.

"Dave's not a man to gossip. I asked, so he told me. Not one good word to say about Baxter. Called him a terrible bully." He looked round at us all. "I actually cleaned that up for you ladies."

Then he said to Betty, "I'll tell you the rest later."

Betty made a vulgar salute with an open pair of scissors.

John's digressions were unusually irritating for me. I wanted to shake the rest of the story out of him. "Keep going, John," I said.

"Baxter stood in front of my desk like a sergeant major." John tucked his thumbs behind soiled lapels. He spoke with his Baxter voice again. "'Mr Souseman, I see from these wall displays you are disobeying my order not to teach that *ridiculous* Theory of Evolution. We are trying to instil a Christian ethos in these boys. You must teach them the Christian truth.' I nearly laughed in his face," John said. "Told him – respectfully as I could – 'I don't do religious education, Mr Baxter. And I don't expect the R.E. Department to do my job. I won't lie to the boys. I'll tell them that Santa Claus and the tooth fairy don't exist either. That's the way I teach.' Baxter thought it over. Hard faced. Stared at me a *long* time. Neither of us looked away."

John checked we were all still listening and fought a smile that would ruin his mime.

"'We *do* have a dress code for the staff, Mr Souseman. It is to ensure a certain level of professionalism and decorum. We have to set an example to the boys, you know. As headmaster, it

19

is incumbent upon me to ensure that all staff comply with these regulations.'"

The girls in the office laughed at John's pantomime.

John held up a Baxter finger to rebuke us. "'You, Mr Souseman, are a mess. You smell like an ash tray and look like you slept in a hedge.'"

We roared with laughter and outrage. None knew whether to fully believe John.

His performance as Baxter continued. "'How can you expect the pupils to take you seriously and respect you as a man of learning if you look like a vagrant? You must make a concerted effort to clean yourself up, Mr Souseman. Your attire is both unprofessional and unseemly.'"

"Did he really say that?" Dorothy gasped.

"Exactly as I said," John nodded, "More or less."

For a moment, we were paralysed with disbelief.

"Even *I* think that was harsh," said Betty.

Dorothy looked concerned for John.

Joan tutted. Her grey bun disapproved.

When he had elicited enough sympathy, John continued.

"I didn't know what to say. Completely stunned. Then, I got shirty. 'Where're these regulations written?' I asked him. Baxter looked surprised. Like I'd told him to bugger off. He probably thought I'd back down when confronted."

"He doesn't know you," I said.

"It gave him something to think over. He took a step back when I challenged him. Stared angrily at me. The fool hadn't looked to see *if* we have a dress code." John looked round in appeal. "You'd think he'd have checked that."

I looked across at Betty. Her eyes rolled in amusement at John's dramatic turn.

"Baxter stepped up again. Put his fists on my desk. 'I assure you, Mr Souseman, the new staff dress code *will* be typed up by Mrs Bedford today. All staff *will* be issued with a Revised Staff Handbook by the end of the fortnight. You *will* be expected to comply with school policy just like everyone else.' Baxter shook with fury. His head nearly burst into flames. Then he stomped out."

John spread his hands in conclusion. "Dave Handel's right: Baxter's a bully."

20

Most of us nodded agreement.

Betty smirked across to me. "Bullying Baxter'd," she said.

John and I laughed. It was a quip worth repeating.

Dorothy sucked in a breath.

"Betty," Joan said, "I'll not have that language in here."

"Yes, mother."

When we had settled again, John continued. "If that git pushes me, I'll bring the Union down on him. I'll not be bullied. I'm not that scruffy."

Betty searched for my eye contact but I looked down.

Joan spoke up, "John, it would be a very different matter if you were a poor teacher. He shouldn't be making personal comments like that. That must have been very hurtful for you."

"Yes. Come to think of it." He commiserated with himself. "No shortage of poor teachers in this school. Can't control a class. Whose results are dismal. Not me. Baxter's got a thing for me. Definitely."

John looked like a boy crying to Mummy.

True to his word, Baxter had set Mrs Bedford to work. The Revised Staff Handbook was born by the end of the week. Before the days of capable photocopiers, such publications had to be shipped to a professional printer. The completed draft document, containing Baxter's amendments was sent to the General Office to be packaged and posted. By some inexplicable mischance, one of the pages – the one dealing with the new staff dress code – never made it to the printers.

Such were Mr Baxter's orders for haste, that the Revised Staff Handbook was delivered to each member of staff before it had been checked for errata. A delay would have spared him the public embarrassment of discovering that page six was faced by page nine. The missing sheet was never found.

We waited for Baxter's explosion, but it never came. He could prove nothing.

I would find out later that John Souseman represented everything Samuel Baxter detested. John was an excellent teacher and easily the most intelligent member of staff. His yearly exam results proved this beyond doubt. John's academic credentials did nothing to appease the headmaster, however. He could not

21

abide John because he was godless. Worse still, he was proud to be an atheist. An ignorant atheist could be evangelised, but John was a thinking atheist – the very worst kind. Ironically, John's fine academic pedigree made him more of a threat. Baxter's values as a martinet were also offended by John's smoking, drinking and dishevelled appearance.

John was a born teacher. He took all the school's vagrants and miscreants into his classes and infected them with his passion for biological science. He could turn an O-Level 'C' into an A-Level 'A' without fuss or fanfare. He joked with his pupils, cajoled or harassed them as required. A personality cult had stirred up around 'Souser', and the boys worshipped him. On a Thursday afternoon, the Science Club boys even wore wigs to look like him.

Baxter could never approve of a teacher who allowed himself to be laughed at.

While John was inspiring and intuitive, Baxter had always spoon-fed his pupils dead ideas in mechanical monotones. Their revenge was to call him 'Boring Baxter' behind his back – and he knew it.

Not long after his arrival, Mr Baxter declared his prowess to the Chancery Grammar heads of department. He told them he had routinely achieved all 'A' grades in his A-Level English classes. John ran this past Dave Handel, of St. Ethan's Grammar, who confirmed it. But Mr Handel's explanation illuminated what the headmaster had failed to mention. As head of department, Baxter had exercised his privilege. He garnered only the very best pupils for himself – those who could secure top grades without being taught at all. It was no marvel that his results were immaculate: he taught only a handful of the highest achievers.

As a teacher, Baxter had been a fraud. He took the best for himself and left his subordinates to sort the others out. This did not bode well for the future of Chancery Grammar School.

Chapter Three

"I'll go – as long as you don't think it's a date." John blew smoke out the biology store window.

I gasped in response to his comment.

After his long exhalation, he gave a cheeky grin. "Gotcha there," he said.

Indeed he had. For the last five minutes, I had worked up the courage to invite John for Sunday dinner with my parents that weekend. Traditionally, Harry had accompanied me, but I had invited John in his place. There were obvious issues that made this moment uncomfortable: I was recently single; John was pathologically single; we were long-standing friends, and I had just invited him to meet my parents. Before I clarified the point, John's joke had blown all the toxic complexity out the window.

I slapped him with a nearby Bunsen hose.

"Now that's sorted," he continued, "Don't let the word out. It'll ruin my chances of pulling this weekend. Local totty would be heartbroken to hear I've been scooped up. Prize catch like me." He sucked in the rest of his cigarette like a spaghetti string.

"Just tell them you're helping a friend through a rough patch," I said.

"It'll ruin my bad boy image." He shrugged.

"I'll pick you up at 4:30. Wear something smart – and clean."

It was John's turn to laugh, off guard. "I've something fits that description: Dad's old suit."

"Oh good. I've never seen you in a suit."

"He was nearly buried in it. Undertakers whipped it off him before they screwed the lid down. Almost fits me."

"John, you're a disgrace."

"If only his legs had been the same length."

I shook my head on my way to the door. "4:30. Smart and clean."

John lived in Grampton, a little village, four or five miles outside Chancery. In 1975 it was hardly more than a few short streets with a petrol station, post office and pub. But that was about to change, as a building contractor had recently purchased several acres of farmland, with planning permission for a major housing development. The local farmers considered The Cartwright's Inn to be their own social hub and the height of culture. Grampton was on the up.

John's semi-detached house had flaking paint, turning grey. Everything outside seemed to have a beard of moss on it, particularly his driveway. The lawn was similarly unkempt.

Just after 4:30 p.m., I rang the doorbell. John opened the door and stood back. With a sweep of his hand, he invited me to comment on his transformation. His hair was neatly creamed back and parted. It had also endured a trim. He looked like a Prohibition Era gangster. His suit, while old, was well turned. I could not help judging the symmetry of his trousers legs, but they were actually the same.

"John never told me that he had a younger, more handsome brother living with him. I am Rose. Delighted to meet you."

John bowed low. "The pleasure is all mine, Madam. John asked me to accompany you tonight – he has urgent business with some local totty."

This shared amusement was a cover. Our relationship had just taken an unfamiliar turn. I was still anxious my motives would not be misread: John was just a friend. Tonight would help us feel less alone, when we returned to our empty homes. But we would certainly be going home alone, I told myself.

At my parent's front door, I thanked John for the effort he had made.

"You deserve an effort – even if it's only me," he replied.

That touched me deeply. I considered giving him a kiss on the cheek. This impulse died when I noted a muesli of dandruff in the fold below his jacket collar. From instinct, my hand lifted to brush it away – as I had done for Harry a hundred times – but I winced at the idea of touching John's crumby skin flakes.

There and then, before the evening had really begun, I confirmed to myself that John and I could never be more than friends. Chemically, we were not compatible – no matter how funny or gallant he could be.

24

John noted my pause. "I presume you have a key?" he prompted.

My parents' dining room table had a modest diameter. This reflected my father's belief in the fellowship of family meals. He liked us to sit close together, within range of each other for better conversation.

When we were dating, Harry had been invited for Sunday dinner. While he could avoid it, Harry's cowardice spawned creative excuses every week. He did not like my father's direct manner of speaking and often referred to the appointment as 'The Sunday Inquisition'. Once we were married, Harry could no longer avoid The Inquisitor. Every Sunday, my father nailed Harry to a dining room chair with genial conversation. Harry perspired liberally.

His guilty conscience contributed to his anxiety. He never believed me that my parents were ignorant of his betrayals. Suspicion comes freely to those who are dishonest. He could not believe my promise of secrecy – especially when he had caused me so much hurt.

Actually, I had told my mother the truth about Harry. I also told her not to tell Father. No doubt, she had told him and warned him not to let on he knew. So there we sat, each Sunday evening, everyone knowing and affecting not to know.

John, on the other hand, found my father engaging. After all, John had no filthy secrets, no fear of a clumsily decanted word.

We sat opposite each other, between my parents. John discovered an early rapport with my father but did his best to include us in all his topics. When the men burrowed deep into social anthropology, however, Mother and I began to discuss the absolute necessity of new dining room curtains.

"Woman's objective, conscious or subconscious, is to catch a high status male with plenty of resources," John lectured my father. "Preferably one who will invest time and resources in their offspring. Clearly, Peter, better-looking females will find it easier to catch high ranking males."

"Naturally." Father made himself dizzy from nodding.

"Men look for females with genetic markers for child-bearing and nurturing: rounded hips, large breasts – "

25

Just then, Mother and I reached a natural lull in our discussion. The word "Breasts" resonated like a fart in a prayer meeting.

John rushed to conclude. " – and the like. That's why millionaires marry models, and road sweepers settle for ogres."

Father nodded and chewed down a smile. He scratched at his mouth slowly for cover.

The clock ticked.

"Would you like a little taste of brandy before your coffee, John?" my mother asked, gathering in our trifle bowls.

I began to manoeuvre the crockery in my mother's direction.

John looked awkward. "Yes please, June. And, if you don't mind, I'll just nip off to the loo."

After John had tiptoed out, Father smiled broadly. "I think it's for the breast," he said.

Mother twittered on her way into the kitchen. I snorted a laugh.

Father gave my hand a reassuring squeeze, while we listened to the kettle boil in the kitchen and the lavatory seat drop upstairs. His silences never alarmed me and I predicted his topic before he broached it.

"Which solicitors are you using?"

"Bardell and Spenlow."

My father laughed and patted my hand. "His old firm. Good choice. Maximum embarrassment and discomfort for the filthy sneak – presuming he turns up to the hearings, of course"

Mother brought in the good tea pot and a plate of fanned biscuits. She had heard Father's last comment. When she sat, she copied him and placed her hand over mine.

"How long must you be separated before you can divorce?" Father asked.

"Two years. That's presuming he does not want to contest it. It could take up to five in that case."

"A long wait to finally be rid of him. What about the money he took?"

"It's gone – probably spent."

"A small price to be rid of him. A man spends a month's salary on an engagement ring as a prologue to marriage. He probably figured he was owed it. "

26

"He figures he's owed anything he wants," Mother said.

The toilet flushed upstairs.

"Our money is yours," she continued. "Better you have it when you need it most. It'll be yours soon enough anyway." She slipped an envelope into my hand. "We want to help you through this, dear. You have enough to concern yourself, without worrying about money too."

I gave their hands a squeeze. My tears spilled out and Mother's soon followed. Father nodded.

We listened to the bathroom taps.

"John appears to be a good friend," he said.

I wondered whether he would ask the obvious question.

"You will need a good friend to get you through the briars," he said. "If a woman were ready to put in the effort, he could be domesticated to a tolerable degree." He paused. "I don't think it will be you, though." Father had always known me well.

"No, it won't be me," I said, and we heard John's tread on the stairs.

"Is there no human spirit in your belief system, John?" The Inquisitor began, handing John a brandy and ushering him into the living room. "If you don't mind, dear, John and I will retire to the lounge," he said to my mother as he went. "Leave the dishes and I'll help you with them later." It was a dutiful gesture, but my mother had never left dirty dishes sitting in thirty-five years of marriage.

"Rose doesn't mind helping. You two go and browbeat each other. We have things of our own to discuss."

We cleared the table together in silence.

I had the feeling this had all been prearranged.

Through the door I saw John lower himself into an armchair. "Sorry to disappoint you, Peter. I don't believe in the paranormal. Consciousness is simply electrical discharges in the brain."

Mother washed, I dried.

"You've lost weight, love. Have you not been feeding yourself properly?" she said.

"I needed to lose a bit anyway."

27

My figure had grown too matronly for my own tastes – Harry's too, evidently. Perhaps, it had been comfort eating. My bust would always be weighty but, recently, my other rolls had shrunk to modest lumps. Soon, they would smooth down and leave me trim, as I had been in my teens. Misery was whittling me a youthful figure. My body rallied to advertise its fertility before it was too late.

My most bitter complaint against Harry was he had left me no children. Men I could do without, and loneliness was only a state of mind. My womb was the real emptiness inside me.

"You can eat here as often as you like," Mother said.

"I know." Long pause. "It's hardly worth the effort to cook for one."

"Our door is always open. This is still your home."

"I know, Mum." I kissed her cheek.

Going back to live with my parents would have broken my heart. I was lonely in the house, but I would not surrender my independence.

"When all this divorce fuss is over, you can find a good man to keep you."

I let that hang, unanswered.

It was naïve to feel optimistic about future romantic prospects. I have always been shapely, but I am no beauty. Neither am I particularly charming. At thirty, I felt I had little to offer a suitor.

Harry must have understood the vulnerability of ordinary women.

For women, it is a depressing truth that the majority of us are unremarkable. This is our horrible secret. Most women do not have sufficient beauty, intellect, wealth or status to make them invincible. The same could be said for men, of course, but it does not haunt them the same way.

My generation, born just after the Second World War, had very different expectations of gender roles than those upheld today. Opportunities, particularly for women, were as limited as the selection of television channels. There were only three: spinster, wife or widow. At school, we learned typing – to earn a living, until we snagged our man – and Home Economics – for when we were housewives. Although I prospered at secondary school and achieved excellent A-Level results, no one ever mentioned that I should consider university. Think of the confusion it would have caused for a woman to be called a Bachelor of something.

Women are trained from infancy to be mothers and home-makers. We have gender programming toys to thank for that. Buy a little girl a plastic baby or a miniature kitchen and she will play at being mummy. Buy her a beautiful princess and she will dream of marrying a prince. Such girls grow into disappointed young women, wondering why they did not qualify for the dream. The kitchen and the prince they graduate to are often less stimulating than their plastic predecessors. But little girl's dreams linger inside every woman; dreams more fragile than a fairy's wings.

Harry would mine this simple truth until it caved in around him. Ordinary women are afraid of being ignored. Flattery makes them feel special. They will fall in love with a man who makes them feel special. Harry had reasoned that sex with multiple ordinary women was better than sex with only one woman.

No, I would not be replacing Harry with another man.

"Right, that's all done. Let's put a nice pot of tea on for the boys," Mother said.

As I drove him home, John dipped his cigarette through his opened window. I hated the smoke and even considered the chill blast of air preferable to it. To compensate, I turned the car heater up full.

When I pulled up outside his house, I kept the engine running.

"Good chat with your dad," John said. "Refreshing to find a theist open to other beliefs." He flicked his cigarette stub through the window gap. "And doesn't treat booze like the devil's phlegm." He nodded in agreement with himself. "My folks hated drink. Worse than murder."

"I didn't know your parents were Christian," I replied.

"More religious than Christian. Maybe that's why I turned out," he swept his hands down over himself.

"An alcoholic atheist?"

"Ouch." He sniffed the window. "Kick a guy when he's down."

29

My own upbringing had been Christian but lacking in dogma. My parents believed we are saved by grace alone. Other Christian families we knew found security in strict codes of conduct. I was encouraged to make moral judgements for myself. Our household was governed by reason. If it was not Biblically prohibited, if conscience gave it a pass, and no one would come to harm, then it was permissible.

Reason was given broader roots through my wider reading. My father especially encouraged this. I graduated quickly from nursery stories to adventures and the classics. In my father's library, nothing was off limits. To him, an idea was good only after it had been challenged, and so, he let me discover dangerous new ways of looking at the world. I tore through his fiction and histories, then complained that he had only boring stuff left to read. One morning, strictly from boredom, I dabbled with the ethics of Marcus Aurelius. From him, I learnt two things: that I preferred good storytelling to good argument, and that I was in desperate need of a library card.

Before it became a modern trend, my parents decided to be my best friends. This tactic ensured we were never alienated from one another. Some parents forbade their daughters to pierce their ears; Mother did mine as I squealed into the kitchen sink. Most of my friends were forbidden make-up or trendy hair styles; Mother experimented on me with various tints, dyes and highlights – she even discovered a permanent pink that required emergency professional attention.

And so the contract was formed: Christianity would not be an imposition. I would comply until I was old enough to decide for myself. When that day came, it was not a difficult decision. I wanted to live a good life, and I enjoyed the idea of a friendly, omnipotent God.

With a long inhalation, John wound up the car window and popped the handle. He opened the door a fraction. "Well Rose, thanks for a good night. Hope I didn't let you down."

"Not at all." I feared the silence and the inevitable awkwardness of our parting. "I'm sure you wore Dad down. Mum will take him shopping tomorrow, when his resistance is still low. He'll be all argued out. He'll just nod and say 'Yes, dear' for a few days. You'll probably see new curtains next time you're back – "

"I'd be honoured to do it again, sister."

With that, he squeezed my arm and got out of the car.

There had been no awkwardness. John had pronounced me his sister. He may have used the word deliberately. Tonight had answered that question for both of us.

That night in bed, however, it plagued me. Was I so unremarkable that even John Souseman did not find me attractive?

Chapter Four

That Monday, our first visitor to the office was Charlie Bakewell. He was always welcome and often called to speak to Joan. They had been close friends for many years. She was nine years older than Charlie and had overseen his early days as a Sunday School teacher. Recognising his enthusiasm for working with children, Joan had encouraged him to teach. He had originally intended to enter the ministry but, as a teacher, he took every opportunity to win young people for Christ.

Charlie was head of the Religious Education Department and founder of the school's Christian Union Society. The Bakewell family were highly regarded in local Christian circles. They had also produced an Anglican Bishop to keep Charlie company in the glow of holy ordinance.

Charlie had paid a price for his commitments, however. Still a bachelor at thirty-nine, Charlie lived at home with his mother. His time was dedicated to extending the family of God rather than extending his own.

After a brief word with Joan, Charlie waddled over to me. He parked his baggy body on the corner of my desk and crossed his legs, bracing a knee between meshed hands. It was not a particularly masculine posture. His numerous little bellies rolled together, forming terraces between his waist and chin. Enough jelly remained to lap over his belt.

He looked to the ceiling for words, while I lamented the stapler that had been absorbed into his splayed buttocks.

"Rose, my dear," Charlie said, like a grinning sponge-cake.

I made a mental note to swap staplers with Dorothy.

"Rose, my dear," he sighed, "We need a cook for the Christian Union camp next weekend." He waited for this to sink in. "Are you free?"

My first reaction was to lie, but Charlie was smiling down at me. That made him hard to refuse. He probably knew that I had little else to do with my weekends. My marital situation was common knowledge by then. It was not the first time Charlie had asked this favour. Once, I had abandoned Harry for a weekend to cook in a youth centre kitchen. Unfortunately, he had not starved in my absence. That had been almost two years ago.

Charlie smiled like he was gazing into a box of pastries. He radiated optimism. This weekend would have both icing and fresh cream.

"Charlie, my dear, you know I'm free. I don't even have a spinster's cat to look after." I conceded, "It may even beat watching television until it closes down."

"Of course it will." He bounced up and gave me a clumsy hug.

My stapler clattered to the floor.

"You'll be doing a great service for the Lord," Charlie said. "Besides, you won't be in the kitchen alone: Dorothy is coming too."

"Dorothy?" I leaned sideways, past Charlie. Dorothy, at her desk, feigned surprise.

"She recommended you when the other girl dropped out," he chuckled.

I leaned past him again. Dorothy smirked at her clever trick.

And so, that next weekend, I found myself ladling sustenance for fifty enthusiastic pilgrims. Boys and staff alike had their plates heaped high with the improbable positivity of Charlie Bakewell and the word of the Lord.

Our temporary residence was a faux castle. It was owned by a once wealthy family, who found themselves associated with the Christian Union Society at the same time they found themselves no longer wealthy. The grounds had become a National Trust forest park, converted, in various parts, to include a nature reserve, water sports centre and caravan site.

The castle shrugged off dark winds from atop its mound, while our coach juddered a winding path to its thick, old doors. The driveway was long and anchored by several oaks. The October gales had stripped them, but they endured, clutching their portions of earth and sky.

I sat at the front of the coach. It was actually a glorified bus, with impossibly hard, shiny bench seats to which no buttocks could adhere. Dorothy slipped around beside me. Charlie had briefly occupied the seat behind us. From the moment the coach left Chancery Grammar, he bounced around the aisle, conducting the boys through juvenile camp songs.

It was Friday evening and already dark. I could see myself and Dorothy reflected in the black windows. From every angle, I was miserable. My expectations of the weekend ahead could not even have filled the overnight case on my lap.

Dorothy prattled on, but I hardly listened. I concentrated on not being dislodged from my seat by the sideways pitching of the coach. Both my feet were braced for this purpose. This weekend would measure my endurance. The quivering lights of the castle drew near but were overwhelmed by the gathered gloom. Once we had lurched to a halt, the boys cascaded from the coach and into the orange light beyond the pitted doors. Their arrival brought fresh echoes to the grand halls and chambers. In their wake, they would leave many scuffs and stains on the hard-boiled floors and furnishings.

The boys stampeded to claim their beds, while Charlie directed Dorothy and me to garrison the kitchen. He did so without his usual toadying: his hectic schedule had begun.

All the necessary supplies were in the kitchen awaiting us. The room was long, sided with generous work surfaces. The cupboards were old solid oak, their doors in need of lacquer. An assortment of supermarket boxes was already stacked on the worktops. Within were the ingredients for each meal, themselves in numerous boxes and tin cans. Each large box had enough for one meal sitting. Every box had been labelled with its day and meal. Charlie was well prepared.

A ruthless old AGA stove dominated the near end of the kitchen, close to the door. Its red iron doors would bite off a slow hand. Two battered old cookers stood on either side of it. Everything was clean but showing wear. At the far end of the kitchen, a wide rolling shutter covered the serving hatch.

Over the next few hours, Dorothy and I familiarised ourselves with the stock while the staff galloped boys around the dark castle grounds.

Friday's supper and Saturday's breakfast were simple affairs. Immediately after supper, we packed bag meals for everyone. This would be a roving lunch for those abseiling the hills and kayaking the lake until dinner. Our real work began after breakfast on Saturday, when the last echoes of the boys had settled. Dinner was to be a two course meal.

The dynamic in the kitchen was much better than I had expected. Dorothy enjoyed it like her first adventure – even with the considerable work we had to complete. At this Christian Union weekend, she laboured for a higher purpose: William Butler, was assisting Charlie. William had travelled up in his car, arriving shortly after us. Little Dorothy was shimmering with the possibility of being almost in love. Her willingness to help with the cooking was a means to an end. She knew William contributed to the extra-curricular life of the school. He was an ambitious company man. She wanted to share his contribution. They both had aspirations: for one, a career; for the other, a husband.

Because of the busy schedule, they spent most of the day apart. Every time the team returned to base, William would slip into the kitchen on some pretext. Their time together was brief but succulent.

This excitement was a distant memory for me, and my remembrance was smeared with betrayals. I did my best to be sympathetic to the lovers – in a superior kind of way. Without seeming to pay attention, I observed them. In one corner of the kitchen, he stooped over her. His baritone murmur tugged playfully at her apron strings. She giggled and scolded with affected disapproval. At the end of the ritual, he would leave with a reluctant kiss from her reserve. Part of my amusement was their physical mismatch. He was the size of a bear, with forearms as thick as her legs. I wondered again what feminine qualities he saw in her.

While we prepared Saturday's dinner, Dorothy nattered continually. William had picked her a posy of flowers from the garden. They looked more like weeds to me. These emblems of devotion, in a chipped mug, decorated the window sill above the sink. She gazed at them the whole time she spoke.

Much of her chatter was forgettable until, she said, "I'm not sure William knows what he wants."

This took a moment to register with me. I had been filtering out the nonsense but this comment dropped like a plate and caught my attention. I paused from laying down the pasta layers of a lasagne tray.

Dorothy wanted to talk about relationships. It was a topic I had avoided until now. At every mention of William, I had resisted the obvious inquiry: "And how are you two getting on?" She would have to learn the final solution to the masculine question for herself. Although I disapproved, I was pleased she trusted me enough to allow me to peek into her box of trinkets.

"What man ever does?" I said, and resumed my pasta layers.

"He seems to be two different men."

"Really?"

"Sometimes he wants to be with me, and other times he's withdrawn," she said.

This was interesting. Unfortunately, it sounded a little too familiar. I did not believe that all men were like Harry, but this was suspicious.

"When we are alone, he's all mine," she continued. "When other people are around he hardly acknowledges me."

"What other people in particular?" Women, I suspected.

"His friends, the other teachers."

Better to make sure. I probed subtly. "Are they all male members of staff?"

Dorothy was silent.

She turned to face me, up to her elbows in suds.

I searched her face.

She frowned.

"Actually *yes*," she said after deliberating. Her brow uncreased. "Now I think back, it's when he's around the other men." She smiled. "I never noticed that before."

I had accidentally restored her faith in him, the poor thing. She could not see that he was embarrassed to be seen with her. As an ambitious man, he sought approval from his peers. He worried they would think it a ridiculous mismatch. When the novelty subsided, he would sniff the air again for the scent of another woman.

"He must be shy," I said.

"Dear love him," she cooed. "Who would want to be a man, afraid of his own feelings? He's such a big, cuddly dummy."

After a pause, she added, "Thank you, Rose. You are very wise."

She turned back to the sink and gazed past her weed posy, through the window, over the rolling garden that became thicket and trees and, eventually, sky. There, the clouds bore her gently aloft.

I was almost sick in my mouth.

For the next hour and a half, Dorothy and I worked in harmony. Occasionally, I caught her watching me. As I drew breath to ask her if there was something else, she spoke.

"Rose, I'd like William to serve the food with me."

That was unexpected.

She continued, "It was his idea. He'll come here as soon as he's free – if you don't mind."

"I don't mind at all," I said. No doubt it would be the bonding experience of a lifetime for them.

Moments before we were scheduled for dinner, Charlie shuffled into the kitchen. He grazed his eyes over the food trays in expectation. "Oh goodie," he said to Dorothy's bread and butter pudding. "Could I have that for my main course?" His fingers strayed towards it.

"Don't touch!" Dorothy's tea towel lashed out at his legs.

"You'll make a fat man very happy," he said.

"Out, Charlie," Dorothy said, "or you'll be on dishes after dinner. The hatch is going up now." She added a fake frown.

"Who's a Bossy Boots?" he said to me.

I had known Dorothy for two years. Only this weekend, a new persona had emerged. This shocked little office girl was capable of humour. It hardly counted, ordering Charlie around, but I had not imagined she was capable of that either.

Charlie snatched a biscuit and whistled into the dining hall. There, the riot of charging boys began to subside. He was the master of ceremonies at these events. His schedule told us that Grace would be said at 5.30p.m., once we had raised the serving hatch.

I rolled up the shutter and its clatter announced food to the gathered mob. Dorothy and I wrestled the arrangement of platters, stockpots and trays into place. In the distance, Charlie patted down a hush and spoke to the fidgeting herd.

"And now, gentlemen, the Headmaster will give thanks for the lovely meal we are about to enjoy. Let us pray."

I exhaled with horror.

37

My throat twisted in panic.

Baxter was here! Without a doubt, I would have to face him. On this occasion, I copied Dorothy's attitude of shock, hand to mouth. We stared at each other.

"The headmaster?" Dorothy whispered. Our playfulness had disappeared. We were guilty little girls in trouble with teacher.

"Why is he even here?" I said.

"And look at the state of us." She looked at me, my apron, my face and she swallowed a lump.

"What do we care?" I said, but my indifference was feeble. I brushed hands over my apron, smoothed my hair and rearranged a stack of dinner plates on the wide sill of the serving hatch.

"Oh God," I said.

"What?"

I appealed to her. "I don't want to sit with Baxter over dinner. I'll stay here and serve. William can help too. Three isn't too many. I'll do the mash first, so you two can stand together."

Dorothy pouted as Baxter's prayer rumbled in the distance. It wound on for several minutes. God was surely impressed. While it continued, William tiptoed into the kitchen, gently closing the door behind him. He spoke with a hush. "Hey there," he said to Dorothy. I got the slightest nod of recognition.

"I'm going to stay for a while – to make sure you aren't swamped," I said. That earned me another nod, but it was clear I was no longer welcome.

Befitting his rank, Baxter was first in the queue to be served. Charlie was close behind him, chatting without the formality of a subordinate. The headmaster moved before me, nodding along to one of Charlie's anecdotes. Without looking up, Baxter took a plate and scanned the food trays. There was no selection beyond lasagne, mashed potatoes and garden peas, so it was not a long decision.

I had these brief seconds to see Baxter up close. As I had previously thought, his face was roughly composed. He was not conventionally handsome, but there was a distinction to his hard jaw and cheekbones that matched his broken nose and thick neck. One ear had cauliflowered and old scars ran parallel to his wide brows. His face had bolstered too many scrums. During our first encounter, however, I had not noticed his incongruous eyes. These did not belong in a battered face. In them were gathered the blue and the black of the firmament. And, in a blink, they were focused on me.

"Ah, Mrs Maylie." Surprise registered in his raised brows. He was genuinely off-guard but controlled his face. In the pause, he assembled a platitude. "I see Mr Bakewell has you hard at work. Giving up your weekend is a noble sacrifice," he said.

There still remained an awkwardness between us. He could trot out fancy words but I was not fooled. I dolloped a serving of mash onto his plate.

"I trust," he paused momentarily, looking me in the face. Then he smiled with amusement. "I trust you have not laced my servings with poison, Mrs Maylie?"

"Perhaps, Mr Baxter, I'd have been better prepared if I'd known you were coming."

William served his lasagne and peas.

Baxter moved on to Dorothy who could not bring herself to look directly at him.

"And thank you too, for giving up your weekend," he said.

Clearly, her name was not as memorable as mine. For some reason, that delighted me.

"Yes, Mr Baxter. Enjoy your meal." She bobbed with a little curtsy. "Would you like custard with your pudding, Headmaster?"

I shook my head.

Chapter Five

The serving hatch was overcrowded with three servers. William could manage the mash and lasagne, a utensil in each paw, while Dorothy administered peas to plates and custard to bowls. I was not needed there. And, since my dialogue with Mr Baxter, I felt less inclined to hide in the kitchen.

"You two can manage without me," I said, after ten more diners had passed.

Dorothy warmed into a smile. "Yes, thanks. You go and enjoy your meal while it is still warm."

"This woman's work is easy," William said, and got their bonding experience off to a shaky start.

Dorothy and I had been scheduled to eat after both courses were served. Our meals were in the oven, wrapped in foil. I stood with a foil-covered plate and considered my options. The castle's kitchen, unlike its homely equivalent, was designed for bulk food preparation, not for dining. It had no tables or surfaces where I could comfortably sit to eat. I had to use the main dining room and risk another exchange with Baxter.

The staff ate at the far end of the hall, removed from the chaos of boys. Charlie and Baxter sat together, their empty plates in front of them. Charlie was on one corner, with the headmaster on his right, facing my approach. They were mid-conversation when Charlie spotted me, bearing my meal.

"Rose, let's get you a place," he said, pulling out the seat to his left. This put Charlie between Baxter and me, although he was still looking across me.

My peripheral vision caught Baxter inspecting me, head to foot, then lingering on the top of my apron. I sat and removed the foil from my plate.

"Lovely grub, Rose," Charlie said. He seemed oblivious to the tension my arrival had caused.

"Yes, Mrs Maylie, some very fine victuals. Most felicitous," Baxter said, nodding.

I am sure he expected me to ask for an explanation of his words. Even if I had not understood, I would have died before giving him the satisfaction.

"That's Samuel showing off," snorted Charlie. He added, "English teachers are smarter than everyone else, you know."

"So I've heard," I said.

"But only from English teachers," Charlie finished.

"It is difficult to find respectful staff these days," Baxter said, standing. "Mrs Maylie," he paused, "Would you like some tea?" Baxter was smiling. I had not believed the hard slabs of his face could arrange themselves in that manner.

When he said my name, I had jolted. Baxter probably considered himself witty. He had structured his comments for effect. I thought it unlikely that this good humour was a common occurrence. It was not consistent with my profile of him.

"Tea, Mrs Maylie?" he repeated.

"Yes, please," I said, searching for a neutral tone.

"Not for me. I'll have a quick prayer with the senior boys before the service starts." Charlie said, much to my alarm. He rose and pushed his chair in. I was hoping he would register the appeal in my eyes and rescue me. I would have accepted the invitation to a prayer meeting, even if it meant leaving my dinner unfinished. Better still, he could have invited Baxter to join him. But Charlie's baggy form receded from the dining hall, a number of sixth form boys being drawn into his wake.

When my eyes reverted to front, they caught Baxter's. He had deposited our cups of tea and resumed his seat.

"Thank you," I said.

The next minutes would be filled with platitudes on neutral topics before Baxter finished his tea and withdrew. It was that or uncomfortable silence.

"I hope you don't find this awkward, sitting with me, Mrs Maylie," he said.

This was much more frank than I expected.

"Should I?"

"Well, I think you may remember the little fracas of our last meeting."

"It does come to mind, now you mention it."

He laughed.

That irritated me. It was more evidence of his condescension.

I studied the new light of his face. He was being sincere.

41

"Let us not continue fencing, Mrs Maylie. I was less than socially adept during our first exchange." He gauged my reaction.

The resolute focus of his eyes unsettled me.

My mouth was too full of lasagne to reply.

"I hope you will forgive my coarseness. Sometimes I am perfunctory with my terms of address, especially when I am under pressure."

"Mmm," I replied.

"Good. Then, perhaps, we can forget it ever happened," he said, without disengaging his eyes. Their combustion was most disconcerting, and I blushed. I looked away, prodding lasagne onto my fork. This ferocious scrutiny required a clever riposte.

"I expect we can do away with the demeaning name badges, then?" I almost asked.

Baxter finished his tea and sat back. He placed both hands palm down on the table, as if to launch into orbit. "I hope you will excuse me, Mrs Maylie. I'm afraid I have to go."

The boys in the hall returned their dirty dishes to the serving hatch and meandered towards the main hall for the praise service. They clumped and shoved but their behaviour was moderated by the headmaster's presence.

"Mrs Maylie, some of the staff are having a game of 'Scrabble' this evening, after the boys have gone to bed. I do hope you will find the time to join us. I plan to demonstrate to Mr Bakewell just how much smarter English teachers are." He smiled at his own humour and the stony angles of his face softened.

"Thank you, Mr Baxter. I'll see if I can."

When I had agreed to work in the kitchen that weekend, Charlie advised bringing plenty of warm clothes. The castle was old and drafty. At this time of year, even with the central heating at full blast, the halls were only warming up at midday. The kitchen was an exception, however. The vicious old AGA drew directly from the lake of sulphur, where tortured souls cook for eternity. It was always on, and the kitchen was always warm. At midday, when the rest of the castle had warmed, the kitchen became a smelter's furnace. Charlie's advice had been well intended but was based entirely on his own experience of the castle. He never worked in the kitchen. He only visited long enough to snatch desserts. As a result, the warm jumpers I had brought were unsuitable for the majority of my stay.

Dorothy and I wore light T-shirts under our aprons. In this condition, I met Mr Baxter: my T-shirt clinging to my figure. Only my apron preserved modesty for my bosom. It was no wonder his eyes snagged on my mid-portions as I crossed the dining hall. While regrettable, this had been unavoidable. I would not feel self-conscious because Mr Baxter might notice that I had breasts.

Dorothy and I retired to our rooms after setting the tables for breakfast. Charlie had a selection of boys assigned to washing dishes. It would have taken us all night without this intervention.

With my limited selection of clothes on the bed, I considered my options. I would need something comfortable and warm, especially sitting in the dining hall this evening. With this in mind, I opted for comfortable slacks and polo-neck jumper. It was a matter entirely beyond my control that these garments happened to be figure-hugging. A glance in the mirror told me I looked well.

For the game, a space had been cleared in the dining room, close to the serving hatch and the warmth of the kitchen. As the light withdrew, heat was again at a premium.

William and Dorothy were first in place with the 'Scrabble' board. I sat across from them, with one seat empty on either side of me. William was snugly beside Dorothy, his arm curled around her narrow shoulders. When Mr Baxter entered, William's arm slowly withdrew and he adopted a more upright posture.

"I think we have enough to get the game going," Mr Baxter announced from half way across the dining hall. "If no one objects."

It was my turn to survey Mr Baxter's figure as he walked towards us. He wore dark suit trousers, an open-necked shirt and a black jumper. His clothes indicated he would not be dispensing with formality this evening. He was stocky and filled his clothes well enough but there was little merit in that unfinished face – except for his eyes. Overall though, he was not displeasing to look at.

43

Mr Baxter sat to my left, beside William. With a forward shuffle, William brought his chair upright and detached from Dorothy. She remained in his shadow, shielded from the headmaster. "Charlie Bakewell is policing the dormitories. He will not be down for some time," Mr Baxter said, his hand already inside the bag of letters. He withdrew a tile and sneered at it. The bag was passed round to determine who should act first.

"X," said Mr Baxter.

"E," said William.

"O," said Dorothy.

"C," I said, showing the evidence. I drew out my letters and placed them before me. When I passed the bag to Mr Baxter, he lifted his eyes to mine. He had recently found something of interest in the lines of my jumper. Clearly, Mr Baxter was a breast man.

While the others considered their letters, I swept back my hair into a ponytail. It took a moment to apply the bauble. It was such a fiddly thing. While my arms were up, Mr Baxter could not concentrate on his letters. He stirred restlessly. I was amused that my little display had worked. Now I was ready to play the other game.

Mr Baxter clearly expected to win the 'Scrabble'. Words are the province of English teachers. Lowly Administrative Assistants and a physics teacher would have no chance against the headmaster's erudition.

"Abalone," I said, after a moment of arranging the letters in front of me. "I believe that's ten for the word – 'E' is doubled – twenty, because it passes through a double word square, and another fifty, because I used all seven letters. Seventy. Who's going to keep score?" I was enjoying myself already.

Mr Baxter scrutinised the board. "I believe you are right, Mrs Maylie. Well done." He frowned. "I think we have a contest on our hands."

"You are only contesting for second place, Mr Baxter," I said.

He smiled. "The game is still recoverable. And I enjoy a challenge, Mrs Maylie."

I flicked a look at Dorothy. From within William's shadow, she was frowning at me.

44

Mr Baxter mused over his tiles and produced 'ornate', (using my 'N') to represent his immense learning.

"Hmm. That's only twelve. I still have some way to go," he said.

"There is a significant luck element," William added.

"True," Mr Baxter nodded. "But skill will prosper in the long term."

"We could declare me the winner and start again, if you like," I said.

Mr Baxter laughed with astonishment.

"What does 'abalone' mean?" Dorothy whispered to William.

He was mildly irritated by the question and said nothing.

"My dear, eh – I'm sorry I've forgotten your name," Mr Baxter said.

"Dorothy Giles, Headmaster."

"Dorothy – that's right." He had never known her name to forget it. "I believe abalone is the little sea creature, a mollusc, whose shell gives us mother-of-pearl."

"Yes," William said.

"Mother-of-pearl is often used as inlay on guitar fretboards," Mr Baxter said, completing the lesson. "Isn't that right, Mrs Maylie?"

"I thought it was a bird," I lied. Men feel less threatened by stupid women.

The game continued, with Mr Baxter making some impressive gains. He still lagged behind me, though. William gave a reasonable account of himself, but Dorothy showed everyone that she was a dimwit.

William sighed and laid down 'sub'.

"I'm afraid I'm going to have to challenge that," Mr Baxter announced. "'Sub' is a prefix. The rules prohibit prefixes."

William flushed and stammered, before managing a defence. "I meant it as the short form of submarine."

"Abbreviations are prohibited too," Mr Baxter countered.

"Are we playing all those rules? It's the only word I could get."

"We have to play by the rules, Mr Butler. They give the game meaning."

"You could do 'bus'," Dorothy said, summoning all her courage.

Everyone looked at her.

She slowly receded into the shade again.

"I'm afraid 'bus' is an abbreviation too. It's short for 'omnibus'." Mr Baxter smiled, not at all awkwardly: he was in control.

I felt some sympathy for William. He had been hoping to engage the headmaster in some friendly conversation and impress him.

"I didn't make the rules," Baxter said, but it was clear that he would not concede the point.

"Oh, that's all right. I'll take these back," William said, lifting the offending tiles. He smiled tightly and his dark eyes flicked around.

No one spoke.

It was an uncomfortable situation, and all of Mr Baxter's making.

"Dorothy, it's your go," I said, rearranging my letters. The good humour had gone but we were contracted to see the game to its conclusion.

About ten minutes later, Mr Baxter laid down 'laser' over a triple word square, for a mere fifteen points. I looked to William for a reaction but saw none.

I cleared my throat and said, "I challenge that word."

Mr Baxter flinched, as though he had caught himself in his zipper.

"On what grounds?" he said.

"'Laser' is an acronym."

"Really, Mrs Maylie, of what?"

"William will know. He is a physics teacher."

We looked to William for confirmation.

"Eh, mmm – it is." He flushed deeply and looked like he would kill me.

"It's something about light being amplified," I pushed.

"Well, Mr Butler, what does it stand for?" Baxter said.

Reluctantly, William conceded, "Light Amplification by the Stimulated Emission of Radiation."

Baxter looked at me. It was a gaze without expression. He was waiting for my next move.

46

Help came from his left. Help for him; betrayal for me. William said, "Laser is in such common usage that it could be considered a word in its own right."

"Like 'bus'?" I said but no one appeared to hear.

"Ah, a word in its own right. You are most kind, Mr Butler," Baxter said, his eyes unwavering. "Does that satisfy your curiosity, Mrs Maylie?"

"Curiosity?" I could feel anger flaring.

"Let's just play on," William said.

Dorothy murmured agreement from beyond his shoulder.

They were all regarding me now. William and Dorothy prayed to avoid confrontation. Baxter glutted himself on my defeat.

"Perhaps Mr Baxter would like to tell us which rules he wishes to enforce, and which inconvenient ones he will disregard," I almost said. "If you don't want to play *that* rule, I don't mind." I said. "I didn't make the rules."

Baxter broke off his penetrating glare. "Yes. Play on. It is getting late," he concluded.

I cannot remember the final scores exactly. All that mattered was being twenty-five points ahead of Mr Baxter. Dorothy and I were left to clear the game away. The headmaster strode off, muttering a bland farewell. He had a long drive home. William scurried after, to lock the outer doors behind him.

"You were flirting with him," Dorothy said.

"Who?"

"Mr Baxter, of course. And he's married."

"No, I wasn't. Why would I flirt with someone I dislike?"

"I'm not sure you dislike him as much as you say," she said.

"What utter nonsense you have in your head, Dorothy." I paused to think of a better defence. "I challenged Baxter on his 'laser'. He embarrassed William too. I defended William and neither of you had the guts to back me up."

That silenced her. Harry had taught me the strength of a well timed accusation.

Dorothy reset our places with breakfast cutlery. "Did you notice how he ignored me?" she said.

"Consider yourself lucky that Mr Baxter does not lech over you. I would rather be ignored."

"No, William! He ignored me – when the headmaster came in."

I remembered. "You are imagining things, Dorothy. He was just getting in a better position to play the game."

"He never spoke to me once the whole game. I could hardly even see the board."

"You should have moved, or said something to him. Men are not mind readers. You must spell things out to them, Dorothy. He was using his little brain to think up new words."

She had been content to hide behind William. I was sick of her helplessness.

"You're probably right, Rose."

"Again," I said.

I could see no future in their relationship at all. He would desert her when a fully developed woman showed interest in him. It was doomed to failure – unless he wanted a porcelain doll that could cook, clean and bear miniature ceramic children. For the short term, I would keep her optimistic. When she was finally rejected, I would help her reform into a wiser woman.

Returning to my room, I passed Charlie's door. It was slightly ajar, and Charlie quickly emerged to determine whether I was staff or an errant child.

"Oh, Rose. It's you," he whispered. His face looked like dough in the pale light. He was in his pyjamas, but I affected not to notice this.

"Yes. I thought you were going to join us." I copied his hushed tone.

"I was, but the boys wouldn't settle. You know what they're like." He opened the door, nodding at the junior sleeping bag and the casualty on the bed. "Bumped a bed post and lost a tooth. A big pillow fight got out of control. Blood on the carpet. Don't worry, it's already cleaned up."

As a woman, it must have been my job to clean carpets. "Oh dear," I said.

"I'll watch over him. We need more staff at these weekends. I knew we were undermanned. That's why Sam agreed to join us today. I presume he's on his way home."

"Yes. About fifteen minutes ago."

"He'll have a long drive home in the dark. How did you two get along?"

This last question had been so surprising that my response was incoherent.

"Was it awkward?" he asked.

"Why would it be?"

"After your little disagreement a while back," he said and smiled.

"You knew about that?" I scowled. "Why did you leave me alone with him?"

"Well, I thought it would force you to make peace, and –" he interrupted himself.

"And what?"

"Nothing."

He was like a boy with chocolate lips denying the missing cake.

"Charlie! And what?"

"Oh, I'm useless at this," he muttered. "He told me to."

I did not understand. "He *what?*"

"He told me to leave you two alone. He wanted to apologise." Charlie looked pathetic.

"Really?" I said, after a pause, but the question was unnecessary. "Charlie Bakewell, I had no idea that you were capable of subterfuge."

"No, I'm useless at secrets. I wouldn't last a minute under questioning."

It occurred to me that Samuel Baxter was a contradiction.

Sunday morning was clear but lightly frosted. The coach was fully loaded, except for Dorothy. She had forgotten her grudge and accepted William's offer of a lift. I had the full width of a front seat to slip around on. Using my overnight case, I jarred myself into the corner and waited while the driver stowed baggage.

The oak sentinels on the winding driveway no longer looked haggard. They remembered that summer had just passed and spring would come soon to thicken their limbs. They would endure the harsh winter ahead with defiance. Why should they not lay claim to their own portion of the sky?

49

I closed my eyes and felt the half-warmth of sun on my face.

Chapter Six

There are two types of people who are happy: the ignorant and the deluded. From Harry's departure in August 1975 until Christmas Eve, I had convinced myself I could cope perfectly well.

I was one of the deluded.

Christmas is a family celebration. I had my parents and cherished their love but it was not enough. At thirty, I had always expected to have my own children. I wanted to watch my parents fuss over their grandchildren. Christmas brought these dreams to the fore again.

For our first Christmas, Harry and I bought a plastic tree and a string of unreliable lights. Christmas morning was spent laughing ourselves senseless on cheap bubbly. We took turns to guess which broken bulb had prevented the chain from working. The forfeit was a gulp of wine. We never identified the bulb. Passion overtook us, and we made love beside the tree, while the turkey petrified in the oven.

The very same tree squatted in the roof space on that Christmas Day. I was disinclined to stir the dust on those memories. Neither had I bothered with festive decorations around the house. It would take more than that to bring me cheer. I lay in bed all Christmas morning, my pillow slip wet with recollections.

I determined to get a cat in the New Year. That is what spinsters do. Every cat comes with guaranteed affection. Dogs are stupid and driven by their appetites. They reminded me of Harry.

Even John Souseman, once interminably single, fared better than me. On the first day of the new term, the secretaries had much gossip to catch up on. John called in, seemingly for chalk. This was timed to coincide with Betty's first cake. He lingered long enough to be offered a seat. He had played this trick several times before. He was in good spirits for the beginning of term and I was not the only one to notice. Betty began to forage. John had witnessed her nosing around often enough to know what he was in for. She sat opposite him in the circle and her questions came in a flurry.

"Did you spend Christmas at your parents again, John?"

"No. Called in for a few hours."

"Did you have Christmas dinner at theirs?"

"No."

"On your own, then?"

"No," he said.

"Well, where did you have it?"

He paused, "Girlfriend's place."

"Girlfriend, John?" Betty smiled like a hungry vixen. "Are you not mistaken, John? It sounded like you used the word 'girlfriend'."

All conversation in the office was on hold. All eyes were on John.

"No mistake," he said, and could not suppress a smile.

"Truly, Christmas is a time of charity," Betty said. "When did you meet her?"

"At university."

"Were you a couple then, or just friends?"

"Dated a little," he sighed, growing tired.

"Tell us about her, John," she said.

John used a defensive tactic none would have predicted.

"She's great breasts," he announced.

That shocked us to silence.

"John!" Joan said, eventually.

"Too much information," Betty conceded.

Dorothy had spilt tea on her tunic.

"More cake, John? I think you've earned it." I passed the tin over to him.

"Wouldn't say no." He winked, confirming our pact.

After the dust settled, Joan said, "Bill Logan had a heart attack on Boxing Day."

Bill Logan was our vice-principal.

"Is he all right?" I asked.

Everyone was hushed.

"I spoke to Bill's wife, Jennifer. The doctor's said it was mild, as heart attacks go. He has taken it as a warning, though, and will retire early."

"That's terrible," Dorothy said.

"Better he walks out than is carried out," John said. "He'd do with losing weight. Retirement will suit him fine. Do him a world of good."

"Jennifer was saying it has shaken them all up very badly. He was working too hard here. It's renewed his perspective on family life, she says – especially over Christmas."

"Yes, I'm sure," I said.

"They'd run you into the ground here." John nodded to the headmaster's office, "Especially Baxter. He's here until all hours. Expects us to do the same."

"You'll live forever then, John," Betty quipped. "You're out of here before the bell's stopped ringing."

"The point is," Joan said, "The poor man has been given a second chance. He was a good VP and a friend to many, but we will have to do without him."

Already, we had started to talk about Bill Logan in the past tense.

"Does that mean there will be a new vice-principal?" Dorothy said. There were cogs creaking in her head: she could be married to a vice-principal some day.

William would have applied for the job, had it been advertised, but Mr Baxter had his own policy on recruitment. He used the Old Boy Network. It took very little cake for Mrs Bedford, the headmaster's secretary, to tell us the rest. A phone call to the headmaster of Elmfield Grammar – our nearest rivals – had elicited a recommendation. After a short interview, with Mr Baxter alone, the position was awarded to Mr Jack Dawson. He had formerly been a head of department in Elmfield. It was quite a jump to vice-principal, but Mr Baxter had been assured he was easily up to the job.

Mr Dawson was released by Elmfield and was in Chancery Grammar by the end of the week. Bill Logan was allowed to see out his three months' notice on the sick. Everyone was saying how decisively Mr Baxter had acted. How generously he had treated Bill Logan. Everyone, that is, except William and Dorothy.

On his first day, Mr Dawson was given a privilege that Mr Baxter had not even allowed himself. As part of his guided tour, he was introduced to the secretarial staff. Mr Baxter was rarely in the General Office and spoke no more than was absolutely necessary – something I claimed credit for. Today was different, however. He was showing off to his new disciple.

The headmaster entered, his gown billowing, and Jack Dawson lingered behind him. Mr Baxter's vigorous stance declared ownership of everything and everyone in that room. It could not have been more obvious if he had urinated in the corner.

"Mr Dawson, this is the General Office. It is small, as you can see, but well appointed," said the headmaster.

The two men were physically contrasted. The headmaster was thick-bodied and compact; the new vice-principal was tall and lean. His reedy frame was accented by a close-fitting suit jacket. His dark hair was lightly oiled and kinked. Shadow dusted his lower face, where a caterpillar moustache clutched his top lip. Beneath this, he wore an impudent smirk. He looked raffish, like a secret agent loitering in a casino. His eyes darted over us and I wondered whether he was taking Mr Baxter seriously. He seemed to be aware of some joke and was looking around for someone to share it with.

"Are they good workers, Mr Baxter?" Dawson winked at us behind the headmaster.

I already liked our new vice-principal. Purely from curiosity, I noted he was not wearing a wedding ring.

"Mr Dawson, I can vouch for every one of them," Baxter said, looking at the cornice.

"Thank you, Mr Baxter," Joan said, rising. "Mr Dawson, I am Joan Spenser." They shook hands. "I am the office manager – not that my girls need much managing. They are all very good workers."

While Joan talked through the services we could provide in the office, Mr Baxter loomed toward my desk. To my absolute astonishment, he stooped and spoke to me in a low voice.

"Mrs Maylie, I wonder if I may have a moment of your time this afternoon. Something has occurred that I wish to discuss with you."

I flushed deeply but my voice did not waver.

"Of course, Mr Baxter. I will contact Mrs Bedford and make an appointment that is convenient for us both."

"Very good."

54

Then he was gone, conveying Mr Dawson from the office as soon as Joan had concluded. We were silent until they passed beyond our foyer window.

"Well, that was interesting," Betty said.

I said nothing. I was busy thinking what I could have done to warrant a personal interview with the headmaster. His awkwardness had been obvious when he spoke.

Later that morning, I went to make my appointment.

It had been over six months since I had last been inside the headmaster's office. Dr Thompson had been headmaster then. It had served perfectly well as an office for many years, but now, Mr Baxter preferred to call it a 'study'. I wondered whether it would look more academic because of the change.

The headmaster's secretary had a separate office, adjacent to his. This was little more than a cubicle of comically small proportions. It was an architect's afterthought, barely fitting a desk, chair and filing cabinet.

Convention dictated I request an audience with the headmaster through his secretary. Mrs Bedford would tell me a time when his schedule was free.

"He's available now, Rose," she said through her television-screen spectacles.

I was not ready for this. I was not yet mentally prepared for a meeting with him just then.

"I think he said he wanted to see me in the afternoon."

Mrs Bedford's face snapped shut like a bear trap.

"That's typical. He never checks his diary. He is out at the Headmasters' Conference after lunch. It'll have to be now. He'll have to leave in an hour if he's going to make it in time. Really, Dr Thompson was never this disorganised. It's a wonder Mr Baxter can even do his own tie in the morning."

Christine Bedford had been Dr Thompson's secretary for almost twenty years. Over the years, their communication had become intuitive. His retirement had ended the golden age of Christine's career. Rumour had it that she would be retiring soon herself.

She swept aside a paper bundle to find a beige plastic intercom on her desk. It was about the same size as a writing pad, with a chunky buttons and the shadow of a speaker under

55

its grill. "I hate this thing. *He* had it installed. *He* said it would be more efficient. I never had a problem communicating before, mind you. Dr Thompson –"

"Christine, I can come back," I said. "Tomorrow would be better."

She craned forward and jabbed the intercom button. Her voice was vinegar. *"Mr Baxter.* Rose Maylie here to see you." She waited before remembering to disengage her finger from the machine. It fizzed in reply as soon as she did so.

The intercom squawked and, a moment later, Mr Baxter filled the doorway.

"Ah, Mrs Maylie. I'm afraid I'm in trouble with Mrs Bedford – again." As ever, he spoke formally but a luminous intensity in his eyes showed amusement. He smiled. It was self-assured, but it did not reassure me. I could not relax in his presence. Nor could I predict which way our meeting would turn.

"If it is convenient for you, Mrs Maylie, and if Mrs Bedford permits, perhaps we could meet in my study. It should not take more than a few minutes," he said. Without waiting for my reply, he turned on his heel and withdrew. His gown licked at the door frame as he took the corner.

Mrs Bedford's face wrung out a silent curse and she recorded the appointment in her desk diary.

When I emerged from her office, I found Mr Baxter holding his study door open for me.

"Do have a seat, Mrs Maylie," he said. The frequent repetition of my name sounded false.

As I had suspected, the room's change of title had done nothing to increase its academic credentials. It was still modestly sized. Bland oyster wallpaper sucked the colour from everything. The furniture had not even been rearranged from Dr Thompson's layout. A knotty old desk still sat between narrow windows, and upright chairs occupied either side of the desk. That was where the similarities ended, however. Mrs Bedford had spoken of the differences between the headmasters. Her meaning was now clear.

This scene was like an explosion in a mail sorting office. Dr Thompson's old trays for incoming and outgoing documents teetered with stacked paper. They threatened to surrender their equilibrium at the slightest breath. Copious boxes and folders slumped all around the headmaster's desk. Even the visitor's chair, where I was expected to sit, held bundled documents between its arms.

Mr Baxter scooped these up, without apology, and found a patch of carpet on which to file them. His own desk stored numerous poster-sized rolls of grey schematics. He tiptoed behind his desk and reclaimed a chair.

"You will note the mess. I have not yet fully moved in. I'm organising a filing system at present and keep getting interrupted."

"No doubt," I said.

He was seated but his posture remained upright.

"I am sure you are wondering why you are here, Mrs Maylie."

He paused.

I was beginning to wonder whether he expected a reply.

"A crime has been committed, Mrs Maylie. A grave injustice has been done. And I am going to see that justice is carried out," he said.

I thought of the staff handbook's missing pages. A wash of dread burned in my stomach. Something dangled at the back of my throat but I could not swallow.

Baxter steepled his fingers under his chin and considered me deeply.

"Laser is indeed an acronym, Mrs Maylie. You were correct to challenge my word."

Ten seconds must have passed before I understood. He referred to our game of 'Scrabble'. I unknotted my oesophagus while he snorted at the joke.

He was absolutely hilarious.

"There are few people who will stand up to the headmaster, Mrs Maylie, and those are people whom I like to have on my side," he said.

He still had not explained the purpose of our meeting. Although, now I was more at ease.

"You see, Mr Dawson has asked for his own secretary – if he is to be expected to do the job properly. While I would dispute whether this is entirely necessary, I would like to accommodate him, at least for a while. I am sure Mr Dawson

57

will work out fine – his references are spectacular. I understand, though, that he has not been a vice-principal before. He will need some support, Mrs Maylie."

He leaned forward, pushing the inference at me.

"I see," I said, but I did not. I wanted Mr Baxter to discontinue his stare.

"He will make the adjustment in good time but he will need somebody to help him," he dabbed his chin, "Make the transition."

"Yes, I see," I said, and I was starting to.

"The appointed secretary may also be required to organise him, Mrs Maylie – perhaps the way Mrs Bedford graciously organises me." He faked a smile. "You see, Mrs Maylie, we were very lucky to get someone at such short notice. Bill Logan left us in a difficult situation – my prayers are with him. It was most unfortunate. I felt that prompt and decisive action was required to get someone for the job. Elmfield were very good to let Jack Dawson go at such short notice. I think we owe it to Chancery Grammar to give our new vice-principal the best support we can provide." His eyes soaked my blouse.

"And you would like me to recommend one of the secretaries for the job?" I said.

He smiled at my playfulness. "No, Mrs Maylie. I want you to do it."

It was around that time Dorothy started confiding in me. One Tuesday morning in January her old car succumbed to the frost, and I received an early phone call. I gave her a lift to and from work. Before the journey home, I invited Dorothy to dinner at my house. This woman of twenty-nine phoned her mother for permission. It was reluctantly granted.

"It's nothing fancy, I'm afraid," I said, hanging our coats under the stairs.

"Oh, that's fine. It'll be nice not to have to cook tonight."

"You cook for your folks?" I said.

"Oh yes. Mother grumbled that she would have to do it tonight. She complained about her back." Dorothy sat at the table while I peeled and chipped a few potatoes.

"I have wine, if you are feeling daring," I said. But I was sure she would not.

58

No, I better –" she interrupted herself. "Yes, why not? Where do you keep your glasses?" She was on her feet, awaiting direction.

I indicated a low cupboard where Dorothy found the wine. She twisted the foil wrapping on the bottle as if that would be enough to open it. I handed her a corkscrew from the cutlery drawer.

"That foil will pull off, but most people just cut round the rim," I said.

The bottle was over-sized in her hands, but I let her wrestle with the corkscrew. My hands were covered in potato starch. My primitive corkscrew was a simple crank, relying on the Principle of Moments. In the hands of the inexperienced, that often failed. Brute force worked much better. Dorothy grunted like she was dislocating a shoulder but twisted the cork free. By the end of it, her face matched the Bordeaux in colour.

Chips fizzed in the pan, fish fingers thawed under the grill and the extractor fan hummed. Dorothy filled our glasses before she made a confession.

"My car didn't break down this morning," she said. "I wanted someone to talk to. That's all."

"I'm happy to listen," I said. It seemed to be the correct response.

"I shouldn't be bothering you with my problems."

"A burden shared is a burden halved." It was a horrible cliché but people say these things to comfort each other.

"William has broken up with me." Her jaw quivered. She fought for control but tears broke free. Others followed this trail and Dorothy looked down to hide her face. She breathed steadily and did not sob.

I worried about the fish fingers. They would need turned under the grill.

"I'll get you a hanky," I said and patted her shoulder. "Tissues are something I have been buying a lot of recently. It's okay to cry when you have to. It's not a sign of weakness."

I flipped the fish fingers over and passed Dorothy a box of tissues. The first one sat ready like a white flame.

"I am sending Harry the bill for all my tissues, in fact," I said.

59

She snorted a laugh and looked up. Her eyes were puffy marshmallows.

"I could have it as part of my divorce settlement."

Humour does not solve our problems, but it is a distraction. She appreciated my attempt to comfort her.

Nothing more was said about her break-up while we ate. For a quiet half hour, we sat on opposite sides of the table. I finished before Dorothy and topped up my wine glass. She was a slow eater and very precise in her movements. With great daintiness, she squished the last of her mushy peas to the back of her fork.

"I'm absolutely stuffed, Rose. Thanks so much." Her cutlery sat exactly parallel.

She sighed and leaned back. "I could burst." She patted her stomach but, to my eyes, it was enviably flat.

"They were comfort portions. A good feed helps at times like this," I said.

"Well, *apparently*, that's what I need."

"What do you mean?" She was talking about William again. I topped up her glass. Wine in, truth out.

"He has been hot and cold for quite some time. Remember, I told you about this kind of thing when we were away at the CU weekend."

"Of course," I said.

"Well, he's been getting worse lately." She toyed with a strand of hair and drank some wine. "This is going to my head a bit – but I do like it." She sniffed.

I nodded for her to continue.

"Well, I confronted him about it." She puffed up at the memory. "It took all my nerve. You know how useless I am with confrontation, Rose. I'm pathetic." She took another tissue. "He was round at Mum's for dinner on Sunday, then we usually walk to the evening service – our church is just down the road. I'd planned what I was going to say while we were walking alone. I kept doing a countdown in my head before I would speak. Eventually, I did. I just said to him, 'William, I want to know if you are serious about this relationship.' And it came out just the way I had planned it – only my legs were shaking at the knees. The effort nearly killed me."

"How did he react?"

"Well, he was walking on my right, but I was too scared to look at him. He stopped in his tracks and looked at me. No expression. I had to wait forever for an answer. I didn't have anything else prepared." She dabbed a tear from her cheek.

"What did he say?" I asked.

"He said 'I don't know'. Just like that. And I said, 'Then why are you here?' He took that as me asking him to leave. I wasn't. I didn't." She blew her nose and paused a moment. "'I'll walk you home' was the last thing he said to me. But I said, 'Don't bother!' and I pulled my hand away. And he just walked behind me all the way home." She deflated into the chair.

"Oh, you poor thing." I reached across the table to touch her arm.

Her tears streamed. "I went to my room and cried all night. Mum and Dad were suspicious but I couldn't face all the questions. I told them I wasn't feeling well and had sent William home."

"Have you spoken to him since?"

"Yes. It got worse. He slipped me a note yesterday in the office," she said.

At the mention, I remembered his unusually hasty visit.

"It just said: 'We have to talk. I will come round to your house at seven'." There was spice in her tone.

"That was blunt," I said.

"That's William – when he wants to be. Well, he was there exactly on time, which is incredible for him. He's normally late. I think he parked up the road until exactly seven before coming to the door."

"How was it?"

"Frosty. I sent him into the lounge to talk to Mum and Dad. That's the usual thing we do. I made tea in the kitchen. I knew by the look on his face that he was dead serious. Maybe even angry. The whole time I was waiting for the tea, I was a quivering wreck. I knew then it was over. I just needed to hear it from him. It made me feel numb."

I rubbed her arm. It brought memories of my own break up. Dorothy offered me a tissue. My tears showed we were kindred. We were spinster sisters: a fellowship of tears and suffering. It was enough to make me forget my usual disdain for her.

61

After a cough, she continued. "We sat in the back lounge, away from Mum and Dad. He started talking. He said he'd asked himself whether we were meant to be together. He said he enjoyed my company, but he wasn't sure he was physically attracted to me." She brought a fresh tissue out and held it to her eyes.

"Oh, Dorothy. You poor thing," I said. It was as I had predicted long ago.

"No. I'm all right," she said. "I'm not as bad as I thought I would be. Let me finish telling you. He started blaming himself. He said it was all his fault –"

"It is!" I interrupted.

She tried a ragged smile for me. "He said I was a lovely girl." Tears rolled freely and her chin crimped. "And that I deserved better than he could give me. He said I had a lovely temperament and was easy to talk to. But he said that wasn't enough for him. I asked him if he had met someone else," she said.

"Good girl."

"He said no." She closed her eyes and dabbed again.

It would not be long before William would be touring bars with his rugby pals. Sooner or later, he would hitch up to a sturdy lass and have thick-necked children.

"I believe him, Rose," she said.

And I had believed Harry.

"He has been busy at work and spent his weekends with me. He wouldn't have had the time. It was just something I had to ask." Dorothy had risen in my estimation. A tough fibre ran through her. Today, she had sat in the office and worked normally, without the slightest indication that her world had dimmed. She had kept her own counsel until now.

"It's his loss, girl. You'll find a man who knows what a treasure you are: one who'll have the sense to hold on to you," I said.

"I'm not so sure, Rose. I worry about that. I didn't have any boyfriends before William. I don't get out. I live at home with my parents."

Inspiration glimmered for me. "Sister, there are some things that can be fixed," I said.

"No dates, if that's what you are thinking, Rose."

"No. Better than that," I said. "You could move in with me. I have plenty of space here. We'd be there for each other." It was my turn to babble now. "We could take it in turns to cook. Think of the fun it would be."

Dorothy frowned with speculation. "We do get on well together," she said. "But what would Mother say?"

"Oh damn your mother, you are nearly thirty," I wanted to yell at her. My hopes were hobbling away on a Zimmer frame.

"Sod the old girl!" Dorothy suddenly announced.

"Dorothy Giles!" I said, laughing.

She giggled. "I'm virtually their servant, anyway. I work a full-time job, then cook, clean and wash while Mother complains about her back. It'll do her good to get up and about."

Our sisterhood was confirmed with a hug, more tears and nose blowing. Dorothy would break the news to her parents and move in by the end of the month.

Chapter Seven

"I liked the look of Mr Dawson," I said.

"Huh. Two types of people get a glowing reference: those who deserve it, and those their employers want rid of," John Souseman replied.

"He was quite charming when he was brought to the office."

"Yes, Rosie. You're such a good judge of character."

I frowned at John with mock annoyance. He had promised to tell me about his love life if I completed his worksheets on the Banda machine by break time. The biology store was a good choice for privacy. The window was open, and John's cigarette hand was resting on the sill.

"You win," he said. "Frowning defeats logic every time. Dawson's the greatest vice-principal ever."

"I think it's just too early to making judgements about the man," I said.

"Baxter never brought him to see me. Funny that." John took a long draw and blew smoke out the window. The January wind blew it right back in his face. The store stank.

"You could just go outside," I said.

"In this weather? Could catch my death out there," he said.

"Right, John. Where is the gossip you promised me?"

While he made our coffee, John filled me in on the details, the bulk of which Betty had already uncovered. Some interesting points emerged, however.

"Why did you split up last time?" I asked.

"I didn't like the sight of dead bodies; she didn't appear to mind them."

"John, I thought you were going to be serious."

"No really. She was at my cadaver table, first year medicine. We dissected Bertie. It was so romantic. We dated a few years, then she went to Africa. Voluntary service."

"Is she back here for good?" I said.

"Depends on your definition of 'good'. She's living here full-time. With her two kids."

"Really?" I was not sure whether he was joking. His face said he was not.

"Yes, the full contingent: kids and husband."

"Oh John," I said, without censure. "What are you getting mixed up in?"

"Ellie has a bit of a divorce going on – like yourself."

Divorce and adultery were shocking in 1976.

"It's very easy in her company. Life makes sense when she's in it," he said. He was a re-animated version of himself these days. "Actually," he held up a finger, "it's more chaotic. I'm up all hours. Hardly get any sleep. I've to wait 'til her kids are in bed. She wants to protect them."

"So, when do you see her?" I said.

"About nine. I stay until 1 a.m.. Drive home half-pissed."

Drink driving was not shocking in 1976.

"That's a bit risky, John."

He swatted my concerns away. "Drive slow. That's the trick."

"But how can you work the next day?"

"I've been doing this gig –" his finger circled in the air, "long enough to wing it. I know my stuff."

"As long as it doesn't affect your work," I said. "Baxter will be waiting for you to slip up."

"I need a life, Rosie. Ellie makes it worthwhile. She's worth more than this – and you know I love teaching." That was high praise indeed. "She could be the one. Can't let her being married get in the way. I'm in too far for that."

"At least you're a fool for the right reason," I said.

I had no sooner arrived back at my desk, than Joan rushed over to me. Her face was flushed with concern.

"Mr Baxter wants to see you. Right away," she said, eyes wide.

"Oh." I could not think why. "Did he say what it's about?"

"No, but he had the devil's own scowl on him," Betty said, from across the office. "You might like to clear your desk out."

"Very funny, Betty," I said.

Joan looked like she might cry, Dorothy mouthed "Good luck", and Betty drew a finger across her throat in a comic gesture that, all of a sudden, was not so funny.

I knocked on Mrs Bedford's office and pushed the door. It was locked.

Mr Baxter, hearing my knock, opened the door of his study. The vigour of his movement made me flinch, and he saw it.

"Please come in," he said with a broken edge in his voice.

The little progress our relationship had made over the last six months was lost in that instant. I became indignant and would not be dictated to. I did not move from my position. It was an act of defiance to counter Mr Baxter's spectacle. "What seems to be the problem, Mr Baxter?" I said.

It was his turn to flinch.

His face darkened and his burly chest drew in the atmosphere.

He held it within.

Then he laughed. As he did so, he deflated. "My apologies, Mrs Maylie. I cannot confront you in this manner and expect to survive. Please forgive me." His eyes illuminated those words and revived my favour.

I walked past him and sat upright in the chair facing his desk. I demonstrated displeasure in my posture: stiffness of neck, angle of chin, firmness of lips.

He watched this from the door.

"Would you like some tea, Mrs Maylie? The pot is still warm from break-time." His words led him to a cluttered tray across the office.

"I had to make it myself, you see. Mrs Bedford is off sick today. Actually, I'm having a devil of a time without her. She is absolutely invaluable to me."

I could have said something affirmative, but I left him in Purgatory.

"Tea?"

He was already pouring for both of us.

"Yes, please. White. No sugar."

"Ah, she speaks. I am forgiven," he said.

A smile almost broke free before I could suppress it.

Mr Baxter returned to his desk, once we both had tea.

"How do you feel Mr Dawson is settling in?" he asked.

"I think he has a lot to deal with. He's making the adjustment," I said.

"Today, I asked Mr Dawson for the minutes of the heads of department meeting that took place last week. Mr Dawson

66

wrote the minutes during the meeting. He told me he passed them to you for typing. Is that correct?"

Again, Mr Baxter's enquiries baffled me.

"Yes, last week."

"And you typed them?"

"Yes."

I developed the sense that I was being accused.

"And returned them to him?"

"He collected them from his tray, on my desk, in the office."

"Did you see him collect them?"

I thought back.

"We all did," I said. "The office was full. He stayed some time and spoke to everyone – especially Betty. He left with his mail, some other papers and those minutes."

"Hmm." Mr Baxter chewed on an idea.

"What's this about, Mr Baxter? Is there some question about my work?"

He moved the idea to the side of his mouth. "I am in receipt of two conflicting stories and I am not sure how to proceed," he said. "Of course, I believe you, Mrs Maylie. I think, however, that one of you must be mistaken."

My story would need verified.

"I will return in one moment, Mr Baxter," I said, on my way to the door.

Back in the office, the girls were all around Joan's desk. All work had been suspended as they awaited the outcome of my trial. Moving directly to my filing cabinet, I extracted the appropriate document. All eyes were on me. I could have said something to alleviate their anxiety, but I enjoyed the drama of being centre stage. Without expression, I strode from the office and back to the headmaster.

"Ah, the minutes?" he said.

"No, the carbon copy. Mr Dawson has the minutes." I handed the document to Mr Baxter. "Note the completion date in the top right corner. That corresponds to the job entry in my diary."

"You keep a log of everything you do?" he said, surprised.

"I do."

"Mrs Maylie, you are impressively organised. This makes everything clear."

A swell of pride took me. I sat upright and drew my arms back a little. My posture reminded him of how well organised I was in all respects. Mr Baxter's gaze was drawn by my movement. He peered past the carbon sheet just long enough to refresh his memory. After reading the minutes, he began chewing again.

"It seems we are both victims of skulduggery, Mrs Maylie."

"Really?"

"Mr Dawson is evidently finding it difficult to meet the demands of his new position."

"And the skulduggery?" I asked, amused by his archaic words.

"Mr Dawson suggested you had lost the minutes."

"He what?" I was outraged. Just that morning, I had spoken in his defence.

"Your diligent record-keeping has proved your competence – not that I ever considered this more than a minor oversight," he lied. "But today has been unduly awkward for me with Mrs Bedford's absence."

Mr Baxter probably expected me to have sympathy for him. I was too busy filling up with indignation. "He accused me of losing the minutes. That is ridiculous," I said.

"Actually, it was only something he offered as an aside, to explain the delay. It was a ploy to buy himself some time. He did not put great emphasis on it. I suspect he did not think I would follow up. But I am meticulous about some things, Mrs Maylie, and the truth is one of them. It is very important to me that my people tell the truth and keep my confidence. Relationships are founded on truth and confidence, are they not?"

The question surprised me, coming out of his homily. I was hardly listening to him; Dawson was undergoing torture in my head. "Of course," I replied.

"Well now, I have a problem," he said, "And you, Mrs Maylie, are the solution." He spoke with a self-conscious, dramatic style. I wished he would stop addressing me so formally. In normal conversation people do not use each other's names. His speech was too formal. But its cadence was pleasing, like that of a classically trained actor. I imagined what it would sound like if he called me Rose.

"I do not wish to add pressure to you, as I know you are very busy in the office, but I would like your assistance in –" he paused, "– managing Mr Dawson."

"Managing?" I asked. "I'm already his secretary."

"*Managing* would include keeping a detailed diary of Mr Dawson's activities, to assist him in the efficient discharge of his duties. He may need more of a guiding hand than I originally believed. I assure you, I will be looking into his previous career at Elmfield Grammar in much more detail. I have some colleagues there, with whom I used to play rugby."

"Would you like me to report on his daily progress, Mr Baxter?"

He considered the suggestion. "I feel it would be prudent to keep a file on Mr Dawson's successes and failures – just in case we need to call upon our records, as you did today, Mrs Maylie."

"As you wish, Headmaster," I said.

He liked that. I saw the approval in his penetrating eyes.

"Needless to say, Mr Dawson need not be made aware that such records exist," he said.

"Naturally."

His eyes lingered and he smiled like a Caesar. "In the absence of Mrs Bedford, I would like you to act up as Headmaster's Secretary," he said.

"As you wish," I said.

"I will only impose three conditions," he said.

I prepared myself for condescension.

"That you begin at once; that you do not interfere with anything on or in my desk and –" he paused for dramatic impetus, "– that you do not keep a file on me."

I laughed in spite of myself.

Joan, Dorothy and Betty were all at their own desks. The wait had been longer than their curiosity could bear.

"You were right, Betty, I have to clear out my desk," I said.

They froze when I spoke. Betty's face went slack and an apology died in her throat. Joan shuffled over, full of grief. Dorothy bit her lip and checked her name badge.

69

"I never thought –" Betty said.

"Oh, pet," Joan said.

Conscience got the better of me. "Oh, I haven't been fired," I said, like it was an accidental misunderstanding. "He wants me to be his secretary while Christine is away."

Joan's hug switched from commiseration to congratulation. Over her shoulder, Betty stuck her tongue out. I acknowledged it with a smirk.

"You should have seen your faces," I said, once Joan had released me.

"I was hoping to take your chair, Rose. I've had my eye on it for a while," Betty said.

"But Mr Baxter looked angry earlier," Dorothy said.

"A minor issue that I cleared up. He has asked me to start right away."

"Then you mustn't keep him waiting, my dear," Joan said. She removed lint from my cardigan. Her next words were rheumy with emotion. "I'm so proud of you. My girl. If you need any help, you know you've just to ask. Don't be scared of him. Any friend of Charlie Bakewell's can't be that bad."

Like a good daughter, I gave her another warm hug. I left with my desk diary, fountain pen and handbag. My mug stayed in the General Office, as I had no intention of spending my breaks alone. Christine Bedford rarely joined the office girls, but that was her own choosing. I would do this job my own way.

Mr Baxter was waiting at the door of his study. He nearly smiled as he unlocked my new office. "It is very cramped, I'm afraid, Mrs Maylie, but I hope to do something about that quite soon."

"Please, Mr Baxter, call me Rose. I think surnames are very impersonal."

He blinked at the idea. "As you wish, but only when we are alone. To maintain a professional formality when others are present, I will address you as Mrs Maylie. Please do not take it as an insult when I do so."

"And when we are alone together, call me Samuel," he, pointedly, did not say. The omission was obvious. He set the office keys on the desk and explained the functions of the intercom. This he achieved without once making eye contact. "Good luck –" he paused, "Rose. If you have any difficulties, I'll

70

see if I can get Mrs Bedford on the line. I will phone her later today for a prediction of how long she may be ill – not that one can accurately forecast such things."

And he was gone.

The office was claustrophobic. It had been warmed all morning by central heating and weak sunlight. Stale aerosol polish stifled the air. I sat in Christine Bedford's chair and pondered the unknown order of her filing system. The phone gave a long ring, indicating an internal call.

"This chair has great lumbar support," Betty said.

In January 1976, Christine Bedford was stricken with sciatica on the week that Mr Baxter had two evening meetings; thirty-eight letters (fourteen requiring prompt replies); countless internal memos and calls; an after-school meeting with the heads of department; lunch with a visiting cardinal; and an unpleasant interview with John Souseman. By the end of the week, sciatica looked like the easier option.

Mr Baxter provided me with a list of additional duties for me to carry out, many of which required me to be his mobile writing pad. It was beneath his station to make his own notes. Therefore, I had to shadow him for his most important meetings.

Mrs Bedford had endured significant upheaval with the retirement of Dr Thompson. This was aggravated by the additional duties Mr Baxter attached to her role, all because he refused to carry a notepad. The trauma of the headmaster's heavy dependency had sent her off sick.

While it was challenging, I enjoyed the novelty of the extra responsibility. The pay was better too. On that first day, I got a memo: 'RM, I informed Bursar you are acting HM Sec. Has adjusted your pay accordingly. SJB.' I was impressed by Mr Baxter's consideration. Just how much consideration, I would be able to calculate when I saw my next pay slip.

At meetings with governors, heads of department, and the academic staff, I was invisible. Only Mr Baxter addressed me directly. Staff briefings, held at 8:45 a.m. every morning, were the most intimidating of all. In the staffroom, the "*Academic* Staffroom", I was thoroughly out of place.

71

The staff slowly gathered to their cliques from around 8:15am. Almost exclusively male, dark suited, gowned and dusted with chalk, they sat in rigid armchairs. Their conversation was a balance of erudition and complaint. Some foraged through newspapers, collaborated on a crossword, or inhaled their morning coffee. However they occupied themselves, they all deserved to be in that members' lounge. I had entered on the wisp of Mr Baxter's gown. Only the Physical Education master and I did not wear the same academic shroud as everyone else. In his blue tracksuit and white shoes, he was more conspicuous than me – like a canary among crows.

A bell rang in the corridor outside the door – one of Mr Baxter's new initiatives. He had ordered extra bells in several placements around the school. The bell directly outside the staffroom was a strategic message to staff: lounging had been abolished by the new headmaster, for all but the headmaster himself. There was no bell outside his study door.

The staff fell into a grumbling hush. Mr Baxter folded his hands behind his back, under the wings of his gown. His chin was tilted up. The vice-principal, Jack Dawson acted as master of ceremonies and announced items of lesser consequence. He and the headmaster met before the briefing, every morning, to agree an agenda. Mr Baxter would keep the most significant items for himself. His talent for dramatic embellishment was best reserved for such matters. He was especially fond of items that demonstrated his efficiency or promoted controversy. Today's announcement met both these requirements.

The minor issues concluded, Mr Dawson indicated the headmaster would speak. Mr Baxter stepped forward. "God willing, I will be meeting with an architect this evening concerning plans I have drawn up for developing the school's facilities. As you know, the school building is old – some parts of it date back to the mid-nineteenth century. The newer parts of the building, built after the Second World War, are not entirely ideal but will suffice for the meantime. I have established a ten year plan to rejuvenate the school building and maximise capacity. The population of Chancery town has surged, but we have not grown at the same rate. We find ourselves oversubscribed and under-resourced. I intend to do something about this and will be presenting our case to both the

Department of Education and our own Board of Governors. Inevitably, there will be some considerable funds to raise but, I trust, I will have your backing and your prayers through what may be an arduous campaign."

There was a pause, then a cawing of approval from the crows. The briefing was concluded by the 8:50 a.m. bell. It was time for roll call. The staffroom flapped with black birds in a widening gyre, whisking up books, registration folders and sheets of paper. They spiralled and swirled through the door, scattering into the corridors and the rooms beyond.

Mr Baxter remained solid, unmoved by the wind that carried his subordinates away. When the staffroom was empty, he granted me a smile.

Chapter Eight

Mr Baxter's evening meetings were with an architect and, on another night, the Board of Governors. Minutes were taken for both meetings by Mrs Maylie, Acting Headmaster's Secretary. How impressively she had progressed in her career.

The architect meeting was to study building schematics and discuss their numerous permutations. I was not encouraged to look at the technical drawings. The headmaster had simply requested that I return in the evening to document the meeting and its outcomes.

I had no more interest in the governors' meeting, nor was I even required to take the minutes there. The governors – twelve local business men, gnarly and wise – had appointed one of their own number to act as secretary and chronicle their deeds. It was left to me to issue cups of tea, coffee and biscuits where required. After that, I had no other role for the evening. While the group were still settling down and there was sufficient conversation to cover my retreat, I whispered to Mr Baxter that I should probably leave.

"Not at all," he said. "I want you beside me. You may yet be needed, if only to note down any matters arising that require my action." Something in his demeanour told me that he would appreciate an ally. I took my place beside him.

The boardroom was conservatively decorated with an old table for fourteen and a sideboard for crockery. It lacked the grandeur one would associate with government. As the meeting continued, the tedious issues drove me to consider the portraits of forgotten dignitaries, dangling on the walls around the room. I could see only three walls without turning, but every character in these portraits, painted and photographed, appeared to have been holding his breath too long. One gentleman was standing beside a horse – or, if he was a dwarf, it may have been a large dog, and it too was suffocating for art's sake.

Mr Baxter cleared his throat and brought me back to the present. He had dashed notes on an envelope and read it before responding to a question. "Indeed, Mr Chairman. I have met with him and am in the closing stages of having some workable plans. We may be available to go to tender within the month," he said. His face was stony but I noticed a minor quivering in the

74

envelope he fiddled between his fingers. Mr Baxter was anxious to impress his new employers. He surged from his seat and produced the rolled architectural plans from beneath the table. "Gather round, gentlemen and see for yourselves," he said. With bold movements he took control of the meeting and spread the treasure map before his crew. Once the governors were engaged with the drawings, Mr Baxter stepped back and spared me a look. He raised his eyebrows in relief that he had won their approval.

It was interesting to me that even the headmaster was accountable. There was a limit to his power and he depended on the favour of these pirates more than he liked.

The meeting concluded informally, which caused some alarm to the governor secretary, who rushed to record final comments in the minutes. Then Mr Baxter was surrounded by governors, who wanted to shake his hand or grip his elbow, the way men do. The chairman, Mr Boyce, a short, swarthy gentleman, with a black dyed, hair-sprayed comb-over, shook hands with the headmaster like he was operating a sturdy water pump.

"Great job. Super job, Samuel," he said, working Mr Baxter's arm with each word. "This bodes well for the school. We have a man of vision at the helm. Start at the centre and work out. Excellent idea. Worth every penny."

I was sorry I had not paid more attention in the meeting. Something of significance had passed and I had missed it. I recognised that Mr Baxter had sold the building project to the governors. More than that, they were celebrating him as a visionary. No doubt they also prided themselves on having appointed him as headmaster.

As the last governors departed, I returned to my office to collect my coat and bag. A fierce gale was whipping the car park. I buttoned my coat in the foyer, readying myself for the dash to my car. Mr Baxter ushered the last of the school's patrons to the front door and into the tempest. We stood in there with only the sound of the rain's assault. His stony face slumped up to a tired smile. He was momentarily stripped of all pretence.

"Thank you, Rose, for coming. And thank you for staying, although I'm sure it bored you."

75

"No. I don't mind, Mr Baxter. I'll not pretend it was interesting, but it was good to see your project receive approval."

"I think, when we are alone, I would rather you called me Samuel. You were right: surnames are very formal."

I did not know what to say. I uttered a trite, "Thank you, Samuel" to fill the space.

"Good night," he said and opened one of the doors for me.

I hardly noticed the buffeting wind or stinging rain. The light from the door Samuel held lit my path to the car.

John Souseman was the first visitor to my office on Friday. Unfortunately it was not a social call.

"Baxter wants to see me," he said. John looked dreadful, as if he had slept in a hedge. His eyes were shot with capillaries, his hair was matted and he had not shaved for days.

"Does he?" I said.

"Need to know what it's about."

"Well, I didn't even know he had asked to see you."

"He phoned biology directly."

"I'll find out if you like." I was about to press the intercom button, when John stepped forward.

"Wait," he paused in thought. "I'll go back to class. Phone me with what it's about. Make the appointment for after school. That'll give me time with Cruiksy." John was concerned about something.

"Why do you need Danny Cruikshanks?" I asked.

"Union rep." Given John's history with Samuel Baxter and their previous confrontation, it was logical to presume their meeting would be unpleasant.

"Want to know what Baxter's shooting before I go in. Old Cruiksy'll back me up – it's been a long time since he killed someone."

"Very well," I said. In my role as headmaster's secretary I had to strike a fine balance between loyalty to a friend and professionalism.

As John was leaving, he ducked his head back in to the office. "Rosie, any chance of a lift home? My car's off the road today." His top lip curled under his beakish nose.

It was not good news for John when I phoned the biology store. "Mr Baxter tells me he wishes to discuss your recent timekeeping," I said.

"That's arse," he said. "Still, could be worse. Book me seats for two. Cruiksy is sharpening his commando knife."

I had to inform the headmaster that John would be bringing his union representative to the meeting. I thought it best to convey this face-to-face.

"What does he mean by bringing the union into this?" Samuel said. His face darkened and he flexed his hands on the desk. He looked down at them and frowned. "The highs never last long in this job, Rose. It is a difficult balancing act at the top." After a considered pause he said, "If Souseman wants to play that game, that is fine by me. You will have to sit in on the meeting and officially document his verbal warning. I was just going to rebuke him, but now it can go on record."

"As you wish, Mr Baxter," I said. He did not notice that I had not called him Samuel. He was probably so used to the more formal version.

My next thought was to warn John that he had inadvertently raised the stakes of the game. However, self-preservation encouraged me to say nothing. If John had been late for work, that was his affair. His decision to hide behind his union representative was his own decision too. I could not jeopardise my working relationship with the headmaster to warn John. He would discover it for himself soon enough. It also occurred to me that Samuel may have been testing my loyalty by telling me these things in advance.

"I spoke to Mrs Bedford on the phone," Samuel said. "She expects to be back on Monday."

I could not read any emotion in his face. "That's good news," I said.

After a pause he said, "Actually, I am a little disappointed. I do not look forward to the scoldings. You would make an excellent headmaster's secretary, Rose."

"Thank you," I said. I felt like curtseying before him.

He was an unpredictable, contrary man. There were two impulses within him: one overly formal, the other emotionally expressive. On most occasions, the formal man dominated the expressive one. Infrequently, the expressive Samuel would wrest control, but his coup was short-lived.

Danny Cruikshanks had been a Paratrooper in the Second World War. There were many legends concerning him, among staff and pupils, but he never spoke about his wartime experiences. Some of these legends were that he had been among those to assault Pegasus Bridge and that he still had the fragments of a German bullet, grenade or *Panzerfaust* lodged in his leg, back or brain – much depended on the tale-teller. Danny was aware of these rumours but did nothing to dispel them. It was not that he enjoyed them; he just understood the futility of such a venture.

On the occasions when I had visited the biology store, Danny had always been welcoming. To members of staff, he was a gruff uncle; to the pupils, he was an absolute tyrant. He had a traditional view of discipline, explaining himself between slaps. It would be easy to assume that he was hated by the boys for this, but most of his methods were commonplace in 1976. Not commonplace, however, was his use of the phrase: "It's a long time since I killed a man!" The recipients of such a warning usually believed they were next. Danny Cruikshanks had adopted John as an apprentice. It was convenient that John's mentor and friend could also defend him through this court-martial.

Danny's moustache entered my office first. It was so voluminous that it may well have concealed a commando knife. The moustache claimed most of his jowls and tailed down to his jaw. Its white bloom contrasted with the tight brown dome of his scuffed head. The remainder of his white hair fought a retreat and made a last stand on his top lip. It gave him a fierce look that even intimidated some of the staff. This was shaping to be an encounter that would put Samuel Baxter's fortitude to the test.

"Tell that damn bounder we are here!" the moustache said, but the eyes above it twinkled. He was going to enjoy this.

I gripped my writing pad, checked the pen in its spiral binding and pressed the intercom button. "Mr Baxter, Mr Souseman and Mr Cruikshanks are here to see you."

"Yes, Mrs Maylie, accompany them in at once – and bring your note pad."

"Yes, Headmaster," I said. No doubt the headmaster's last comment had been intended to shock the opposition, but the moustache did not even twitch.

Outside in the corridor, John winked at me. He tried to straighten his collar and jacket, but his efforts achieved nothing. His movements were also unusually stiff.

Danny Cruikshanks rapped the headmaster's door and strode in without waiting for confirmation. "Right, let's get this started, Mr Baxter," he growled. "We haven't got all day." Danny snapped toward a chair and sat down.

There were limited seating options in Mr Baxter's study. The headmaster had foreseen this problem and had borrowed two chairs from the boardroom. John occupied one of these, and I sat in the other. I repositioned it off to the side to have a good view of all their faces.

The headmaster began, grandly, to lecture John. "Mr Souseman, I spoke to you previously about your lack of professionalism in how you dress yourself for work. Observing your current dishevelled appearance, I continue to be appalled. You make very little effort to present yourself as a serious professional. It has also come to my attention that you were late for work this morning. This kind of thing will not do at all. It is entirely unacceptable to be habitually turning up for work late, shabbily dressed and missing the staff briefing. Mrs Maylie, acting as my secretary, is here to document that you are being given a formal verbal warning under the school disciplinary code."

Danny Cruikshanks had been regarding the headmaster with a fixed stare. If Mr Baxter noticed this, he showed no signs of being intimidated, but he did blink heavily when Danny barked out his first protest.

"Now listen here, Baxter! This is nothing but a damn nonsense," he said. He did not shout, but his tone belonged on the parade square. "Members of staff are late every day, and you do not hound them. I know, because I have asked around. You have not rebuked one other member of staff about poor time-keeping – and there are plenty who deserve it. I'd also like to see what evidence you have that Souseman was late. It is clear you didn't see him arrive into school, because you were taking staff briefing. So, where is your evidence?"

Baxter glared back at him.

"You also jumped to the conclusion that he is habitually late," Cruikshanks continued. "From hearing of one lateness, you have presumed that this is a habit. It's a damn nonsense. Besides that, Baxter, you have a history of singling Souseman out for your abuse.

"That's Mister Baxter to you!" the headmaster snarled.

"I'll call you mister when you start acting like a gentleman and not a playground bully." Cruikshanks rapped his knuckles on the arm of his chair. It sounded like a rifle being cocked. "And furthermore, Baxter, your comments about his appearance are insulting. He wears a shirt, tie and jacket as required by the staff dress code, yet you still challenge him."

"The man has not shaved for days." The headmaster stabbed a finger at John.

"For all you know, he is growing a beard," Cruikshanks scoffed. "But you haven't even asked him. Do staff need your permission for that too? This is nothing more than harassment. Souseman's results speak from themselves." He rapped the chair again. "Souseman is the best science teacher I have encountered in nearly thirty years of teaching. His exam results put the rest of us to shame. You cannot deny he is an effective teacher. The only logical conclusion is that this harassment is based on nothing more than your own personal prejudice."

"It certainly is not!" Mr Baxter spat the words.

"Well, *Headmaster*, I'll tell you what is going to happen. You have Mrs Maylie here record the verbal warning on Souseman's record –"

John jolted. "Steady on!" he blurted, but fell silent as Danny raised his hand.

"You record this warning and I'll have the National Executive down here tomorrow, balloting our members on industrial action." Danny's eyes calculated range and trajectory to target.

Mr Baxter paused. His mouth twisted as he considered his next move. "It is not long until your retirement, Cruikshanks. You're an old soldier. You know that this is the first skirmish of a long war. And I can promise you, sir, that you will not be in Chancery Grammar to see the end of *this* war. When John

80

Souseman is making his last stand, you will not be at his side."
Baxter sneered his last words, and I did not like to see it.

It was the old soldier's turn to pause.

"Your threats are empty, Baxter. You cannot touch me and
you damn well know it. You're nothing but a pompous fool. I've
seen a dozen of your sort scarper at the first sign of a real fight."

Mr Baxter sat back in his chair with an affectation of calm.
His voice was deliberate when he spoke. "On the contrary Mr
Cruikshanks, that was not a threat. I would not threaten you, or
your retirement. I actively encourage you to retire, and to do so
at your nearest convenience. You see, I can have you replaced by
someone young, vital and half the price. I am sure you have been
considering it. While you are here, you should also consider the
generous enhancement package offered by the Department of
Education for those applying for voluntary redundancy."

It was a bribe and a dirty trick. Just then, I was glad
Christine Bedford would be returning on Monday.

"I think you have given us our answer," Danny said with
contempt. "We have nothing more to say." John followed as
Danny stood. They walked from the study in silence.

I remained seated, affecting to be absorbed in my notepad.
Mr Baxter drummed his fingers on his desk. I wanted to
transform into a wisp of smoke and drift away unnoticed.

"What have you written in your notes, Mrs Maylie?"

We were alone, but I was back to being Mrs Maylie.

I showed the headmaster my page of shorthand
hieroglyphs.

"Please throw that in the bin," he said. "I want no record
of that meeting." He only half looked over to me.

"Will there be anything else, Headmaster?" I said.

"No," he nodded to the door, "You may go."

I decided my day's work was complete. My duties as
headmaster's secretary were fulfilled for the day, even if it was
half an hour early. On a whim, I called into the staffroom. After
school, a different set of rules existed there, as the academic staff
abandoned it to the cleaners. John and Danny sat in corner
armchairs and the room was otherwise empty. They were busy
with a debrief when I entered.

"Good girl, Rosie. Was worried you'd forgotten my lift home?" John hailed me.

I noted that the kettle was coming to the boil and I hoped there would be enough for three coffees. Danny was on his feet and produced three mugs from the cupboard under the sink.

"Have a seat, Rose. I'll do the coffee," he said. His bark had gone. The only remnant of his confrontation with Baxter was a crease in his brows. He brought the coffees over to our corner armchairs, and we sipped in silence for a while before anyone spoke.

"You're screwed, Souseman," Danny said. He smiled, contradicting his persistent frown. I only knew this because his moustache turned up at the corners. His mug disappeared under the shrubbery while he sipped.

"Thanks for that," John said.

"Baxter was right: I'll not be here much longer, laddie. I'm counting the days."

"You've got years left yet," John said. "You're only about fifty-five."

"Fifty-seven. That's old enough to go. The Department will make my pension up to sixty, if I take a redundancy. And that's what Baxter wants."

After a pause, John said, "I'm screwed, then."

I nodded.

"You need to get yourself squared away, John," Danny said. "Baxter will be looking for something to use against you. Make sure you take care of business, so he has no grounds for complaint."

"You should move to another school," I said. "Baxter will keep a detailed file on you from now on. That's what he does."

"Don't be worrying about me," John said. He knocked back the last of his coffee and winced at the movement. He rubbed his neck. "I could use that lift home now, Rosie."

While I did not object to giving John a lift home, I did not want Mr Baxter to see me doing it. The headmaster may have thought I was colluding with his enemy – which I was. For some reason, that concerned me. Even though I would not be his secretary on Monday, and I disapproved of his methods, I did not want him to think I had sided against him. A lonely woman, going through a divorce, needs to keep her options open. Mr

Baxter represented an opportunity and I would not carelessly squander it. I wanted to be a headmaster's secretary.

"Rose?" John asked.

I looked at my watch. "Sorry, John, I was just thinking that I'm not due to knock off until five. You know what Baxter is like when it comes to timekeeping."

"I think I may."

"Very good. You'll have to wait. Or Danny may be able to give you a lift?"

Danny shrugged. "I'm going the other way."

It was difficult to explain. John had a bluff exterior but he was a sensitive soul. I opted for another tactic. "I'll only be twenty minutes, John. I'm happy to give you a lift, but could I ask a favour in return?"

"You may."

"Would you hide in my car boot?" I almost said. "Would you walk to the corner shop on Hill Street and get me a bottle of milk? My bag is still in the office. I'll get you the money after."

"Just a pint? No problem," he said.

When John emerged from the shop, milk in hand, he found me parked on the kerb only a few metres away. He did a double-take, laughed and carefully lowered himself in to the passenger seat.

"Didn't want to be seen with me?" he said.

Surprise was required for my denial to be plausible. "What? No. That's not a nice thing to say, John." Again, this was a trick I had learned from Harry.

"You should have said. I don't want trouble for you. You know that." John was too clever to be deceived.

"I did need the milk," I lied. "And I wasn't needed at the office – so I thought I would save you the walk back to school." I paused. "But, yes, it did cross my mind that it would be a little awkward if we were seen driving out together. I did not plan it like that. That's just the way it worked out."

"I can't complain," John said.

The route to John's house took us to the limits of the Chancery town and beyond its suburbs. Just before Grampton village, where John lived, I slowed at a T-junction, about to turn left. On that late January afternoon, it was already dark. My headlights illuminated the area ahead where a road sign had once stood. It was now two twisted metal posts, their concrete feet uprooted. Behind it, there was a large hole in the hedge. John cleared his throat.

"What did you say was wrong with your car?" I asked.

"I said 'it's off the road'."

"It certainly is, John. Off the road, through a hedge and upside down in a field."

John sniffed. "Thought Baxter wanted to speak about that. Crapped myself. Imagine the police coming to the school. Baxter would've exploded."

"Mr Baxter would not forgive that easily," I agreed. "Are you injured?"

"No. I'm fine. I wasn't hurt. Too busy sleeping." He lied. I remembered how he had been favouring his back and neck.

"How did you get to school this morning?"

"I spoke to the farmer after the crash. I know him. He was grand," he laughed. "Then I started out to school."

"You walked? That's about six miles."

"Closer to eight," he said with misplaced pride.

"No wonder you were late."

Just then, I noticed another car's lights growing in my rear mirror. I made the left turn.

"It's too far for a lift in the morning, sister. Thanks for the offer." He climbed out stiffly, with a grunt.

I had made no such offer.

"Get yourself a bath before bed. I'll pick you up in the morning and take you home too. After that, make your own arrangements."

"You're the best, Rosie," he said.

Chapter Nine

My week with Mr Baxter had a greater impact on my future than I expected. In that January week in 1976, an interweave of consequence was at work. My two late evenings in work were of the most significance to Dorothy, meaning that when she needed my counsel, I was unavailable. The Thursday evening of the Governors' meeting was her crisis point. She kept everything to herself on that Friday, but erupted on Monday morning.

"We're engaged!" she declared.

I was stunned.

Betty's jaw slackened before she could compose herself.

"Congratulations," Joan said.

Betty shot a look over to me, while Joan hugged Dorothy. "Well done, Dorothy," Betty said. "Let's see the hardware."

My recuperation required effort. When I did speak, it was in a murmur, and I only added to the artifice of congratulation. It seemed appropriate.

"William asked me on Thursday night. Of course, I said yes immediately, but we didn't want to announce it until we had the ring." Dorothy bubbled and duly extended her left hand, thumb pushed under her third finger.

The ring was unremarkable, with a full stop of a diamond, hardly visible to the naked eye. Of course, we all cooed over it as a lavish display of taste and wealth. It is much the same when viewing a friend's newborn child. The standard responses of "how lovely!" were doled out. In truth, I pitied Dorothy. She probably imagined the tug of the ring's extra weight on her arm, just as she imagined the enormity of William's love.

"I'm absolutely delighted for you," I said. "Have you set a date?"

"July," she said. Her eyes cast round for our reactions.

"I'm sure you'll get the weather in July. There's something special about summer weddings," said Joan. "It gives an extra measure of hope." She gave Dorothy another hug, wringing from her whimpers of delight.

"I got married in November," I said, but no one paid attention.

Betty stood at her desk and counted her fingers. "That's almost five months. When's the baby due?"

She had meant it as a joke, but the possibility knotted in my throat. I was appalled. Had Dorothy condemned herself to a loveless marriage for the sake of a child? I hoped she had not been so foolish. Her life was normally governed by fear. Surely she was incapable of the irresponsible passion required for pre-marital conception. She was desperate for William's approval but I could not believe she would trade her chastity for marriage.

"That's horrid," said Dorothy.

"Betty! Behave yourself," Joan said, frowning over her glasses. "Don't listen to her pet," she said to Dorothy.

"Sorry. Only joking," said Betty, smirking.

I winked at her. Betty and I would be having the same lunch break. There was much to discuss.

As the morning progressed, I tried to corner Dorothy alone. I was sure an explanation would be forthcoming. She remained elusive, however. Either she was in the company of others, or on some urgent errand whenever we risked being alone. At break-time, she was last to bring her chair into the circle and sat between Joan and Betty, even though they had to shuffle over to give her room. Mostly, I was curious to see how far Dorothy would get on a diet of pure hope. I wanted to know whether she was sure of her decision.

It was Wednesday before Dorothy was stranded alone in my company. Joan was on an errand and Betty had ducked out to the toilet. Dorothy looked up from her desk to see me looking at her. I had been staring over, willing her to notice.

"I am delighted for you," I said, "And I trust that you will be happy together."

She looked uncomfortable.

I continued, "William couldn't manage without you, I expect, and came to his senses." I imagined he had returned with a posy of weeds slumped over his thick knuckles. "It's a sign that you are made for each other," I said. "You'll be very happy, have lots of babies, and you won't have to work here anymore. I am delighted for you."

Dorothy's famished little face wilted. "Thank you, Rose," she pined. "I'm sorry, I never got to speak to you. Please don't tell anyone what happened before. That was just a bad patch for William and me."

"Of course I won't say a word, you silly thing. That's nobody's business but yours," I lied. Both Betty and John already knew everything.

Apparently, William had called to see her on the Thursday, wringing with remorse. His apology was unreserved. A fear of commitment had caused him to invent foolish reasons to break up with her. He was miserable without her and never wanted to be apart from her again. Not only did he beg her forgiveness, he said she was his soul-mate, and he wanted her to be his wife.

I was sure she romanticised the event far beyond its actual proportions.

It sounded pathetic.

"That's lovely," I said.

"Your mascara is running, Rose," Dorothy said.

It was a cheap brand and forever doing that.

In spite of our recent reversal, Mr Baxter called me to his study. We were to discuss the progress of Jack Dawson, to whom I was still assigned. Our meeting was scheduled for after the final bell. Christine Bedford sneered at me when I entered her office.

"My replacement has arrived," she said.

"Oh, Christine, that's not true," I said. "How is your sciatica?"

"I'm sure you'd love to know. If it wasn't bearable, I wouldn't be here. Would I?" She had a sharp tongue of late and had changed from the woman who had quietly supported Dr Thompson. "My hip is not the real problem, Rose. It's my nerves. He has them in tatters." She jabbed a thumb through the wall to the headmaster's study. "It's like having another child. And I've done my share of that. It's a young woman's game, doing everything for him." She stood, hands on hips and rotated her waist in a wide circle. "Sitting doesn't help," she said.

"I came to see Mr Baxter."

"Of course you did, girl. Go on in. He should be waiting, unless he's off doing something he hasn't told me about."

I knocked on Mr Baxter's door.

"Enter," he said with grandeur.

I took a deep breath. He was seated at his desk, writing hastily. "One moment, Mrs Maylie. I promise not to keep you."

He gestured to a chair with a flick of his eyes. When he finished writing, he looked up with an amused expression. "You braved the perils of Scylla on your way in here." He waited for my reaction.

I remained silent.

"My apologies, Mrs Maylie. A classical reference. *The Odyssey.*"

I offered no recognition.

"On Odysseus' voyage home he encountered Scylla, a six-headed, man-eating monster," he said.

"I shall make a point of reading it." I said.

"Never mind. It probably wasn't funny anyway," he said. His smile flattened with disappointment. "That was a bad business on Friday." He paused, either for effect, or to measure my reaction.

I constructed an impassive look while his sharp eyes scanned me.

"I understand you are friends with John Souseman," he continued. "It is a difficult business and I have thought it over. Perhaps I was a little reactionary concerning his lateness. But I'm not a man that reacts well to defiance." He squeezed his hands together. "All things considered, I will let that incident remain undocumented. It was no one's finest hour."

I wondered whether Mr Baxter was expecting me to relay this message to John.

Again, he studied me for a reaction.

"On to other business then," he said. "In the morning, I will be reminding Mr Dawson that it is his responsibility to organise the school timetable. I am not sure whether he has experience of this. As a safeguard, I asked Bill Logan to write a schedule for him to follow. Mr Logan is recovering well, thank the Lord." He waved the schedule in his hand.

"I am very glad to hear it," I said, although I had been aware of it for some time.

"Mrs Maylie – Rose – I would like you to help Mr Dawson implement this schedule."

So I was Rose again. That informality was a sign of his favour, but the memory of how he treated John was still fresh. I felt a long way from returning to a personal form of address with Mr Baxter.

"Very well," I said.

"I am sure you would like a copy of Bill Logan's schedule?" he asked. The angle of his head indicated playfulness but I could not think why.

"That would be helpful, yes."

"And you shall have one. Or as many copies as you wish," he said, pleased with himself.

"Thank you," I said. His boyish enthusiasm was almost amusing. "You may consider this quite odd," he said. "But I have ordered a photocopier. It will be delivered tomorrow. I concede to being rather excited about it, too." He may have expected me to congratulate him.

I had heard of such machines being used, but the technology was relatively slow to catch on. They were expensive and notoriously difficult to maintain.

"It is a clever, labour-saving device. It should also prevent mishaps, like the one we almost had concerning Mr Dawson's lost minutes. It will copy an entire page with just the touch of a button," he said.

"That should be useful." I wondered whether to say his name. He had called me Rose twice. Perhaps he was due a Samuel. He had practically apologised for his actions against John.

It was too late.

I had left it too long.

I would say it next time.

"I want to run an efficient system and save unnecessary paperwork," he said. "Imagine how much time it will save you when making multiple copies of a document. The salesman tells me it is possible to tap in the number of copies you want, press Start, and simply walk away. The machine does the rest. You could type something else, answer the phone," he wafted a hand, "Or whatever else you do."

"Our lives will never be the same," I said.

"Ha! Yes, I see." His finger waggled and he smiled. "You mock me. Perhaps I'm getting carried away. But we will see. Slowly, my plans are coming to fruition." He gestured to the piles of box files, papers and assorted mess. "Do not presume that this is an indication of a disorderly mind, Rose. Quite the contrary: it is a testament to my patience. I have tolerated the disarray of my workspace only because it is necessary. This will all change very soon. I spent my first week in Chancery Grammar in this office, assessing where I could make improvements. I plan to build something great here, and the humble photocopier – which you dryly dismiss – is an important brick in the edifice. Come September, all will be impressed." He pulsated with significance for a moment. "Well, I digress from the original topic. Have you anything on Mr Dawson that needs to be included in his file?"

"Not so far," I said.

"Well, I have." His wrist flourished. "Take note of the following," he paused and I readied a fresh page on my notepad.

I was glad to focus on a task at last.

Mr Baxter began, "Date: Friday, January 23, 1976. Mr Arthur Edwards, Head of modern languages, was looking for Mr Dawson, who had not turned up to his timetabled class, teaching O-Level French. Mr Edwards set the class to work and went in search of Mr Dawson. He found the vice-principal's office door locked but believed him to be inside it, nonetheless. Mr Edwards lifted himself up and looked through the window above the door, whereupon, he observed Mr Dawson asleep on his desk."

"Eh, pardon me, Samuel, should that not be 'asleep *at* his desk'?"

He smiled and nodded. The 'Samuel' was acceptable. "Well, you would think so. In his defence, Dawson might be able to say that he had been working at his desk and slumber overtook him. No, not Jack Dawson. He was actually lying *on* his desk. He had cleared its contents onto the floor and stretched out for forty winks."

I snorted. "Asleep *on* his desk it is, then," I said, writing.

"To continue – Mr Edwards persevered in knocking the door until Mr Dawson was eventually roused from his slumber. Mr Edwards then reported the incident to me."

"And what did Mr Dawson have to say for himself?" I asked.

"We have yet to see." Samuel checked his watch and smiled primly.

I felt a sudden alarm. I was about to witness another disciplinary action. "Surely, you don't expect me to stay?" I said, my eyes widening.

He smiled at me. "My dear, Rose. I have tarnished myself enough in your sight," he said. "And Dawson is not to know we are keeping a file on him. Mrs Bedford will write the minutes of this incident."

I was very glad to hear it – and also that he had addressed me as his 'dear'.

He looked at his watch. "In about ten minutes, the angry Mrs Bedford will caw through her intercom that Mr Dawson has arrived for our appointed meeting. You will be long gone by then, but I will keep the report for you to read on Monday."

Standing behind his desk, he withdrew to the corner. From a peg, he flourished his academic gown and donned it like a shadow. With that, his formality grew. The headmaster ushered me to the study door. Before we had fully reached it, the door swung in with a sharp rap, and Mrs Bedford frowned at us. "Mr Baxter, Mr Dawson is here for his meeting," she said. Behind her, Jack Dawson loitered. He looked neither concerned nor uncomfortable. His casual manner suggested he was ignorant of the meeting's real purpose.

"Hello, Rose," he whispered to me as I slipped past. "I'm getting my wrists slapped again," he said. His caterpillar moustache arched into a sneer.

In spite of my disapproval, I wrestled down a smile. His bravado was difficult to condemn. It is easy to make heroes of those who do not play by the rules. Samuel would have quite a job chastening Jack Dawson into place.

One month later, at our Tuesday afternoon meeting, the headmaster and I discussed his vice-principal's failings. The file on Jack Dawson had thickened with misdemeanours since his January disciplinary meeting.

"It absolutely will not do, Rose." Samuel stubbed his finger onto his desk. "I cannot wait forever in the hope he will shape up. Dawson is a skiver of the worst kind. He has absolutely no work ethic. He defies me openly and will not take reproach. He can weave a credible excuse for everything. That business about his back injury, for instance: he has not produced one shred of medical documentation to prove it."

Samuel referred to Dawson's excuse for lying on his desk. He had claimed that an old back injury had flared up, compelling him to lie down on his desk to straighten out. He had surely passed out with the pain. It was an excellent excuse, and difficult to disprove. Samuel, although sceptical, allowed Dawson a week to provide a doctor's report to corroborate his claims. A month later, Dawson still had no proof.

"He is very plausible," I said.

"Plausible, yes. That's the trouble. I want to believe him. It is easier to believe him than to replace him. Unlike most people, he cannot be intimidated. He is utterly fearless and indifferent to what others think of him."

"His crimes are all minor. It's nothing scandalous that −"

Samuel's broad hand went up, a finger extended. His eyes were wide, as though I had uttered a voodoo curse. "Do not say that!" he said. "That is precisely what I fear. For a hundred and twenty years, Chancery Grammar has been a beacon in this community." The finger swelled to a fist. "Left unchecked, Dawson will bring us to infamy. I cannot permit that to happen. While I am headmaster, I will do *anything* to defend this school's reputation." His fist shook, as he choked meaning from his words.

This was a little melodramatic. Jack Dawson had been late to class; he had missed whole classes; he was conveniently sick during the school examinations − which he was tasked to oversee; he was absent most Mondays and, on Fridays, slipped out early. He was a man of several minor defects. We all have them; Dawson's were all simply work related.

"That's very pessimistic," I said. We were more familiar by this stage and Samuel did not flinch when I contradicted him. Our relationship was strictly professional, however. His desk was the barrier between us. Our words could be frank, but rarely personal.

"Dawson is a drinker − and you know how I feel about that. His self-indulgence knows no end. To my shame, I did not properly research him before appointing him vice-principal. I only learned last month that a rumour was circulating around Elmfield Grammar two weeks before I looked for a candidate to replace Bill Logan."

"What was it?"

"That he might be in the habit of visiting prostitutes." Samuel shook his head. "I am looking further into the matter. I pray to the Lord it is just a rumour and nothing more."

"Here in Chancery? I had no idea we had such a thing."

"Apparently so." Samuel lowered his head and massaged his lumpy brow with his finger tips. "He will ruin us, Rose. I must replace him."

"He will be hard to remove."

He looked up slowly. "I agree." A light kindled in him. "But he can be pushed aside. I am extending the senior management of the school. I need a good man; someone in whom I have an absolute trust."

In my experience, there were few men to fit that description. A name occurred to me and I smiled. "Charlie Bakewell."

"Exactly, Rose." Samuel returned my smile. "We think alike." In the pause, he examined my face as if for the first time. He cleared his throat and continued. "Charlie is perfect for the job: thoroughly conscientious and he has a real heart for the school. I have discussed it with him and he spent the evening praying about it. This morning, he accepted the position. In September he will become our new vice-principal."

"I cannot think of a better man."

"The best man," Samuel said. "Indeed, he was best man at my wedding."

I nodded as if surprised, but Joan had told me this long ago. She would be delighted for Charlie. She looked upon him as a younger brother. Joan had badgered him to develop his career, but Charlie always resisted. "The Lord will provide," he had said. It seemed he had been right.

"You may have noticed, Rose, when you were acting as Mrs Bedford's replacement, that I prefer to start each day with Bible study and prayer, alone in my study. I feel this helps to calibrate my daily decisions. Prayer is the foundation for righteous living, after all. Charlie, however, puts me to shame," Samuel said. "He has always been thoroughly prayerful and, for him, everything is in God's service. He asked to start our management meetings with a prayer." He looked to the cornice. "I am a spiritual man, but it had never occurred to me that I should pray with my enemy. I had never considered that to be the solution to my problems with Dawson. Charlie's suggestion was a timely rebuke for me."

"It amuses me to imagine Dawson, sandwiched between the two of you, praying."

"What finer way to torment him?" Samuel laughed. "He will tender his resignation within the week."

Since Harry had deserted me, my own spiritual observance had wilted. At first, I began to miss a few Sunday services; eventually, I missed them all. My Christian faith had been something I shared with Harry – although mine had always been the stronger. It was something I thought would bind us together. Church was supposed to remind us of our commitment to each other. For that reason, I liked to sit with him at the front, near where we had said our vows. When my marriage dissolved, my faith did too. The day Harry left me was the last day I prayed. Until God cleared his account and gave Harry testicular cancer, I would pray no more.

"What has kept you from our table so long?" my father said, passing John the butter dish.

"Trouble of the worst kind, Peter," John replied.

"Ah. A woman." Father nodded slowly.

My mother and I shared a look.

John ran his finger around the lip of his wine glass. "Rose waylaid me tonight with the promise of fine food."

"How was your roast, love?" my mother asked him.

"Perfect, June. You are a maestro."

"He is a charmer when he wants to be," she said to the rest of us. We laughed because my mother rarely said anything amusing.

"Tells us about Ellie," I said to John.

His eyes narrowed at my betrayal – he had successfully deflected the topic so far. Now he had no option but to tell his story. He briefly recounted their days as medical students but shuffled around the topic of her marriage and pending divorce.

"She's a doctor in The Royal now?" my father asked.

"Cardiology. She has a real heart for her job," John said.

I tutted at his weak pun. Mother laughed after a five second delay.

"I am sure she works very long hours," Father said.

"She's a locum, and fits work around –" John realised his slip, "– her other commitments."

"Around her family?" My father poured him more wine. "There, John. That will steady your nerves."

John dropped his head and snorted a laugh. "It all comes out eventually," he said.

"There's no judgement here," Father said.

"We look forward to your visits, John," Mother said. "Bring Ellie next time, if that helps you make it here more often."

"Thank you," said John nodding. "I will try," he fluttered a hand, "babysitting arrangements permitting."

John had a clear road ahead of him. He would inherit an emotional fortune. All he had to do was make the transition from shambling bachelor to responsible stepfather. I tried not to mind that another of my friends was slipping from my life.

"I'll bring Ellie to the evening of Dorothy's wedding. Then the office girls can pick her bones clean," John said to me.

"I'll not be going," I declared.

"Why not, Rose?" My mother started forward.

"If I'm not a good enough friend to invite to the whole event, I'll not be going at all. And I certainly won't be getting them any presents."

My father, and John sat back. This was not a man's discussion. It had more to do with hurt feelings than abstract principles.

"When were the invitations sent out?" Mother continued.

"A couple of weeks ago."

"And did you not get one?"

"The General Office girls got one collectively," I said, folding my arms with disgust. I told them of the incidents leading to Dorothy's engagement. My mother nodded. John knocked back his wine and Father worked at a food fragment behind a molar.

My mother patted my knee and said, "She may regret abandoning her friends some day, but you shouldn't take it personally, Rose. Weddings can be expensive things."

"I can't imagine her packing the rafters with friends, Mother."

"Now, Rose. Don't be unkind," she said.

95

"Did you invite all of your work colleagues to your wedding?" John asked.

After some consideration I said, "That's not the point. Dorothy led me to believe that we were special friends."

"Would you invite her to your wedding, if you were getting married in July?" John pushed again.

"Have you got yourself a new car yet, John?" I asked.

"Let's retire to the lounge John," my father said, "Or you'll end up walking home. I have a new brandy for you to sample. It's an XO." As they withdrew from the room I heard his advice to John. "Logic has nothing to do with it –", and they were beyond earshot. Perhaps he was right.

The month of June brought with it a pleasant surprise. The headmaster sent round a memo to all 'ancillary staff', as he called us, that we would be allowed almost the same summer holidays as the teaching staff. Even more pleasantly, we were to receive full pay for our seven weeks off. This was unusual: we normally only got a month's leave in July. His rationale was that the buildings should be cleared for the construction of the school's extension. The only stipulation was that the last two days of our term were to be spent packing all office equipment and supplies into crates. This was not as onerous as it sounded. It offered a change from our normal working routine, which I found refreshing.

I tried to imagine what the face of the school would look like when we returned for the last week in August. If only I had paid more attention to the architectural drawings, I would have known exactly what to expect.

Jack Dawson called into the office to collect his mail and have me appoint his next task. This was established routine. He rarely spoke to me beyond the direct exchange of information, and he never lingered to exchange pleasantries. Today, however, he had found something worth lingering for.

As the day's work would be manual, Joan had given us permission to work in casual clothes. Dorothy was dressed like a Mormon in a long skirt and blouse. These were as prim as they were ill-suited to hot, dusty labour. Joan wore loose slacks and a summer blouse, but Betty and I both wore light jeans and casual tops. As befitted the fashion of the day, our jeans were close fitting and flared at the knee. Our tops were similarly fitted.

Mr Dawson took a long time sorting through his papers – all two of them. While I watched, he looked over the top of his letters. Following his line of sight, I saw that Betty was the real focus of his attention. She was quite glamorous, her hair drawn into a high tail, golden skin on her slender neck and arms. Her top was snug, and her jeans bloomed neatly with her hips. She looked statuesque, when she was not talking, or chewing gum. Presently, she was reading a file, absently toying with a side lock that had broken free of her ponytail. Jack Dawson was hypnotised.

"Mr Dawson, I'm sure you will pardon us. We are very busy in here, clearing the office," I said. He did not respond. To him, my voice came from the bottom of a mine shaft. "Mr Dawson. You mustn't stand around. We are far too busy today. We have only two days to have this cleared."

At my stronger tone, all work in the office stopped.

Dawson snapped awake, just as Betty caught his stare. His conversation opener sounded strained. "I haven't seen the plans. My security clearance isn't high enough." He wet his lips and the caterpillar stirred. "I think Mr B. is going to build a prison block under the school." He began to recline against the mail rack beside him. "Rumour has it that Science is expecting three classrooms, but no one knows for sure." He arched an eyebrow. "It's all very secretive." He winked at Betty and the caterpillar twitched. "Have any of you lovely ladies seen the secret plans?" he said.

Thankfully, no one paid him any attention. I finished filling a crate with folders and began labelling it. Joan and Dorothy were emptying a filing cabinet together, and Betty consigned her file to a waste bag. Mr Dawson had picked a poor time for a conversation.

"How is the new timetable coming along, Mr Dawson?" I asked. "You must be nearly finished it by now. Bill Logan always had it done by the end of May. It's June now, the end of term, and the staff will be expecting their copies."

That shifted him. "It's all in the bag, as they say." He stood upright. "I'd love to stay and chat, but I have to keep looking busy. The headmaster's spies are everywhere, you know." He

97

stalled on his way to the door and scavenged another look at Betty. "Who is the lucky little filly that's getting married?" He had asked no one specifically, but we all stopped to listen.

From the back of the office, within the filing cabinet, came Dorothy's tweet: "That's me."

"Well done, my girl. Good show. Caught yourself a fine man." He paused. "We're all invited to the evening do, I hear?"

Dorothy's pause was heavy with regret. "That's right," she said. I could just see her accompanying wince.

"I'm looking forward to seeing you ladies there. I may even lure some of you beauties onto the dance floor." He was looking directly at Betty as he said this. More than that: he licked his lips, like a randy old fox.

"Bring plenty of money, is my advice," she quipped and met his lurid grin without flinching.

Jack Dawson swallowed hard, blinked twice and left the office.

"Some chance," Betty added to the three ladies staring at her.

Chapter Ten

In spite of my resolution, I went to Dorothy and William's wedding function in July 1976. The lure of Jack Dawson's antics was too strong to resist. True to the rest of my promise, I did not get the Butlers a present. I was sure their real friends would provide those in abundance. I did not intend to stay much more than an hour and only arrived in time to see the bride and groom's first dance. It was enough to show my face and pass a few pleasantries.

On my way to the function room, I passed through the hotel bar. John was deep in the throng, ordering drinks and did not notice me. Rather than wade through the crowd, I continued in search of Betty. If there was to be any pleasure this evening, it would be in her company.

Dorothy and William's first dance was announced by the DJ as he cued up "Save Your Kisses for Me". Alone on the dance floor, they were orbited by spots of coloured light. From the edges, hushed onlookers gazed sympathetically. I paused in the smoky half-light to observe and felt a tug of sympathy too. Dorothy was in danger of being trampled to death. William's hulking shadow would have been enough to crush her sparrow bones. His slow dancing added considerably to this likelihood. She looked like a little flower girl, while he slouched over her and enfolded her in thick arms. His tailed morning coat stretched tightly across his back and grew wide at the seams. Their movements together were far from harmonious. In his maul, she was jerked across the floor. He had the grace of a bear lurching over hot coals. She strained up and cooed encouragement: that his clumsiness was unnoticed, that he was doing well. I wondered whether she would offer similar reassurances later in the bridal suite.

When the rest of the wedding party straggled onto the dance floor, I returned to the gloom, searching for Betty. I scanned each of the circular tables in turn. Furthest from the dance floor, in the far corner, sat Betty. Her seat was among a cluster withdrawn from the table. As I drew near, I recognised the profile of Jack Dawson at her ear. The slow music resonated through the room but not so much to ruin conversation. With Dawson at her ear, Betty was nodding agreement to whatever he was saying. She raised her brows when she noticed my approach. I smiled to her but Dawson was too busy narrating to notice me. Betty's eyes rolled up with mild exasperation.

"Hey, Rose," she said. Her voice was a giddy pitch and her cheeks were flushed. She saluted me with a gin and tonic as I sat opposite her.

Dawson leaned back and nodded to me.

"Get yourself a drink," Betty said. Her glass made a circle to indicate the fresh gins on the table. "Have one of mine. Jack has been trying to get me drunk all evening."

A vulpine grin spread across his face. "Have a drink indeed," he said. "Someone should appreciate my generosity." He spoke clearly, over the music, but slower than usual.

Betty reached up and patted the side of his face. Her hand lingered there longer than required. "I appreciate it. Just not the way you are hoping for."

He kissed her cheek and produced his own dark drink from the shadows. He tapped his chest. "My lady, it's only your charming company I seek – and perhaps a little breakfast."

Betty laughed. She was no longer repulsed by him. Her body language and the friendly pat said they were more familiar now. Something had grown between them. Betty was too much at ease for only a few hours in his company.

Jack rose slowly and straightened his jacket. "If you'll excuse me ladies, I must speak to a man about a dog. I think he's over at the bar." And he strolled off into the noisy fog.

When my eyes returned to Betty, she was smiling.

"You two are quite familiar," I said.

"We've been out a couple of times since term ended." I arched a brow and Betty laughed into her drink. "You should see your face, Rose. Yes, this is our third date. We've been to the cinema and a restaurant. Today, before this," her gin made another circle, "we had dinner in the hotel."

"How has he been?" I asked.

"An imperfect gentleman," she laughed, "but I quite like that. And he pays for everything. He's never boring. Keeping him in line is half the fun."

"In that case, you must be well suited," I said. Betty was worldly and could take care of herself. The relationship would

100

develop at her pace. I wondered whether to mention the rumour about his prostitutes.

The music swaggered on, sentimentally. Women tugged their reluctant men up to dance or danced in circles among themselves. Married couples swayed together with modest reserve and unmarried couples in a hopeful clinch. A grandmother, her shoes off, danced a slow jive with an infant flower girl. Dorothy and William were deep in the tide.

"Look at the state of that," Betty said, pointing to the dance floor. I aligned myself to see where she pointed. It was not William Butler's lumbering, as I had first suspected. It was John Souseman.

Normally, dancing couples would hold their partner for intimacy. John was clinging to Ellie for support in a battle with gravity. He slouched on her, arms draped over her shoulders, tugging her forward. Ellie was trim, pretty and did not look accustomed to strenuous labour. Her face was twisted with justifiable complaint, but John was unable to help himself.

Suddenly, affronted by her protests, John straightened, disengaged his choke-hold and swaggered like a one-eyed pirate. He tottered on wooden legs and swayed to right himself. Ellie frowned with disgust. He extended an arm towards her but she flicked it away and stepped back. It was a tiny gesture, but it impacted on John like a punch to the head. He tottered forward but his pickled brain was not up to the task. His right leg tangled with his left and momentum pitched him forward. With nothing to support his weight except a half-placed leg, John was beyond recovery. He landed on his right knee and, soon after, his face. Over the music, I heard the sickening slap of his face on the floor. Gravity had won.

An empty space cleared around him, as he writhed on the floor. People stared down with horror or pity. Complete strangers had expressions of empathy but Ellie, John's beloved, had none. With a snarl, she turned on her heel, summer dress twirling, and strode out of John's life.

William Butler began casting around for someone to take charge of John. The job would naturally fall to one of his close friends.

I said a quick farewell to Betty and took my leave.

William scooped John up to his knees and the crowd obscured my exit. John could be someone else's problem for a change.

Late in August, I returned to work. The scene was blend of wonder and chaos. Mr Baxter's changes swept from the school gates to the front doors, on a carpet of retextured tarmac. The new car park had consumed a portion of the front lawn, but this sacrifice allowed generous parking accommodation. This had been long overdue. I would no longer have to worry about someone stealing my parking place if I went out during lunch. There would be plenty to spare.

The scuffed old doors had been replaced by sheets of double-glazing and polished aluminium. Somehow, the school's plaque had been mounted between the doors' glass sheets. I had never seen this done before and was most impressed with the headmaster's attention to detail. The foyer, however, was where the real grandeur began. Smooth, white plaster and wide glass sheets brought light to sweep visitors towards the new General Office enquiry window. The office itself was much enlarged. Through its door, there was the barrier of a chest-height desktop, where staff would bring their enquiries. Beyond this, spaced generously, were the secretaries' desks. For the first time in my experience, I would not be working in a cramped office. The desks were wide and the chairs supportive. Filing cabinets, too many to count at a glance, stood ready to store our intelligence. The office had widened into the car park. Above the windows, on the sloped roof, skylights pumped filtered sunshine straight to our desks. Mr Baxter had ordered it, and it was so.

Joan and Betty were there ahead of me. They sat in silence and pivoted their chairs around to take in the wonder. I looked through the enquiries window and noted that the old paved courtyard between us and the Geography Department had become a garden, in the early stages of bloom. No weed yet dared its wide beds or freshly unfurled lawns. I wondered if it would soon become 'The Baxter Garden' in honour of its visionary. I had to admit, these changes were much more extensive than I had originally conceived. Even though builders were still on site attending to minor items, it was a marvel that so much had been completed in seven weeks.

After we had quenched our awe with a cup of tea, we set to work. While it was new, the office still needed to be organised. We would be thoroughly occupied before we could begin the usual paperwork for the start of term. The old records and supplies had to be unpacked from crates and given their place. It was a considerable job, which would take the three of us half the week.

The two days before the pupils' return were unusually frantic with paper work and form-filling. Samuel's new photocopier had its own little room and was almost as useful as he had promised. It lightened the burden of duplicating, but it had not yet learned to feed itself individual sheets from large documents. With its help, we rushed a week's administration through two days.

Those who benefited from the new building thought it a triumph. Unfortunately, that only included the headmaster, office staff and the Governors. The teaching staff were bitterly disappointed. Many tried to remember the exact wording of the headmaster's announcement that morning in the staffroom. Most were sure he had mentioned new classrooms in his grand scheme. What he had actually said was coincidentally vague: his 'ten year plan to rejuvenate the school building and maximise capacity' meant he would expand the pupil intake. While that would increase the money received from the Department of Education, it would necessitate some short-term discomfort. That discomfort took the form of six 'temporary modular classrooms', squatting beside the playing fields. Samuel reasoned that the administrative centre of the school had to be upgraded before the rest of the buildings expanded. The modular classrooms would alleviate overcrowding, while pupil numbers could rise annually by thirty, for three consecutive years. Every new class would require a new teacher. With Samuel in charge, Chancery Grammar was thriving.

But teachers are notoriously difficult to please. The more cynical ones saw only the headmaster's disregard for the academic staff. He was overcrowding the school so he could draw a bigger salary, they said. On top of that, these temporary 'huts' were an eyesore.

103

Samuel ground a forefinger into his desk. "The 'nerve centre' of the school was overdue this upgrade by at least a decade," he said. "It is no longer a source of embarrassment, Rose. Our visitors may wait in a well appointed reception area; the General Office is extensive and includes a Reprographics Suite; the Headmaster's Study is now fit for purpose and the Board Room is a marvel of which we may be proud." He had asked me to come and see him. I suspect he wanted to impress me with the majesty of his new office.

"Reprographics suite?" I asked.

"The photocopying room," he said, with a touch of patronage.

"It was the word 'suite' I was having difficulties with. 'Suite' implies luxury."

"Well it is, practically." The mounds of his lumpy brow folded in the middle.

"A suite, with a row of one photocopier," I said, and enjoyed teasing him.

"Some people are impossible to please, Mrs Maylie. I hope you are not one of them."

He was seated across his new desk. It was three times the size of its predecessor, as wide as a king's dining table. He had also appointed himself a throne. Yards of leather were wrapped over its broad frame, before it had been stuffed with a thousand goslings. The final apparatus was a cross between a chair and a booth. The visitor's chair I sat on was much more modest, suitable only for a Third World dictator.

"Well, what do you think?" He swept his arm to include the expanse of his new study, its en suite bathroom, sofas, coffee table, bookcases, circular dining room table, chairs and ankle-deep carpet. There was an adjoining door into Mrs Bedford's office – itself much enlarged – and double doors to the reception.

"Are you planning to live here?" I asked.

"Ha! I certainly could. If only I had thought of making one of these a sofa bed." He was not distracted by my sarcasm. The little boy wanted approval for the things he had built. Anything less was irrelevant.

"I am sure Mrs Baxter and your family would miss you," I added.

104

His response was unexpected. "Huh! An unlikely occurrence." He launched himself from his booth and strode to the double doors. "Let me show you the boardroom. Even you will be impressed, Rose." The eddies of his forward surge flushed me into the corridor behind him.

The boardroom was impressively landscaped, doubled in size – not counting the kitchen anteroom. The most imposing feature was the new table. Its golden cherry expanse shone like a savannah sunset, and the curvature of the earth could be seen in its length. Along its sides, numerous chairs diminished off into the distance. The esteemed portraits had resumed their positions around the walls, with new frames to match the table. Their smudged faces looked on at the realisation of Mr Baxter's dream.

"What do you think, Rose?"

"That's a big table."

"It is a grand table. My gift to the governors, if you like."

The governors' gift to themselves, I thought. "Indeed," I said.

"Now they have been honoured, they will be more generous. The six extra classrooms pleased them, and the increased pupil intake – with its increased budget – will please them further. It is a cynical way to conduct business, Rose, and it's not one I like. I signed on to be an educator. Now I am managing a complex business enterprise. The two do not always sit well together."

"I'm sure they are very pleased with you," I said.

He was not diverted from his lecture, however. "More money will mean more jobs and more resources in the classrooms. This is where good business sense meets good educational practice," he said. "The town of Chancery has grown by over ten thousand in the last decade. A thriving school must accommodate this increased demand."

I was thinking that the money for such a grand table could well have paid for a real classroom to be appended onto the school building. It startled me when Samuel tapped into this thought.

"The table is an extravagance, some may say."

Actually, everyone was saying it.

"But bricks and mortar classrooms will come – and not singly – a whole wing, with two storeys." He spoke like a general planning a coup d'état.

When I turned, he was standing closer than I remembered. He was close enough for me to inhale a gossamer tail of his aftershave. It tingled on my neck. His eyes scanned mine for recognition.

"I should be getting back to work," I said.

"Probably," he said, eyes undiminished.

"Thanks to you, I have a lot of photocopying to do," I said. His hypnotic spell was broken only when I turned.

In the corridor, just as we parted company, he spoke again, "Mrs Bedford has announced her intention to retire in June. The headmaster will be looking for a new secretary."

I nodded and a curious heat rose in my throat.

"But he will not have very far to look," he said. With that, he smiled and returned to his study.

Samuel's Reprographics Suite soon became our Photo-gossiping Room. Within this secret space, Betty sat on a table and updated me on what I had missed of Dorothy's wedding. I scanned pages into the copier purely as a pretext, lest Joan catch us doing nothing.

"After Ellie's sprint for the door – and you after her – big William and his best man helped John up."

"He shouldn't drink so much."

"Well, that was all he wanted to do, especially after Ellie left. John thought he'd buy the teachers a round. Off he staggered to the bar and ordered fifteen gin and tonics –"

"Fifteen?" I said, touching Betty's forearm in alarm.

"Fifteen," she nodded. "The barman told him it would take a while. But, when he had finished, John was nowhere to be found."

"What?" I could not help laughing, despite my concern.

"Danny and Jack found him in the hotel garden, asleep on a bench, with a rose in his mouth." Betty shook her head. "The bar man wouldn't let anyone touch the drinks until they'd been paid for. They frogmarched John back in and handed over his cheque book to pay the bill. I was coming back from the ladies' and saw John trying to sign it. He had one eye closed to help him see straight, and Danny held him upright. I'm sure his signature was illegible."

"It's illegible when he's sober," I said. "How did he get home?"

"He didn't – not that night, anyway. Danny and Jack took turns sitting with him until the function was over. They fed him water for an hour or two – not much use, though. Danny took him back to his place and John slept on a mattress in Danny's garage."

"The garage? That's not right," I said.

"He wasn't safe to be let in the house. He could have been sick, or messed himself."

I could not argue with her logic. A question now hung in the air, and I wondered whether to ask it. While I paused, Betty lifted a packet of business envelopes from a shelf. "How do you know John slept in the garage?" I said.

"Jack phoned Danny the next day to check up on him," she said.

I narrowed my eyes at her. " Were you there when Jack made this call?"

Betty rocked back her head and laughed. "Let's get some work done," she said and swatted me with the envelopes on her way to the door.

Charlie Bakewell enjoyed the celebrity of being the new, and second, vice-principal, especially when he visited the office. Joan mothered him, fussing over his new status. It would not have surprised me to see her lick a handkerchief and daub a spot on his cheek. This day, he had toddled in to drop off some mail.

"And how are the girls coping in this dingy little office, then?" he said, with a child's grasp of irony. His pudding face showed delight. He had said the opposite of what he meant.

"Oh, Charlie. How is our new vice-principal?" said Joan. Without waiting for an answer, she was up from her desk and gave him a clumsy hug.

The new office layout offered plenty of places for visitors to sit. There was even a spare desk and chair, should the need ever arise to employ another secretary. Dorothy's desk was also unoccupied: she had been off sick since the first week in September. With all these surfaces available, Charlie chose my

107

desk on which to splay his bulk. I had been typing with my audio headset on, when I saw him descend to my desk.

"No!" I held out my hand. "Not safe."

Charlie's face inflated with surprise. "Oh!" he said and waddled over to Dorothy's chair.

Joan and Betty froze to observe me. A look of disapproval flicked over Joan's face. With the headphones on, I had spoken louder than intended. I removed them.

"Sorry, Charlie," I said. "These things make me shout."

Charlie inspected Dorothy's desk and found the modern design was not nearly as robust as its predecessor. "I'd have crumpled that like a cardboard box," he said. "Thanks for the warning, Rose." He rumbled Dorothy's chair across the floor towards me. When Joan and Betty resumed their work, Charlie spoke in a hush, "How is Dorothy? I hear she's off sick."

"I've no idea," I replied.

"I thought you might know. I know you two are close."

A scathing comment sprung to mind. "She may have a cold or something. People often get colds after long flights."

"Long flight. Honeymoon. Yes. It could be a cold," his eyes gleamed. "Or an upset tummy." He smiled and his eyes widened. Charlie was being ironic again. His eyes locked on mine, for the flicker of a clue. He tested me, with the subtlety of a clever infant.

"Charlie, I have no idea. Honestly, I would say."

His jowls opened while he searched my face, then he nodded with belief. "You would tell me – if you'd heard anything," he said. After a pause and some nodding to himself, he said, "How is John then?"

I shrugged.

"I saw him at the wedding," he said. "Poor fellow."

I nodded slowly.

"Jack helped him," Charlie continued. "That was a very decent thing to do." He looked across the office at Betty, but she was busy typing, and did not notice. "And how are *you* managing, Rose?" he said.

This was a question that most people had stopped asking me. It had been over a year since Harry and I had separated. Even close friends could not sustain active interest in my troubles for that long. With enough time, people assume you are over your trauma, or that it has grown manageable. Their own lives crowd out their sympathy. Apart from my parents, few kept up the vigil for me.

I reached over and squeezed his hand with gratitude.

In the three years I had known Charlie, I had never heard him disparage anyone. He was gifted with a remarkable sympathy that instinctively understood others, even if he disagreed with them. He did not shift like a chameleon to avoid conflict, nor did he search for approval. This is characteristic of the weak in faith, not Charlie. For all his childish simplicity, Charlie was adamant in his beliefs. He lived to be an exemplar of Christian love. While he would seldom evangelise adults, his interest in people frequently produced the same results. Charlie's concern touched me deeply, and I regretted that I had grown so cynical. He loved good news and foraged for it everywhere. He would never rejoice in misfortune or be diminished by another's success. For these reasons, I found him a challenge to be with: he reminded me of the good person I had wanted to be.

Of course, not everyone felt the same way about Charlie.

John squinted at my words. "That fat poof should mind his own business," he said.

"John!" I was shocked by his response. "Charlie asked after your well-being because he is concerned." I had called in to biology to see John on my way back from an errand to reunite a boy with a packed lunch. The bell had just rung and, between periods, I found John sitting out the back of his biology store, smoking on the fire-escape stairs. It was a mild afternoon, and he was enjoying the blend of fresh and toxic air that was peculiar to his habit. I sat beside him but, after his abrupt response, I wondered why I had made the effort.

"If you don't want to talk to a friend, I'll leave you alone."

John put a hand up to stop me rising.

"Hang on." After a pause he said, "Just feeling sorry for myself. Doesn't help, people gossiping about me."

"You make it hard for them not to gossip."

He shrugged and sucked on his cigarette. "And I've an issue with Bakewell too. Not my favourite person. Far too good to be true."

109

"What can you mean?" I found it hard to believe that Charlie had aggrieved someone knowingly. It must have been a misunderstanding.

"Effective immediately, Bakewell teaches human reproduction to the junior school – in RE. *Fait accompli* for us in biology. Danny just got a memo. No discussion about it. We'll be teaching creationism next. Bloody nonsense. Shows the benefit of having your nose up the headmaster's arse."

I understood John's point, although I could see no harm in moving human reproduction to teach it within a moral framework. With John, however, it was better not to press the point. He was tenacious in an argument.

"It's very suspicious," he said. "Most staff would run a mile rather than teach it. And Bakewell's an odd one. What grown man prefers children to the company of adults. He's rarely in the staffroom beyond briefing."

I was disgusted with John's cynicism. He had grown bitter recently, and it was clear Charlie was an easy target for his ridicule. I spoke with a stern voice. "Charlie has a different outlook than you. He has dedicated his life to evangelising the pupils. *That* is why he is rarely *lounging* in the staffroom. *That* is why he has few friends among the staff. He is doing what he thinks is best for the boys. Charlie has done nothing to you personally and he does not deserve this slander. Perhaps you are just bitter because there is nothing you can do about this decision." As I spoke, John turned to view me with surprise.

He slouched when I had finished and drew in the last of his cigarette. "Sorry," he shrugged. "You're probably right."

I thought a change of subject would improve matters. "You've spoken to Ellie?" I said, after a pause.

"On the phone."

"What was the problem?"

"Too much drink. She wants someone responsible, around her children, and so on." With his middle finger, he flicked the butt, launching it into an arc to the grass below.

"That sounds fair," I said.

"In theory." He faced me. "I was never drunk around *her children*. Haven't even met *her children*. So, she wants responsible even when I'm not around her children."

"Then you'll have to prove yourself to her," I said.

"Is it irresponsible to get drunk?" he asked.

"Depends how drunk."

"Knew you'd take her side. Anyway, she needs some time to think. Ball's in her court."

We could hear a turmoil of boys from the corridor inside. They were waiting for John to let them in.

"Back to the grindstone," he said, staring into the distant.

"Will you be all right, John?" I asked.

He shrugged. "I'd do without drink and fags – if she asked me to. Not sure I'd do too well without her, though."

We stepped inside the biology store and he hauled the fire door shut.

"Fifteen gin and tonics?" I asked.

He grinned. "Not all for me. Anyway, how'd you hear?"

"Can't say."

"Betty Trent?"

"Possibly."

"She's sore I got more of Jack's attention than she did," he laughed. "Good bloke, he is. Turned out to be a mate." He winked a farewell and disappeared into his laboratory.

It was some time before I got Betty on her own again. That afternoon, Joan left the office on an errand. Betty had just redirected a phone call, and, as she put the handset down, I asked, "And how did you get home from the wedding?"

She grinned, while considering her options. She looked around the office to confirm we were alone then said, "Jack and I had no cash for a taxi." She raised her brows and nodded.

"So you got a room," I said. This confirmed my suspicions.

After a pause, she laughed at me. "No, I'm only joking. I'd love to string you along, Rose, but nothing actually happened. Jack and I danced, he bought me drinks, he tried it on at the hotel, I told him to get lost, we shared a taxi and I got dropped off alone. He asked to come in. He promised to behave – lied through his teeth, of course – but I went home alone. That's the truth."

"Are you two an item?" I asked.

She shrugged. "He wants to. I'm for taking it slow."

"Good for you," I said.

111

Beyond the glass panels we could hear Joan clip clop down the corridor. The artificial silence that descended when she entered made her pause at the door.

"What were you two gossiping about?" she asked.

"Rose is pregnant," Betty said.

With only a few minor revisions during the first week of the Autumn term, Jack Dawson's timetable for the new school year was a success. Any doubts about whether he was up to the job were put to rest. Samuel was encouraged by his efficiency and even speculated that Mr Dawson had straightened himself out. The vice-principal's attendance had even improved, having gone a full term without an absence. It was Friday, 14 January, 1977 – the day of Dawson's first sickness – before we learnt the truth.

A young, female substitute teacher rapped the glass panels at reception. "Excuse me, I can't find 2X1. I'm supposed to be covering for Mr Dawson." She spoke politely but with confidence. She knew this was someone else's mistake.

I looked her over, as far as the reception counter between us allowed. She was dressed like a fortune-teller, but I tried to view her with sympathy. Chancery Grammar was an old school and the room numbering was often confusing. Many staff would get lost on their first day of work.

"You should have been given a cover slip this morning by Mr Bakewell. Do you have it there?" I said.

She passed it through the opening and leaned an arm on the counter. Her cheap jewellery jangled like voodoo charms. While I read the details of her deployment, she continued, "I've been to the classroom. The boys are not there."

"Well, Miss –"

"Ms Walton," she corrected.

"Ms Walton," I said to the feminist, "I will walk you over to 121 myself. It is easy to get lost." I was sure she tutted when I said this. The whole way there, neither of us made any attempt at breaking the silence.

Room 121 was empty. She had not been lost.

"They may have been sent to the library. The head of department may know," I said, more to myself. She did not reply.

Arthur Edwards, the head of modern languages, was busy teaching when I interrupted and asked for his assistance. Like an old gent, he called the boys to attention when we ladies entered the room. He set the class a passage to translate while he would assist us. It took him two minutes on the phone to determine 2X1 were not in the library. As he worked in the room adjacent to Dawson's, Arthur was certain no class had been waiting in the corridor between periods.

"Boys have a way of making their presence known," he chuckled and pushed his glasses up his capillaried nose. "I'll just check the department timetable." He referred to a wallchart in the anteroom off his classroom. He muttered in German. I could not understand his words, but they were certainly expletives. When he turned back to us, a frown crumpled his foggy brows into a single cloud. "I don't recognise this class number. Could it be a misprint?" he asked me, ignoring my gypsy companion.

"It's possible. I suppose," I said. "Why do you think that?"

"There's no split in the junior school. We have only five classes. In languages, each class is a full form class. All our rooms are big enough to hold thirty boys. I have never heard of an X class in the junior school."

I understood what he was saying. In the junior school, the pupils were grouped according to their school houses: Hawthorne, Jones, Lockwood and Walker, named after the school's original benefactors. All classes were conducted in these groups, and each was named according to their house initial. There was a 2W, 2L, 2H, 2J but no 2X.

"And look where these classes fall." Arthur Edwards jabbed his index finger back and forth between the first two periods on a Monday and the last three on a Friday. He pulled his timetable off the noticeboard and it quivered before me. "Look at when Dawson has timetabled these classes." A dark flush had overtaken his scalp. The deep red made his grey tufts appear white.

"You don't think he has created a phantom class," I said, "To have those periods free?"

"I'll have his bloody job for this!" The words spat from him. Arthur Edwards had transformed from a jovial little gentleman into a berserking savage before my eyes. As he

113

stomped off to see the headmaster, I wonder whether I was pleased that Dawson had finally hanged himself.

Ms Walton, I suppose, had a half-day and returned to her caravan.

Chapter Eleven

As he did more frequently now, Samuel phoned me on my internal line. "Rose, I need to meet with you after school."

"I can guess what this is about," I said.

"Good. Bring your pen. We'll be opening the Dawson file again."

Samuel's spacious new desk had lockable, filing cabinet style drawers. In these, he kept his most sensitive documents, including the staff personnel files. He had the only keys, and no one else was allowed access to the drawers.

Mrs Bedford swept me through the adjoining door with dismissive wave. I closed the door behind me. Samuel was waiting over at the armchairs. Of late, we conducted our discussions there. He had taken the initiative to reduce the formality between us, and I enjoyed the privilege.

I sat and crossed my legs. My new skirt and blouse fitted neatly. Over the last few months, I had been disciplined in my eating habits and had shed several pounds. For this reason, I had refreshed my wardrobe. Samuel's eyes nourished themselves on the swell of my bosom. I had grown accustomed to this but could not acknowledge his habit. That would have embarrassed him and put a distance between us.

"What are we to do with this rogue?" he said and opened Dawson's personnel file on his lap.

"Do you have enough for a dismissal?" I asked.

"Unfortunately not. He will, of course, claim the phantom class was an accidental error."

"A very convenient error, in his own favour," I said.

"But when he discovered the error, it was too late to change the timetable, et cetera." Samuel shook his head with frustration. His fingers drummed the manila folder on his lap. "It gets worse, Rose. This is only part of a greater concern." His tone warned of bad news.

"What is it?"

"I have investigated in more depth the rumours about Mr Dawson's leisure activities. My enquiries led me beyond Elmfield Grammar and to the Constabulary itself. I have a friend who is rather high up in Chancery station. He told me that Dawson consorts with a woman, who is known to the police – and I put this as politely as possible – as a brothel keeper. This 'madam' has been arrested on a number of occasions. I am not sure whether Dawson is involved in the business side of the affair, but his relationship is certainly more than casual, if you know what I mean. The last thing this school needs is for Dawson to be on the premises during a police raid." Samuel shook his head, which appeared too heavy for even his thick neck. He steepled all his fingers and braced his elbows on the chair's arms to stabilize them. "He will bring scandal upon us. And I will be blamed for appointing him vice-principal." An irony occurred to him, and a smile glimmered. "An appropriate job title, don't you think? Principal in charge of vice."

After a moment's thought, I said, "Then we must get rid of him."

"He always has a lie or a loophole prepared," he replied.

"If he is arrested, you could fire him."

"Yes. I believe the formal term for it is 'gross moral turpitude'. I'm no expert in this subject either," he managed a smile, "but an arrest would indicate that he is not fit to hold a position of responsibility over our pupils. The parents' outcry would be horrendous if we didn't sack the scoundrel." He massaged his temples while saying this.

Something occurred to me. "Samuel, he could not prepare a lie if he did not know what he had done wrong," I said.

He dropped his hands and frowned to understand my cryptic message.

"I'm sorry, Rose?"

"He cannot have a defence prepared if you pursue him for something that he has not done wrong," I said.

"You will have to give me an example, my dear," he said with excessive patience.

I sighed deeply. I had thought him capable of more mental agility than he was currently demonstrating. "Simply put, we could set him up."

Samuel blinked twice.

I continued, "One of Dawson's responsibilities is to organise and administrate the external exams. He alone is responsible for O-Levels and A-Levels in the school. If you were able to prove that he had botched this job and compromised the integrity of the exams –"

"We would be able to fire him," Samuel said.

"Exactly."

He pondered a moment.

"There are two problems with this grand scheme, Rose: it would be very difficult to find evidence of his malpractice; and this would bring disrepute to Chancery Grammar."

I thought about these objections for a moment. "Actually, praise would given to the headmaster who acted promptly to minimise the impact of a vice-principal's misconduct," I said.

He actually considered this, rubbing his lumpy forehead with a fingertip.

"And," he continued, "It would be easy to prove his malpractice if we contrived it ourselves."

"Yes," I said with growing enthusiasm.

"That suggestion is completely immoral, Mrs Maylie. Frankly, I am shocked that you could suggest such an objectionable and base practice." His eyes pinned me to the back of my chair.

In the silence, I felt that I had taken a foolish risk. With shame, my head fell and I could not meet his gaze.

Just as I was preparing an apology he said, "Nevertheless, It is a stroke of brilliance."

I looked up and he was smiling, with the same fixed eyes.

"*Finis coronat opus*, as the Romans used to say: the end crowns the work. We must do it for the good of Chancery Grammar School – before this rogue brings our name to infamy." His eyes were exultant, whether at his own dramatic turn or at our proposed scheme, I could not tell.

I was glad I had not apologised.

"We work well together, Rose," he said. "We must talk more of this on Monday. Unfortunately, I do not have time now. Mrs Bedford has me meeting some boy's parents this afternoon." He bounded up as if he had just thrown off a burden. Bowing politely, he opened one of the double doors for me. I paused a moment to straighten the creases in my skirt and was again aware of him cataloguing my movements. I would not have been surprised to feel his hand on the inside curve of my back as I passed him. But it never came.

117

Our next meeting finalised the details of our venture. This shared venture strengthened the bond between us. Evidence of this was Samuel's willingness to talk about himself and, most notably, his personal life. The conversation came about when I had asked for time off later in the week to see Mr Spenlow, my solicitor. After Samuel had probed, and found I would share the details of my failed marriage, he reflected upon his own. Our conversation lasted long after the school had closed.

From the age of nine, Samuel James Baxter had been the only boy in an entirely female household. His father had returned from the Second World War with a pathological drink problem. Three years later, he had wrapped his car around a telegraph pole and died. He had survived the war but not the peace that followed. Samuel was left with his mother and two older sisters. His mother was an inspiration to him. Her grief, although colossal, did not overwhelm her. She made a brave effort to fill the role of both parents. She was strict with her children but had a particular indulgence for her son whom, she said, was the image of his father.

The children were pushed to excel at school, worked in the family clothes shop at the weekend and attended church on Sundays. Life was structured and Samuel was at home in the company of ladies. This was made easier as they attended to his slightest whim. This he admitted freely to me, chuckling with the memory.

At university, Samuel met his wife, Helen. Back then, she astonished him with her intellect. She also was from a well-to-do local family, and they believed they had much in common. Both studying English literature, they were in many of the same tutorial groups. It appeared to be a match contrived by God Himself.

When their university days were drawing to a close, Samuel confessed that he was stricken with the impulse to consolidate his life. He would soon be looking for a job – beyond selling clothes – and did not want to add loneliness to the uncertainties he would face. Life would be better with its variance limited. With this reasoning, he asked Helen to marry him. Her reasons for accepting the offer were not something he could speculate on. Helen was a strong woman and not given to outpourings of emotion. Then, he had taken this as a sign of her caution; now,

118

he conceded, it had more to do with indifference. She may have accepted his offer because he was a solid prospect financially and socially.

If alternative careers did not present themselves to the young English graduates, they had two family businesses to fall back into. Helen originally aspired to be a journalist. This issue was resolved within the first few months of marriage when she fell pregnant with twins: a boy and a girl. At around the same time, Samuel had wandered into St. Bartholomew's Grammar, his former school, to visit the headmaster. It had been entirely a social call, during the summer holidays after his graduation. His headmaster congratulated him on his first class honours degree and offered him a job there and then. Thus began Samuel's dual careers as teacher and father.

The two roles beginning together may have been the reason why one of them suffered immediate decline. To prepare himself for a teaching job – a career for which he had not trained – Samuel felt compelled to put in many extra hours. Often he arrived home later than Helen thought reasonable. She believed his work day ended at half past three. He argued that English teachers had the heaviest marking load of all staff. He focused better on his work at school, rather than at home. Two young children could be quite a distraction.

Helen coped with difficulty. The demands of the babies had to come first. As a result, she was unable to pay much attention to her husband when he came home. When the evening came and the children went to bed, Helen had little engaging company to offer. Numerous minor resentments consolidated between them. They had not been married long enough to build a secure foundation before the twins had arrived and they both felt the strain. With hindsight, Samuel agreed it would have been more prudent to wait until they had been married at least two years before considering children.

As it happened however, Samuel threw himself into his work. Helen had to be grateful that he was providing a stable income while she remained at home. He never disparaged her housekeeping, and her skills as a mother were unquestionable. The trouble was, she never had any time for him. If anything, she may even have resented his liberty, while she was tied to the home.

119

Possibly to compensate for his disappointment at home, and to increase his salary, Samuel had pushed himself for promotions. He was respected by his colleagues as a solid practitioner, a loyal member of staff, and he had the favour of his headmaster. He ascended through the ranks of house master, head of department, and eventually a vice-principal. These elevated positions provided a better living for his family but, inevitably, deprived them of Samuel's company. He recalled with genuine regret the week nights when he had only an hour or so with his young children before they went to bed. After that, he was committed to the paper work that came with his additional responsibilities. Even while he was vice-principal, he continued to teach English. His life, after all, was measured out in red pen.

At work, he was an alpha male, but the dislocation from Helen gnawed at him. He confessed to being unusually sensitive to his own failures and, every year, vowed to find balance between work and family life. Ironically, it was the two months of the summer holidays that were always a chore. Instead making the most of his family time, he confessed to feeling like an outsider. He concluded that Helen and the children lived more harmoniously when he did not interfere. Always, he looked forward to getting back to work.

Years progressed and his children grew. He found he had little rapport with them. He countered this by being a disciplinarian but he knew that had not improved matters. His children had not been inclined to rebel, as it happened – their relationship with Helen was too strong for that. The twins, Jack and Laura, grew to be responsible young adults, if a little serious for their age.

Samuel was now forty, married and in teaching for eighteen years. He had long since stopped accounting for his time from home, and he was not missed. He and Helen had always been at least civil to each other, but civility, he said, could be the worst indifference.

"Will you be changing your surname," he asked, "When you are finally divorced?"

"I've certainly thought about it."

"What's in a name? That which we call a rose by any other name would smell as sweet." He was quoting Shakespeare, and it confirmed his fondness for me.

"Thank you, Samuel," I said and did my best to blush like a young maid.

He held the door for me as I left his study. As I passed him, an impulse took me and I kissed him quickly on the cheek. "Thank you, for being so kind," I whispered and, before the incident gathered momentum, I walked down the corridor and out to my car.

I had not considered the consequences of my actions until I was behind the wheel. Nothing had passed between us about which we needed to be ashamed. In any case, shame did not fit in to my new outlook. Thanks to Harry, I believed I was owed my share of happiness. Pleasure was in such short supply that I would take mine where I could find it. As a Christian man, and a married one, Samuel might have had more difficulty with my last familiarity.

As I drove from the car park, I looked over to his office window. There he stood, at the window, watching through the blinds. At that distance, and on the move, I could not judge his expression. I knew only that he watched.

"Dorothy is pregnant," Joan told Betty and me at break.

It was January and Dorothy had been mysteriously ill for a number of weeks. In the three years that I had known her, she had not been sick as many days as she had since getting married. I imagined she felt insulated from the consequences, now she no longer needed to work for a living. William was making enough money to support them both, and she could allow every little cold to knock her off her feet.

When Dorothy had been in school, I noticed an aloofness about her. She stuck her nose in the air when Betty and I bantered. The new Mrs Butler did not approve. Betty and I agreed: Dorothy now thought herself better than a spinster and a prospective divorcee. She was married to a teacher and he was going places. Now she was more accomplished than us. It made her even more so because she was to be a mother.

"And she is leaving work," Joan said. "She handed in her notice but will see it through on the sick."

121

"Leaving work?" I asked. Betty and I would be photo-gossiping about this soon. "The poor thing. Have you been to see her, Joan?"

"I have." She dropped her head with maternal concern. "She is very worried about this one."

Betty was first to pick up the cue. "This one?" she said.

"I can tell you now, although you know how secretive Dorothy is about her business. This is not her first pregnancy."

And it was all apparent to me.

"How many has she lost?" Betty asked, for I could not speak.

"Two," said Joan.

"My God!" Betty said.

"The poor thing," I said.

Betty looked at me and we both winced. We had been cynical fools. Dorothy was not aloof, she was grieving. It was no wonder she could not laugh at our banter. How trivial we must have sounded to her after losing two babies.

'Operation Dosser', as I liked to call my joint project with Samuel, had to remain dormant for some months before we could act on it. For his malpractice with the timetable, Dawson was given a final written warning by the Board of Governors. This would stay on his record for a year and gave Samuel and me plenty of time to implement our plan. Fearing further misdemeanours would cost his job, Dawson behaved like a professional. His phantom French class periods were allocated as extra cover duties, taking the weight off those staff who actually earned their wages. Samuel insisted that Dawson meet with him every day at the end of school, to ensure that he was still present.

Wednesday, 21 April 1977 brought Phase One of our scheme by recorded delivery. Since January, we had anticipated this day: the day when O-Level and A-Level examination papers were delivered in five sealed cardboard boxes. Our conspiracy began by manipulating Dawson's exposure to these sensitive documents.

The courier arrived just after midday. From my copy of his timetable, I knew that Dawson was in a class and would soon be on lunch. I signed the courier's docket to acknowledge receipt but did not phone across to modern languages to notify Dawson of their arrival. Instead, I moved the five boxes into the reprographics suite, where they would be safe.

At the end of lunch I phoned the staffroom. Another teacher answered the call but it was passed to Dawson. "Mr Dawson, it is Rose. The O-Level and A-Level papers have arrived. They are stored in the reprographics suite for now."

"That is lovely, my dear. Would you arrange for the caretaker to send them to my room?" he said. There, Dawson had a lockable metal filing cupboard for securing the papers away. The headmaster had replaced the old wooden one in January when we had first conceived our plan. It was a much more secure unit, significantly better than its predecessor. The security of these exam papers was so important that only Messrs Baxter and Dawson held keys to it.

It was not a widely known fact, however, that each of these filing cabinet locks had a three digit number inscribed on it. A careful observer would find it on the lock's front plate. This number, given to a locksmith, along with a small fee, allowed additional spare keys to be ordered. I had such a spare key to Mr Dawson's filing cupboard.

"I will, after lunch. Will you be in your room last period?" I said, knowing he would.

"I have a blasted double with the fifth form. I'll be there," he said.

"Remember your meeting with Mr Baxter at 3:30 p.m.."

"How could I forget? I've been looking forward to it all day," he sneered.

With a curt farewell, I returned to my salad. Today, I would have to eat lunch at my desk. Joan and Betty were out to lunch separately, so I used the opportunity to phone Samuel with an update.

Hello, Rose," he said.

"The eagle has landed."

"Pardon me?"

"Elvis has left the building"

He laughed, "It appears he has taken your senses with him. I presume you mean the papers have been delivered?"

"If you prefer a prosaic way of saying it, yes, they have," I said. Perversely, I found it exciting to be part of a secret enterprise with Samuel. This was my first conspiracy – not

123

including my intervention with the new staff handbook, of course. Jack Dawson had eluded the consequences of his other crimes and, to my mind, our scheme was justifiable. If all went according to plan, Dawson would be dismissed and someone useful promoted to his place. It did not please me to consider the personal cost to Dawson: losing his reputation, job and career. I was too excited by the thrill of potentially getting caught.

"I will keep him from 3:30 until 4:00 p.m.. Just be sure to avoid being seen. I presume you have your key?" he said. He referred to the copy of his own key to the filing cupboard. This was the third key that Dawson knew nothing about.

"Of course, I do. It sounds like you don't trust me," I teased.

"Now you know that is not true, Rose. When it is done, phone me and I will release him."

As requested, I had the boxes delivered to Dawson's classroom but late enough that he would have no time to check them, especially with a class present. He should have locked them in his filing cupboard for inspection and sorting later that day. It was vital that they be verified promptly, for the examining board would need to be notified of any missing or incorrect papers.

Jack Dawson was reasonably punctual for his meeting with the headmaster after school. When I imagined their meeting was sufficiently underway, I lifted my secret key, a key to Dawson's classroom and a document wallet, slipping from the office without a word. It was a commonplace action and provoked no response from Betty, who remained to answer the phones. Joan was out of the office, querying some documents with the bursar, but she would return soon. A thrill ran through me. No one guessed at my subterfuge and none would have believed it, had they been told.

The corridors were empty of boys, for the most part. Discarded crisp packets, sandwich crusts and forgotten sports bags remained in their place. My journey to the Modern Languages Department was uneventful. While I walked, I went over the mission in my head. My principal concern was being caught inside Dawson's room. The plan would unravel if I was seen there, after school. The cleaners were beginning their work rounds, with usually one cleaner for every two departments. Teachers walking past were another threat. To ensure I would have a few minutes undetected, I walked the length of the corridor, casually glancing into each room – five in all. Dawson's was the first I passed. It was empty, as expected. The echo of my steps announced my presence but I did nothing about this on my initial pass through. I considered carrying my shoes, but to be found doing so would create instant speculation.

At the end of the languages corridor, I continued on to geography. There, I noted the cleaner busy in one of the rooms. It would be some time before she made it to Dawson's room, at the end of her route. When I reached the stairs, I increased my pace. I looped back to the central staircase and returned to the ground floor. From there, I could return to Dawson's room. In my heightened state, I imagined my clip-clopping steps returning along the languages corridor drawing suspicion, especially if they stopped short of the corridor's full length and the clunk of its swinging doors. It was much better that I take only a few light toe-steps beyond the fire doors before confronting the door lock. I did so with great care, bringing the heavy doors together lightly.

When I tried the door of Dawson's classroom, I was disappointed to find it unlocked. I had hoped for some little challenge – a lock to jemmy with a badly cut key – before I completed my mission. In keeping with the rest of life, there was only disappointment. Within, I still intended to work quickly and closed the door gently. The filing cupboard was at the front, near Dawson's desk. I trod lightly and closed the distance. My copied key, was snug between my curled forefinger and thumb. It even quivered slightly with anticipation. I wondered how I would explain myself if Arthur Edwards walked in.

The key slipped in. It had been well cut and filed to match its partner. But really, I need not have bothered. Dawson had not even locked the cupboard doors. With a tut, I opened them and looked over the shelves. All were empty, but for a box of tissues and a packet of chalk. If the examination papers were not there, I could not carry out my plan. It was inconceivable that

125

Dawson should move them to another store. That would require effort.

I cast around Dawson's classroom to locate the missing boxes. Each was the size of a typewriter and would be difficult to miss. As I looked, I was able to characterise the teacher and the man. The pupils' desks, far from the customary neat rows, were in complete disorder. There were few distinguishable rows at all. The floor was littered with crumpled papers, sweet wrappers, pencil sharpenings and dissected pens. Worst of all, there were 'mushies' – wads of paper chewed to pulp – stuck to the ceiling. Boys were at liberty to chew sheets of A4 and hurl them to the ceiling, walls or even at the teacher. Most alarming were those spattered around the blackboard. I imagined the daily riots, and shuddered. For Dawson, I had a moment's pity, but little sympathy. Through laziness and carelessness in his teaching methods, he had allowed this to happen. The classroom walls exhibited no pupils' work. This room was little more than a holding centre for boys unlucky enough to have him for a teacher.

Dawson's desk was a similar testimony to his indifference. It hunkered in the corner, strewn with papers several inches deep. I could see pupils' scrawled work, which must have been months old. They knew it would never be marked. A crooked pile of French text books slumped against another pile of dictionaries. Some artistic wag had drawn a leaking phallus along the white page edges of the stack. The marker pen had faded somewhat. It was unlikely Dawson would reconstruct the book pile to preserve this art work each time the books were collected in. It was easier to conclude that these texts were never used. Dawson's own leather satchel slouched on the window sill. It had a layer of chalk dust on its top flap, unmolested since he first brought it to school. His chair was the only well used resource in this dismal failure of a classroom.

After a moment, I noted the five boxes of exam papers under the desk. This was Dawson's idea of secure storage. This further example of malpractice cleared my conscience of its last reservation. As surely as anyone deserved to be fired, it was Jack Dawson. The rest of my mission, I executed without the slightest regret. I even enjoyed the thought of Dawson discovering what had happened – if he discovered it at all.

126

With the key, I sawed through the tape sealing one of the boxes. It proved useful for that task, at least. Inside, the exam papers were sealed in polythene packets, according to their subjects. Again, I used the key to saw these open and extracted an O-Level mathematics paper. This went into my document wallet, ready for transport. To delay the discovery of my intrusion, I moved the opened box to the bottom of its pile under the desk. There it would not be immediately obvious.

Down the corridor, I heard a door close.

My complacency flushed away on a wave of adrenalin. I froze and listened.

Someone was walking up the corridor. The shoes did not resound like my own. It must have been a man. Arthur Edwards, most likely.

"Oh God," I said and cast around for somewhere to hide.

There was no room under the desk, thanks to the boxes. I doubted I could slip to the back of the room in time. Even if I got there, the window in the door would put me in full view of a casual glance.

The footsteps continued. Mr Edwards was humming. He did not carry his tune well, though.

With a desperate hope, I opened wide the nearest door of the filing cupboard. It was enough to hide me from passing view and I hoped it did not look obvious. Mr Edwards could still enter the classroom. I had not ruled that out. I would need a cover story for being in the room.

"Mr Dawson forgot this folder," I practiced in a whisper. *"Oh God, let him keep walking."* I stood frozen behind my makeshift screen. I did not know I held my breath until the swinging doors clunked together, signifying Arthur Edwards' exit from the corridor. God bless those clunking doors. It was not long before I used them myself on my return to the office.

It would be at least a day before Dawson bothered himself to process the papers, by which time it would already be too late. The mathematics paper was to be held by Samuel, who would duly "find" it after sufficient time had passed.

Chapter Twelve

It was usual for the headmaster to patrol the playground in the morning, with his attention normally dedicated to areas where the highest volume of boys gathered. That next morning, however, he had a very specific route in mind. As Charlie Bakewell was available at the time, he joined Samuel. The trip turned out to be a short one, primarily because it took them past the middle school cloakroom. It was 8:20 a.m. and few boys were in that early but, with uncanny sensibilities, the headmaster spotted a suspicious cluster of boys in the area. His subsequent official incident report stated that he had witnessed four pupils hastily copying questions from an O-Level examination paper into jotters, notebooks or homework diaries. He recognised the source as an examination paper as it was a distinctive light blue document.

The headmaster sent the boys to sit outside his study, minus the exam paper, while he and Vice-Principal Bakewell made directly for Mr Dawson's classroom where another disturbing discovery awaited them.

"Dawson was sitting at his desk when we entered," Samuel told me.

"Did you see what I meant about the mess?" I asked.

"That's the point, Rose. The place was scrupulously clean. Apart from the warped filing cabinet doors, there was no mess. His desk was clear. Everything was neatly stacked on the shelves. Even the chewed paper you mentioned was gone."

"Nothing?"

"Not a trace."

"That's very strange." I said.

"Stranger still: he greeted us like welcome friends and directed us to the filing cupboard – not that we could have missed it. Its doors had been broken open and the mechanism had been bent into uselessness. It looked as if a crowbar and considerable leverage had been used on it."

"That wasn't me," I said, somewhat obviously. "Who could have done it?" I asked.

Samuel looked more than a little disappointed at my question. "Certainly not the boys who are about to be punished for it."

"Oh dear," I said. Only then did I realise that our scheme required scapegoats. I had thought that Samuel would stumble upon the paper, somewhere innocuous, in an act of serendipity. That might have appeared suspiciously implausible to Dawson, though. For the plan to succeed, it was vital he did not suspect a conspiracy against him.

Neither had I considered what would happen to any boys who were found in possession of the exam paper. They would probably have to be expelled from the school. In my haste to collaborate with Samuel and ruin Dawson, I had caused significant damage to some promising young lives.

Revenge has a way of claiming unexpected casualties.

"It could only have been Dawson who broke into the cupboard," Samuel said. "I am sure, after our meeting yesterday, he returned to his classroom. Most likely, he checked off the exam papers against the order list. As he did so, he discovered the opened box and the missing paper."

"He should have alerted you," I said.

"And that is the absolute cunning of the man. He has shown himself to be a foeman who is worthy of our steel," he said. I think he was quoting again. "He had not secured the exam papers when he should have. For this, he was culpable. Even if he could not check them with pupils in the room, he was expected to lock them away. He knew I would have enough to sack him – especially under his final written warning. No, Dawson worked a wonder here." He shook his head. "He must have unpacked and checked the papers – even ticking to indicate that the missing maths paper was present. Then he locked the filing cupboard –"

"And tidied his room," I added.

"Yes," he reflected, "I suppose so. For the cunning devil knew it was soon to be a crime scene, and he didn't want the place looking untidy." Samuel actually laughed, with amusement and exasperation.

"When did he break in?"

"Certainly after the cleaners had gone. They would have noticed something so obvious as bent doors on a secure filing unit. Logically, Dawson destroyed his own cabinet when all but he had left the building.

"His first day working late since he started here," I said.

"Now I think on it, I don't recall seeing his car beside mine when I was leaving. It is always a squeeze to get in, but I remember the door opening wide because the wind caught it. I was glad his car had gone. It would not do to dent a colleague's car before firing him." The headmaster and two vice-principals were privileged among the staff to have their own designated parking spaces beside the school's front doors.

"He probably drove out," I said, "and then returned on foot."

"Very good, Rose. You are thinking like a criminal. The back gate would be easy to climb and he has keys for all the main doors. He probably used a wheel brace from his car to assist him in doing so."

"I'd have used a jack too. Squeeze that into a gap and the rest is easy," I said.

Samuel nodded his approval. "Most likely."

"Was his classroom door forced?" I asked.

"There was probably no need. The cleaners leave them unlocked all the time. The brilliance of it is that Dawson's cover story is plausible. It is not hard to imagine a boy or two who stowed away until everyone was gone, et cetera." He dismissed the rest with a backhand flick.

Back in the General Office, I felt as though I had gatecrashed a wake. Charlie sat in the chair bedside Joan Spenser's desk, his shoulders slumped and his head bent. He spoke into clasped hands with a voice soaked in disappointment.

"I can't believe any of them could have done this," he said. Charlie, of course, knew nothing of our conspiracy.

Joan patted his knee and nodded.

Charlie continued, "They're all good boys. Jason Maguire goes to my church, sings in the youth choir. Andy Evans is a chancer at times, but a good lad. Davy Green and Jake Cunningham have never been in trouble in their lives. I can't understand this. What were they thinking?"

This was the human consequence of my actions, and I had not prepared myself to face it. Four innocent boys facing the end of their grammar school careers, bringing shame to their families. This was not an acceptable price, even if we did implicate Jack Dawson. I sat heavily in my chair. I thought of

130

how glib I had been when proposing this scheme to Samuel. I had not foreseen these consequences, but he must have known scapegoats were inevitable. He had chosen to leave the paper for pupils to find. He knew boys would be caught in the net with Dawson and he must have considered that acceptable. To my mind, that was callous.

Charlie continued, "They're saying that the exam paper was just lying there in the cloakroom." He shrugged.

"That sounds unlikely," Betty said. That earned her a look from Joan.

"But I can't believe one of them would break into the school and crowbar a secure filing unit open. It's a bit advanced for someone that age."

"What will happen about the exam?" Joan asked.

"The exam board will have to set another paper. That one cannot be trusted," he said. "They should have something prepared as a backup." After a pause, he concluded, "And they'll have to send it out to all schools."

Joan added, "Everyone will know it's because of Chancery Grammar."

"I'm afraid so," Charlie said, shaking his head, "Mr Baxter will not like that one bit."

"Will he make an example of those boys?" I asked.

Charlie nodded slowly. "I'll see what I can do about that." He deflated into his chair. When he spoke again, his voice was softer, without great conviction, "We'll try to find a measured approach." After a moment's reflection, he sat up straighter, as if he was preparing himself for exertion. "These boys have been foolish – if what they say is true – but they are not guilty of a real evil. It was opportunism that overcame common sense. It can happen to all of us at some time or another." I imagined Charlie was making reference to a missing pastry his mother had left to cool on the sideboard. His face folded with anxiety. Ahead of him was an unpleasant task connected to his new responsibility. Eventually, Charlie puffed up and stood. "Boys are much better to deal with when they are still young and innocent. I just hope I can do some good here."

Charlie and Samuel met together, to discuss the appropriate disciplinary measures. The boys were sitting in the reception area, awaiting parents who would take them home early. I attempted to busy myself with ordinary things to occupy my mind. I managed to do this, all the while, expecting Samuel to contact me. He did not do so until late in the afternoon.

"I have to strike a balance between punishing guilt and deterring such crimes in the future," Samuel told me. He was sitting at one end of his three-seater sofa and I was at the other.

"But the guilt is ours," I said.

He held up a finger. "Not entirely. Those young men availed themselves of information to which they had no legitimate right."

"We made it possible."

"They should have had the moral backbone to resist temptation and report the matter to a member of staff. That would have been the correct course of action," he said.

I wondered if he was toying with me. The shadow of a playful smile crossed his mouth, but that was no indicator that he did not believe what he said.

"Will you expel them?" I asked.

He looked up to the cornice as if receiving divine guidance. "I would like to expel the rogue that broke into the filing cabinet. The boys, unfortunately, must go but they are not beyond my help." He paused, no doubt, to allow me to ask how.

I resisted.

"If I told you the boys were to be expelled, I am sure you would challenge me, just as the Reverend Bakewell spent an hour doing this afternoon." Samuel smiled at his own dark humour. "The boys and their parents have been told that it is best if they move on. I have spoken to Jim Murray, headmaster of Elmfield Grammar, and he assures me he can accommodate all four boys. I vouched for their previously clean record. They can start there as soon as next week."

"That was very generous of him," I said.

"He was reluctant at first, then I reminded him how much he was indebted to us for taking Jack Dawson off his hands." he smiled. "And, when he had stopped laughing, he agreed to do me this favour."

"He has a cheek," I said.

"The irony is not lost on me. In attempting to oust that rogue, Dawson, we end up giving four good pupils to our rivals at Elmfield. If I ever have the opportunity of doing Elmfield a disservice, I assure you, I shall jump at the chance."

"At least those poor boys will not have to suffer too much," I said. My heart lifted a little.

"That was not my only reason –" Samuel had started to say but was interrupted by the phone. He frowned over at it, as if the ringing would cease at his disapproval. As he could not intimidate it to silence, he answered it.

"I told her no interruptions," he said, half to himself, as he crossed to his desk. His tone to Mrs Bedford was dry. "Mrs Bedford, I am sure this is a matter of the utmost urgency."

From my place on the sofa, I could make out her scratchy voice but not the words, as she made her case. Samuel exhaled with disapproval as he listened to her.

"But I do not want to speak to him, Mrs Bedford. Tell him something –" he looked over at me and I read fear in the widening of his eyes. Their blue light was scattered and watery. "All right, then. Make the appointment. Tomorrow." He dropped the telephone receiver into place and looked to me with blank petition.

"What has happened?" I asked.

He exhaled heavily and steadied himself on the desktop.

"A reporter from the Chancery Chronicle. He wants a statement concerning the leaked exam papers."

There was no evidence of who informed the reporter, but Jack Dawson's name sprang readily to mind. I wondered what he would have to gain from this tactic, except to disgrace the headmaster. I doubted Dawson could suspect us of a conspiracy against him. He may simply have enjoyed the idea of Samuel being in the firing line for a change.

When Samuel returned to the sofa, he descended into dark speculations. His left fist crooked to support his temple, the elbow digging in to the arm of the sofa. This was unusual for him, as his posture was normally exemplary. He crossed his legs, turning his body away from me just perceptibly. He withdrew to brood over his new problem. Immediate action was required to prove my usefulness.

"Let us think of how best to contain this problem," I said, "Or even turn it to our advantage."

133

"These deeds return to plague the inventor," he mused. "I intended to deal with this supposed security breach confidentially. The exam council is very discrete with matters like this – a phone call would have done it. But now, it is all out of the box. I feared a scandal. It will destroy the professional reputation for which I have sacrificed so much. This reporter, Paddy Audley, is a hack and gossip-monger of the worst sort. I've read his articles before, and they are nothing but sensationalist tat." As he spoke, Samuel's left hand unclenched and shaded his eyes.

"Let's investigate this Audley and see what more we can find out about him. It pays to know our enemies," I said, attempting optimism I did not feel.

His hand moved from his brow and he looked at me. "*Our* enemies, Rose?" Some of the flame rekindled in his eyes.

"Yes, ours, Samuel." I nodded.

He extended his right hand and I took it.

For half an hour, Samuel and I considered the best strategy for dealing with the prying reporter, Paddy Audley. His surname had jarred a memory of something I had recently typed. It had been a mundane administrative task, itself entirely forgettable, but I remembered making the joke "Audley enough" in my head when I first encountered that name.

On this whim, I dashed to the General Office to retrieve the document. No more than fifteen paces brought me from the headmaster's office to the reception area, where Jack Dawson was waiting. He sat in one of the armchairs, presenting his relaxation to any who would view him. His long, thin legs stretched out, crossed at the ankles. His hands meshed on his waistcoat and his head rested on the wall behind, without displacing his neatly creamed hair. The caterpillar on his top lip arched at my approach. I faltered in my stride and slowed before him. Foolishly, I thought he might have something enlightening to say about the day's events.

"Ah, Rose." His brow animated but his head remained static. "Terrible business today. I'm trying to see the head."

"I am meeting with him at present."

"You've been at it a long time, my dear. Will you be finished with him soon?" he said with a lecherous grin. His eyes slithered over me, top to toe and back again, recording and rating.

I felt as if he had slid a hand inside my blouse. Without responding to his vulgar comment, I strode into the office and attempted to slam the door. This was made to look ridiculous by the newly installed door closer. Fortunately, it was late enough that no one else was in the office to see it. Cursing Dawson fluently, I sorted through my files and found the document I sought. The thought of walking past that creep again made me wince. No doubt, he would rate me on the view from my rear.

"I hope we will be able to keep this from becoming a scandal, Rose," Dawson said to my back as I gusted past him. I understood the implications of what he had just said. The document in my hand, however, could just insulate Chancery Grammar from such a disaster.

"He cannot possibly suspect we had a hand in this," Samuel asserted.

"We must not underestimate him," I said.

"What can he actually know about our involvement, though?"

"He only knows that, while you were meeting with him, the papers were stolen; that you want rid of him; that you found the papers." I counted these off on my fingers.

"The rest he may only suspect."

"Whether or not he suspects your hand in this, I know he would enjoy seeing you suffer the shame of a scandal," I said.

Samuel's considered the pen resting between his thick fingers. I shuffled a little closer to him on the sofa and laid the document on his leg.

"Do you notice anything familiar about this?" I asked him and watched him closely for recognition. He ignored the page, however, and concentrated solely on me.

"I have noticed you are sitting very close; I noticed your hand brush my leg; that you smell like sweet vanilla and it would be the most difficult thing in the world not," he inclined his head, "To kiss you now."

And he did.

We breathed the same air.

On my third breath, I pulled back slowly – not because I wanted the moment to end – because it is a woman's

135

responsibility to control how passion is expended. Samuel searched my face for signs of disapproval. There were none. He leaned in again, to resume, but I leaned away just enough.

"Later," I said. "We need to concentrate on our problem before we –". I left that sentence deliberately unfinished.

He looked at me, lulled, but said nothing. After a moment he nodded, a smile growing. "You are quite right, Rose. We have much to discuss and there will be plenty of time for –" he said.

Chapter Thirteen

In matters of conscience, it is worth remembering that some people can forgive themselves for a lot. I was embarking on an adulterous relationship with a married man, knowing full well how damaging this could be to those affected. I had been a victim myself. This hurt was something I wished on no living being – except Harry. In spite of this, I continued. My logic was influenced by my own losses: I had suffered much and was owed my portion of happiness. This, I would extract greedily, whenever an opportunity arose.

My parents would have certainly disapproved. They would have highlighted the hypocrisy of my actions, and no argument could have opposed their objections. But this was not a matter of reason or logic: this was an issue of my desperate heart. I would not pass by my last chance for happiness. All along, my humble dream had been to share a home with someone I loved, who loved me in equal measure. That was worth a charge of hypocrisy.

My Christian upbringing had been worthwhile in establishing family values. It sculpted me into a forgiving, patient wife and made me easily exploitable. However, Christian values failed to deliver happiness or security in this life, as far as I was concerned. I was no longer naive enough to expect anything better in the next life either. What use is a moral code if it brings no benefits? I dispensed with it rather promptly, at the first touch of Samuel's lips. My principal concern was my own well-being and whatever that entailed. For the time being, that included my relationship with Samuel Baxter.

It was early evening when Samuel and I left his office. There was no sign of Jack Dawson: it would have been unlike him to work late two days in a row. Samuel's car was parked just outside the school's main doors, but he walked me across the car park. We were confident that we were alone. The empty spaces in the car park demonstrated this.

After a long kiss, he said, "Life offers few opportunities for real happiness. This may be one of them, Rose." His deep voiced rumbled through me, close as he was. There was a thrill to his touch. "I had determined to let things happen by themselves, if they were meant to be."

"Do you not feel guilty, then?" I asked.

He flinched slightly but considered the question. "God has brought us together," he said. "He has us working together and He has given us these impulses for one another." He nodded approval of this flexible logic. "This is His will. He led us to each other and we should make the most of it."

I had abandoned my conscience, while Samuel had another strategy, one that conveniently compelled him to pursue what he wanted. I would not challenge his self-justification; it suited me just fine.

"We must operate with the utmost secrecy, however," he continued. "If word of this were to leak out, it would destroy the good name of our school, not to mention what it would do to our families." He studied me. "We should allow this to flourish before we decide on more suitable arrangements."

"I agree. Besides, you may grow bored of my attentions and regret you ever seduced me. It could all be over in a month," I said.

"Seduced you, Mrs Maylie? Is that what I did?" he laughed.

That next morning, at the appointed time, we waited for Paddy Audley of *The Chancery Chronicle*. I met him at the General Office and showed him in to the headmaster's study. Samuel rose from behind his desk, and greeted Mr Audley formally with a handshake and a hard smile. I took my seat beside the reporter, across the desk from Samuel, angled to face our visitor. Samuel and I had hoped this would prove off-putting for him.

"Mr Audley," the headmaster began, "This is Mrs Maylie. She is here to act as a witness to this interview, which I will also take the liberty of tape recording."

"I see," Audley replied, a little baffled.

Samuel produced a small tape recorder, about the size of the spiral bound notebook that fidgeted on Audley's lap. He positioned it on the edge of the desk, equidistant from interviewer and interviewee.

"I say, is this really necessary?" Audley asked.

In our preparations, Samuel agreed that he had to control this situation. That included directing the conversation. For a

138

long moment, Samuel made no response to Audley's question, beyond shifting his lumpy brow. When he did eventually speak, it was to ask a question, rather than answer one.

"And why do you think we are taking such precautions, Mr Audley?" Samuel spoke as if to a delinquent boy, with whom he was showing unusual patience.

"This is very defensive of you. Very defensive indeed," Audley said.

I studied the little man while he protested. He had wispy hair on top but longer, lank strands clutched at the sides. Some of this excess on the sides he had redirected, to compensate where it was lacking. To top the absurdity of the comb-over style, his roots were grey by an inch, missing the brown dye that matted the rest. Neither did Audley's ratty little face win my sympathy. To us, he was a threat.

"Mr Audley, I would hate there to be some confusion or ambiguity concerning the statements I am about to make. Mrs Maylie and this tape recorder are simply my means of ensuring that not one word is misinterpreted or wrongly attributed," Samuel said. He sat back in his chair, confident that he had the upper hand. After some consideration of the cornice, he continued. "After all, the consequences of an exaggerated report of this trivial incident would be damaging to Chancery Grammar School and *all* its pupils."

"I am not looking to damage the school," Audley said, as if wounded.

"Mr Audley," Samuel shot forward and held up a reproachful finger, "I read your newspaper every week. I know how you love to groom minor inconveniences and oversights into scandals. That is how you sell papers."

Audley sat back as if slapped in the face. He smoothed a strand of hair and flattened it to his crown, thinking of some defensive response. Before he had composed it, the headmaster spoke again, with a much warmer tone.

"But that need not be the case here, Mr Audley. I have the relevant information for your report, but I'd like to discuss two other issues first. I hope they will be of interest to you."

"Go on," Audley said, suspicious of the headmaster's changed demeanour.

"The first concerns our school magazine," he paused. "We are looking for a new printer to produce it for us. The final figures are not quite available now, but I understand that we need about eight hundred copies run off each year. That figure will increase to one thousand copies, when we increase our pupil intake over the next few years." Samuel gave a final dramatic pause, observing Audley's reaction. "Our current printer has been finding the job difficult to keep up with," he concluded.

For a moment, Audley did not react. Gradually a smile accumulated on his face, but it was not one of amusement. He knew he was being bribed.

Each man watched his opponent.

When Audley's head tilted, as if to speak, Samuel broke in.

"Do you think *The Chronicle* would be able to cope with this type of work, Mr Audley? I understand it has just bought itself some expensive new presses."

Vinegar tinged Audley's reply, "Yes on both counts, Mr Baxter."

I wondered whether another article about an attempted bribery would be in the sidebar, attached to the "Examination Paper Scandal" article.

"*The Chronicle*'s directors, of whom I am one, will need to meet and discuss that matter," he said.

The headmaster smiled like cracked masonry. His eyes were molten with intent. "And the other matter." Samuel produced the document I had retrieved from the General Office and read the file with exaggerated interest. "I see that Audley Junior is with us, and in the Fifth Form." He paused and looked up, with his eyes only, and waited for Audley's confirmation of his last point – as if there was any doubt.

The reporter sighed and crossed his arms tightly. From the side, I saw his Adam's apple bob with anxiety. When he eventually spoke, his voice crackled with phlegm. "Yes. So?" he said.

"I was wondering how all of this would affect him," Samuel said. "I'm sure it would be upsetting for him to have the good name of his school run through the mud."

"It would not affect him in the slightest."

Silence, boiling with omen, brewed in the air between them.

140

"I see from his grade profiles that he may be struggling. As you know, we require our boys to get at least eight 'C' grades at O-Level if they are hoping to come back for A-Level study. Does he intend to return next year, Mr Audley?"

"I believe so."

"Then I trust he will find all the assistance he needs in securing a place next year," Samuel said, smiling like a pope.

Audley nodded for a moment. His next words jerked out of him and he jangled like a marionette. "I note you are not yet recording this part of the interview, Mr Baxter!"

The headmaster wore a counterfeit surprise but there was a surge of heat from his eyes. "Are we ready to start the interview?" he said. Leaning over, he pressed the two buttons to begin recording. The tape fissled like leaves, before running quietly. "Here is our statement, Mr Audley, concerning the forced entry and subsequent compromise of the examination papers." He handed a typed sheet across his desk to Audley. "Mr Audley has been handed the school's official statement, a copy of which will accompany this tape on file."

Audley looked at the short paragraph and read it with a glance.

"Mr Audley, do you require any further clarification about the school's official statement?" the headmaster said.

Paddy Audley glared at the page as if the real statement would magically appear. He gave a snort to register his disappointment when it did not. "I see you mean to have it all your own way, Headmaster," he said.

"What other way is there, Mr Audley? My way is best for this school – and its friends."

"Your way is thoroughly corrupt," Audley said, standing abruptly. From my seat, I watched our typed statement drift to the carpet. He trod on it as he turned towards the door.

After Audley had left, Samuel spoke. "He is a dreamer."

"I hope we have not made an enemy of him," I said.

Long after the school had emptied, Samuel and I retired to the sofa in his office. He finally allowed himself to relax in my presence and talked, at length, of his concerns about the article Paddy Audley could write. The words poured from him. While I saw no profit in these speculations, I was pleased he shared his

141

concerns with me. For him, discussing his apprehensions was a significant step. He had lowered the draw bridge and raised the portcullis.

I sat at one end of the sofa and Samuel stretched out its full length, his head on my lap. He was rewarded with a fingertip massage of his face: eyes closed, breathing deeply as I traced the contours of his unfinished face. Just then, I realised it had grown handsome to me, despite its disarrangements. A warm aura ran up to my elbows with each line my fingers followed. This was an epiphany for me, and one to which my mind often returned in the future. At the beginning of our relationship, our love multiplying its substance, we were thrilled by every moment stolen together. Samuel had been under threat and he had sought my counsel. We worked in unison and, I believed, we would endure. I believed in us.

Small mention was made in *The Chancery Chronicle* of our troubles:

'On the evening of Wednesday 21 April, there was a break-in at Chancery Grammar School. A classroom was vandalised and a secure filing cabinet damaged. As a precaution, the school has informed the local examinations board that new O-Level mathematics examination papers will be required, as the current paper may have been compromised.'

That was the best outcome Samuel could have hoped for. Whatever his reasons, Paddy Audley had refrained from doing us harm. Samuel's promises were not forgotten. When the O-Level results were published, Audley Junior was allowed into the lower sixth form, even though he was below the minimum grade requirement. The school magazine was also run from the *Chronicle*'s presses, with the expectation that this arrangement would continue in future – an enterprise worth several hundred pounds each year.

The new academic year, September 1977, brought with it a few notable personnel changes. Chancery Grammar's expanded pupil intake required six new staff, interviewed in June, starting in September. Samuel, with the indulgence of the Governors,

142

altered the staffing structure, adding two 'senior teachers' to his Senior Management Team. William Butler was one of those promoted. His long tongue made him eminently suitable for the role. Dorothy had had her baby in August and would probably never have to work another day in her life.

Danny Cruikshanks had applied for voluntary redundancy the previous November, which the headmaster accepted with enthusiasm. Danny began his retirement early with a non-actuarially reduced pension and a handsome lump sum. Mrs Bedford flew off on her retirement broomstick and was replaced as the headmaster's secretary by Mrs Rose Maylie –former Administrative Assistant. Dorothy was replaced by Miss Lorna Herriot, who made up some of the shortfall in the General Office.

My promotion meant my summer holiday was much reduced, only two weeks in all. This did not trouble me in the least: I hated to feel alone in the emptiness of my house. The General Office staff had their usual four weeks holiday in July, leaving the headmaster two weeks to train his new secretary to his own exacting standards. The second half of July 1977 was exciting and passionate. I felt like a dating teenager again, as we kissed and fondled whenever the notion took us. In that fortnight, Samuel and I were insulated from the outside world. With no one else around, he cast off formality and rank. As the school was officially closed, we experimented with an unprecedented level of familiarity. Within Samuel, however, there remained an awareness that he was acting improperly. It would not be correct to call it guilt, for he could reason that away to his own satisfaction. He needed to know that I could be trusted, that our love would remain a secret until the appropriate time.

"Do you know the etymology of the word 'secretary'?" Samuel asked me as I buttoned up my blouse.

"Etymology? Isn't that something to do with insects?" I asked.

"I'm not fooled by your word play, Rose. I still haven't forgiven you for your 'abalone', fifty point word score."

"Seventy points, actually. And no, I don't know the origins of the word. Teach me something else new today." I straightened his tie and flicked the end of it on his chin.

His thick hands almost encircled my waist. "It comes from the Latin 'secretarius', meaning a confidential officer or confidant," he said. "It is a position of trust."

"I see where this is leading."

"Not to labour the point," he said, "I just fear the consequences more than you do."

"It is simple, Samuel. I won't say anything because you don't want me to. I don't want to lose you. Trust me."

"I do trust you. I'm sorry."

"Besides, I quite enjoy having a secret. It makes life interesting again. I haven't felt this frisky for years." I brushed a hair from his lapel. "Now, if we're finished with the 'dictation', I need to powder my nose."

In those early days, we limited our contact to after school sessions. It would have been suspicious if Samuel left home to make evening visits without a clear purpose, and he did not want to rush things. In the periphery of my thoughts, there loitered a concern that we had not yet fully defined the term 'appropriate time' for when we could reveal our relationship. Early on, I was not particularly anxious to clarify this. Long-term thinking of that magnitude seemed presumptuous. I half expected the affair to dwindle with Samuel's feelings of novelty; the other half of me hoped furiously that it would not.

At a time when new prospects were dawning for me, John Souseman's world was growing dark. When he missed the first week of school, it occurred to me that a friend should make contact. Reaching him by phone was unsuccessful, so I was compelled to call round. Friday evening seemed the best time to visit – it was not like either of us had a social life.

In my friendship with John, I had been inside his house many times. It was at least three months since I had last seen him, and longer since I had visited. I was not expecting the scene that greeted me.

From his driveway, still sitting in my car, I could tell he had let the place fall into decline. Like his personal grooming, John had a relaxed attitude to the order of his house, for his garden, even more so. His front lawn had always been patchy, thanks to the attentions of neighbourhood dogs. Now, it was more of a nature reserve than a lawn and had begun to creep towards the front door, reclaiming the driveway en route. I frowned at clutches of weed on my way to the door.

After my second ring of the bell, I stepped back to look through the lounge windows. The curtains were closed, their linings nicotine yellow and on their way to brown. There was no evidence of life within the house, beyond what I could imagine evolving on the curtains. No lights were on inside to push back the gathering gloom.

I renewed my efforts at making myself known. Between rings, I thundered on the door until my hand hurt. Some of its flaked red paint adhered to the heel of my fist. I lost count of my ringing and began to reason that John was either not at home, or inside and incapacitated. A slide show of possibilities began to whirl through my mind. He could have been topping up his fluid levels at the village pub. This was quite likely. The other scenario, unfortunately, seemed just as likely. I imagined John's decomposed body slumped in an armchair, his hand stiffened around the neck of a whisky bottle.

I finally lost all patience and embedded my finger in the doorbell button, leaving it there. Eventually, I heard a thump within and the living room curtains twitched. John peeked out at his intruder. While I was glad to see him alive, annoyance stirred inside me. Something clattered in the hall before lights came on within and John's jagged outline appeared spectral through the dingy, frosted glass of the door's panes. His ghastly appearance only increased when he opened the door.

"Rosie posy," he said, throwing an arm out to usher me in. He was pathetically drunk and thoroughly stinking. When he spoke, he leaned sideways on the door frame for balance. Only this spared him the indignity of another fall.

He wore what had once qualified as his best suit – the one he had worn for his first meal with my parents. It was now encrusted with food or vomit. I did not want to look close enough to classify the other barnacles. His equally soiled dress shirt was open at the neck and, by the look of him, I imagined the tie lost in the ditch where John had last slept. His hair was normally wild but was now greased down, and his beard was a collection of matted tufts. My good friend was now a parody of his former self: the efforts he had made to be presentable to my parents were before me in caricature. He was a ruin.

145

"Come in," he muttered. "You're lettin' the smell out."

One step into the hall and I realised he was not joking. A stagnation of bad breath, body odour, cigarettes, sick and urine hunkered in the air. I looked at John but said nothing. He crinkled his face with humiliation. I tutted when I walked into the lounge. The air was mossy with old smoke. Only after I had opened all the windows, was the air thin enough to speak through.

"Do you have a bin bag?" I asked.

"Don't do this, Rose. It's bad, but I'll tidy it myself. Just never got round to it." His eyes watered as he spoke. I tried not to pay attention to his face.

"Two will get it done in half the time," I said.

"Alright," he shrugged, "Useless to argue." John walked to the far end of the lounge as if over uneven ground. He disappeared into the kitchen and I heard him rummage ineptly through drawers. Finally, he emerged with a black bin liner and we set to work. He held the bag unsteady, while I disposed of every item that had no place in a living room. The food tins and cartons were first to go. He had lived out of his larder, eaten tinned food and used the empty tins as ash trays. He had snacked on dry Corn Flakes, straight from the box, munched by the fistful. Cigarette packets outnumbered everything else, followed by the eleven empty whisky bottles.

"Put the water heater on," I said. "You'll be needing a shower. A bath would look like soup after you'd finished."

John nodded and clung to the bin bag like it was his shame.

While John scrubbed off his rind in the shower, I washed dishes. The kitchen was not as bad as I first expected, only modestly grimy. It was helped by the fact that John only had six of everything – he was a bachelor, after all. His dishes did little more than fill the sink, instead of sprawl over the entire draining board. Several new life-forms were attempting to evolve on the worktop and linoleum, but a squirt of bleach ended their struggles. John's fondness for tinned food had contained the worst mess to the lounge area.

Thirty minutes later, John sat in clean pyjamas and dressing gown. His face, free from its straggly stubble, looked freshly smacked. His hawkish nose dipped into a coffee mug and we sat in the silence.

146

"How long were you wearing that suit?" I asked.

"Oh, a week, I think. Or two." His thin lips pinched. "I measure time in centilitres now."

"How many centilitres in a day then?" I had counted eleven bottles of whisky.

"About seventy. Sometimes more," he said without looking up.

"John, you can't go on like this. You're destroying yourself."

During the pause, he wiped his nose on the back of his hand. "Means a lot to me, what you've done." His eyes made contact once, but they had clouded over with self-pity.

I had been in the same dark cell of misery and knew how difficult it was to break out. "When will you be back to work?" I asked.

"Monday, probably."

"The headmaster will want to know why you were off."

"No doubt. Pious Baxturd."

"He has a right to know," I said.

"Listen to the headmaster's secretary," John retorted.

I may have been a little brisk in how I had spoken. "Who have you been speaking to?" I said.

"Danny drops in the odd time. Leaves off his empty whisky bottles."

I ignored his attempt at humour. "What's the matter with you, John?" I said with open concern. "Tell me."

He shrugged. "Everything," he said.

I waited for him to clarify this.

"Ellie broke up with me – for good. It's hard to stay drunk enough. A lot of work." He shrugged off a half-made smile. "Even work's changed. I used to find peace there. Mostly. Danny's gone. He was my rock. Baxter's reshuffled science departments to help Danny's redundancy. Departments have been merged. Jim Tate, head of physics, is head of science now. Three sciences are now one department. Big mistake. I'll be teaching physics and chemistry to juniors before long. It's not the job I signed up for." John's job had been his salvation. It had given him routine and security. "And Der Führer's decision to move human reproduction into religious studies makes me sick.

As if that had anything to do with religion. As if Bakewell would know where to stick it, if he had one."

I held my tongue, in spite of my disapproval. John needed me to listen.

"Best thing about the job is when I'm teaching – I'm not thinking about anything else. But, with these changes, I'm not sure I could face it again."

"You'd adjust better if you laid off the drink, got a decent meal and regular sleep," I said. "I'm sure your mental state would improve if you started looking after yourself.

John heaved another shrug and slurped his cold coffee.

"Why did Ellie break it off?" I said with as much delicacy as I could manage. There was unavoidable abrasion in that topic, but he answered without flinching. He spoke as if the words no longer carried any meaning for him.

"Her husband wormed his way back in."

The condition of his suit, no doubt, had something to do with the dramatic events of their break-up. The rest, I was content not knowing. I was surprised when he continued.

"She gave me the good news on my birthday. In a restaurant. 'Pass the salt and, by the way, Alistair and I are back together.'" After a pause, he added, "Bitch."

Chapter Fourteen

Over two years had passed since my split with Harry. I had heard from mutual friends that he appeared to be happy with his new lover – just as he had appeared to be happy with me. Our separation had passed its two year minimum requirement and I was free to sue for divorce. I did not expect Harry to oppose me on this, particularly as he had left me. I expected he would force the sale of our house to liberate his own portion. I imagined he would keep the full amount of this money a secret from his mistress.

On my behalf, Mr Spenlow poured over the minutiae, while I poured cheques into his company account. By the time I had paid for the divorce, I would have enough only to live in a garden shed. While I was considering the property market, Samuel made a suggestion. We were lying on the sofa, in his study, after hours.

"The problem with your current house is that I am not at liberty to call," he said.

"But you are always welcome," I said.

His smile was full of patronage. "I meant that it is surrounded on all sides by nosey neighbours," he said. "That makes it difficult for us to be together – comfortably together, without worrying about who knows what."

I was not beset with anxieties. Neither did I think my neighbours were unduly interested in my visitors. These were all Samuel's concerns.

"I'll ask the estate agent if he has any lighthouses for sale, shall I?"

"My dear, I was thinking of something a little closer to land," he said.

"A cave, then?"

He snorted with amusement and kissed my forehead.

"Something a little out in the country would be perfect," he said, "Away from Chancery."

I pulled back and stared at him. He was smiling but earnest. I considered his final comment and thought of the subtext: he was trying to isolate me, far from his family. Such a move, out of town, would put me further away from my own family and friends – not that I had many of the latter. My doubts must have registered on my face, because he spoke.

"I only want to call on you without worrying what the neighbours think. I'm well known in Chancery. Hundreds of parents and former pupils know me to see. I cannot possibly know them all by sight." He brought his face closer to mine. "And when I leave Helen, I can move in with you. We can enjoy the peace of the countryside together.

While I resisted allowing a man to influence my decisions, Samuel's logic was compelling. He had said what I wanted to hear, and that decided the matter.

Relationships, governed by arbitrary human nature, are in continual flux. So it was with Samuel and me. That evening, we remained behind in school to carry out, what Samuel called, 'necessary administration'. Upon completion of my secretarial duties, and getting dressed, Samuel was distant.

"What's the matter, Samuel?"

"Nothing. Everything's fine," he lied.

This had developed into a noticeable pattern. We were drawn together by physical impulse, then Samuel would withdraw into a dark corner to gnaw on his shame. He tried not to make it obvious, and I would pretend not to notice. For the next while, we would manoeuvre around each other in a gradually decreasing spiral, until he summoned me and surrendered to his impulses again. A less tolerant mistress would have made her disapproval known. I did nothing, because I understood his ambivalence. A good man should find it difficult to act improperly. Eventually, he would grow accustomed to deception. I could wait for him. In time, his recovery periods would decrease and eventually disappear.

The next day, a Tuesday, I had an awkward collision. It was early in the morning, before 8:00 a.m., and the adjoining door to Samuel's office was closed as usual. The headmaster's car was parked at the front entrance and I supposed he must be in his office, alone. I lifted some letters that needed his signature, rapped on his door and walked straight into Charlie, who was coming out. The moment should have been quite comic. For some reason, though, Charlie was in no mood to make jests.

150

"Oh!" we both said in the collision. I recovered first, but Charlie looked positively horrified to see me at the door.

"I'm sorry, Charlie. I don't usually throw myself at men," I said, my last words dying in the recognition that they were out of place.

Charlie flicked a glance at Samuel who was storing a document wallet in his desk's filing drawer.

"I'm sorry," was all Charlie said as he rushed past me. That he could not look me in the eye, told me everything about the topic of their previous conversation. For all his 'a secretary is a confidential officer' warnings, all his urgings that I tell no one, Samuel had just confided in Charlie about our affair. So heavy was his guilt that he had confided in his closest friend.

Without acknowledgement or greeting, I delivered the letters to the headmaster's desk top. With a crisp tone, I informed him that they required his signature. I turned on my heel, closed the adjoining door and left the headmaster to his own business. In my own office, I considered what Samuel had just done. My throat tightened. I had borne our secret on my own. Anything else would have been betrayal. Unlike Samuel, I held my counsel. But now, we would have to trust Charlie Bakewell to do the same.

Charlie, in many ways, was like a priest. As far as I could imagine – and I shuddered when I tried – he was, as yet, unknown to woman. He was also a confessor of the utmost integrity. If anyone could carry the weight of such knowledge, it would be Charlie. He would tell no one, nor even allude to it when talking to me. No doubt, Samuel had bound him with sacred oaths similar to my own. I knew Charlie would disapprove of the affair in the strongest terms, and he would have said so to Samuel. The discussion between them may even have been heated just before I walked in. That seemed to fit with the atmosphere in the office. I cringed at how my joke had been precisely the wrong thing to say to a man who had just been debating against adultery. It is fortunate that embarrassment is not fatal. In time, Charlie would begin to relax in my company again. Undoubtedly, he would pray for us and the families we endangered, but he would not judge us himself.

I would avoid him for a while, as he would avoid me. When enough time had passed, it would be moved from the

151

forefront of our minds and we would regard each other much as we had done before. One thing was for sure: Charlie would not be asking me to cook at his fellowship weekends again.

In the first term of each new year, it was customary to celebrate the academic achievements of the year before. This grand celebration of erudition was known as 'Speech Night', and its title was an indication of where the real focus lay. Laboured, humourless droning was directed at the assembled governors, guests, staff, parents and pupils. The boys made a mental note to do less well in their next summer exams, to dodge the ritualistic tedium of this night. The prizes awarded to the pupils were scarcely worth the effort. Weighty tomes of pedantry were heaped on them when they stepped up to receive their accolades. The whole event was contrived and choreographed like a state funeral. The pupils' orchestra sat beneath the stage, framed by its stairs. The young musicians belched, twanged and tooted approximations of what composers intended, while parents looked on, flinching behind their smiles.

The front five rows of the audience were reserved for the teaching staff, but they were not allowed to be in place before the proceedings began. That would have neglected an opportunity for the pomp provided by the academic procession. Solemn music resounded while the teachers walked with slow, measured steps down the centre of the assembly hall. Those in the audience must have wondered how any class started on time if teachers walked so slowly. In ranks of two, they paced, blackened in their suits and gowns like undertakers of learning. Their austere formation did not waver. It was as if a giant coffin, poised between them, balanced along the rank of their shoulders.

John Souseman had returned to work by this time and even he did his best to appear sombre. From my aisle seat in the sixth row, I did note, however, that he was the only one sucking a sweet. When they reached the front of the hall, as though on rails, they wheeled left and gowns flourished into seats. John was in the back row of teachers, just in front of me. He winked at me while gathering his robes to sit. I wondered whether he wore a clean suit under his gown.

152

The governors and their guests sat aloof on the stage in two compact rows. Some were partially blocked from my view by the ornamental rostrum. Enough of them were visible, however, for me to notice the self-satisfaction they shared, like twelve Caesars watching the plebeians. But the person on stage who interested me most was Samuel's guest. He was accompanied by his wife, Helen.

The Chairman of the Board, Mr Boyce, opened the proceedings. His swarthy enthusiasm crammed positive buzzwords into his speech. Chancery Grammar School had entered a golden age. Its headmaster was the captain of a great ship, on a voyage of scholastic discovery. On and on Boyce prattled, wringing the last drops from tired old metaphors. Samuel's smile was cemented, but I saw him blink when Boyce concluded with a pun on his own surname: 'Boyce is for the boys'.

Thankfully, mid-speech, John's hand dropped down behind him, between the chairs, bearing a crumpled bag of cinnamon lozenges. The evening was already dragging on, so I felt justified in taking four sweets. Yawning was much less likely if I had a sweet in my mouth. The headmaster rose to deliver his annual report and, somewhere along the back row of staff, a stopwatch clicked. Ralph Preston, head of physical education, organised the staff's annual sweepstake, betting on the length of the headmaster's speech. At least some attention would be paid to Samuel's words – if only the first and last.

My eyes kept returning to Helen Baxter, on the stage beside Samuel's empty seat. Throughout Boyce's speech, she had been attentive, laughing when appropriate, nodding at the chairman's exhortations. Sitting in the front row, raised up on the stage for all to see, it would have been remiss to do otherwise. Now Samuel was speaking, she inflated, perfectly upright. She was anxious for her husband. The attention she paid to his words was either entirely genuine or very well feigned. I believed it to be real: the admiration kindling in her eyes convinced me. She was the triumphant owner of a prize alpha male.

I assessed her, with a superiority born of knowing something she did not. Like me, she had an expansive bosom, although hers had suffered the haul of gravity more than mine.

Samuel was a breast man, it seemed. She had thickened in the middle but carried herself well enough that it was evenly distributed. Her jade dress suit was elegant and well tailored. For my taste, its design was from the previous decade but that was in keeping with her vintage. Without being noticeably comely, she had a pretty face.

After the rituals of prize-giving, it was customary for governors, guests and staff to attend a light supper in the canteen. There were a number of issues I wanted to clarify, and I contrived to wait until Samuel was separated from Helen before making my approach.

"Hello, Mrs Baxter, I am Rose, Mr Baxter's secretary," I said.

She had a mouth full of canapé and could only nod her acknowledgement at first. The light lines around her eyes and mouth creased with humour.

"Mmm. You caught me at my favourite guilty pleasure – delicious pâté. Hello, Rose. I'm Helen. But you've already worked that out." She offered her hand to me.

I shook it, trying not to study her as a secret adversary. "We don't get to see you in the school very often," I said.

"Wives are only wheeled out for special occasions. Did you like the speeches?" she said.

I paused and she cut in.

"Trick question," she said. "Don't incriminate yourself with a lie."

"Or the truth," I said and was proud when she laughed.

"You must have a terrible time of it, keeping Samuel organised, I'm sure."

"Another trick question?" I asked.

"Absolutely not. I'm oozing sympathy for you." Charisma radiated from her. I could see why the young Samuel had been impressed with her wit. She was a strong, capable woman.

Just then, I felt a pressure on my arm and turned to see Samuel standing almost between us. His stoniness reminded me of our first meeting. His face was flushed and the angles of his mouth were rigid. When he spoke, his eyes narrowed minutely. It is in barely perceptible gestures that we express the most.

"Ah, Helen. I see you have met Mrs Maylie."

"Yes, we were just saying how enlightening your speech was," she said. He did not see her wink to me.

"I see. I'm sure, Mrs Maylie, you are finding the whole evening quite tedious. I thank you for attending and showing your support tonight."

"Really, that's quite alright," I said, beginning to understand his subtext. Defiance, here, would do me no good. In the role of dutiful subordinate I would have to take my leave. Samuel was giving me an opportunity to withdraw. Although I knew defiance was counterproductive, I felt Mr Baxter needed to work some more before getting what he wanted. The edge of his formality made me feel especially stubborn.

"I'm sure you would like to go home now, Mrs Maylie," he added in the pause.

"No, I'm just beginning to enjoy myself."

His face slackened at the cheekbones, indicating surprise. He blinked heavily to reconstitute himself. "Goodnight, Mrs Maylie. I need to reclaim my wife. We have our rounds to do," he said. Taking Helen by the elbow, he directed her towards Mr Boyce, the nearest person of any significance. For a second his eyes lingered on mine. They blazed with reproach.

"Goodnight, Rose." Helen turned from his grasp and stepped back to me. She took my hand again. "I'll see you at the next one of these dreadful things," she said, then followed him into the swirl.

I did not even have a cup of tea to nurture while I stood alone. That awkward moment intensified the emotions churning inside me. I saw many familiar faces but none that offered the comfort of friendship. John had surely ducked out long ago and Charlie was nowhere to be seen. I gave Samuel what he wanted: I turned on my heel and left.

That was another lonely evening. I considered my place in the order of things and reasoned my own insignificance. To Samuel, I was dispensable. Given his way, I would be isolated for his use, whenever his conscience allowed. Both my head and heart told me there was no future in the relationship. The more I considered Helen's body language during his speech, the more I saw contradiction. She was concerned that he do well, which did not conform to Samuel's characterisation of her. In his narrative,

155

he described a failing marriage. There was no trace of the indifference he had ascribed to her. Quite the contrary. His representation of Helen had been unfair. That, in itself, became a question. He might have misled me to elicit sympathy. As a lonely woman, I was vulnerable to seduction. In my recollection, he had been the instigator. There was enough haze to make me sceptical. Harry had operated in this type of obscurity. Suspicion was my best defence.

Now I could put a face to one of the potential casualties, I felt less inclined to continue with the affair. Samuel's recklessness made him guilty in my eyes. Knowing the consequences for those who loved him, he persisted anyway. He was the cold and indifferent one, not her. Helen had given up a career to raise his children, and he had repaid her with betrayal. If that was how he rewarded his wife's dedication, I knew his mistress could expect even less.

Over the next week, I tested Samuel's awareness. In school I maintained a civil but formal method of addressing him, returning to the old forms of 'Mr Baxter' and 'Headmaster' even when we were alone. In the first instance he looked askance at me, recognising my shift, but, otherwise, he did nothing. On the Monday of this trial period, I was expecting him to challenge me, or summon me after school. He did neither. The week wore on and he said nothing. Our interactions were all professional. I presume he was content to watch this moral predicament dissolve, without his intervention. Had he really cared, he would not have let our relationship dissipate. Inaction speaks louder than words.

In the affair, he had easy pleasures for the taking. My foolishness had not required him to earn that which he took so freely. Since I had distanced myself, he had interpreted this as the end of our secret contract. It was just as well, then, that I had not been hasty in moving house. A remote country house would be a lonely place, with only my spinning wheel for company.

"I trust you'll forgive me, Mrs Maylie – you are still using that surname?" Mr Spenlow asked.

"Yes."

"Then I trust you'll forgive me if I take some extra concern in your case. The law is said to be dispassionate, but divorces are

156

very personal work. I feel that you and I share a similar interest in ensuring that our Harry feels the pinch." Old Spenlow smiled over the top of his glasses and his forehead wrinkled with it. His baldness was almost complete, but for ghostly wisps that lingered above his ears. More hair cascaded from his ears than remained on his head. The feature that most distracted me, however, was the boundary where his wrinkled forehead met his mottled scalp. Beyond this margin, there were none of the muscles required for expression, and so, it did not ripple. The contrast between the two areas was pronounced, as different as sea and shore.

I realised I was staring at him. He may have retained the impression that I was stupid, if he recalled our first telephone conversation. Thankfully, he was as gentlemanly as ever.

"Mrs Maylie?" he said.

"I'm sorry. It's an emotional time for me."

His head bobbed like a dashboard ornament. "I will not be dealing with your case directly. We have a new matrimonial expert, Mr Larkin. He will be giving your suit special attention. I'm more of a litigator."

"Certainly," I said.

"Good. You may use my office. I have to be in court this afternoon and need to visit another client now." He stood and shuffled round to my side of the desk on bowed legs. He reminded me of an old tap dancer. "I will just send him in," he said. "He won't be a moment." Mr Spenlow shook my hand and stooped deeper in a farewell.

Mr Larkin was more than a moment by my definition, but I did not mind. The longer I was at Bardell and Spenlow, the longer Mr Baxter would have to cope without me. The headmaster would find that Wednesday especially busy: I had scheduled a number of appointments for him during my absence. Without me to organise the necessary documents for each interview, he would be overwhelmed in my absence. Indeed, the required documentation was in a locked filing cabinet and I had brought my office keys out with me. In some ways, at least, Mr Baxter would be missing me.

Waiting for Mr Larkin, I gazed around Spenlow's office. Befitting a man of his status, his desk was grand and robust. It was old and seasoned, like its owner, and the green leather desktop showed significant wear. It characterised a tidy man, but one not preoccupied with appearances. Files and documents sat in a stable arrangement beside the desk, but the room was uncluttered. He did not allow his work to back up. I mused that Spenlow was either efficient or quick to delegate to lesser minions, like the elusive Mr Larkin. The shelves were similarly neat, displaying ledgers, bound in uniform leathers of red, brown and green. They were not for presentation. All had signs of wear. The most worn books waited on the shelves closest to Spenlow's desk.

Before I had the opportunity to rummage through the desk drawers, Mr Larkin appeared bearing a file marked 'Maylie/Maylie'. I had preconceived an image of the man by his name: tall and egg-headed, with wobbling jowls. He was tall, but the rest surprised me: a distinctive figure, almost handsome, with thick, dark hair scooped up and back. He wore a neat beard, squared at the chin. He was not more than thirty-five but grinned with a school boy's impudence.

He stood before me and bowed. "Mrs Maylie, David Larkin," he said, hand extended. After jolting me from wrist to elbow, he sat in Spenlow's chair like it was a sun lounger. Leaning back, he crossed his legs so that one knee rested against the desk top. All the while, he read my file.

I was unsettled by his ease in my company. Spenlow had been much more formal, as he should have been with a client. Larkin lounged in front of me as if we were at the beach. I noted other aspects of his appearance that were consistent with his leisurely posture. He wore a trim black suit, slim-fitting, buttoned and waistcoated. The collar of his white shirt was narrow, his tie a black strip of liquorice – a fashion consciously out of harmony with the flares and wide lapels of 1977. His suit was closer to the early 1960s style, like 'The Beatles' had worn back then. Mr Larkin liked to think of himself as an individual. He did things his own way and outwardly disregarded what others thought of him. Or so I guessed.

"Can I call you Rose?" he said. Coming from the long silence, his abrupt words surprised me.

"If you like."

"I like." He smiled. He was flirting.

158

I could not think of a witty rejoinder, so I arched an eyebrow in a way I thought might register disapproval.

He continued, "Your file tells me that the bank account from which you paid the mortgage was in your name alone for the five years of your marriage."

"That's right."

"And what contribution did —" he checked the file, "— Harry make towards the upkeep of the property?"

"His money went towards housekeeping."

"And what did that include?"

Although his body language verged on casual, his manner was sharp.

"Groceries, utilities, other things."

"Common sense would seem to say that you have sole claim to the title of this property. Unfortunately, the law and common sense have only a passing acquaintance. Legally, Mr Maylie is still entitled to half," he said, peaking his brows.

"Is there any way for me to keep the house?"

David Larkin's head bobbed but not enough to discompose his sculpted hair flick. "Only if you have funds to buy his half, at the current market value."

"Oh," I said. "That's not very likely."

"Think of it this way, Rose: you can make a fresh start in a new house, with all the modern conveniences. There are several new developments in the greater Chancery area that would suit you, I'm sure," he said.

My biggest concern had been losing the house. I dreaded the upheaval of moving, of turning an unfamiliar house into a home.

After a pause, he spoke again, his tone no less factual. "I'd like to take you out to dinner, Rose."

I paused mid-breath with shock and probably flushed with embarrassment. "Yes," I stuttered — far too quickly.

159

Chapter Fifteen

"What are you looking so pleased with yourself for?" Betty said, slipping in to the Reprographics Suite behind me.

"Me?" I asked with surprise. "Why do you say that?" I tapped numbers into the copier.

"Since when do you hum to yourself? Something's up. It must be, you deliberately caught my eye on your way past. And you're photocopying last week's announcements?"

"Am I?" I said. "I must have lifted the wrong thing."

"Now! Before I get bored," Betty demanded.

"I was at my solicitors this morning. They told me I'll have to sell my house, even though I'm the only one who ever paid the mortgage. Harry didn't pay a penny but he can still claim half."

Betty stared at me without expression. "You must be ecstatic."

"Oh, and one of the solicitors asked me out on a date," I said, fighting a grin.

Betty snorted. She was not the girly type to squeal and throw out hugs at any good news. "Things are looking up, old girl. Is he hunky? More importantly, is he loaded?" she said and a grin escaped her.

"Yes, God, I hope so."

"I'm telling Joan," she said, swung the door and strolled into the office. When she was level with Joan's desk she cleared her throat. She said, "Rose is dating her solicitor."

Joan and Charlie Bakewell looked up at her with curiosity. Then they looked around for me. The door to Reprographics was still open and I was biting my lip, conscious of what I had just done. Charlie winked and extended a marshmallow thumb to show his approval. Now that Charlie knew, I expected it would be telegraphed around all the staff.

I confess, it was no coincidence that Charlie was in the office when I chose to use the photocopier. Joan and he met at the same times every week: Monday and Wednesday at 3:30 p.m.. Joan handled Charlie's schedule and administration, just as I used to manage Jack Dawson's – Betty now had that dubious pleasure. Charlie relished tittle-tattle, as long as it was not malicious. I had hoped Betty, Joan or Charlie would hail me in the office, allowing me to mention my solicitor's appointment during the conversation. My news would then have been delivered in front of Charlie. I had not expected Betty to make a comic scene but this outcome was satisfactory. Charlie would carry the message to Samuel.

My news brought another significant development: Charlie would be more comfortable around me again. No doubt my good news pleased him because it announced the end of my affair with Samuel.

The dinner with David Larkin was scheduled for the Friday evening. Under no circumstances would I have agreed to dine on the Wednesday, the same day as my appointment. To have made myself immediately available, would have looked desperate. Friday gave me the opportunity to make preparations and buy new clothes for the occasion. It is much easier to relax when you have confidence in your looks. Smart and fashionable new clothes help considerably in this respect, especially if they disguise the worst bumps and accentuate the best.

By late that Friday afternoon, Samuel had still passed no comment concerning my forthcoming date. I wondered whether Charlie had completed his task and passed on my news. The big clot was probably unaware he was supposed to do this. The temptation to interrogate Charlie with chocolate éclairs was strong, and I only just managed to resist.

Samuel had plenty of opportunities to talk to me when we were alone in his office. He could have used any one of these to comment on the status of our relationship. On Friday especially, I contrived numerous reasons to visit his office while he worked on his own, but again he failed me. His conversation was spartan and functional, never referencing the forthcoming weekend. Short of broaching the subject myself, I could not have done more. To do this would indicate that I wanted his reaction. At times I wonder whether men are capable of noticing anything that is not bouncing or wiggling in front of them.

Every action has an implied meaning: this is especially true on a first date. First dates mark the transition of a relationship from casual acquaintance, or friendship, into a period of emotional investment. During the first date, a woman assesses the level of respect and commitment shown by her suitor. Naturally, in this formative phase, a man should be on his best behaviour, keen to make a good impression. It is also natural to assume that a woman's sensitivity to indifference will be heightened.

Any man who does not already know this, does not deserve to know it. He should be left grunting in the cave of his self-absorption. He does not know these very basic facts because he does not want to know them. Man learned to make fire because he was cold, and being cold made him unhappy. Through experimentation and observation, he learned to kindle, and he was happier. Ignorant men will only acquire behaviour that pleases women when they are unhappy being single men. It is that simple. They should be shunned until they learn to behave or their kind dies out.

David Larkin was one such unenlightened man. With remarkable precision, he did everything a woman on a first date would consider insensitive. He said he would call to pick me up at 7:00 p.m.. For once, I was ready on time. But I need not have been. He was twenty minutes late.

Rather than be troubled parking his car and walking five yards to my front door, Larkin stayed in the car and tooted the horn to signal his arrival.

Standing in my lounge, I shuddered and cursed him.

For the previous twenty minutes I had been expecting the doorbell to announce my beau, bearing an extravagant bouquet. As the time passed, I grew less optimistic, but I would still have been receptive to apologies and excuses.

Larkin's tooting presented me with a dilemma: to reject him immediately for pure ignorance, or give him the benefit of the doubt. My father would not have let me run out to such a dimwit, had I still been living at home. Answering the horn would have sacrificed my feminine integrity. My only option was to ignore him, hoping he would discover his error. From the bottom of the stairs, I flicked the switch to turn the upstairs hall light on. If he noticed that, he would know that I was home, at least. Hopefully he would also take it as a hint that the horn's toot was ineffective as a signal.

My plan worked almost completely.

He did notice the light, and understood that I was home. There he deviated from my plan. He reasoned that the horn's toot had not effectively signalled his arrival. Male logic overcame him. A toot had not done the job; more force was needed. The resounding blast that issued from his car killed all insects in a two hundred yard radius. I cursed him liberally, using words generally heard on a building site.

Further ignoring the horn was useless. He was not sufficiently aware to learn from this lesson. Any remaining good humour of mine vanished, along with any hope for the evening. My last shred of optimism clung to the hope that he would restore himself to my graces that evening. I took my time locking the front door and walked to his car. This allowed him plenty of time to stir himself and, like a gentleman, hold the passenger door open for me. But he did not. He remained in the car, scraping a rough edge off his fingernail with his teeth.

When I opened the car door myself, he leered the length of me. He drove a trendy 'MGB GT' sports car, which was unsuitable for my choice of skirt. My fault, for thinking that solicitors drove saloons, but I tried to recover the situation as best I could. As gracefully as I could, I lowered and twisted into the passenger seat. When I looked, I caught Larkin eyeing my legs as though he planned to wear them later.

"Hello, love. You scrub up well," he said. His abrupt delivery, that I had found so compelling on Wednesday, was now only abrasive. Its charm had evaporated.

I looked him up and down with the same eye for detail, hoping to undermine his confidence. "You are wearing your work clothes," I said. "And the same tie as Wednesday.

"I work late, love. And I only have one tie."

I was supposed to be impressed.

"When you first sounded your horn, I thought one of the neighbours must have ordered a taxi," I said.

"Right." His head jolted upward as he slipped into reverse gear. "Easy mistake to make." By then, I knew the date was a failure. If allowed, it could drag on into an anecdote that Betty would have been proud to tell. She had several folk tales of her own like this: dates that were the equivalent of a car crash.

I passed the journey in relative silence. Larkin gave a commentary on the stupidity of other road users. He drove like he could recover the twenty minutes we had lost from his lateness. At every corner, I braced myself against flailing around helplessly. Once, I even squawked for fear that he would put the car into a slide. Again, he may have supposed I would be impressed with his mastery behind the wheel.

Larkin parked across the road from the restaurant and briskly exited the car. For a moment, it appeared he would perform a conventional duty, opening my door.

Too often I am fooled by hope. This was one of those occasions.

He stood at his door, watching me struggle up to street level. It was best he was not positioned to see my stocking tops and underwear as I sprawled upward.

"Come on, love. Table's booked for half past." He clunked the central locking and preceded me across the road. He did pause at the restaurant door, and allowed me to catch up, but he only did so to adjust his elaborate bouffant reflected in the glass door.

I had seen enough and had enough. A few yards up the street, two young couples spilled from a taxi, fizzing with good humour. I turned sharply, crossing the road and snapped into the taxi's passenger seat. My movements were so abrupt that the old driver fumbled his change and raised an arm to defend himself.

"Strafford Avenue, please," I said with absolute resolution.

The driver studied me for a moment, then turned to his right and saw Larkin gawping into the car. "Right you are, Ma'am," he said. And we were away.

I kept away from the General Office on Monday morning. Betty would have removed my finger nails with pliers to extract every detail about the date. To avoid perjury, I remained in my office and worked through break. It pained me to miss out on the company. Joan was ever thoughtful and sent Lorna, Dorothy's replacement, in with a mug of tea and some jam tarts. Curiously, this made me feel even more alone.

In spite of my best efforts, though, the subject could not be avoided. Charlie Bakewell passed through, en route to visit Samuel in his office. "How was your Friday night, Rose?" he said, tapping a pudgy finger to his nose. He was at the adjoining

164

door when I shrugged. "Sorry to hear that," he said with exaggerated sympathy.

But once he had opened the door to the headmaster's study, an impulse leapt from me. "It was ever so romantic," I said, "And he was *such* a gentleman!"

Charlie held the door half open and wagged a finger at me. "You had me worried there – thought I'd put my foot in it again. Well, I'm glad things worked out for you. And I hope they keep working out." He winked and vanished through the door.

I cringed that I had been so childish, and hoped my tactics had not also been transparent.

"Mrs Maylie," the intercom said, "Would you come in and see me before you go?" Samuel's voice lacked intonation.

"Yes, Mr Baxter," I said, depressing the beige button. The plastic box fizzed into silence. I sat at my desk and considered how long I should wait before going in to see him. It was already well past my normal leaving time. I had lingered, allowing trivial matters to delay me. It would convey the wrong message to dash in to see Samuel immediately; that would appear servile. Neither could I delay too long; that would appear defiant. My thoughts organised themselves like spaghetti. Uncertainties played pantomimes in my head. Had there been a sharpness to his monotone? Had my inflection been too sharp or too brittle? I knew nothing for sure. He might even send me back to the General Office.

I opened the top two buttons of my blouse. After some consideration, that was too obvious. Samuel would spot the contrivance. In some ways, he was more astute than me. I refastened the top one but left the second adrift. This had the benefit of allowing him a view from the right perspective, without indicating an obvious ploy. Button strain across the cleavage is a common problem for generously proportioned women. I checked the angles with a hand mirror. The second button's gap would inflict maximum damage. It restrained the widest part of my bust. That afternoon, that button could have a well deserved rest.

I gathered my notebook, pen, and a deep, calming breath before I knocked and entered.

165

Quite unusually, Samuel was seated at the circular dining table. Leaning forward on his elbows, his chair at an angled towards the door, he half faced me as I entered. A broadsheet newspaper was spread out on the table top. This too was unusual for him.

"Rose," he said, turning towards me, "Have a seat." The tilt of his chin indicated the chair beside him.

"Where would you like me to sit?" I said. It would not do to let him have everything his own way.

"Beside me will do," he said without the formality of our recent exchanges. "If you don't mind."

I withdrew the chair from under the table and pulled it back a foot before sitting. It was still within his reach but required some effort on his part if he intended to make contact. I did this only to gauge his reaction, without wanting to completely discourage him. On the other hand, I could not appear to be actively encouraging him either. The stubborn part of me wanted him to work hard if he was making amends. As a defence, the extra distance would show that I no longer cared for his company.

A quick glance down verified that my angle allowed him to glimpse a lace border, inside my blouse. I readied a fresh page on my writing pad while my eyes were downcast. Only when composed, did I look up. Samuel turned fully to face me, sitting sideways in his chair, one thick forearm resting on the table, the other on the chair back. His hands meshed and formed a bridge. His chunky face was earnest. He watched me and currents of blue plasma broiled in his eyes. I had to look away but resolved not to speak first. He had been dismissive of me on Speech Night. He should be the one to re-establish our connection.

Eventually he untwined his fingers and extended his palms out to me. It was a moving petition, an act of reconciliation. I considered this and noticed the arch of his dark brows. A lump ran a circuit between my throat and stomach.

In his upturned palms, I placed my notepad and pen.

"Will you be making the notes yourself, Mr Baxter?" I said. With a supreme effort, I clamped my mouth against a triumphant smirk.

Samuel jolted in his chair. He saw me chew down laughter and he laughed a little himself.

"Was I being too sentimental, Rose?"

I said nothing.

He discarded my accessories and grasped my hands with renewed purpose. When he spoke, his focus was unwavering. "I have grieved you. For this, I am deeply sorry." He nodded slightly as if to say 'amen'. "On Speech Night, I was afraid you would accidentally stumble and give my wife a clue of the love between us. In my fear, I may have treated you harshly."

"You did," I said, outwardly scornful. Actually, I was swept up on the warm thermal of his words.

"And now I fear I have lost you forever," he said. "And, in losing you, I have lost my last chance of being happy." His voiced diminished to a whisper in those last words.

It worked. I looked down before he could read my face for a response.

"Have I lost you?" he asked, squeezing my hands.

"That depends," I said, still looking down. "I need to believe there is a future in this relationship – that I am not wasting my time."

He said nothing.

I continued, "Otherwise, I may as well wait for someone who will make the commitment I need."

"You do not want to continue as we did before?" His tone indicated surprise.

"That is no longer enough," I said and locked his eyes with mine. I had not planned to say these things when I had imagined our reconciliation. They occurred to me only at that moment.

"I am a married man. What can I give you?"

"Tell me your intentions."

"Yes, that seems fair," he said, looking over my head while he considered the rest.

I knew he must not be prompted or led to say the right things. Those he should discover on his own, or he was not ready for the commitment. He began slowly, "I will have to divorce Helen. Our relationship is all but dead anyway – but for our mutual interest in the children." He searched my face for a reaction, but I deliberately withheld expression. He continued, "She and I have a civilised relationship. I am sure we will be able to reach an understanding. Jack and Laura, however, would be devastated." He stopped and waited for my response.

167

I only nodded.

"And I don't think it's fair to put them through that," he said, "But I don't want to lose you, Rose." After a pause, he continued, "Can we reach an understanding between ourselves – if only for the sake of the children?"

I thought of grubby faced little urchins, a boy and girl, clothed in rags, searching through bins for their next meal.

"How old are they?" I asked.

His eyes flicked up while he brought the twins to mind. "Seventeen."

Not quite little street children, then.

"They are in the Lower Sixth, beginning to study for their A-Levels. It wouldn't be right to put them through a trauma at this delicate time in their lives. That would certainly impact their on school work, and future careers," he said.

"I suppose it would."

Neither of us spoke for a time. I looked down at his hands enveloping mine. His were square and angular, stuffed with rubble, but warm. He squeezed mine before he spoke.

"I know this is a lot to ask, Rose, but I will ask it because I love you." His pause was short but dramatic. "I want you to wait for me – until the time is right. And we will be happier for doing these things in the right order. Then, no one may accuse us of anything shameful –"

"Even though they would be right," I nearly said.

"– and we will be able to hold our heads up and be happily married, beyond reproach," he said, tapering off.

He had said he loved me; that he would marry me. I was sufficiently pleased. He had answered my deepest concerns. This reassurance was important to me for continuing our affair. I was wrapped in the soft fleece of his carefully chosen words. While I believed him completely, there was an incantation in his words that made me want more.

"Helen still loves you. I saw the way she looked at you on Speech Night," I said. My softened tone indicated my last doubts were held by a gossamer strand. Samuel could blow them away with a gentle puff.

"Helen may still love me – or think she does – but not as a wife should love a husband. I am familiar to her: an old friend. More often, she does not consider me at all. We are not lovers.

She no longer needs to play that role." Somewhere in that speech his hands moved to my knees and he leaned in.

"Why do you say that?" I asked

He shrugged. "She no longer needs me in that regard. We are not lovers. It is no longer worth the bother to her. She got what she wanted from me: children, a home, status. It is clear she no longer desires me." He finished with a shrug.

"And she did this deliberately?" I said.

After a moment's consideration, "I suppose not. It would be harsh to accuse her of conspiracy."

"Conspiracy?"

"Something switched off inside her when the children were born. They became her preoccupation and she forgot how to be a wife."

A feminist instinct was rising in me, but I knew a fresh argument now would ruin our reconciliation. As usual, I was wiser when I said nothing.

He continued. "I am still useful for paying the mortgage, the bills and some heavy lifting." His smile grew as he dropped to his knees before me. In what seemed like an after-thought, he added, "We will never be like that, Rose. We'll always be lovers – even as an old couple." His fingers found the opening in my blouse.

This was not a convenient time for that discovery – I thought, we were still negotiating terms. But I could not dissuade him. Because of this, the particulars of our contract had to wait for another time. It was enough to be back together. At least, I had some expectation where the relationship would lead. He had said he would get a divorce after the children's exams. Presumably, that would be after their A-Levels, in two years, or so. I could wait that long. Our affair did not have to remain on hold until then; it simply had to remain a secret.

Chapter Sixteen

Since we had split, Harry and I had little contact. Once he asked me to leave a box of his belongings on the front step, which he collected when I was at work – the locks had long since been changed, denying him access to the house. Among his possessions were several vinyl records. I considered it a sign of healing that I was not even tempted to grill them first. It helped that we hardly spoke. Even while married, we found it difficult to agree. Our last conversation, however, pleased me immeasurably. It was a phone call on an evening in November 1977.

"Hello Rose," he hesitated. "It's Harry here." He spoke mechanically, with a thick tongue.

My stomach tightened. "Yes?"

"About the divorce – we'd like to come to an arrangement."

"Go on."

His tongue smacked and his mistress prompted from the background. "Tell her what we agreed," she said, and not in a whisper. Her voice was strong, edged with impatience. She wanted me to know he did her bidding.

"Rose, we want to get this over with as soon as possible," Harry said.

"I'm listening."

"I will transfer my half of the house to you if you agree not to pursue me for any maintenance allowance." He rushed his speech like a bitter tonic. "We have plenty of money here and don't need anything from you."

"That's *enough*," she hissed. Harry was no more in control of the conversation than a ventriloquist's dummy. He merely brokered an agreement between his women.

"That's fine," I said. "Have your solicitors draw up the documents and send them to mine."

"Yes. Goodbye, then," he said.

I put down the phone without farewell. There was a delightful subtext to this call. When I retold the story to the girls in the office, they thought it fortunate that Harry would surrender his half of the house. I gave what I thought to be the more likely explanation: Harry's mistress did not want him

170

having money of his own. The clever woman had stripped his resources and ensured his dependence on her. I presumed she would handle their finances as she was wealthy in her own right. Harry was probably given a small allowance each week – if he was a good boy. Her control of the telephone conversation justified this opinion.

I never learnt her name, but now I felt a solidarity with his mistress. She had achieved what I could not: she had subjugated Harry. He was in a purgatory of her devising and would suffer countless humiliations until his usefulness expired. She knew what sort of animal he was and would harness him as a deterrent against future disobedience. Initially, she had lobotomised him, removing his power to decide anything for himself; after she had extracted her quota of children – if that suited her – she would emasculate him. After that, he would mow the lawn and empty the bins.

In life, if you can wait long enough, most people get what they deserve.

Harry's new woman was not the gullible fool I had been. She knew the creature and how to cage it. Harry had made the adulterer's cardinal error: he indentured himself to a dominant woman, his intellectual and financial superior. He would never escape.

I informed Mr Larkin, my solicitor, of Harry's offer. While I did so, there may have been a frosty edge to my voice. Mr Larkin was similarly detached when he counselled me to accept Harry's terms. The document was drawn up and passed between us for signature and counter-signature. We moved from 'decree nisi' to 'decree absolute' in the next month.

I was a single woman again.

I began to measure time by how far Samuel's children had progressed through school. Our routine had been fairly steady over the last seven months of our affair. Except for holidays, we would work late until about 6:30 or 7:00 p.m., twice a week, on Monday and Wednesday. From these sessions we snatched only as much as ninety minutes alone together. On a Friday evening, Samuel would tell Helen that he was doing voluntary work with 'The Samaritans' and he would come to my house. That had been my idea. I was on the contraceptive pill. That had been his.

Rogues will often clothe themselves in robes of virtue. As such, 'The Samaritans' was an ideal cover. It was an entirely confidential organisation, secretive about every aspect of its operations, from the identity of its volunteers, to the privacy of its callers. Helen would never have been able to ask Samuel about his evening and expect anything other than a vague response. Neither could Samuel tell her about anyone else involved in the voluntary work. That was confidential also. She had no way of verifying whether he would be where he claimed. Even if she phoned – and he told her it was forbidden to receive personal calls – she could not expect to reach him. Being cautious to the point of paranoia, Samuel told Helen that he never gave callers his real name because of his prominent position in the community and the sensitive nature of his voluntary work. Helen may even have admired her husband's Christian commitment to a charitable cause.

At this, he worked late into the night and returned home exhausted. She could never have found even the slightest trace of another woman on his person. We had all of the possibilities covered in that regard. I had bought Samuel a few sets of comfortable clothes, into which he changed before we began our evening together. These always remained at my house. To remove any telltale scents from himself, he always showered before returning home. He even used the same type of soap that Helen provided at home. As a final routine, I would examine his clothes with a forensic eye, removing any stray hairs or make-up marks.

This system was our pulse. We lived for our Friday evenings together.

In May 1979, Jack and Laura Baxter began sitting their A-Level examinations. I particularly remember the day of the English Literature paper. Samuel had acquired a copy that morning and fussed over the poetry questions. That left me free to join my friends in the General Office for a slice of Friday cake.

John Souseman no longer made any pretence about dropping in accidentally for these occasions: he left his mug on our tea tray and expected that it would be cleaned between his weekly visits. He flattered us, declaring we were much better company than the teaching staff. That we ate better on a Friday, was more like the truth.

Joan was just finishing off some typing, while I helped Lorna measure out the teas and coffees. John was already in place, a circle of one, with jacket over the back of his chair and hands folded in his lap. He watched with Zen contentment as others busied themselves to provide his refreshments. Betty conjured her cake tin when everyone was almost in place. Unusually, Joan had been last into the circle.

"Would his lordship like the first slice of fruit cake?" Betty said, stooping like a butler towards John.

He straightened up to view inside the tin. "That'll do." He winked and helped himself.

Betty continued offering around the circle until everyone had a slice. While we ate, the group fell silent, as the holy contemplation of cake descended upon us. Betty had long since finished her Advanced Patisserie evening classes and tuned her own recipes to a divine frequency. Her fruit cake elevated the soul beyond the constraints of the corporal plane.

It was easy to admire a woman like Betty. She had often said she would hate to be a housewife: she wanted to open her own patisserie, running it as a family business – if it came to that. She would work as a secretary only until she had saved enough capital.

John's first slurp of tea broke the trance of our enlightenment. I narrowed my eyes at him with disapproval – not that he noticed.

"Joan, that typing must have been urgent to keep you away from this cake," I said.

She pinched her lips. "Something for Charlie: a consent form. It has to go out quickly." For some reason, this clearly bothered her.

"Is there something else?" I asked, flicking a look at John. He was watching his feet.

After consideration, Joan answered, "Somebody complained yesterday about the sex education. The consent form will allow parents to have their sons withdrawn, if they disapprove of the topic."

Across the circle, John's heavy lids snapped up as his eyes locked onto me. His body was perfectly still, as he waited for the

173

next words. When I renewed my focus on Joan, she was brushing a crumb from her skirt. It was a long moment before she looked up and said, "The parent didn't think it was the school's job to teach such things. Charlie is *very* upset."

As Joan mentioned this, I remembered an abrupt caller being directed to my line from the General Office. He had insisted that he speak to the headmaster immediately. The tone of his few words told me not to query the request. I had put him on hold, then warned Samuel through the intercom of the agitated caller. That was all I had known of the incident, until now. I had not even connected the dots when Charlie hurried through my office about half an hour later. He and Samuel were in a closed meeting for the remainder of the afternoon. None of this had been sufficiently out of the ordinary, however, to attract my attention or cause me to speculate. At least once a week, there was some crisis that had the management flapping around.

"The consent form should prevent this kind of objection from happening again," Joan said. "Boys whose parents don't want them to learn the facts of life will be taken out of class and sent to study in the library." Then she receded into the fabric of her chair.

"Perhaps, it was best left in the biology syllabus," John said quietly. A considered silence followed and was broken only when John reached for more cake. I am sure a whole minute had passed. "Who is on the rota for next week's cake, then?" he said.

"Lorna," Betty replied.

"Oh, dear," said Lorna, startling, "So soon? I don't think my oven is working properly still." In form, Lorna was a little blond dumpling; her mind was also like a lump of dough. What she lacked in intellect, however, she made up for with her bubbly character. She was impossible to dislike – without a concerted effort.

Lorna's oven was pronounced faulty after her first cake for the rota failed to meet anyone's expectations. After considerable chewing, it was decided that she had baked an eight inch diameter carpet. The only praise it received was from John. Never wanting to offend a potentially man-hungry female, he described her offering as 'quite aerodynamic'. The rest of our jaws were too tired for us to add anything beyond a nod.

"I'll do it then," Betty said, "If nobody objects."

"Nobody does," John added. "I could marry your cakes."

After we had skimmed through several other topics, Betty made the trivial observation that John had a small plaster on the crease of his left elbow. As it was the summer term and a warm day, John wore his sleeves rolled up.

"What happened your arm, Johnny boy?" she said.

John's smile was crooked and disintegrated into a sigh. "I gave blood," he said.

"Not as a donor, surely?"

"No."

"Are you being tested for a disease or something?"

"Yeah. Something."

"What's it being tested for? Do you have an exotic disease?" Betty said. She never liked to leave her curiosity unsatisfied.

John sighed. "Alcohol content."

"Oh!" we said.

Betty cringed and mouthed an apology to John.

Until then, I had thought John's drinking had been mostly under control. He often assured me that he had only a bottle of wine, or so, a night. He had switched from the whisky to make his hangovers more manageable. The idea was that he would be able to do his job properly and stay out of trouble. His attendance remained patchy, though, and Samuel had often mentioned it to me. All I could do was show concern and nag John occasionally.

Ultimately, you cannot save a man from himself.

"John, what have you done?" Joan asked.

He washed his face and forehead with an invisible cloth. "Drunk in charge of a vehicle, they call it."

"How did that happen?"

"Peelers saw me sleeping in the car. Figured I was drunk."

"How did they know that?" Joan said.

John shrugged. "Car was on top of a roundabout."

"This is a disgrace and it will not be tolerated. That man is a dissolute of the worst kind. He is not fit to teach, let alone drive," Samuel told me in one of our afternoon meetings. He was talking about John, of course, but it was August 1979 before he had found out about John's driving offence. The school had opened in the morning to dispense A-Level results to our outgoing Upper Sixth boys. Samuel and I had stayed on afterwards, while all other staff returned to their holidays. For some reason, in the last three months, it had kept slipping my mind to tell him about John.

The Chancery Chronicle was good enough to provide all the details, however. And so, it was here that Samuel first learnt of John's court appearance, the circumstances of his case and the penalties imposed. Much to Samuel's annoyance, in his report, Mr Patrick Audley had dwelt upon Mr John Souseman's place of employment.

"Did you know of this?" Samuel asked, wagging the folded newspaper at me from behind his desk.

"It's entirely new to me," I said. "You know I would have told you of something like this. I know how you feel about protecting the good name of the school."

He studied my saintly expression and appeared satisfied.

"I will be mentioning this to the governors. We will convene shortly, I assure you, to discuss Mr Souseman's future in this school. Anyone who commits such a public disgrace should lose his job. Something has to be done about him."

"What can you do?"

"Gross moral turpitude, is the term for it. I will see to it that his crimes fit that description," and he shook his paper sword. "Otherwise, we shall have him on his outrageous attendance record." He was referred to John's usual three day week.

I would have to pay John a visit soon. It had been a month since I had last done his dishes, and we had much to discuss.

"I think he might genuinely be ill," I said.

Samuel shook his head tersely, lip curled. "His problem is self-indulgence. I can't abide a man who drinks to excess. It is completely immoral. He has no standards whatsoever. That is what comes of being godless. I am duty bound to drive him from our midst by any means necessary. If I fail, he will drag the good name of our school into the gutter, and our reputations with it. I will be blamed for complicity in his crimes, if I allow him to remain in place." He slapped the newspaper onto his desk for punctuation. "When Souseman next hauls himself into work, I will tell him that myself."

This conversation was not going as I had planned. There were some issues I needed to clarify on this, the A-Level results day, and it was most inconvenient that Samuel had found this article in the paper. My objectives required the conversation be steered in another direction.

"Well, don't take it out on me," I said. "It isn't my fault. You think you can speak to me in any manner. Just because John and I are friends, doesn't mean I know everything about him." I walked from his office and into my own. At my desk, I rummaged in my handbag for some tissues, waiting for him to respond. Momentarily, he was before me, arm encircling my waist, his look a blend of patronage and concern. With a free hand, he drew the venetian blinds closed – though the school was empty over the holiday period. He steered me to sit and knelt at my feet, folding my hands in his own.

For an instant, I thought he would propose marriage.

"I am not cross with you, Rose. You are the one I rely on," he said. After a pause, while his eyes soaked through me, he continued, "You are my rock. Without you, I could not cope." Another pause. "If I take you for granted, it's because I know you will always be there. And I love you being there, with me, through everything."

Samuel was working harder than I expected for a general purpose apology. His rumbling voice soothed me. My faith in him was being restored.

"Rose," he said, " Jack and Laura also received their results today."

I knew they had. That was where I wanted the conversation to turn. Today was a reckoning: his children's results would determine the future of our relationship. With them out of the house, he would tell Helen that their marriage was over and – when the time was right – we would reveal our relationship.

"They both did well, three 'A's each," he said, with a glimmer of pride.

"That's very good news," I said, but wondered if it was.

"You know their first choices were both Trentford University. Helen counselled them to stay local and choose there – even though entry requirements were higher. I advised against it but she used every emotional argument she could."

177

"And?" I said.

"Well, their 'A' grades mean that their places are confirmed. Jack will study History and Laura, French." He swallowed something dry, while my eyes slowly closed. His next words were hurried. "I will do everything to get them a house in Trentford, or into the halls." By then, his words were far off. "But Helen wants them to live at home."

"Live at home," I said, as if the words were merely a movement of air. I knew, though, that they meant further delay before Samuel fulfilled his promise to leave Helen. While the twins lived at home, we had agreed not break up the family. For the next three years, they would be studying in Trentford city, fifteen miles away. An easy commute.

"I will do everything I can, Rose. Don't lose faith in me." He put thick arms around me. My own arms, boneless, hung slack.

Fortunately for John Souseman, the Board of Governors did not support Samuel's definition of 'gross moral turpitude'. One of them even accused Samuel of being overly zealous – apparently, his son had been taught by Souseman and thought him a 'top fellow'. However, the governors did concede that Her Majesty's Education Inspectorate should be contacted, so that John's classroom practice could be scrutinised. If his drinking was affecting his teaching, they wanted to know. An inspection would be a matter for the record either way. It could even clear John's name, at least as far as his teaching was concerned. Conveniently, it would also give the governors an opportunity to have Jack Dawson audited at the same time.

Chapter Seventeen

"Rose, this is Mrs McVickers," Charlie said, introducing us.

"Please, call me Pauline," she said to both of us, offering her hand across my desk. She had a genial smile to match.

I stood, shook her hand firmly and smiled, also firmly. "The headmaster is expecting you. Just go on through." I indicated the adjoining door.

"Very good." She disappeared through without hesitation.

Her manner concerned me. It was as if our school was an enterprise the headmaster was managing on her behalf. In that brief moment, I assessed her: trim figure, fitted navy skirt suit with a tapered waist, blooming at hips and bust. Long heels shaped her calves. An up-sweep of amber hair accented a graceful neck and fine jaw. Her voice held casual authority. If she was yet in her forties, she was very well preserved.

I disliked her immediately. She laid claim to things to which she had no entitlement.

Charlie watched her pass from my office into Samuel's study. He was not the sort of man to watch women. His expression held no admiration of her figure. It was not awe but fear that fixed him. When he looked at me, his eyes were wide and his chubby head sank into his shoulders, as if bullets were already flying overhead.

"She's the school inspector," he said.

I nodded.

"I don't like this," he said. I agreed with him, but for other reasons. "When you invite an inspector into your school, there is no telling what they can do. They could go anywhere, look at anything and there's no controlling them. I don't like it. I told Sam. I said to him, 'I don't like it.'" His jowls wobbled.

"Like inviting a vampire in," I said.

It was a month into the new school term when Mrs McVickers of Her Majesty's Education Inspectorate infiltrated us. John told me she had spent most of her time sitting at the back of his classroom, writing notes. At first, the boys had quietly speculated among themselves about the purpose of her visit, and whether she was an inspector or a student teacher. Their suspicions were eventually confirmed when she interviewed a few of them concerning what they had learnt after the first and each subsequent lesson.

"The boys are all taking my side," John told me that Thursday afternoon, while I was giving him a lift home. "They are working harder than I have ever seen them do before. More of them are answering questions too. I used to have to pick on someone to get a question answered. Now the air is filled with hands. They even laugh at my jokes."

"You still tell jokes?"

He shrugged. "I'm not bothered by her. It doesn't take long to get used to having an adult in your class, even a foxy bit of crumpet like her. A couple of times I've forgotten she was there. The boys have amazed me though. They're not going to let old Souser down."

"Has she spoken to you much?" I asked.

"No. Not yet. Hasn't shown me any of her notes either – could you just turn into the village there? I've a message to do." He pointed to the right of the junction I had just approached.

"You're going to the pub, then?"

He paused, probably considering the lie too obvious. He shrugged again. "I suppose I could, now you mention it. Would you like to join me?"

I shook my head and tutted.

"How are you getting to work in the morning – or are you having another long weekend?" I said, pulling over to the kerb outside The Cartwright's Inn.

"The Dodger gives me a lift."

"Jack Dawson?" This was news to me.

"Lives just outside the village. Bumped into him in *Cartwright's* one evening after school. We'd a great laugh. He's been giving me a lift since term started. We've a code: curtains closed means I'm not coming in. He'll wait a few minutes, then drive on. Great guy, that."

"You are two kindred spirits."

"We're certainly fond of the same spirits, anyway," he said, kissed me on the side of the cheek and climbed out of the car. "Besides, the inspector's not about tomorrow. I don't need to be on my best behaviour. Don't you worry." He gave me a wink and was about to close the door when I held up my hand to stop him.

"John, how do you know she won't be in tomorrow?"

"Baxter paid me a visit today. Doing his rounds. Said McVickers had watched me all week and would write her report up tomorrow. No time for classroom visits either. Said he'd spoken to her every day and he was disappointed that she'd praised me. Fascist git."

"He actually said that?" I asked.

John nodded. "Disappointed that she'd praised me." He smiled. "He wants to fire me. Seems he'll have to wait, though." With his grin still fixed, he closed the car door.

In the time it had taken me to complete my turn, he had disappeared inside the bar.

Perhaps it was too much to hope that John could hold himself together for a full week. He could not live moderately more than four days out of seven, and he had used up this week's quota. It would have been much better for him if he had simply called in sick again.

That Friday morning, I passed Mrs McVickers in the foyer. She wore another smart skirt suit, accessorised with a leather business binder under her arm. She acknowledged me with a pert nod, as she passed into the outer corridor. I paused to watch her go, as I had noticed many of the male staff do, but for a different reason. Four steps gave me line of sight and I saw her ascend the stairs that led to the first floor classrooms. It did not take long for me to conclude that, John would indeed be getting a visit today.

On impulse, I considered phoning through a warning to John, but it would do no good if he had one of his hangovers.

I suspected very strongly that John had been deliberately deceived. *Finis coronat opus*, Samuel would be saying to himself: the end crowns the work. Just then, I hated Samuel Baxter. For once, I did not look forward to spending my Friday evening with him. I would be having a migraine that evening.

From John, I later learned the extent of the damage.

By the end of third period on Friday, Mrs McVickers noted a pattern arising with Mr Souseman, one that had not appeared on any of her previous days of observation. John let his classes in, settled them, then handed out worksheets. The pupils completed their work in silence for the most part. The occasional question was asked, but John's replies were not always coherent and were certainly not as convivial as they had been earlier in the week.

Just before break, Mrs McVickers approached John and asked if she might ask him some questions about his week's work. John phoned and told me about the confrontation that afternoon.

"She asked me something about my learning objectives for Friday's work," he said. "I told her 'Look darling, Friday's worksheet day. I test their week's work. From that I'll be able to see any gaps. So my *learning objectives* are to see what they haven't learnt in the week.' I may have been a little sarcastic. She leaned forward into me and wrinkled her nose, like I was wearing piss for aftershave – except I wasn't, this time. Then she said, 'Mr Souseman, you smell of alcohol and it is very strong. You are either extremely hungover or you are still drunk. In either case, you are not fit to be responsible for another class of children. Remove yourself to the staffroom while I consult with the headmaster.' I knew I was in a bit of a jam after that, so I did the only sensible thing I could: I walked down High Street and into the nearest pub for the rest of my breakfast."

It was from this bar that he phoned me later.

All week, Mrs McVickers' sessions with the headmaster had been closed, and I had not been required to sit in and minute them. This was, no doubt, because of my affiliation with John. Samuel was far from stupid. It was more than likely he suspected me of subterfuge concerning John's drink driving charges. Neither did I believe I was missing much, being excluded from these meetings. From what I could tell, Samuel found them both demanding and exhausting. This Friday's session produced results that were much more to Samuel's tastes, however. He was now in a position to rid himself of a man he considered his antithesis.

That afternoon, I typed a formal disciplinary letter, informing Mr John Souseman that he had been suspended (with pay) pending a disciplinary hearing. The charges against him were that he had been teaching while intoxicated, which was in breach of the staff code of conduct, as outlined in the *Revised Staff Handbook*. If only I had thought to bin that page as well.

"One down, one to go. I said I would have him out," Samuel boasted. It was late afternoon on Friday and he emerged from his office, expecting me to share his triumph. Mrs McVickers had left only moments earlier, her case against John held firmly under her arm.

"You didn't get him. He got himself," I said, more than a little tartly.

"Ironically, that dreadful McVickers woman had written glowing reports of his teaching all week. Then he turned up drunk." He stood like a freshly stacked bag of rubble.

"That's nice for you," I said.

He leaned over my desk and frowned at me. "Have you been crying, Rose?" His voice was soft again.

"No. I have an allergy. It makes my eyes runny." I rummaged in a drawer for some tissues.

"I see." Samuel paused. "He is not good for the school, Rose. It is my responsibil –."

"– He is sick," I interrupted. "Alcoholism is a sickness. He can't help it. He is a good teacher when he's not –" When I looked up, Samuel was glaring at me. Then, he turned on his heel and walked into his study, closing the door hard behind him.

Charlie Bakewell would often spend his lunch breaks in his classroom. He had an open door policy for any pupils who wanted to speak to him – or even for those who were looking for somewhere to 'hang out', as they called it.

When Joan and I found him, he was at the far end of his room, sitting on his desk. Around him, a cluster of small boys were being awed by his animated story-telling. Other groups were distributed in clumps around the room, swapping Trump cards, homeworks and sweets. It was an atmosphere in which young geeks could be comfortable.

Charlie spotted Joan and me when we were just inside the door. He excused himself and waddled through the boys towards us. His smile fell as it met our serious expressions.

"We need your help, Charlie," Joan said.

"Of course. We'll use my office," he replied.

183

Charlie's office was little more than a refitted book store next to his classroom. Upon his promotion to vice-principal, the office had been given some new fluorescent lights, a thin carpet and updated office furniture. Its walls were a lively yellow to compensate for the undersized window that did little to light the cubicle.

"Sit, sit," Charlie said, indicating some plastic chairs. He sat in his own and scraped it round to face us both. His manner of sitting forward, hands meshed, signalled that he was ready to hear us.

Joan spoke to him like a sister, not needing the necessary preamble required by friendship. "John Souseman has been suspended. The inspector smelled alcohol and accused him of being drunk. Samuel Baxter is going to fire him."

Charlie's face became a pantomime of sadness as he thought over this. His shoulders hunched, as the trouble climbed onto his back and squatted there.

"What should I do?" he asked.

"Speak to Mr Baxter," I said.

Joan filled in the pause that followed. "John is a good man. He is a very good teacher when he is not gripped by the drink."

I continued, " I am sure I read somewhere that alcoholism is an illness. John is certainly physically dependent on it. He cannot help himself." I needed something else to strengthen my argument. "It would not be a Christian thing to do, to punish a man for something he cannot help. And John needs to be helped, not crushed and disgraced. Mr Baxter has made this a personal crusade to ruin John. He needs to be made to see it from a Christian perspective."

"To do as Jesus would do," Charlie said. Purpose sparked in his eyes. "John struggles to control his drinking. He needs support, not condemnation. I can't say he was right to come into school drunk, but I don't think he can help himself sometimes – we all do things like that sometimes. He is a lost soul."

I hoped then that Samuel had told Charlie about our affair. It was Samuel's indulgence and Charlie could use it to undermine his self-righteousness.

Joan said, "Charlie, you are going to have to stand up for the weak and the oppressed. John needs your intercession." The

Christian imagery was clear to all of us. Charlie's spark kindled within.

"If he is an alcoholic, then he has an illness," he said. "If he has an illness and can no longer teach, he should retire early on medical grounds. He can also get Partial Incapacity Benefit and whatever pension he has accumulated." Charlie sat upright in his chair. The trouble no longer bowed him. "I will go and see Samuel."

It had been their hardest battle yet, but Charlie emerged victorious. He had invoked the headmaster's sense of fair play, and that had failed. He had drawn upon Christian arguments about showing mercy to the weak, but Mr Baxter offered only to accept John's resignation. That was far from good enough for Charlie. When Charlie said he would offer his own resignation too, however, his friend crumbled. Charlie stood strong in his principles. It was clear to Samuel that Charlie would take no part in a regime that preyed on the weak and vulnerable.

Betty said she would bake a chocolate cake, just for Charlie. He was a hero in the General Office, and to me as well.

John Souseman was allowed to retire prematurely on grounds of ill health. The month between John's suspension and his visit to the doctor appointed by the Department of Education allowed him plenty of time for further self-destruction. It was a quick diagnosis. John was granted Partial Incapacity Benefit, as he was deemed unfit to undertake any other gainful employment. The doctor assessing him also noted that he was 'suffering mental disablement brought on by chronic alcoholism'. While this helped his case immeasurably, it concerned us all. It certainly brought tears to my eyes as I copied it into his personnel file.

John's final package amounted to a lump sum of just under £15,000. In 1979, that was a considerable sum. He could also expect modest monthly payments, combining twenty years of pension and benefits. John later joked that Baxter had done him a huge favour. Now he was getting paid to drink, and he earned almost as much each month without having to work for it.

'That dreadful McVickers woman' – as Samuel called her – was unable to expose Jack Dawson in the second week of her visit. Of his teaching, she had merely commented that he had been 'lax in the setting and marking of homeworks' and that his classroom management was 'occasionally less than orderly', but overall he was deemed 'satisfactory'. Unfortunately for the headmaster, none of these failings warranted Dawson's dismissal. They did, however, give Mr Baxter leave to monitor Dawson's teaching even more closely.

Mrs McVickers had also produced words of praise in her report. I thought this uncharacteristic of her, like a shark singing a mermaid's song. She took it upon herself to examine the school's policy documents and her official statement cited honourable mention to Mr Charles Bakewell, Junior School Vice-Principal and designated teacher in charge of the pastoral system. She described Chancery Grammar's facilities for child protection as 'sensible and sympathetic.' McVickers officially recommended that all schools adopt this model for their own pastoral systems.

Charlie was delighted. He was the engineer of this effective system and had made its success his responsibility. While the headmaster was pleased with the positive report, there was still some stuffiness between him and his vice-principal. Samuel had not forgotten the leverage Charlie had applied to secure a sympathetic retirement deal for John Souseman.

"It won't last," Charlie told me. "We did the right thing, and Sam's displeasure is a small price to pay for that. Give him time and he will come round. He always does."

The cobwebs would not be blown away so easily when it came to my own relationship with Samuel. He had withdrawn into himself after I had protested on John's behalf. He must have know I was behind his confrontation with Charlie too. This was not just a feeling of mine; I noted a pronounced change in his attitude to me. Lately, Samuel had missed some of our Friday nights, after my suspicious migraine on the Friday of John's suspension. Before then, he had not missed one. Evidently, he was punishing me.

Of course, each time he neglected me, he offered a more than adequate excuse. Apparently, Helen had been unwell and he had felt guilty about leaving her. I recognised the subtext: he

186

could choose between his women. I needed to please him to be preferred.

It was a game I was not yet in a position to win. I would not be secure until Samuel's twins had completed university, which was the prospect of another four year's wait. I had originally thought it would be three years, but Laura, his daughter, was studying French and she was required to spend a year in France, which would delay her graduation until July 1983. It was likely that his son, Jack, would remain at Trentford for a master's degree, while his sister completed her course.

Chapter Eighteen

Like his recently retired drinking companion, Jack Dawson was incapable of behaving professionally for any extended period. His terms were scored with strategically placed illnesses, mostly coinciding with Liverpool Football Club's big fixtures. But he was always cunning enough to ensure that nothing could be proved. It was the last day of the winter term, Friday, 21 December 1979 when he received his next disciplinary action.

Last days always had something of a party spirit to them. Traditionally, the winter term ended with a half day and a carol service at the First Presbyterian Church of Chancery. While the teachers were thus engaged, the 'ancillary workers' prepared the staffroom and the canteen ladies cooked Christmas dinner. It was only on the last day of each term, when all employees were joined in celebration, that 'non-academics' were invited to the staff party. 'Party' is perhaps a misleading term: the event was normally as dreary as woodchip wallpaper. This year, however, Jack Dawson was to provide the entertainment and much fresh documentation for his personnel file.

"It still feels like we're trespassing here," Betty said, as she laid a paper tablecloth out. "It's the same every year."

"We should have our own little party in the office," Lorna said, unpacking the polystyrene cups into which I ladled warm, mulled wine.

The selection of refreshments was limited. It was restricted by the headmaster's disapproval of all things alcoholic. He only made the concession at this time of year that mulled wine could be served, but he would never have touched any himself.

Betty emptied packets of crisps into large mixing bowls, on loan from the kitchen, and Joan removed the cling film from the canapé and sandwich trays. Most of us nibbled at various somethings while we made final preparations for the returning teachers. The Christmas mood was completed when Joan slotted some Bing Crosby into the tape machine, swirling dusky vocals into the cinnamon and ginger air.

Just as I had begun to relax, Jack Dawson slipped in. He was carrying a five litre stock pot, with a ladle protruding from its lid. Mr Dawson's return from the church was so early that it made me doubt whether he had been there at all. Perhaps another back spasm had overwhelmed him and forced him to lie on his desk for the duration of the service.

"I've just been in the canteen. The ladies there asked me to carry this over." He set it down heavily on the table, which shook the contents of some polystyrene cups over the Santas printed on the table cloth. "So sorry, ladies. That's a bit heavier than it looks," he said.

He looked up at Betty, then down and up again, before his caterpillar lip quivered at head and tail. "You look lovely, Miss Trent. Would you like to try some of my fruit punch? It's a special recipe."

"*My* fruit punch? I thought you said it was from the canteen?" Betty said.

The caterpillar curled while Dawson ladled some into a polystyrene cup and handed it to Betty. She regarded it suspiciously, sipped it, then took a larger swig. After a little cough, she downed the rest in a gulp.

"That is a special recipe. And the main ingredient isn't fruit," Betty said, tapping her empty cup on the edge of the stock pot. "Fill it up."

Not long after Dorothy Butler's wedding in July 1976, Betty had decided that she and Jack were not a safe mix. Since then, their relationship had been on and off – mostly off, until alcohol found its way into their chance encounters. According to Betty, he was a 'friend of sorts' but Dawson still aspired to be much more.

Among his colleagues, Dawson was quite popular. His easy charm and rakish behaviour made him good company for the male staff. The few female teachers that had infiltrated the school, knew to avoid him.

The staffroom quickly filled up as the teachers returned from church. Dawson played host, placed himself behind the drinks' table and administered to his colleagues. A generous pouring hand did much to improve his reputation. His special fruit punch was a gift to his hard-working colleagues, most of whom could not get enough of the stuff. And, before the headmaster had decided to grace us with his presence, the punch had vanished. Its effects lingered on for some time, though. Early on, Betty and I decided it was for the best if the

189

headmaster never knew of the punch's existence. Dutifully, we joined the others in burying the evidence.

As the gathering wore on, the cheer developed to the point where most of the teachers stopped complaining about their terrible lives. As a poor substitute for the punch, the mulled wine flowed. Fortunately, there were a number of additional bottles of it, many conjured by Dawson from a cupboard under the sink. Obviously these had been bought on another budget, unrelated to the miserly stipend authorised by the headmaster. Mr Dawson had done a sterling job

Within myself, however, I longed to be with Samuel. Our relationship remained discrete and I could never have shown him any familiarity when others were present. That was especially true in a situation like this. I knew better than to even look in his direction, so preternaturally cautious was he. Instead, I stood chatting to Joan and Lorna in the overcrowded staffroom. While the conversation was pleasant and friendly, it was not what I sought most.

The general cheer was so good, that Betty loitered with Dawson after he had refreshed her glass at the drinks table.

Moments later, the unmistakable sound of a hard slap interrupted every conversation.

I heard it clearly, fifteen or so feet away, across the room. Only Bing Crosby was unaware of what had just occurred.

All eyes roamed in search of the combatants and naturally alighted on Jack Dawson – one side of his face already showing scarlet – and Betty Trent, for whom the crowd parted as she rushed to the door.

"I'll take that as a no, then," Dawson said to everyone, but no one laughed.

The coven regrouped in the General Office. Betty was sitting at her desk, only partially composed.

"Betty, are you all right?" Joan asked, full of sympathy.

It was obvious that Betty was only just holding her emotions together. Tears poised in the wings, waiting for their cue. She looked at her outstretched palm instead of at us. "I hurt my hand. I'm sure his face will sting for a while."

"What happened?" I asked.

"He groped me," she said. "And it wasn't the first time, either."

Samuel and Charlie joined us. The headmaster bore a frown of disapproval but Charlie was wringing with concern for Betty.

"Are you okay, Betty? I'm sure you're very upset," Charlie said.

The headmaster considered Betty, his demeanour dark. "That is some right hook you have, Miss Trent." His stony brow quaked. Below it, his lips were tight. "If you had made a fist, we may have needed an ambulance for the scoundrel."

"Thank you," Betty said, but her face was uncertain.

"Be assured," Samuel continued, "that I will pursue this matter to the fullest extent. I will not have my female staff harassed and sexually molested. Several members of staff witnessed the whole incident. Mr Dawson has been suspended, pending a full investigation of this matter."

Betty looked at me, her eyes wide. I think she was afraid that she too would be suspended for striking a colleague.

"You're okay," I whispered and squeezed her stinging hand.

"And when you feel able," Samuel said, "I would like you to make a written statement, recalling every detail you can about this incident. Please pay particular attention to Mr Dawson's actions before you were forced to defend yourself against his sexual assault."

Betty flinched slightly with the headmaster's last words.

"I will arrange a disciplinary hearing in the New Year," he said, and one corner of his mouth slipped upward. He was triumphant again.

When the men had left the General Office, Betty spoke with a crackly voice, deep in her throat. "I don't want him to lose his job over this."

"As far as I'm concerned, he deserved to lose his job a long time ago. Especially if he has groped you before," I said.

"Not his *job*. Not over this," she said.

"This year will be difficult enough, without having to drag that dosser around with us," Samuel told me on the first morning of new term. "That dreadful McVickers woman will be

191

back to pick our bones again. I'm honestly sorry I invited the Inspectorate here in the first place."

"Charlie did warn you," I reminded him.

We were in Samuel's study. As it was during normal working hours, Samuel sat behind his great desk. But, in spite of the physical distance, our old familiarity had returned. The thrill had not entirely gone, but it was confined to the recesses.

Samuel poured us a cup of coffee each from his new percolator. I had bought it for him as a Christmas present. Technically, Chancery Grammar had paid for it. For obvious reasons I had not been able to wrap it, or give it to him on Christmas day, but apart from that, it was a present from me to him in all the ways that counted.

Samuel had got me my own photocopier. Actually, he had upgraded the one in the Reprographics Suite, and I had inherited the old one. But, again it was the thought that counted. I suspected that was not all, though. He had just asked me to post a parcel at the end of the school day, on my way home. His tone had been playful when he said it, leading me to believe it was not a regular parcel at all. This shoebox-sized, brown paper package sat on his desk and awaited its address label. It could have been almost anything.

He saw me looking at it as he handed over my coffee.

"It won't be needing a stamp." He winked and inhaled his coffee vapours.

"To whom shall I address it?"

He gave a sly grin. "I will take care of that, my dear." After a pause, he nodded to his cup. "This really is a most thoughtful present. I will be able to offer my guests coffee without having to send for it. You have surpassed yourself, Rose. I look forward to thanking you."

"It has been a while since you've properly thanked me."

"I would be happy to do so this Friday. It has been a difficult wait over the holidays." He was referring to the family commitments that had kept him from me over the Christmas holidays. We had been together for two years and nine months. These holidays were the first in which we had not met. It had not been his fault, however. This time Helen had filled his schedule with family visits and jobs around the house.

"Very difficult," I said. I was going to launch into an inquiry about our long-term romantic schedule when Samuel spoke.

"This Dawson thing. If Miss Trent doesn't write a statement, I won't have enough to push him out. The governors are a timid lot. They won't fire the scoundrel unless they have it all on paper. None of the other staff are prepared to write a statement either."

"Really? She told me she had accepted his apology and did not want to take this any further."

"I think it will be another final warning at most," he said, shaking his head. "That's a contradiction in terms: another final warning. But what else can we do? He will bring infamy upon us and we cannot do a thing about it. We just have to sit and wait."

And so, Jack Dawson was soon to be given the final warning. If he behaved for a year, it too would be expunged from his personnel record, as its predecessor had been.

While Samuel continued to complain about this, I nodded and agreed, but I wasn't listening particularly. I was wondering about the box. As with his conduct on a first date, a man must be very careful about the presents he buys his woman. If everything has a meaning, the woman who doubts her status will find it.

At the end of the school day, Samuel handed me the parcel. It had my own name and address on it, naturally. As instructed, I opened it at home. I was in my kitchen, waiting for the microwave to ping, while I unwrapped it. Decoding its message was as straightforward as interpreting the microwave's chime. Within the box, there were two presents, each individually wrapped. The first was a full set of black lingerie, including bodice and stockings. The second was a copy of *Wuthering Heights*.

So, I was a sex object that needed educating.

I never told him I had read that novel when I was fifteen and, even then, found it mawkish. Samuel probably believed I would be gusted away on its message of enduring love. The lingerie might have fitted me two years previously. I wondered whether this was a suggestion that I lose weight too.

Two years of the contraceptive pill can take a slow toll on the figure – and mine had never been that stable. Some bumps and rolls were back.

It is no news that birthdays can be considered depressing. This is especially so when your life is not ordered to your satisfaction and your hopes remain unfulfilled. April 1980 brought my thirty-fifth birthday and, with it, an internal audit of my accumulated worth. The problem was not in being thirty-five; it was being thirty-five without a family of my own. It had not been presumptuous of me to expect that I might have had children some day – especially when I was younger. But now I faced it as an improbability. My fertility was declining. The future was filled with diminishing returns. I was compelled to seize what I could from the last of my body's potential.

There and then, I decided that I had taken my last pill. Neither did Samuel need to know about my decision. I would happily live alone with the consequences, if it came to that.

John Souseman told me that my problem was not having fulfilled my biological imperatives, most notably the need to reproduce. His delivery of this lesson was not as harsh as it might sound. It was comforting to know that it was normal, at this time of my life, that I should despair.

My birthday fell on a Tuesday, but I would have to wait until Friday before I could expect any extended comfort from Samuel. Joan took charge of the celebrations in the General Office. Betty baked me a special cake shaped like an electric typewriter.

Even that depressed me. When people thought of my life's achievements, the only symbol that sprang to mind was a typewriter. Rose Maylie, Administrative Assistant and Headmaster's Secretary. 'Here lies Rose Maylie. Her life written out in typewriter ribbons.'

Not long after break, Charlie appeared in my office. As usual, he was all smiles.

"You missed the cake," I said.

"No, I didn't." And he unfolded a hand from behind his back, showing YGHVBN and part of the Space Bar folded in a napkin. "Joan saved it for me."

"She will go to Heaven for that."

194

"She's got my vote." He considered the cake for a moment. "Best to get it over with," Charlie said, then filled his grin with a large bite.

"Diet starts tomorrow," I said.

Charlie rubbed his spongy stomach. "Starts after this. I want to lose a stone. Rita says I'm too heavy."

My eyes must have widened because Charlie snorted in response, crumbs tumbling down his shirt. Charlie had never talked about a woman, any woman, beyond those he worked with. In fact, he had never discussed any element of his personal life, beyond church. His statement begged the obvious question, and Charlie was bursting for me to ask it. Before I could even utter it, he was nodding at me, eyes wide, anticipating the question.

"Who's Rita?"

"My girlfriend," he said with childish excitement. More cake cascaded free when he grinned.

I sprang up and gave him a quick hug, consciously dodging dislodged cake. "Well done, Charlie."

He bobbed with animation. "She's a girl in my church. I've had my eye on her for a while, but I'm very shy when it comes to that. I'm not charming or much of a looker, when it comes to it. I know."

"I'm sure you'll be very happy," I said, resuming my seat.

"I'm forty-one. I've never had a girlfriend before. I waited and prayed. The Lord provided. I'm not going to waste my time, either. We're going to get engaged soon.

"How old is Rita?"

"Forty. So we can't hang about," he said.

To answer my quizzical look he said, "It's okay. We've talked about this. It was her idea too." After another pause, he remembered the original purpose of his visit. "Oh. This is for you. Happy birthday. Cheer up too. It all comes right in the end," he said.

He had bought me a frail looking silver locket. It was a lovely thought, but I had no one's photograph to put in it, except my parents'. So that is what I did.

Charlie Bakewell was as good as his word. He did not waste his time. Two months later, he was in the office handing out invitations to his wedding. He bounced into Reprographics where I had been processing a large file through the new copier – the one I had inherited kept jamming. He held a bundle of white envelopes in his hand like a bag of sweets. The amusement on his face showed he enjoyed surprising me.

"This is for you," he said, extending an envelope to me. It simply said 'Rose' on the front. Inside there was a white card inlaid with gold. It was my invitation to his wedding – the full thing.

"Oh, Charlie. Thank you. Congratulations, too. I didn't even know," I said, astonished.

"We got engaged on Friday and spent the weekend organising the rest." His smile was irrepressible.

"Thanks for this," I said, "It means so much." He must have thought of me as a real friend – not like Dorothy. I noted that it was in only a month's time, mid-July. Charlie really wasn't hanging about.

He bobbed forward suddenly and gave me a peck on the forehead.

"It's my honour to have you there, Rose." And he left as suddenly as he had arrived.

Samuel and I did not discuss Charlie's engagement until reclining on my sofa that Friday night. As usual, we were watching television, having dealt with our other business earlier in the evening. It was our routine and necessary to both of us, but for different reasons.

"Did you get your invitation to Charlie's wedding?" Samuel asked.

"I was just thinking about that." I looked up into his cloudless eyes. We often shared concurrent thoughts.

"Are you going to accept his invitation?" he said.

"Of course, I already have." After a minute or more of television, I said, "Why wouldn't I accept his invitation?" I watched his face carefully.

He shrugged but flushed under the close scrutiny.

"You don't want me to go, do you?" I said.

"No, it's not that," he said and thumbed an itch on his nose. "You know how worried I get."

"He's a friend of mine. I thought it very considerate of him to invite me. At least *he* isn't embarrassed to have me around," I said.

"I'm not embarrassed. I'm just concerned about you being in the same room as Helen."

"I'm sure Charlie would know to seat me well away from your wife."

He paused to consider my reasoning. "And how would he know to do that?" he said.

"Charlie is very considerate. He would do that for his best friend."

"What are you talking about, woman?" he said. "Why would Charlie be concerned about you being near Helen?"

"He knows about our affair, doesn't he?" I said, remembering the morning I bumped into Charlie as he emerged from Samuel's study. The awkwardness between us had been palpable. And this was just after Samuel had struggled with his guilt – something that no longer held him back.

According to the look on Samuel's face, however, I was a contemptible idiot.

"How would Charlie know about our affair – unless of course you told him?" he said.

"*You* told him."

"What utter nonsense you talk, woman. I haven't told a soul about us," he said.

I was compelled to believe the determined look on his face. Neither did I want this discussion to escalate into a full argument. I was not feeling up to such a battle.

"Never mind," I said. "Tell me what you were going to say about the wedding."

His shoulders had grown stony and rigid. The middle of his brow overlapped above his nose like slates. It was some moments before he had softened sufficiently to speak with a level tone.

"Helen will be there. I was just going to ask you to be cautious around her. I will have my best man duties and won't always be at her side." He considered how best to phrase the next part. "It would be much easier for me if you did not seek her out and –" he paused. "If you do end up speaking to her, do not discuss me or the family."

197

I watched the television in silence until he spoke again. I knew he was not through with his explanation.

"Helen has been asking questions of late about my Samaritans work. She may suspect something."

A dread impulse flushed through me. This could mean that we were on the verge of full disclosure. In spite of wanting this for several years, something in me felt safe in the secrecy. But if Helen discovered the affair, Samuel would be mine alone.

I tried not to show it, but Samuel's harsh manner of speaking to me that night had upset me deeply. At the time, I was too earnestly holding the broken pieces together to register my hurt, even to myself. That night, in bed alone, I had plenty of time to consider it. Never before had he shown such contempt for me. He made no attempt to restrain his displeasure. I pictured the snarl on his lip in response to my questioning. This marked a boundary in our relationship. Either, he was so comfortable that he could show his true feelings – positive and negative – or his respect for me had diminished considerably. Our relationship had never been entirely secure. A mistress is never sure of her place and perhaps now the cracks were showing.

Samuel was fond of the idea that he was above certain menial tasks. That, after all, was why he had a secretary at work and a wife at home. He never actually put this into words, but it was written in his actions. He never stirred himself to any chore that did not require the professional judgement of a headmaster. He might have always conducted himself as a gentleman, but he also assumed a gentleman's privilege: he acted like a landowner upon whose good will his tenants relied.

From Harry, I had learned to watch my man. Most suspicious are the deviations from normal patterns of behaviour, even small ones. So too, a klaxon blared the day I learned of Samuel's plan to attend the Headmasters' Conference in London the following weekend. This, and the manner in which I discovered it, caused me great concern.

After one of our Wednesday late afternoon dictation sessions in his study, I happened to mention the forthcoming weekend. I was brushing down Samuel's jacket and inspecting it and his shirt for incriminating marks. He stood with lordly composure while I performed this service.

"I bought a new TV yesterday," I said. "We can watch a film on Friday without that snowy patch you're always complaining about. You can concentrate on telling me what you think is going to happen."

Samuel looked uncomfortable. "I can't make it, I'm afraid," he replied after a pause.

I froze. Much news was delivered in that short phrase. "Why? Is something wrong?"

"No, everything is fine. I'll be at the Headmasters' Conference on Friday and Saturday."

I nodded, wondering if I had forgotten about this prior arrangement. If I had known about it, I would have remembered booking his flights and hotel. It was not unusual for him to be going, but I normally took care of the details for him. Here my suspicion was first aroused. Thereafter, everything became subtext.

"Oh, I didn't think you were going to this one," I said. "You didn't have me organise it for you."

He looked at me and assessed how much more information would be required. What he offered next was reluctantly given.

"I organised it myself." He paused. "Helen has insisted in coming and making it into a weekend trip."

I held my breath.

"She has friends in London and has arranged for us to spend the rest of the weekend with them. I am not at all pleased," he added, watching me.

"Why didn't you tell me sooner?" I asked.

When we had been at our best together, I had often flown out to meet Samuel on a separate flight and we had spent the weekend together. He would take a single room and I another, but we would spend our time in only one. His booking was paid for on the school credit card, and Samuel paid for mine with his other card – the statements for which were mailed to the school, not his home. It was a card Helen knew nothing about.

Our emotions had been intense during these secret weekends. Time was stolen, brief and succulent. The last three conferences we spent like this, each one a precious memory to me. Friday nights and conference weekends were mine.

Samuel spread his hands and drew me into his bulk. When he spoke, I could not see his face but his words resonated through me. "Helen only told me about her plans on Sunday. It was her idea to use the conference weekend, so that our flights could go on expenses. This way she will not have to suffer me dragging my heels behind her while she shops on Saturday. The conference keeps me busy and takes care of that little problem too." He drew back slightly and looked down into my eyes. "The truth is that I stalled from telling you because I was dreading it, Rose." He kissed my forehead. "I am a coward when it comes to disappointing you. I didn't want you to be cross with me all week. I know how much these weekends away mean to you. They are everything to me as well. It breaks my heart to leave you."

His words went some way towards warming me, but they could not fill the emptiness. Of course, I played the pantomime of indifference to relieve his guilt about letting me down. He poured out assurances: he would make it up to me, we would get away together soon, et cetera.

Driving home, I knew that I could not face cooking another meal for one that evening. I wanted to be somewhere with the sounds of life. The best Chancery offered was an American fast food shop on Church Street. It was perfectly situated for hungry revellers, spilling from the bars on a Friday and Saturday evening. But tonight, Wednesday, it served busy parents, rushing home with the family's dinner, a teenage couple on a date and a lonely divorcee spinster, feeling very sorry for herself.

Unlike other fast food establishments in town, this glorified chip shop had red plastic seats bolted to red Formica tables. Its patrons had the option to eat in or take away. All the others on Church Street were mere shop fronts, with serving counters two yards inside the door and nowhere to sit.

I took my plastic tray and cardboard cartons to a table and meditated through a damp hamburger and chips. A swirl of people came and went before me but I paid them no attention.

Helen was apparently making more demands on Samuel's time. I wondered if their love was rekindling. As a theory, it explained his failure to visit me over Christmas. It would account for his reduced commitment to our Friday nights. If that was the case, then my role as mistress would very soon be redundant – unless, of course, Samuel was the sort of man who enjoyed the ego boost of having two women attend to his needs.

Chapter Nineteen

Charlie's wedding in July 1980 was my next break from routine. It was also a valuable opportunity to observe my rival, Helen Baxter. Naturally, I had to look my best for the occasion, and this meant spending too much on a new dress, with matching hat and bag. The shoes were a little harder to come by and needed dyeing, but they were worth the effort.

A perfectly groomed July morning awaited the two families and guests at the First Presbyterian Church of Chancery. It was this kind of morning that compelled humanity outdoors, where families picnicked on sunshine and photographs were taken for albums. Everything was at its best, vibrant with life's colour.

Charlie looked as smart as a barrister, although his face was unusually waxen. His Brylcreemed hair was a shiny version of its normal style. He welcomed me at the door of the church, offering me a soggy hand to shake. I jangled his limp arm and struggled not to comment on his obvious nerves.

"You look very well, Charlie," I said, "like a handsome prince. Rita is very lucky."

He nodded with gratitude but could only manage a heavy exhale in reply. He looked like a criminal awaiting sentence and, in his anxiety, he forgot to let go of my hand. Perhaps he hoped I would drag him off to safety. I smiled and patted his forearm before leaving him to puff over the other guests arriving behind me.

Coming from the sunlight into the vestibule of the church, made the interior appear gloomy. As my eyes adjusted to the subdued light, a solid outline I knew well filled itself out into Samuel Baxter. He was standing beside the two doors that led to the aisles, directing guests to the groom's or bride's side. His left arm pointed like a traffic policeman's toward the door on my right. The unfinished masonry of his face shaped a rough smile. "Mrs Maylie," he said.

"Headmaster," I said continuing past him. I did not mind the formality. He had told me it would be so, and we had shared many familiarities on the previous night. My usual Friday evening had been swapped to the Wednesday that week to discuss Samuel's expectations. The change of routine was refreshing.

As we had previously agreed, I sat in a pew about a third of the way toward the back of the church. The only choice left to me was whether to sit in the middle or right sections of the groom's side. I chose the middle for its superior view.

Helen was sitting on the right side and, as wife of the best man, she was in one of the front rows. From that distance, I could not really observe very much, except that she was turned round to share a humoured conversation with someone behind her. She was probably ecstatic with Samuel's prominent role again. From my seat, her hat looked like a wilted blue sombrero.

The church was not long in filling up. Joan Spenser arrived with her husband, Derek. They were about to pass my pew when Joan recognised me. Her face showed conflict as she considered joining me. My pew did not offer a great view of the ceremony. Her compassion for the lonely spinster won, and she grabbed at the elbow of Derek's suit to manoeuvre him back.

"Derek, we'll sit here with Rose," she said, stepping in beside me, still tugging his elbow. "Rose, I don't think you've met Derek."

Derek leaned forward, past Joan and offered me his hand to shake. He would have looked quite distinguished once, but now there was an explosion of capillaries over his cheeks and nose that made him look like an old sailor. "I don't like the holy end, myself. This is much better," he said, flinching when that earned him a prod from Joan. I liked Derek immediately and hoped we would all be at the same table for the wedding breakfast.

Organ music began foaming through the pipes, but it was not the wedding march. Only then did I noticed Charlie, Samuel and the groomsman, walking past to the front of the church. At the front, Charlie crossed his arms in a self-hug and exchanged well-wishes with some of his guests. Samuel talked softly to him as they walked to their positions just right of centre. Here they joined the minister in awaiting the bride and her entourage. At one of Samuel's assurances, Charlie nodded but I could not see his expression at that angle. I imagined Samuel advising him on the therapeutic benefits of adultery if his wife grew boring.

As usually occurs at these events, nothing happened for a long time. We in the congregation whispered, fidgeted and fanned ourselves with orders of service. The organ music was frothed to waist height now and was thick enough to make wading difficult. Charlie kept gawking behind him towards the vestibule, on his guard.

I looked back there myself and I could hear the photographer issue his instructions. Somewhere beyond our sight, Rita posed with her father and bridesmaids. Flashes rattled off the walls like a miniature storm. As I looked round again, the minister leant forward to Charlie and said something. The organ stuttered short, ending one piece and filling its vats for another. Just then, I was aware of Joan pushing up beside me.

"C'mon girls, budge up," Derek said.

I looked to the end of our pew to see Betty squeeze in beside Derek. She was flushed from the shame of being almost as late as the bride. When she leaned forward to pull the creases from her skirt, she saw Joan and I watching her. She gasped out a little laugh when she recognised us. "I just grabbed the first pew that wasn't full," she whispered, "And here you all are." This was evidently her first meeting with Derek too. "You're probably Derek, then," she said to him.

"Probably," he replied.

The organist became vigorous with his pumping and stamping. He stomped out the wedding march and the congregation stood with much muttering. This limited my view of the future Mrs Bakewell as she made the last steps of her spinsterhood, but I had a narrow field of view when she levelled with my pew.

It is customary at weddings to remark upon how beautiful the bride looks, how fine her dress, her hair and all the rest. As such, Rita presented a church full of Christians with a great moral dilemma. From my poor position, even I could see that she must have bought her dress in a closing down sale at a charity shop. She probably reasoned it would do well enough for one day. Physically, she was sturdy, with a boyish face and hair styled like a German Army helmet. But what most appalled me was how she walked. Rita did not measure her pace to the tempo of the music; she towed her aged father along beside her. Her carriage suggested she was rushing through a supermarket, rather than preparing for solemn vows. When she walked down the aisle, it was with rounded shoulders, as if she carried shopping bags instead of a bouquet. She finally parked her father, by stopping beside Charlie, to whom she gave a curt nod. She rotated to face the minister and another nod initiated the proceedings.

At first, Reverend Ackroyd was unusually tense for a man so used to his profession. He stuttered a little for half a minute until he warmed up to the proceedings. The address was a stock sermon about the sanctity of marriage, the two becoming one flesh and other conventional nonsense. I had been a subscriber to these ideals long ago. My experiences had taught me otherwise. If or when Samuel and I got married, I would retain a healthy scepticism and a separate bank account.

The ceremony was a success, in that both bride and groom agreed to the marriage and no one claimed knowledge of lawful impediments. Beyond that, it was forgettable. Outside the church, we threw little pieces of coloured paper at Charlie and Rita for reasons that have never been made clear to me. After that, Betty and I did our best to stay out of the crush, but Joan dragged Derek into the middle of it.

Charlie had calmed considerably. He smiled for the well-wishers in the sunshine, his face glowing like a peach. Rita held her bouquet like a toolbox by her side and took awkward instructions from the photographer. The poor man was having a difficult job earning his commission.

At the point when the newly-weds disappeared down the road in a silver-grey Rolls Royce, Betty and I regrouped with Joan.

"Where is Derek?" Betty asked.

"Oh, he's gone to the car already. He says he needs to warm the engine, but he's really having a smoke," Joan said.

"Presumably, you aren't supposed to have worked that out," I added.

Joan smiled.

"Men," said Betty. "What tiny little brains."

The wedding reception was at the Glendinning House Hotel, a large country manor, converted and extended. It was a few miles outside Chancery. Betty and I had originally planned to meet and share a taxi, but we eagerly accepted Joan's offer of a lift.

Derek had no sooner parked up, than Joan was out of the car. She explained her haste: "I want to get some photos of Charlie and Rita." From her handbag she produced a new compact camera and patted it. "I bought this especially." With that she was off towards the hotel's main entrance.

Derek opened his car door and extended only one leg out. He half turned to Betty and me in the backseat and spoke. "You girls go on without me. Today has little enough peace and quiet to it. I'll sit here and enjoy it while I can."

"You sit there, Derek, and smoke your brains out," Betty said.

He jolted and, after a moment, started to laugh.

"I might as well take what I can get. Lord knows there's probably no real drink to enjoy at this one," he said.

"If there is, I intend to make the most of it," Betty said.

The hotel grounds had been sculpted to allow as many photographic contrivances as possible. Plants were trained up and over Corinthian arches in little bowers, with convenient seating for all the family. Arbour, gazebo and summer house were twisted with the blossoms of synthetic vines. These had endured more seasons than their natural rivals, but they were now in need of renewal. From afar, and to the camera, they would look real enough. Only close inspection showed the fraud. The sunshine and rain had jaundiced them, far from the healthy pinks and whites of their real counterparts. An oriental bridge spanned an artificial pond that was fed by a stream, which, at source, issued from a garden hose. Over the bridge hung a weeping willow that never really cried. I never looked, but I imagined the fish in the pond were rubber facsimiles.

"This looks like a garden centre," I said to Betty.

"I hate weddings," she replied. "Let's hope Derek is wrong. I'd love some free champagne right now. About a pint should get me started."

Although Charlie and Rita were both chronic Christians, they had not stinted on the alcohol. Inside the hotel foyer, a waistcoated boy waved his arm over a table full of drinks, only one quarter of which was dedicated to cordials and fizzy drinks. The rest had enough champagne flutes to occupy John Souseman for a day, had he been invited.

"Would you like a drink, ma'am?" the boy said.

"Oh yes please," Betty replied.

When we each had a glass in hand, Betty winked at me and said for the waiter's benefit. "We should take some champagne out to Joan and Derek."

After a pause, her meaning registered. "I'm sure they would appreciate that." And I fought off a rising smile.

The young waiter only registered his suspicion on our second return visit for more. That time, our errand had been on behalf of Jill and Jeff. They were as thirsty as only made-up people could be.

"I'm sorry, ladies. These drinks are for wedding guests as they enter the hotel," he said, reddening at the collar. Perhaps that was just as well, for it was going straight to my head and I would need to pace myself until the meal.

"Yes, Rosie, we don't want to do a Souseman," Betty said. Her meaning was clear. We found ourselves a leather sofa in a corner of the bar lounge and chattered without consequence. The room filled slowly with cheerful babble.

About an hour later, Derek and Joan found us, her arm hooked through his as they walked. She was propelling him around to meet people.

"There you are," she said.

"Obviously," said Derek.

"Get yourself a chair, dear," she said, taking the last one available.

"I'd rather get a room."

But he was spared the bother of doing either.

The groomsman cleared his throat and announced from the door, "Ladies and gentlemen, there will be a group photograph on the lawn. The bride and groom request your presence." He was a man in his late fifties – clearly a Bakewell, but taller and much leaner. His face was sharper than Charlie's and only the outside track of his hair remained. There was a familiar set to his eyes and mouth, and he spoke as a man accustomed to audiences.

"Who is that?" I asked.

"That's Stanley Bakewell, Charlie's brother," Joan said.

"Is he a teacher too?"

"No dear, he's the Presbyterian moderator," Joan said.

No wonder Reverend Ackroyd had faltered. He was not just giving an address, he was being inspected by his boss.

The line-up was a dreary affair. The bride and groom shook hands with their guests as they filed into the function room to eat. The line moved like a dying worm. I had just been to the toilet before joining it and thought I would probably need to go again when I had finished. Joan and Derek had already passed through, but Betty and I were together because she had accompanied me to the toilet.

Charlie gave my arm a welcoming squeeze when he shook my hand. "Thanks for coming. I hope you are enjoying yourself, Rose" he said. He turned and introduced us to Rita. "These are the girls from the office, Rose and Betty."

That was my first close-up look at the new Mrs Bakewell. My previous observations had been sound. From a distance and under a veil, I could not have seen her boxer's nose and square jaw. "You got lovely weather today," I said.

"Yes, lovely. Thanks for coming," Rita said and jolted my hand. "Stanley will show you were you are sitting."

Our table was situated in the far corner. That was only fair, as family would populate the better positioned tables. In my approach, I could see that Joan, Derek and another couple were already in their seats. Betty whispered to me on as we weaved between the round tables. "She's a real looker, Mrs Bakewell."

"I'm sure she is lovely," I said. "Charlie is not a man to be impressed by looks. She must have character."

"She'd need something," Betty said. "Look who it is!" she said to the other couple as we approached our table .

At that, Dorothy and William broke off their conversation with Joan. William managed a tight nod and Dorothy smiled at us. In previous years she might have gawped. Some things had changed about her in the years since I had last seen her.

It had never occurred to me that Dorothy and William would be invited. Now it seemed obvious: William was a sycophant who put himself forward for anything that would make him seem useful. His tireless lapping had got him onto the Senior Management Team. No doubt, he now had Charlie thinking he was a great fellow too.

"Here we are, Rose. Sitting together. Put the spinsters in the corner out of harm's way," Betty said.

I had Betty to my left and Dorothy to my right. William was beside her and engaged in a conversation across the table with Derek. Joan was beside Betty. Opposite me were two seats for another couple who were soon to join us. I forgot their names as soon as I had heard them. I am sure one, or both, of them worked with Rita doing whatever they did. William and Derek were tasked with making polite conversation with the strangers. We girls were too involved in catching up.

"And how old is Sally now?" Joan said. I had just tuned into the conversation.

"She'll be three in August. She starts nursery in September," Dorothy said. She had a firm pride to her words. "She is quite the little madam."

"They don't stay babies very long," Joan said.

"Does she take after Daddy for height?" Betty said.

"Yes, thank goodness." Dorothy's words were steady. "I was worried about that. Thankfully, she does."

"You are looking well," I said.

"Yes, your face doesn't look a day older," Betty added. "You make me sick."

Dorothy laughed without her usual shock. "You're not looking bad yourselves. I see the cakes haven't added anything to you."

This provoked the usual chorus of self-deprecating comments that assembled women make about their figures and looks. After that, the conversation continued at a natural pace. The difference now, however, was that Dorothy had her own opinions and would offer them freely. It was good to see her again and hear about her daughter. The child seemed to be a sparky little character, even accounting for her mother's bias in exaggerated anecdotes. Sally was their only child. Two miscarriages and a difficult pregnancy had made Dorothy and William decide that one was enough.

While Dorothy was talking about Sally wanting to pick her own clothes, my eyes drifted across the room to the top table. The meal was well underway and Samuel was engaged in a light conversation with Charlie's ancient mother. Her back was so bowed that her chin was among her roast potatoes. I watched his efforts at speaking clearly to her, while food grew cold on his fork.

For no particular reason, I was feeling very sorry for myself. Weddings can often be the cause of that for people in my situation. I looked across the room at the man I loved, the one I was waiting for. He had promised to make it all right again, if only I was patient and kept our secret. With a turn of my head, I considered Dorothy while she chattered on. She had done everything correctly, as I had initially. We had suffered different kinds of grief, but she had been rewarded and I disappointed. Were it not for the paltry hope that Samuel represented, I would have nothing at all.

Having just turned thirty-five, I was waiting for a dishonest man to live up to his promise. If it did not happen soon, my few remaining hopes to conceive would shrivel up. The last three months without contraception had been fruitless. Dorothy had a husband and child, but I had neither. I was happy for her, genuinely. For myself, I was determined, if I could not have both husband and child, I would have the child. I was prepared to live with the scorn if that was the price of snatching what I was owed.

There is a limit to how entertaining speeches can be with a Presbyterian moderator present. Charlie's words were simple and it was touching to hear him choke up when he talked about Rita as his soulmate. Samuel's speech was remarkable only for avoiding the obvious swipes at the groom for marrying very late in life, to the only woman he had ever dated. The closest Samuel came to humour was when advising the couple never to go to bed with an unresolved conflict: it was better to stay up and fight, he said. That caused only a murmur of amusement.

Throughout his speech, my eyes roved the room. Samuel had instructed me not to spend the wedding day looking over to him: people would notice that kind of thing. He said I was not to show undue interest in his words. In fact, he would prefer that I feigned very little interest in them. In that regard, he need have had no concern. The lack of interest I showed was genuine. The tedium of the speeches was compounded by my urgent need to return to the toilets. I had drunk too much champagne to be able to hold off for much longer.

Without my conscious intervention, my eyes frequently returned to Helen Baxter. She was at one of the centre tables, sitting beside another woman, slightly older than herself. I guessed that her companion might even be Charlie's sister-in-law, both their husbands being engaged at the top table. Mrs Baxter was not facing an audience herself, as she had on Speech Night, and was not required to demonstrate obvious approval of her husband's speech-making. It did strike me as odd, however, that she hardly looked in his direction. Occasionally, she whispered responses to the older lady, but mostly looked down into her folded arms.

My scan of the room showed me another thing, one that gave me greater understanding of Charlie Bakewell. Apart from William Butler, there were no other teaching staff at the wedding. I wondered how many had been invited to the evening celebrations.

I leaned across Betty and asked Joan for an approximation.

"None," she replied.

"That is surprising."

"Not really," Joan said after a pause to toast the bride and groom. "Charlie is very private. He has never mixed much with the staff. His time is dedicated to the boys. I imagine he is hardly in the staffroom enough to socialise."

"That makes it a greater honour that we were all invited." I said.

After the speeches, toasts and cake cutting, the guests dispersed so the hotel staff could prepare the room for the evening function. While we moved to other reception areas, the staff laboured to clear a dance floor and a small band set up their equipment. Charlie and Rita made their rounds of the guests and I dashed to the toilets. Betty's mission was to occupy another sofa in the bar lounge.

Purely by coincidence, I was exiting a toilet cubicle while Helen Baxter reapplied her lipstick in the mirror, over one of the sinks. She looked up at the movement behind her and recognised my face. A moment later, she recalled my name. "Mrs Maylie, I believe" she said and turned to face me. She twisted her lipstick and returned it to her little blue bag. Her wilted sombrero looked no better up close, but I was sure it must have been very expensive.

"I love your hat, Mrs Baxter. It looks like something from a London fashion house."

"Please, call me Helen," she said.

"Then you will have to call me Rose."

"That sounds fair. How are you enjoying the wedding?"

"It reminds me that I'm divorced," I said. Helen's eyes widened slightly. "But apart from that, I'm having a good time. They certainly got a lovely day for it."

"Did you enjoy the speeches?" she asked. I paused. "I trapped you with that one before – on Speech Night – didn't I?" she said. Before I could respond, she laughed at her own joke.

I took that as a natural lull and made to leave. "Enjoy the rest of your evening," I said.

Before I had taken two steps, however, Helen spoke again. "Don't go yet. I need to speak to you. I followed you in here."

I put my hand on to the door handle to steady myself. Words of doom were about to be spoken.

"I need to talk to you – about Samuel. But not in here," she said.

A thrust of pure adrenaline dashed through my throat – in which direction I could not tell.

She stared, waiting for a response.

"Yes. It is busy here. Someone is sure to come in," I said and tried not to sound defensive. I wanted witnesses if she tried to murder me for sleeping with her husband. If we were to have our final showdown tonight, it should not be in a place that would ruin the good cheer of Charlie's wedding. I scanned the size and shape of Helen Baxter. It if came to a violent confrontation I was hopeful that I could out run her – especially in those heels. The hotel gardens seemed the obvious choice. She could be waiting there, while I ran down the road, hem in one hand, high heels in the other. I could flag down a taxi before she realised I had gone.

"Will you meet me in the garden? By the bridge. In ten minutes," she said. "I don't want Samuel to see us speaking."

I was torn between cowardliness and curiosity. If this was to be the confrontation between wife and mistress, then it was no less than I deserved. I had known what it felt like to be betrayed but I had continued regardless. My theory that life owed me something better felt hollow just then. The last tattered scrap of my honour said I was ready to answer for my crimes: that was the least I owed her. It would be better to face my accuser than be cowardly and run away from the issue. Running was the kind of thing Harry would have done. I would prove to myself that I was better than him.

Helen was waiting at the oriental bridge, leaning on the railing. There was a large glass of red wine in her hand. She had control over the situation, at first, being able to assess my strength as I approached.

I thought it best to say as little as possible. What I did say, should be controlled and civilised. It was reasonable to assume that she would do most of the talking.

"I'm sure you're wondering why I want to talk to you. You probably think it odd that I asked to meet you in secret," she said.

I smiled awkwardly.

"You're divorced – sorry to cut straight to the point, but we can't stay out here all night. I understand your husband cheated on you too."

"Too?" The word escaped me. I wore shock all over my face.

"Yes, I've known for some time now," she said.

Every instinct called me to slip off my heels and grab that fistful of hem.

"What did you do when you found out about your husband's betrayal?" she continued, but I could not respond. Once again, acute anxiety brought me to mental shutdown. I was aware of holding the rail and swallowing heavily, staring into her face.

Helen actually laughed a little and shook me gently by the arm.

That was inconsistent and strangely sympathetic towards an arch-enemy. I thought, perhaps, she was charging me with

213

hypocrisy for making another woman suffer the heartache I had been through.

"I know it's a shock," she said patting my hand. "He doesn't seem the type." Her throat crackled at this. "I used to think he was an honourable man. He is proud of his reputation, but he is far from honourable."

Realisation settled on me like the first sunshine: she did not suspect me.

"I knew I had to speak to you," she said. "You have been through this with your ex-husband. I thought, if I spoke to you it might give me some direction. And you might be able to shine light on who his other woman is."

My eyes widened again.

"I know I am asking a lot, Rose. It is a very personal thing I'm asking you to do —" Her voice broke up and she looked away.

There was a moment of silence and I offered her a tissue from my little cocktail bag.

"Of course I will help you, Helen," I said, lying.

"Thank you so much." After another silence, she continued, "What did you do when your husband cheated — and you found out?"

"I was a fool. Harry had many affairs. Each time, I confronted him and tried to forgive him. He pretended to be sorry each time. We ended up moving around a lot, away from his tarts," I said.

"That is no life. Did you have any children?"

"No." I swallowed hard. "And I used to think that was a good thing. Now, I wish I had something to show for my troubles."

"Yes, at least I have that," she said. "Would you like some wine. I'm sorry I never thought to bring you out a glass."

"Yes, please." I took a good swig from her glass and returned it. It had lipstick on opposing sides now. It made me smile to notice that. "I thought marriage was for life," I said, "and made too many excuses for Harry. He walked over me because I let him."

"How do you think I should approach this?" she asked.

I hated myself for saying this, but it was necessary – for both his women. "You should leave him. I wish I had left my cheating husband when I first found out."

Helen took her time to think before she spoke again. "You are right, Rose. He is cheating; our marriage is broken and neither of us wants to fix it."

"How did you find out – if you don't mind me asking?"

She took a sip of wine before she began, offering her glass to me afterwards. I shook my head.

"It was an accumulation of little things. For a long time he has been doing charitable work with the Samaritans. That used to be only on a Friday night and he would get home late. More recently, though, he has been going there on Tuesdays and Thursdays too."

"Three times a week?"

"Yes."

I exhaled heavily and gripped the bridge rail. Helen looked over at my reaction. "Three nights a week?" I said. After a pause, "That's very suspicious." My knees trembled. I wanted to crumple to a heap. Samuel Baxter was cheating on his wife with two mistresses.

"It is sickening that he is hiding behind charitable work. Sickening," she said.

"You must have more than just suspicions, though?" I asked.

"I have found hairs on his clothes. Sometimes there is a scent to him, not perfume, but not something I ever buy. Trust me, I've checked everything in the house to be sure. It's not hand soap either. It's on his skin."

The hairs and scents were certainly not mine. I had been too organised and careful for that. Samuel could have followed the same routine with his new mistress. It seemed unthinkable that he would be careless after all this time. My only explanation was that Samuel had decided, consciously or subconsciously, to get caught. He was not a risk-taker in life. He knew that he was going to be discovered and he must have welcomed it.

"What colour were the hairs?" I asked, wondering if she would suspect me if they were brunette.

"Strawberry blonde."

215

"That's why I knew I could trust you, Rose." She laid a hand on my arm and offered me her wine glass.

I took it. My troubled mind could not conjure a rival woman with that hair colour.

"Besides, Samuel is forever telling me how often you two argue at work. He can be very arrogant and you don't put up with it. 'That dreadful woman' he calls you, I'm afraid to say.

Recognition choked me on my last mouthful of red wine. Much of it found its way up my nose.

Helen patted my arm and steadied the glass in my hand.

It was some moments later, and another swig, before I could speak. I guessed at who his second mistress was, but I could not share my new knowledge with Helen. I had to control the flow of information until I could figure out a plan. "Has his behaviour changed recently?" I asked.

"Yes, that was another thing I noticed. He has always been quite tactile and amorous. Recently, though, he has stopped coming near me. We've hardly made love in the past nine months," she said.

"Nine months?" The absolute bastard. I took a steadying breath. This could not get any worse. I had been his mistress for the past three years and three months. Clearly, his stamina was not up to servicing any more than two women a week.

"I haven't suspected him all this time," she said, to excuse herself. "Only in the last few months, after I noticed the signs." To her credit, Helen's powers of observation were considerably better than mine.

"A scandal is the last thing he would want," I said, looking at Helen. "How soon will you leave him?" I asked.

"When I have solid evidence. Jack and Laura are absolutely itching to move out. It won't impact on them so badly."

I was wrong: it was getting worse. I doubted there was a single truth he had told me.

Helen continued and I stared off, over the artificial pond. "Mind you, they hated having to live at home. All of their friends had flats in Trentford, but Samuel insisted."

"Did he?" The bastard had told me it was Helen's wish.

"Oh yes, he even bought them a car to share. When that wasn't enough, he bought another, so they had one each. He said he wanted to keep the family together." My heart wrung for

216

Helen, as her voice creaked over those last four words. I put an arm around her and she rummaged in her tiny blue handbag for a handkerchief. She had to catch the tears before they ruined her make-up.

Samuel Baxter had engineered to keep his children at home, so he would not have to commit to me. And why would he, I thought. After all, he was getting it all his own way. It made no sense to buy the goose, when he got the golden eggs for free.

After a half minute's silence, she turned, grasping my hand. "Will you help me find evidence against him, Rose? Without that, I've nothing. He finds it easy to lie. He would tell everyone the divorce is my fault. I'll not let him do that to me."

"I will, Helen," I said, and this time it was the truth. "But I'm not sure what help –". And then it occurred to me. He had a credit card she knew nothing about. "Did you go to London with him at the end of May – to the Headmasters' Conference?"

She frowned, while shuffling through memories.

"No," she said.

"He said you did."

"That is where we must begin."

Chapter Twenty

Helen Baxter returned to the wedding reception first. I stood at the fake oriental bridge for many more minutes alone. I felt sorry for myself, certainly, but I was also formulating a plan of action. Before she left, I had given Helen my phone number. She agreed to phone me on Sunday for an update.

It impressed me that I did not disintegrate with the news of Samuel's betrayals. Either I was made of strong fibre, or I was conditioned to expect disappointment. It was clear that I had to act promptly. I no longer wanted Samuel. Even if there was a tug of war over him, I was unlikely to succeed. I had other plans for him. A direct confrontation would not strengthen my position. He could not know that I was aware of his other mistress, nor that I knew he was verging on separation and divorce. Each of these obstacles I intended to deal with in turn. I also had my job to protect. I could not break up with Samuel and expect to remain his secretary for long. Only through guile would I prosper.

"I wondered where you got to." Betty said. She was sitting at a table beside the dance floor, protecting our drinks. Mine was untouched, hers half empty. I had missed the first dance and the arrival of many more evening guests.

She looked up at me. "Have you been crying?"

"God, no. It's hay fever. I was out getting fresh air. I don't feel well. Too much champagne. I'm sorry, but I'll have to go home," I said.

"You're deserting me?"

"Would you rather I did a Souseman?"

"It would brighten this place up," she said. "You go on, I'll get a lift with Joan and Derek." She nodded over to the couple slow dancing.

I scanned the floor and saw Charlie and Rita locked together, swaying left to right. They were oblivious to everything and everyone. Dorothy and William were up there too, still ridiculously out of proportion. Samuel was dancing with a bridesmaid.

Another sweep of the room showed Helen. She watched me from across the dance floor, beyond the swirl of colours. She had replenished her wine glass and with a tiny gesture, saluted me. She drank, knowing that her husband would disapprove. But what did his approval count for anymore? She was beginning to emerge in her own right and that was an early expression of her independence.

"I'll see you soon," I said to Betty. "Be sure to give my apologies to Joan."

It was 7:00 p.m. on a bright amber Friday evening, and I did not wait long for a taxi.

"Where to, love?" the driver asked.

"A number of places. I hope you don't have any bookings for the next hour," I said.

First, I went home, changed into some casual clothes and collected my work keys. The taxi parked in my driveway, its meter still running. Just before 8:00 p.m., the driver pulled into the front of Chancery Grammar school. I had debated whether I was doing anything illegal. That was unlikely. I was an employee returning to my place of work and I had a set of keys in my hand. The taxi driver would hardly consider my actions suspicious. With this in mind, I acted in the open. Actions that happen in the open rarely appear suspicious. After opening the front gates, I got back into the taxi again. The school's drive was long enough to justify it.

Outside the front doors, I said, "I'll only be a moment. I've just to fetch something."

I was into the school without a fuss. The governors had never invested in a burglar alarm, but that would hardly have stopped the headmaster's secretary. I was in a position of trust.

Passing through my office, I picked up a notepad. I unlocked the connecting door to Mr Baxter's study and a few more steps took me behind his desk to his extravagant excuse of a chair.

My supporting role in trying to have Jack Dawson fired had required that I order a secret copy of his filing cupboard key. The same process could be applied to the filing drawers of the headmaster's desk. To these, he had always denied me access. I had a spare set of all his other keys, but not this one. He had not trusted me, evidently. How suspicious some people can be of those they are supposed to love.

I found and noted the three digit serial number inscribed below each of the keyholes. Both locks bore the same number: 614. I recorded it on a corner of my notepad. Chancery's locksmith had always been most helpful whenever the caretaker ordered duplicate keys. Chancery Grammar had its own account with him, but I consider the few pounds I would pay for my copied key worth it. I would not risk this appearing on the school account: the bursar was known to scrutinise every invoice. The expense and the extra effort would guarantee security.

After locking the front doors and securing the gates, I told the driver to take me home.

Stage two began in the morning. Scarcely had Mr Chambers of the aptly named 'Chambers' Locksmiths' rolled up the shutters, than I was waiting beside him for the shop to open.

"Hello. I wonder if you could help me? I've just bought a desk at an auction. It has one of those lockable filing drawers. The only problem is it doesn't have any keys. How hard would it be to get some ordered?"

"Well, love, those locks all have a three digit number on them. If you get that, I can –".

"Six, one, four."

"Oh. Right you are then," he said. "Give me a moment and I'll check my stock." He disappeared into a recess behind the counter and sorted through metal hoops, each filled with tiny keys. He returned the one bearing the 600s. "Here we are, 614," he said, holding it between finger and thumb. "One or two copies?"

Two fitted my cover story better.

In July the school was closed. The headmaster, along with all his office staff, had a month's holiday. To err on the side of safety, however, Helen agreed to ensure that Samuel was well occupied on the Monday after Charlie's wedding – her phone call to me on Sunday had confirmed our pact. He would be conscripted to take her on a shopping trip to Trentford, far away from the school, and they would be there all afternoon. Even without these precautions, my appearance at the school would not have been suspicious. Though the building was officially

220

closed, there was still mail to be sorted or a thousand administrative tasks to which a lonely spinster could attend. It would have looked suspicious, however, had Samuel come into work and found me sitting at his desk, sorting through the contents of his filing drawers. The extra precautions were needed for that reason.

It was a very good sign that I had to unlock the school gate myself. It was tempting to consider locking the gates again but anyone coming in after me would immediately have thought it odd that my car was already parked inside.

The location of the headmaster's office was problematic. It was on the ground floor and overlooked the car park. It also had large windows. While this was good for making the office airy with natural light, it was not good for a novice secret agent. Neither could I tamper with his venetian blinds. He always had them exactly horizontal during the day and only shut them when during our after school dictation sessions . In the summer holidays he was never in school at night and altering them would have signalled intrusion.

The headmaster's parking space was unoccupied. The mission was off to a good start. I parked and went directly to my own office where I switched on the photocopier. In case there should be any problem with that –it had a history of disappointing me – I also fired up the one in the Reprographics Suite. Sleepless nights planning this had improved my efficiency.

Samuel had always been most fastidious about opening his own mail and managing his desk. He had never considered that his secretary should have a copy of his desk drawer keys – although I had copies of his other keys. I was about to find out why.

Out of breath, I unlocked the connecting door to Samuel's study, but did not open it until my photocopier had finished warming its toners, its red light turning green. The study was a little musty and smelt of its last layer of spray furniture polish. I did not dare to linger in there. My imagination had no problem conjuring the sounds of a car engine, rumbling into the car park.

Not for the first time, I knelt behind the headmaster's desk. I had to stay below the level of the windows, as any car driving into the car park could expose me. To sit on Samuel's throne would, similarly, have made me visible. I worked the lock on the

221

right side first to access the two drawers on that side. Despite a badly punning name, Chambers' Locksmiths was a fine institution. Its key slotted perfectly into place. The top drawer was shallow and contained only routine items of utility: a stapler, staples, paper punch, scissors, a bundle of disposable pens and so forth. Below it, the second drawer was deeper. Within, it was well organised. Papers were bundled together with elastic bands. They were easy to sort for their relevance to my mission.

It is ironic that an organised man does a lot of work for prospective thieves. Samuel's neatly bundled credit card statements were a more welcome parcel than his gift of *Wuthering Heights*. I expected their reading would be more enlightening too – but that was a luxury for later in the evening.

To minimise my time in the headmaster's study, I removed October 1979 to June 1980's statements from the bundle and relocked the drawer. I ran two copies of these from my photocopier and only took a moment to scan the result. There were a number of items on it that Helen Baxter would find interesting, including a sizeable transaction to The Grahamsbridge Lodge and three visits to London restaurants. He appeared to have eaten well on all three occasions. Scattered throughout the statements there were transactions in a number of well known ladies' clothes shops. It was enough to hang Samuel if his Helen had not received any of these items as gifts.

I laughed to myself. The Christmas gift of my own photocopier had not been such a failure after all. So far, the old girl was on my side and working perfectly. From that position, I also had a clear view of the car park and down to the front gate. For now at least, the way was clear.

I put the nine copied statements in a manila folder on my desk, returned to Samuel's study and restored the original documents to their place in the bundle. A search through earlier statements showed me that Samuel had been lying about his reasons for being unavailable at Christmas. Another trip, this time to Edinburgh, appeared in place of the family commitments he had claimed. I told myself I had suspected this all along.

The left side of the desk held the big filing drawer, which took up its full depth, front to back. Kneeling again, I unlocked it and pulled it open. Inside, neatly tabbed suspension folders hung between rails at the drawer's edges. Each tab bore the name of a member of staff.

Of course, I looked at my own file first. It held nothing more than my application form and a few doctor's notes to explain a handful of absences. There was nothing in it to indicate that I was of special importance to him. Had there been any such evidence, I would have been very tempted to remove it.

Jack Dawson's folder was predictably fat but it contained nothing new to me.

There was a break in the alphabetical ordering of the folders: I noticed J. Souseman lurking at the back of the row, not far from D. Cruikshanks. Former members of staff had been consigned to the back of the drawer, just in front of the unlabelled spare folders.

My only reason for being in that drawer was curiosity, but it seemed logical that I should investigate everything since I had come this far. Really, I was looking for something else to use as leverage on Samuel. I already had enough to end his marriage, but I wanted a little something else too. Perhaps he had been foolish enough to have buried a keepsake from his latest mistress, or from me.

It is a human tendency that if we have something scandalous, dangerous or precious to store that we do so somewhere secure but easily accessible. With this in mind, I pulled out the unlabelled spare folders from the very back of the drawer. Two of them were almost full of letters.

I could not risk reading them fully in Samuel's study or while I waited for them to scan through the photocopier. I skimmed through enough, though, for my world to lurch on its axis. My heart shuddered, and tears streamed my cheeks as I jabbed the copier button. The machine was blind to the meaning of the characters it faithfully reproduced, two apiece, but the secrets of that correspondence broke me.

With trembling hands, I restored Samuel's desk and study to its former condition.

I was so anxious, that I could not trust to memory what I had just done. I returned to his study to double-check the drawers were ordered and locked as I had found them. I checked the floor for any debris and returned his seat to its approximate position.

223

The consequences of a mistake at this stage would be devastating on the remainder of my plans.

Sitting in my car, I realised that I had left the main photocopier switched on in the Reprographics room. I had been so thrown into disarray that I had forgotten all about it. I put this right at once.

I knew that Tuesday evening was one of Samuel's extra so-called Samaritans evenings and considered it little risk to phone Helen at home. We arranged to meet in a local supermarket car park that evening. The shops were all shut and the car park was empty except for a learner driver receiving instruction.

Helen's white Ford Escort was not difficult to spot. I swung the car round to face the opposite direction from her so we were able to talk, window to window, without getting out of our vehicles. I had seen that in a film once. Drawing up parallel to Helen, I wound down my window. She did the same.

"This is very cloak and dagger," she said. Her face was pale without make-up and she looked dark under the eyes. She had been crying recently.

"I didn't know where else to meet you. Somewhere we wouldn't be seen together."

"That's fine. I know you need to protect your job."

I showed her the large brown envelop I had for her. "There are several things in here that will upset you," I said.

"It is past that now. I would rather know the truth, no matter how harsh, than live a lie." She bit at one side of her lip.

"There are nine credit card statements and some love letters from his mistress, Pauline McVickers," I said. "You have enough to prove his infidelity. It is essential that you leave me out of it, though. I have included a copy of the key to his desk drawers. You should say you went to the school one evening, took the serial number from the locks, got a key cut and then searched his drawers."

Helen nodded while I talked her through her story once again. She should claim to have waited until that 'Samaritans' evening and accessed the school with the keys he left at home. I described the two offices, mine and Samuel's, telling her where she would have found the relevant documents and how she had copied them.

It was a plausible story. The school had no active security measures and only a padlocked gate to bar access. No one living in the area would have considered it unusual to see cars coming and going in the evening – whether during the holidays or not. Samuel did keep his work keys at home. He was such an organised fellow that he had separate key rings for work and home. When he came home, he detached the two and hung the work keys on a hook in the kitchen.

Helen asked a few questions to clarify the narrative and repeated it back to me perfectly while tears streamed freely from her worn out eyes.

Watching her recital brought me to actual grief. Once again, I had involved myself in a scheme with Samuel without fully considering the casualties. Mrs Baxter, or the idea of her, had always been a remote, frigid presence to my mind. She had been the obstacle between me and happiness. She possessed something she did not know how to look after. It struck me as grossly peculiar that I, the author of her unhappiness, coached her through the process of dissolving her marriage.

"I will face him tonight," she said. "Thank you for helping me, Rose. I know you didn't have to risk everything for me. I will always be in your debt." She daubed her eyes and started her car.

I attempted to trot out a gratifying cliché but was too choked to finish it.

She smiled with gratitude and drove off.

Through the mist of times past, I used to think of Samuel's divorce as something liberating for us both. I imagined it would be the beginning of contentment. Now, up close, I understood that I had lied to myself for the last three years. Samuel Baxter was no more worthy than Harry Maylie.

The love letters I had found in his drawer had been from Mrs Pauline McVickers of Her Majesty's Education Inspectorate. When Helen threw Samuel out, he would run to one of us, perhaps even both – it was unlikely that he would make do with only one woman when he could have two. I considered it unlikely that he had told McVickers about our affair. That would have been ridiculous: admitting professional misconduct to an inspector.

225

If a scandal broke and sullied the good name of Samuel's school, it would be career suicide for her to be associated with him, and she struck me as a career woman. I doubted she would let something like an affair with a disgraced headmaster slow her down.

When Samuel was to be released from his marriage, it might not be into my arms at first, but I could be patient. Although I detested him, I still had use for him. I remembered how, when threatened by the journalist, Paddy Audley, and the examination paper scandal, Samuel had relied on me. I hoped that the upheavals in his imminent future would drive him to seek comfort in me again.

Chapter Twenty-One

Samuel was unable to meet with me that Friday in July. He apparently had a cold and a very sore throat. In his thoughtfulness, he did not want to infect me. I oozed sympathy over the phone but enjoyed that his life was in serious turmoil. Helen had surely confronted him and sent him packing. He was either in a bed and breakfast, or with his other mistress. His biggest concern would be that word of his disgrace would spread. It would be another week or two before he could settle into a routine with me again – if he ever managed it at all. I was prepared to make that short-term sacrifice for victory in the long-term.

Eventually, of course, he would have to tell me that Helen had thrown him out. He did so during our next Friday night meeting. When I answered my door to him, he was standing there with a sports bag in hand. I gave him a frown, affecting confusion.

"I thought I might stay over tonight – if you don't mind," he said. There was a glimmer of mischief in his eyes. He probably thought to surprise me with his astonishing news.

"I don't mind," I said. He was waiting to deliver his punchline, so I obliged with the rest. "Will Helen not notice you are gone?"

"I have left her," he said, stepping into the hall.

I threw my arms around him in a grand display of gratitude. It was better to do so because my face had contorted to a sneer at his lie. "Oh Samuel. I have waited for this day for so long," seemed an appropriate thing to say.

After much hugging and sentiment, I took him by the hand to the bedroom. As far as Samuel knew, he was being rewarded for his commitment. That evening and well into the next morning I worked him repeatedly. He marvelled at my renewed enthusiasm for his body. If he had not already made up his mind, he would be evaluating which mistress he would commit to for the long-term. That is, presuming he was intending to stay with either of us. The rekindled flame between us may have increased my equity.

"I should leave Helen more often," he said.

227

"I will have worn you out before you reach fifty," I said. "Then I'll look for someone younger to satisfy me."

He leaned back and looked at me. After a moment he smiled. "You are very playful tonight. And still full of surprises." Between his physical exertions, Samuel had a restless tension to him. I knew him well enough to expect he would want to clarify our position. As we were entering a new stage in our relationship, he would need to outline his terms. He had always found it irritating when I pressured him for reassurances. This time, however, I was playing a different game: I would pretend that I was in no hurry at all.

When he was curled up beside me in bed, exhausted, I thought the time was right to open a discussion. His eyes were closed, his head nuzzled into my shoulder and I stroked his hair.

"I imagine this is a time of great upheaval for you," I said to the ceiling. "You will need time and space to adjust to being single again before you decide what to do." I imagined how he would have expressed these same sentiments to me. It was better that I pretend they were my own ideas, in that case.

He stirred and propped himself up on his elbow to see my face. His eyes were heavy and puffed. "Sorry?" he said.

"You need to get through your divorce – if you choose to go that far – before you decide what to do next."

"I will be going that far. I promise you."

"We need to do this in the right order too. We don't want people saying that we did anything dishonourable." I was leading him.

"I told Helen I didn't love her any more. She actually agreed and we parted on good terms – for the sake of the family."

More realistically, there had been a big confrontation and the proof against him had been irrefutable.

"I'm cold. Cuddle up." I tugged him back to his former position where he could not see my face.

"Does she suspect that you have a mistress?"

"I'm not sure."

"All that trouble we took was worthwhile," I said. "We cannot waste those efforts by acting hastily now. We have plenty of –"

Samuel was up on his elbow again and looked at me with curiosity. "Rose Maylie, you are an astonishing woman. Other women in your position would be clamouring for an engagement ring."

"I have one of those already. It is overrated."

"I see, Mrs Worldly Wise," he said. As he was curling up again, he muttered, "Full of surprises."

I smiled at the ceiling and wondered if I was pregnant.

Just over a week later, on Sunday, 10 August 1980, I was to take John Souseman round to see my parents. We were running a little later than usual because John had needed a bath to make himself presentable.

These days, he was tolerably sober most of the time. He had learned to strike a balance, buying only three bottles of wine each morning. Under his own initiative, he had trained himself to mark his drinking day into thirds. John was normally an early riser, and so he used meal times to divide the days up. On the rare occasion that there was wine left over at a cut-off period, he was to pour it down the sink, rather than have more later. The theory was sound but ultimately flawed because it relied on John to be self-regulating. Sometimes he would skip meals to get more out of the wine; sometimes he would have all the wine, then visit the The Cartwright's Inn for supper. On the brighter side, John said there were days when he had slept through the morning and bought only two bottles for the day to keep himself afloat. Similarly, there had been a few days when he had not finished his bottles and had willingly fed them to the kitchen sink. This might seem wasteful but John would not have been able to sleep for thinking about the leftover wine.

There was hope for him yet. He was not entirely at the mercy of the alcohol and his limits were realistic. Beyond that, he had no ambitions. Whether or not he was drunk, John was still a gentleman. He was a better man at his most drunken than Samuel Baxter leading an assembly in prayer.

At John's own request, my father no longer offered him any brandies. Old Peter was hardly up to it himself now, anyway. Seventy was closing in on him and brandy gave him heart burn.

I stood outside John's bathroom door and knocked. By this time, he had given me a copy of his house key. I had phoned my parents to warn them of our expected lateness, but I had been a little too optimistic.

"John? You haven't drowned, have you?"

"Would I tell you if I had?"

"That's good. Just checking," I said. "We need to get a move on. Mum's roast will be turning to stone in the oven."

"Here! Speaking of ovens. Guess who we saw last night?" John said.

I frowned, unable to make the connection.

"No? Ovens, cakes. Probably think I rambling again," he said.

He was right.

"Who did you see?"

"Betty. From your office." After a pause, he added, "Trent."

This was of marginal interest, but the oven connection was still tenuous. "Where did you see her? She can't have called round."

"We saw her at Cartwright's."

"What was she doing there?" I asked.

"Huh, selling vacuum cleaners," John laughed. "What do people do at an inn on Saturday night? She was looking to pick up a rich farm boy who's none too bright."

"Who were you with – you said 'we saw her'?"

"Dawson. I see a lot of him in the holidays. Good drinking buddy. Helps me stick to the limits – well, the extra limit I allow myself on a pub day."

This was shaping up to be an interesting story after all. From memory, Betty and Dawson were a volatile mix.

Splashes stirred as John got up out of the bath. The plug gurgled a moment later to support this theory. He was a few minutes drying himself before he opened the door and emerged in his grey bathrobe. I tried not to look too closely at him: I did not want to know whether the robe had once been white. I remained at the bathroom door while John walked down the hall to his bedroom.

"You'll stay there, Rosie, unless you want the shock of your life."

"You've no worry there. Just finish your story."

"Right, hang on 'til I get dressed. I can't do two things at once."

We were in the car before John was sitting still enough to concentrate on his narrative.

"Jack and I were propping up the bar —you've been to Cartwright's?" he asked.

"No."

"Big, horseshoe-shaped bar in the middle. We were on the left, facing the front wall where they've a big TV. The football was on. Not very interesting. Jack likes it more than me. He had some money on the match. TV is also near the double doors. It's our favourite spot. We get to see the telly and the talent."

"I hope this is going somewhere," I said.

"About 9:00 p.m., Betty came in with a few friends. She'd been upstairs having a bite to eat."

"Jack nearly fell off his seat when he saw her. He'd just been talking about her."

"What'd he say?"

"Couldn't get her off his mind." John dismissed the rest with a flick of his hand, "And stuff like that." I grimaced. "He didn't go straight over to her. He let her get a booth with her friends and settle in. The place wasn't too full. It never is. I like that," he said.

"Focus, John."

"After a while, she spotted us and she came over to say hello. She's a decent sort like that. Jack has obviously been forgiven for his Christmas grope, but I could tell she was a bit edgy. Dawson was on his best behaviour. Very charming. He has a way with the ladies. We weren't too drunk to socialise – at that stage – so Betty invited us to join them. We dragged over a couple of stools and joined them in their booth. I blathered away to one of her friends. I forget her name. Not very bright. Jack stayed with Betty – but not too clingy. She was happy enough, laughing at his jokes and all."

"I hope there is a good bit of gossip coming."

"Oh, yes. By last orders at 11:00, Jack could hardly bite his own finger. He started telling Betty that he couldn't stop thinking about her. He said he wanted to look after her."

"That's more like the Dawson I know," I said.

"Betty took it in good humour. Bouncers were calling time and clearing the inn. Jack asked Betty if she'd wait for him, while he went to the toilet. She said their taxi would be waiting outside. Jack didn't want to leave it at that and decided to forgo the toilet trip. He followed her outside but her taxi wasn't there yet. He was really busting but he said he'd wait with them while the taxi arrived. Again, Betty was okay with that. Trouble was, the taxi was quite late. Jack ran off to an alley between Main Street and the car park to relieve himself. Just as soon as he dipped into the alley, the taxi pulled up. Betty shouted out to him that they were going and the fool came running to the car to say goodbye."

"I think I know where this is going," I said.

John was gurgling with suppressed laughter as he told the rest. "The girls were all sitting there in the taxi. Three in the back and Betty in the front. Dawson bounded up to Betty's window and calling for her to wind the window down. I was about six feet away and saw Betty's face twist up in horror. Eyes standing out of her head, her jaw hanging slack. Then the girls in the back of the taxi started to roar and cackle, so I looked at Jack. Poor guy had forgotten to put his todger away and he was too drunk to notice."

"Oh my God. That's terrible." I said, thinking just the opposite.

"It gets worse. Jack eventually caught on that something was wrong. He zipped himself up as casually as any man could in the circumstances. The girls in the car took it all in good humour – he clearly didn't do it on purpose. Even Betty looked sorry for him. The guys in the police car across the street didn't think it so funny, though. Two big peelers got up out of the car, all slow – the way they do – and started to cross the road. Jack had no idea they were coming. I couldn't get the words out quick enough, before Betty shouted for him to run." John punctuated his story with a wheeze of laughter.

I had to admit, it was good gossip. I couldn't imagine sharing it in the office, though. We had reached our destination, so I parked my car in my parents' drive and cut the engine. Neither of us was going anywhere until John finished.

John cleared his throat and continued, "I'll tell you, Jack Dawson can run. He was away like a whippet, through the car park, over a hedge and into the field beside it. He was gone before they'd made it halfway across the road. If he'd been in the town, they might have been able to catch him but the peelers are too lazy to chase a guy across a field. They did stop Betty's taxi from leaving, though, and questioned all the girls on who he was. They only did that as it didn't involve any running."

"What did the girls say? Did they give his name?"

"I don't know. I started walking straight away. I didn't want to be questioned too."

"Well, that's no good, John," I said. "You have to finish the story."

"Ask Betty tomorrow," he said. "You'll see her at work."

The despondency of a Monday morning is magnified by the length of the break preceding it. A regular Monday, after a weekend off, is bad enough, but all my reserves of fortitude were required for the first day back after the summer holidays.

We office staff were alone in the school, apart from the caretakers, and even the headmaster was absent. This additional freedom was very welcome. For the first hour, we met in our happy circle and drank coffee. Much semi-personal news was shared and commented on. Lorna confided that she and her long-term boyfriend had been talking about getting engaged. This brought Joan to reminiscing about how Derek had proposed to her at the Eiffel Tower with ice cream on his top lip. Betty and I murmured a quick exchange while she did so.

"Have you heard from him?" I asked.

"He phoned to apologise, for about the tenth time."

"What about your friends?"

"They wet themselves laughing."

"Do you think the police will find out his name?" I said.

"Probably not. We said we'd never seen him before. They could have asked in Cartwright's, though"

"It's dreadful – not knowing."

"He's been so sweet. And he was very charming on the night. He's like a little boy sometimes."

"Were you not disgusted when you saw – you know."

Betty shrugged and smiled. "I've seen a few before. It was more funny than anything. It was an accident."

Our chatter was interrupted by the wallop of the post being dropped onto the reception counter. It was our regular postman but none of us had bothered to learn his name. He usually just delivered, said hello and went on his way. Today, though, he frowned at us and paused.

"I'm sure I know who you're all talking about," he said.

We all stopped our conversations and looked at him.

He put his hand up and conceded. It was as though we had shamed him into retreat.

"Who are we talking about?" Betty said to him.

"That teacher who's been arrested."

Our shared alarm told him that we still did not know.

"Oh God," he said and looked appalled. "I'm sorry."

"Who? Who was arrested?" Betty said with rising urgency.

"The paper's in the van. I'll get it for you," he said and disappeared.

While he was away, no one spoke. Betty stared at me. I imagined how long it would take the postman to walk to the front door and back again. He was longer than I imagined. Concern overwhelmed Betty and she stirred from her seat, pacing before the counter for his return. She kept looking over to me. At least twice she exhaled heavily and wiped her hands on her skirt.

The postman returned with *The Chancery Chronicle*. He laid it folded on the counter and backed away. "I'm sorry to bear the bad news. You can keep that. I'm finished it," he said, like the gift of a newspaper would ease our troubles.

Betty unfolded the paper and read the headline. I could not see it from where I sat. For a long moment, her eyes drank in the first paragraphs of the article. She shook her head and read it again. Betty had never been one for dramatic outbursts. "Oh dear God," she said slowly. She put her hand over her heart and looked to me. By her face, I could tell that she was in shock.

She walked slowly into our circle again.

"I can't read any more," she said. She sat staring into a void.

Shaking her head with disbelief, she gave the paper to Joan. Joan's only concern was for Betty, and she reached out to comfort her.

Betty's voice creaked, "You need to read it." And she squeezed Joan's hand.

Joan fumbled the glasses on the chain at her neck and held up the paper. Her arm weakened as she read the article, again and again, like the newspaper was getting heavier. Her head soon followed, borne down by a burden. The *Chronicle* slumped into her lap. With shaking hands she supported her face. A gasp shuddered from her.

"What is it?" I said.

Joan did not speak and Betty picked up the paper again. She showed Lorna and me the headline: "Grammar School Vice-Principal Arrested."

On the morning of Sunday, 10 August 1980 the police arrested the vice-principal at his home. They did so in the early hours of the morning and with an impressive show of force. Two squad cars of uniformed constables secured their prisoner, while another carload of detectives searched his house. A white transit van was also standing by, in case a significant bulk of goods needed to be seized in evidence.

In the absence of hard facts, the reporter, Mr Paddy Audley, had inflated the tale and threw in some quotation marks. To date, all he could confirm was that the charges were related to several allegations of gross indecency against children. An anonymous police source indicated that detectives had been investigating Mr Charles Bakewell for some time. Beyond that, the police could not release any specific details. I imagine Audley had a police source who tipped him off when a big case was breaking. He must have been delighted.

Scandal had come to Chancery Grammar School, but its courier was not the vice-principal Samuel had expected. The subsequent revelations would send out shock waves through the education system and the Christian community for years to come.

There are a few stock reactions when receiving news that undermines our fundamental beliefs. The most common is denial. After Joan had moderated her breathing and reread the article, she shook her head.

"I don't believe this," she said.

"You don't think he was arrested?" Betty asked.

"No. Yes. Of course he was arrested. But I'm sure it's greatly exaggerated. It's probably a misunderstanding." Joan's head continued to shake as she spoke. "Charlie cannot be guilty of this. Gross indecency? He is one of the most decent human beings I know. This is the work of Satan."

"I'm sure you're right, Joan," I lied.

Betty followed, "Yes, it's bound to be exaggerated. *The Chronicle* blows everything out of proportion."

Joan was silent for some time, while she chewed at the inside of her mouth. The colour had bled from her face completely. With a heaved breath she eventually said, "I can't stay here today, not while all this is going on. I'm going round to see Rita. Betty, log this as a sick day for me."

Betty replied, "I think we should all go home. We don't want to be here – especially if someone phones and asks about this." It was a sensible comment, especially as we lacked direction from the headmaster today.

"I agree," I said. "I'll stay and answer the phones. I think that should fall to the headmaster's secretary."

"Yes. Go home," Joan said. Her walk to the door was slow and mechanical. Her usual vigour had burned off and the last of her strength was spent in keeping herself upright.

It felt unusually lonely working in my own office, so I took Joan's empty station. The bigger office was almost no better and, when not interrupted by phone calls, I had time to reflect on the case against Charlie.

In a crisis, people revert to clichés. For this type of situation, the favourite is: 'There's no smoke without fire.' Without presuming him guilty, I considered the clues that had been before me. There was the injured boy in Charlie's bedroom at the Christian Union weekend. How Charlie had petitioned to have sex education moved out of biology and into Religious Education, so he could teach it. The complaints about his explicit discussions of sex in the classroom. How Charlie had placed himself at the hub of the pastoral system, where any concern about abuse would be investigated by him – a practice praised by the inspector Pauline McVickers. My personal fondness for Charlie had to be put aside. Regarding this

236

objectively, I had to admit, it did look substantial. Ultimately, it would be decided by the individual charges against him, and the number of his accusers.

Under normal circumstances, I would have expected Samuel to be in school, but since he was not, I phoned him at his new number – a small furnished flat outside Chancery. There was no answer. That could have meant a dozen things, but I was not in the mindset to speculate.

Between 9:00 a.m. and noon that morning, almost every phone call I received was from a reporter looking for Samuel Baxter. Few believed that he was not in school. Several of them asked me for a comment. There was no temptation to see my words appear in the national papers. I declined to comment.

Just before lunch, another call came through.

"Hello, Chancery Grammar School," I said.

"It is so good to hear a friendly voice." It was Samuel.

"Oh, Samuel. I tried to phone you earlier but couldn't get through."

"You have heard, then. Are the other secretaries in the General Office with you?"

"No. I sent them home."

"Good. I was about to do the same. I will brief them in the morning. No one is to say anything to the press."

"I have been saying 'no comment' all morning."

"Very good. I am with Rita Bakewell," he said, but I did not imagine she was within earshot. In a lower key, he said, "I will call this afternoon. You should go home now too."

This crisis was exactly what we needed to bind us together. It was my opportunity to prove myself indispensable to Samuel, just as I had done facing a scandal before. It was hard to imagine Pauline McVickers, a school inspector, holding by his side: she would need to get herself as far away as possible.

In the ten or so years that I had known Samuel, I had never known him to go a day without shaving. This day was an exception. His chin was frosted with patches of grey stubble. It was rough against my neck and cheek when I hugged him. His body had softened. No longer was he tight across the shoulders

237

and neck. His eyes were rheumy and glazed. Their broil had dimmed.

His breath shuddered while we embraced in my hall. I dared not pull back to look him in the face. He was proud and considered it weakness for a man to cry. My warmth brought the emotions surging from him. In public he could be the rock but, with me, he was exposed.

"We'll get through this," I whispered to him. "Together."

"This is my worst nightmare," he said, his voice cracking. "A scandal bigger than I could ever have imagined has crashed upon me."

His best friend was in prison, awaiting notice of whether he could be released on bail, and Samuel's thoughts were for himself. If anything, Samuel Baxter was consistent.

I drew back and looked up at him. "I don't believe for one instant that Charlie Bakewell is guilty of these crimes. Do you?" I said. This was the rallying speech I had outlined in my head.

"I pray he isn't." Samuel had taken up his Christianity again. "I can't believe he did those things. That is not the man we know," he said.

"There has been a misunderstanding. It will all blow over soon. His name will be cleared."

Samuel's brow slumped. "He – there were some complaints about him in the past, but I dealt with those. He explained them. They were minor things. I believed him. I still believe him. He is not a villain. This is some parent overreacting because they don't know how to look after their own children. They resent Charlie being close to their boys, when they aren't."

I knew that a change of topic was needed if anything good was to come of this liaison.

"You are worn out. I have the hot water on. I will run you a bath," I said.

He gave a half-shrug and kissed me on the forehead.

"Thank you, Rose. I knew I could rely on you," he said.

There was room enough for two in the bath. For a while at least, Samuel's brow uncreased. We moved from the bathroom to the bedroom, where I did my best to ease his troubled mind. The lull did not last long, however. Eventually, his thoughts returned to his predicament.

"They arrested him in the early hours of Sunday morning," he said. "It was just getting light. I suppose, at about the same time, the police phoned me. They said they wanted access to the school premises." His barrel chest filled up with a great breath. "Of course, I had no idea what they were on about. I thought it might be a prank call at first. But it was Inspector Walsh on the phone. I've met him before at various functions and he is distantly related to Boyce – chairman of the governors. He said Charlie had been arrested and explained why." Samuel paused to digest the memory. "Walsh said they had a warrant to search the school. They were only interested in Charlie's classroom, his office and any other areas where he may store his materials. They demanded his personnel file and anything I had on record about him." He shrugged. "What could I do? I had to cooperate. I met them at the school. There were about dozens of them, with two vans and squad cars. I had no idea what they were expecting to find."

"Did they take much?" I said.

"They filled one van with cardboard boxes. They emptied his drawers, filing cabinets, shelves, everything. I sat in the classroom next door and listened as they gutted the place."

After a long silence, I said, "Will you stay tonight?"

"The governors are having an emergency meeting. I have to be in school by 8:00 p.m.. I will return after that."

"Do you need me?"

"Very much, but it is a closed session. Much will be discussed, but very little of it will go in the minutes," he said.

Chapter Twenty-Two

It was the next morning and I was making us breakfast in my kitchen. Samuel had stayed the night again. He told me that the meeting of the Board of Governors had been very awkward, which was not unexpected in the circumstances.

"Boyce led the discussion," he said.

"Although, to call it a discussion would presume that the outcome of the meeting was a matter for speculation. Boyce is a businessman – a successful one at that. 'Get on the wrong side of him and he will make you regret it,' my predecessor, Dr Thompson, had advised me. He said if I won the governors over, I would thrive. I am certainly on their wrong side now."

"It's hardly your fault," I said.

"According to how they see it, it is very much my fault. Boyce told me there was no fire without smoke." Samuel frowned. "A clever turn of phrase, but his point was most serious: if during the proceedings, I am seen to be in any way at fault, then my head will be on the block too. In their opinion, I should have spotted the signs. I should have suspected my closest friend of being –"

"Well, let us hope it will not come to that," I said.

"I'm sure it will," he said. "I am not guilty of genuine wrong-doing: I was simply in the big chair when disaster struck. The governors are doing what they can to limit the damage. Charlie will be ordered to resign, innocent or not. They plan to meet with him if he is released on bail – which is not guaranteed. In their favour, Boyce did promise to reinstate Charlie, if he is proved innocent."

I could not bring myself to say 'poor Charlie.'

"From this point on, he is now to be described in the papers as 'former Vice-Principal Charles Bakewell.'" Samuel made quotation marks with his fingers as he said this. "His career is over. Even an innocent man could not recover from this. My career will probably follow."

I expected it would.

In less than a week, Charlie Bakewell had been bailed and released. Under the conditions of his bail, he was not to contact any pupils or ex-pupils of Chancery Grammar School. Neither

240

was he to return to the school premises while pupils were there. He was further to exclude himself from any activities that would bring him into contact with children. The detectives set about consolidating their case against Charlie. They would be investigating his past twenty years as a teacher in Chancery Grammar, contacting a significant number of his former pupils. If the initial charges were true, they would surely find more misconduct, if they dug deeply enough.

I wondered how poor Rita would receive her new husband upon his return.

The evening after Charlie's release – Friday, 29 August – the governors reconvened. It was another abrupt session, containing no discussion or debate.

"They must have met some time before this, without me," Samuel said to me later. He shook his head in disbelief. "Boyce spoke for everyone again. He had it all written down. Charlie was at my end of the table, beside me. The governors had clustered at the bottom end of the room, like we were diseased and contagious. Hardly one of them could look Charlie in the eye. There was no social chatter at that meeting, I assure you. They were there for an execution. All the governors heads were down, while Boyce read out the sentence." Samuel made a fist and held it to his lips. "Damn that Boyce. He is colder and harder than all the others combined. He spoke like a judge, without wavering, without emotion. *He* had no problem looking Charlie square in the eye."

"What did he say?"

"Effectively, that the accusations against Charlie made him a liability to the good name of the school. Boyce ordered him to accept a redundancy package that they had drawn up. He said it included a generous financial incentive to see him through this 'period of adjustment'. I remember that little euphemism." Samuel's fist reappeared. "Bastard!"

I had never before heard Samuel use unparliamentary language.

"Boyce said they had taken Charlie's twenty years of service into account. They offered him £35,000 but insisted on an immediate decision." Samuel took a deep breath and looked to

241

the ceiling. It was clearly an effort to prevent the gathering tears from cascading down his face. It failed.

I was glad we were in my home that evening and hugged him. He took several moments to compose himself and shear up the fractures in his voice. "Charlie sat in his chair like a dying man. He endured it all, like he had no reason left to live. All he said to them was, 'I understand why you are doing this.' And he took the money. £35,000 may sound like a lot of money, but Charlie is only forty-four. He is a long way from retirement."

I was thinking how the same governors had paid only £15,000 to get rid of an alcoholic. Crime did pay, after all. The greater the crime, the more money was required to send the perpetrator away. Not thinking it suitable to voice this, however, I said, "Did Charlie try to defend himself?"

Samuel shrugged. "He knew it was a *fait accompli*. At the end, just before he left, he said, 'I want you all to know that I am innocent. I did not do those things, but I don't blame you for how you are treating me.' I showed Charlie out but I could not linger with him. They were far from finished with me. I was next on the scaffold."

"He has always been a Christian example, Samuel. He will get through this. If anyone can, Charlie can do it," I said.

"I suppose so."

"And when you went back in?"

Samuel's face broke up into a flinty smile but his eyes had none of their old luminosity. "They couldn't look at me either – even Boyce had trouble facing *me* down. He told me to appoint a new vice-principal, one to replace Mr Bakewell." Samuel paused.

"There's nothing sinister in that," I said.

Samuel held up a finger. "He said the replacement should be someone capable of running the school, should the governors deem my resignation necessary."

"Oh!"

His smile collapsed under those words. "Boyce couldn't look at me when he said that last bit. I hope it tortures him to ruin an innocent man."

"Who did you recommend?" I asked.

"William Butler. He is best equipped to inherit this poisoned chalice."

"At least they aren't promoting Dawson," I said.

Samuel's smile returned. "That could be my ultimate revenge. I think they would see through that, however." He snorted at the irony. "That cockroach will outlast us all."

The detectives had been hard at work, since the initial complaint in July 1980 but it would be several months before the case came to trial. Joan had told me that, in her church, there was a prayer group asking the Lord to prove Charlie's innocence, that all might see His glory and come to believe. The optimists dwindled in number, however, as the nature of the allegations unravelled in the newspapers. Paddy Audley was aflame with sibilance and metaphor. A 'shock sex scandal shook Chancery,' apparently. *The Chronicle* declared our 'once proud grammar school' to be 'the sex scandal shamed school' or even 'the paedophile grammar school', if Audley was in danger of repeating himself. It was as if the systematic abuse of children had been our secret agenda all along. And almost one hundred and twenty years of hard-won achievement crumbled in an instant.

Audley cranked out stock characterisations of a villain, stalking the school corridors like a spectre with a taste for young boys' blood. Although he had probably never read the text, he likened Mr Bakewell to 'a Jekyll and Hyde character'. He theorised that Bakewell had cleverly manipulated his way into power with the sole purpose of controlling his prey. The fox had been put in charge of the chicken coup. Apparently, Bakewell had also held a spell-like sway over the headmaster, who would concede to any of his demands.

These caricatures were easier to broker than actually investigating the psychology of the man. The nature of his crimes was shocking in the public mind, and any attempt at empathy with him would have been reviled. No one could try to understand this kind of man. For the sake of the children, the people guilty of these offences must be burned in effigy by the whole community. No one could stand beside them and continue to be accepted.

Behind the hyperbole and generalisation, however, there lay the conspicuous truth. Even before the trial concluded, there was a sense of inevitability. The accused had to be guilty. Paddy Audley's unnamed police source was often paraphrased when he reported any updates in the case. The very number of charges that the police had brought to court, seven in all – each from a different accuser – demonstrated that the accused could not be innocent. It was not one isolated complaint from someone with a grudge or an anti-Christian agenda, as many of the faithful had believed. According to the 'police source' there were several other complainants, all young men now, who had refused to come to court.

It did not seem likely, then, that the Lord's strong arm would be flexing itself for Charlie Bakewell.

The optimistic became confused. If they were smart enough, in time, the enlightening power of cynicism would set them free.

It had worked for me.

Since the case against Charlie had developed, I had been able to account for all of Samuel's movements. When Helen had expelled him from the family home, he had taken up in a small furnished flat just outside Chancery. Now he was living with me. When he was not with me in school, he was with me at home. Having him all to myself again, I made sure he was well occupied. I was determined to get pregnant. That I had full possession of him, entirely for my own use, was a victory over his other mistress, Pauline McVickers.

Six months later, in February 1981, the Crown was ready to bring its case against Charlie Bakewell to court. In the lead up to this, the majority of the school staff had been interviewed by detectives. Hardly any substantial lines of enquiry were developed, however, as few staff had anything more than personal opinion or anecdote against him. A number were quoted as saying they had concerns about Charlie for some time, but none had passed these on to the headmaster.

Samuel was very thoroughly questioned. Every incident was brought before him. His memorandums and professional responses were scrutinised. The detectives' questions mostly focused on whether he had known about the abuse, and why he had not done enough to follow up the significant complaints he had received. It was an especially harrowing time for Samuel that aged him physically and caused him to shed a stone in weight.

244

I was extremely thankful that the trial took place during term time. It was not something that I was keen to sit through, but I attended the first one with Samuel, who was required to be available, lest he be called as a witness. From then on, he attended on his own and found it extremely exhausting. Most difficult to bear, was the sight of his best friend in the dock, lashed with outrageous accusations. Samuel was also terrified that either the defence or prosecution counsels would call him to clarify some point.

While the court was preoccupied with assessing Charlie Bakewell's guilt, *The Chancery Chronicle* attributed blame much more liberally. Paddy Audley would not be denied his coverage of this scandal. Samuel watched impotently as the reporter scribbled feverish notes during the trial. Audley even had the impudence to ask for the headmaster's comment at the close of the day's proceedings. Samuel, of course, said nothing.

"Charlie explained this incident to me," Samuel said and waved his hand over the newspaper on his desk. It was a Thursday evening, late in February, and we were still at school. Samuel had asked me to stay with him when he had seen what was in that day's paper.

Audley, I am sure, was delighted to report that the father of one of the complainants had phoned Mr Samuel Baxter. After a brief consultation with Bakewell, the accusation had been dismissed as the concerns of an overly solicitous parent. The headmaster had not investigated the concern thoroughly.

"What was the accusation?" I asked.

Samuel looked uncomfortable, and it was a moment before he answered. "The father complained that Charlie had rubbed talc into his son's groin."

"Oh!"

"Charlie said that was an exaggeration. He said he had rubbed it on his back but had flicked it round the rest of the boy. He didn't want the child getting sores from being damp."

"And you believed him?"

"It was Charlie," he said, like that should explain. "He is my best friend. Of course, I believed him. I thought he was just being too paternal, that's all. We did have cross words about it. I told him he had to stop smothering the boys. He quoted the

Bible: 'Suffer the little children —" Samuel flicked his hand at the rest. After a moment's consideration, he continued. "Actually, you walked into him while he was leaving. You two nearly collided in that doorway." He gestured to our adjoining door.

I remembered it well. I had mistaken Charlie's dark expression for reproach when Samuel had told him of our affair. How blinkered I had been, to think that everything pertained to me.

"Now it looks like I helped a serial child abuser," Samuel said. He put his hands over his face. I went round to his side of the desk and cushioned his head against my stomach.

"Anyone would have given their friend the benefit of the doubt," I said.

Still seated, Samuel put his arms around me and sobbed.

"People will understand. The governors will know you were protecting the good name of the school." His sobbing continued and I looked down at him. He needed me.

Gradually, Samuel recomposed himself and stood. He restored his embrace and held me for a long time before speaking again. "I am sorry, Rose. I shouldn't be disgracing myself in front of you."

"There is no disgrace. I am here for you, as I promised I would be." I tried to remember if I had actually promised that. It sounded appropriate all the same.

He nodded to the *Chronicle* on his desk. "That rag implicates me. Audley has made me out to be complicit in —" He did not finish.

"You did what you thought was right, Samuel."

"That was not enough, though."

I paused before asking my next question. "Was that the only incident you knew of?"

He shook his head, then buried it in my neck. Warm tears ran freely off his face.

While the Thursday news report had been bad for Samuel, the Friday one was savage. Three more plaintiffs alleged that they or their parents had complained to the headmaster about Bakewell's improper conduct. These accounts came on the same day in court because the accusations were being dealt with

246

chronologically. It seemed Bakewell had been much more flagrant when his good friend was headmaster.

One incident particularly turned my stomach. The identities of the complainants were protected by the courts, but I wondered if I had crossed paths with this young man. The alleged incident dated back to October 1975, at a Christian Union Society weekend. The boys had been engaged in a pillow fight in one of the dormitories and the plaintiff had received a head injury. Bakewell had taken the lad to his own room and administered first aid. There was a spare bunk bed available in Bakewell's room and he had insisted the boy sleep there. The youngster had been keen to please his favourite teacher, after disappointing him with his misbehaviour. Bakewell had promised to watch over him, lest he had sustained a concussion. During the night, however, the lad was awakened as his teacher groped him, his arm deep inside the boy's sleeping bag. The boy cried out before scuttling back to his own room and the safety of his fellows.

While the council for the defence attempted to discredit this allegation, it was another clear example of the accused's depravity. My biggest outrage was that the clownish Charlie Bakewell I had known had never really existed. I had seen this boy, asleep on the bottom bunk and thought nothing more of it. The more I read, the more I found myself agreeing with Audley's assessment of Charlie as a predator.

Samuel's negligence was highlighted when the young man testified that his father's complaint to the school had been trivialised by the headmaster. The portrait of Samuel Baxter was that of a credulous fool. The headmaster's reply to the father – and it was read to the court – was that Mr Bakewell had been checking the boy's body temperature for fear he had slipped into a coma, brought on by his head injury. Bakewell had also told the headmaster that the boy had been crying out in his sleep and was probably delirious at the time. At no stage had Mr Baxter forwarded these abuse allegations to Social Services, the Education Board or the Board of Governors.

I worked hard all weekend to assuage Samuel's fears. All my efforts were undone the following Monday morning.

247

As usual, the week started with a full school assembly. Each year group would cluster in designated bands across the width of the hall. The first formers stood at the front of the hall just before the stage, the upper sixth boys were at the back. Staff interspersed themselves along the avenues between the year groups and up each side of the hall.

I had been to few of these events myself, but I knew how Samuel liked to conduct them. Each followed the same principles of ceremony: announcements, act of worship, homily, benediction. There was reassurance in routine, after all.

As a measure of how stressed Samuel had been that day, he had forgotten to pick up the announcement sheet I had for him. He could not possibly have remembered all the day's items without it. As soon as I realised his oversight, I snatched it and dashed towards the assembly hall.

Normally, a senior member of staff at the front of the hall would be keeping an eye on the back corner of the stage for the headmaster and vice-principals. Silence would then be called, while the triumvirate waited in the wings. It was at this point that I reached Samuel. He, William Butler and Jack Dawson all turned to see who was clopping down the side of the stage towards them. In the wings it was shadowy but there was no mistaking Samuel's squared form, shorter than Butler and wider than Dawson.

"Your announcement sheet, Headmaster. Sorry, I forgot to give it to you." I whispered, aware that the assembly hall was fidgety but quiet.

Samuel tilted his head and nodded. "Mrs Maylie, you are indispensable," he whispered back.

"We were just having a panic," Dawson said, leaning a little too close.

When my eyes adjusted to the gloom, I saw Butler had a pen and scribbled note in his hands. He made no acknowledgement of my assistance, though: now that he was a vice-principal, he was civil to his subordinates only when he required their assistance. He knew how his career would unfold.

"My thanks again, Mrs Maylie," Samuel said. "Gentlemen." And they paraded in wedge formation to the centre of the stage. For the novelty of seeing Samuel in command, I remained and watched. My heels would certainly have disturbed the peace, had

248

I retreated across the stage. The wedge formation swung slightly until Samuel was perpendicular to the grand lectern, front centre of the stage. The headmaster, with royal prerogative, surveyed the assembled body. Their uniformity, the ordered rows, the upturned faces pleased him. It was something over which he was still master, when all else spiralled out of control.

Then the pupils began to hiss.

It must have been prearranged by the sixth forms, for that is where it started. From the back of the room it issued like poisonous gas. Boys in other forms understood the message and joined in but few at the front would put themselves at risk.

I stepped out from the wings, giving myself a quarter view of the hall.

Samuel drew in a massive breath and braced the lectern with his thick arms. It shook when he roared into the microphone that trembled in front of him.

"Si-lence!" His face was contorted and his mouth snarled with horror and rage.

The ferocity of his bellowing cowed the majority of boys for a moment.

"This behaviour will not be tolerated!" he spat his words and the lectern quaked. The microphone and speakers squawked with feedback, as the equaliser had only been set for normal speech levels. The feedback became a persistent whine as if it joined in the chorus of disapproval.

The hissing had briefly subsided as the headmaster's fury crashed through them, but it never completely died.

"You are dismissed!" he roared.

"No, *you* are dismissed!" some anonymous heckler shouted from the back ranks. That brought scattered laughter and, with it, a new wave of bravado that revived the hisses.

"Staff, move the boys through the exits," the headmaster ordered. Slowly, the boys obeyed. The hissing dwindled then died as the boys skulked through the doors.

Samuel remained in place. His hands crushed the rim of the lectern while he surveyed the student body for ringleaders. He needed to make an example of someone. Any boy who was laughing at his expense would do. But none presented themselves. They were unnaturally sullen as they shuffled out of the hall.

Another step forward brought me a full view of the hall.

Only the staff remained in place. Some lined its edges, some stood between the vanished year groups. Very few of them had helped the headmaster. Samuel's gaze swept over them, noting those he could. Then he pivoted on his heel and strode to the rear stage door. His eyes were locked far ahead of him. His vice-principals duly followed. There was a distinct smugness to both their grins, but only Dawson acknowledged me with a wink.

For the lack of anything better to do, I returned to my office. I had never seen Samuel so angry and was not confident he would want company very soon after that traumatic event. Ten minutes after the bell for period one, my intercom crackled: "Rose, come in, please." It was most unusual for Samuel to address me informally over the intercom. Anyone could have been standing in my office. I did not reply to the intercom but hurried in at once.

Samuel was slouched on the sofa. He had not even taken the trouble to remove his academic gown. He normally wore this to assembly and on patrol around the school but avoided sitting in it because it creased easily. He slumped there like a man who had forgotten dignity. "Lock the doors," he said, waving his hand. "Tilt the blinds. Then come and hold me."

When I was finally by his side, Samuel stretched out, resting his head on my lap. It was in this position that it had all started, all those years previously.

"I'm sorry you had to see that," he said but his voice lacked its normal resonance. "I assure you, my assemblies are never like that." Needless to say, it would be his last.

"They need someone to blame," I said. "You shouldn't take it personally."

"No. It was very personal. But the real damage is professional. That will get back to the governors. If Butler is half the sycophant I think he is, he will contact Boyce directly. I am ruined."

I agreed with his assessment but said nothing. My job was to show him support. I stroked his head and the cracks in his face gradually eased apart, leaving only creases.

"I have always tried to do the right thing in my life," he continued. "I never believed Charlie could do those things. There was always an explanation that was easier to believe than face the alternative. I trusted Charlie."

"Do you still think he is innocent?"

"How can I?" he said. "If the testimony against him is true, he is not the man I thought I knew. But it is not as if the complaints were put before me all at once. In court, they are discussed all together, but for me they were spread over many years."

We stayed there another half hour before the phone rang to disturb us. We ignored it, but it was enough to announce that he could not remain hidden in his office.

I wanted to ask him what he would do, after losing his job. Wisdom told me that might not be a sensitive question.

I would have to wait until he had been reduced to nothing.

Samuel's meeting with the governors was on the evening of Tuesday, 24 February 1981. It was the same day Charles Bakewell was found guilty of four charges of gross indecency and sentenced to seven years in prison. The conviction caused Samuel much dark brooding but he said very little. He was more preoccupied with his own fate.

No moss would be found growing on James Boyce, Chairman of the Board of Governors. He had phoned Samuel at work as soon as the verdict had been announced. His words had been terse and unambiguous: the Board of Governors were meeting and Samuel was required to attend.

"I want you there with me, Rose," Samuel said, standing beside my desk.

"If you wish. Will the governors allow it?"

"I no longer care. I am through trying to please them. Tonight they will hang me for doing what I thought was in the best interests of the school." He gathered charge like a dynamo as he spoke.

I placed my hand over the fist he had made on my desk. "Damn them," I said, quietly. "I will record their kangaroo court on my notepad."

"Yes. Record everything. My speech is ready." He patted his breast pocket.

251

Chapter Twenty-Three

The meeting was to begin at 7:30 p.m.. Samuel and I had not left the building at the end of the school day. We made the most of his office sofa while we still could and were already seated in the boardroom at 7:10 p.m., when the first of the governors arrived.

Samuel had wanted to have some control of the situation. On that evening there was none of his usual welcoming palaver as the governors straggled in. They could find their own way and sit before us in uncomfortable silence until Boyce was ready to begin. Their physical discomfort was almost amusing. Mr Tweed, the first to arrive, had possibly assumed that the boardroom would be empty. Too late, he walked through the door to see Samuel and I already there. His step jolted and he looked back up the corridor. Finding no allies there, he decided to brave our company.

"Hello," he said, but Samuel only nodded. I looked down to my notepad.

Mr Tweed, quite predictably, sat at the far end of the grand table. He looked around uncomfortably. The school's once proud forefathers looked back from the walls. No one spoke.

Two more governors arrived together. Their conversation stopped abruptly when they saw Samuel at the head of the table. Again, they took up seats at the far end of the room. Before very long, eleven governors were in attendance. They waited on Boyce, their chairman, before proceedings could begin. There was a sullenness to the atmosphere, a fatal seriousness to every man. None of them exchanged anything beyond a greeting with their colleagues.

Samuel Baxter sat like a monument to Caesar. He did not stir in the long minutes while his jury assembled.

Finally, Boyce arrived. His dyed cardboard comb-over hairstyle was like a black cloth on his head. He carried two large envelopes under his arm. He stood at the door a moment and regarded his headmaster. Boyce had a flair for the dramatic. If Samuel had returned his stare it would have become a contest. But Samuel was immovable and his face expressionless pointed straight ahead.

Boyce laid an envelope in front of Samuel and strode to his seat at the opposing end of the table.

Samuel's eyes flicked down to the foolscap envelope but he did not move to retrieve it. His left hand remained clenched in his lap, his right closed over it. To fetch the documents would have been to surrender his control. He would not be dictated to at this late stage.

Boyce sat amidst his colleagues and scanned their faces. A few nodded for the proceedings to begin. "Mr Baxter," Boyce said, opening his envelope and reading from his first document.

Samuel's eyes bore into him across the long table.

"We are aware that these past six months have been harrowing for you. The strain of a child sex abuse scandal has caused all of us great concern. Now that Charles Bakewell has been pronounced guilty, the school will become the focus of an investigation. The manner in which these allegations were dealt with will be a matter for close scrutiny. Doubtless the press will be involved, along with the Education Inspectorate. They will be looking for a scapegoat, someone to blame for their mismanagement of these allegations." Boyce cleared his throat. "We acknowledge your commitment to the school through five years of solid development. In this time you have expanded the pupil intake, improved the school buildings and brought this old establishment into the twentieth century. We are, therefore, grieved to hear of the ill health that has been brought on by the pressure of recent events."

This was not the trial that Samuel was expecting. I looked at him from the side. His eyes had narrowed and the fist in his lap was drawn tight.

Few of the governors could sustain eye contact, as Samuel had observed before.

"As much as it pains us," Boyce said, "We understand and regretfully accept your tendered resignation."

Samuel flinched. He was not ill. He had not offered to resign. This was a sentencing rather than a trial. The defendant was not required to testify in his own defence.

Boyce paused. He may have expected the headmaster to protest. Beyond a cold stare, Samuel did nothing.

"In that case, " Boyce resumed, "your press statement has been prepared. You will find it in the envelope, along with your P45. As you will be on sick leave for the remainder of the

253

academic year, you will continue to receive your monthly salary. Until then, Mr Butler has agreed to act up."

Boyce was locked in a stare down with Samuel.

In uncomfortable circumstances, a minute can seem like a very long time.

"Do I even get to speak in my own defence?" Samuel said.

"No," Boyce replied.

A few of the governors shifted their positions.

"And if I choose not to play along with your game?" Samuel said with a hiss.

"You will be fired, on the spot, for gross misconduct," Boyce replied. There was no bluff in his flat expression.

Samuel, no doubt, considered himself out of options. He could accept this face-saving withdrawal with four months' more pay, or his contract would be terminated on the spot.

The former headmaster rose steadily. He lifted his envelope and left the boardroom without a backward glance.

When my eyes returned from the closing door it was to see all the governors watching me. Suddenly, I was very out of place. "Shall I go too?" I asked, my voice tiny with humiliation.

Boyce nodded.

I had written nothing on my notepad.

On my way past the headmaster's study, I called in. I had expected Samuel to be saying farewell to his former domain, but he was not there. Neither was his car in its parking place.

When I arrived home, I saw he had parked in my driveway. He had his own front door key and was already inside. I forgave him for not waiting for me at the school. He must have bolted from there as soon as possible. It was most telling that he had fled to a place of comfort. And he knew that I would be following close behind. He was waiting for me in the lounge and patted the sofa beside him when I entered.

I sat beside him, angled towards him on the edge of the sofa. "I am glad that's over with," I said.

His voice was steady as he spoke. "I am glad that is over too. I have been preparing for that since Charlie was arrested." He patted my hand.

"What will you do now that you are no longer Headmaster?"

He blinked heavily at the reminder then squeezed my hand. "Rose, this is an opportunity for us to make a new beginning." His face was earnest and his eyes were a weak, watery light. "I will be going away from Chancery and I want you to come with me." He searched my face for a reaction. Quickly, he offered more detail. "My sister runs a branch of the family business in Trentford. She has allowed me to buy into it and assume partnership in its running. I never expected to go into teaching in the first place, if you recall. I know the retail business because that is what I grew up with. It seems a fitting way to occupy myself until retirement."

"I see," I said. "And you want me to go with you?" I said.

He stared at me. "Rose, I want you to marry me."

I laughed with all the scorn that I could muster.

"Only six months ago, you made a fresh start with that McVickers woman," I said, sneering. "Where is she now?"

He recoiled as if I had slapped his face.

"I would no sooner marry you than return to Harry," I said. "There was a time I dreamed of you proposing. But now you are a *nothing*." I emphasised that last word. "I can find a shop keeper to bed in any high street." The bile I had stored up for the last six months poured freely. In the back of my mind lingered the regret that I was not yet pregnant. I had not planned to play the last of my cards this soon, but Samuel's proposal brought it all forward.

Samuel was wide-eyed and slack-jawed. He had no idea who I was.

"You are a treacherous snake," I said. "I have known about McVickers since your paedophile best friend's wedding." His eyes widened. "Helen and I had quite the conversation. She told me about your extra Samaritan evenings and I knew straight away. I even gave her the evidence of your adultery."

He eventually rallied to defend himself from the surprise attack. "Don't talk nonsense woman. How could you have?" he said.

"Helen confronted you with your credit card statements. Did you never guess how she got them?"

"She told me that she used my work keys to look through my study desk," he said. His eyes narrowed in disgust. "Did you help her do that?"

255

"Help her? It was me!" I exalted. "I ordered a copy of your key from the locksmiths – just as I did for Dawson's filing cabinet. I did it on the night of Charlie's wedding." Here, I paused for effect. I had practised this speech a dozen times. "And I went through *all* your drawers. And I didn't just copy your credit card statements."

Samuel Baxter exhaled heavily and his head shook. He put a waxen hand up to his temple to steady it. "You..." He could not find the air to finish.

"I photocopied every note, every memo, every complaint you filed on Charlie Bakewell. You tucked them in a folder at the back of the drawer, where no one would ever think to look."

He stared at me with absolute horror. "You can't have."

"Yes. I photocopied everything and gave it to the police! They were most appreciative. Until then, they had an open folder on Bakewell but didn't have enough to prosecute. My parcel got their investigation rolling nicely."

Samuel plucked at his collar. He struggled to rise from the sofa and swayed as he did so. After two steps he turned slowly to regard me. His frown amused me. "You deliberately set out to ruin me?" he muttered.

"When I heard from Helen how much you had lied to me, yes," I said. "You lied about leaving Helen, about your children not wanting to live up at university. You had me as a plaything but had no intention of committing." The words spat from me. "I wasted five years on you and you would have strung me out further had Helen not confronted you. So, yes, I went in search of evidence to end your marriage. It was just my good luck to find evidence of your corruption – or incompetence – too!"

He stood shaking his head. "Have you hated me for six months? How cold you are to play your part so convincingly."

"You taught me that," I said, for I did not like the truth I heard.

"And what did you teach me?" he replied. "To be an adulterer; to deceive and cover my tracks."

"You were a natural at that! All I wanted was a good husband and to be a mother. But you gave me nothing."

Now it was his turn to laugh. "Was that why we had all the sex? Because you want to be a mother? You must have stopped your pill in August, then?"

256

"April," I said with gritted teeth.

His smile stretched and he nodded. "I had a vasectomy after the twins were born. I was never going to give you children."

It was my turn to reel with shock.

"Get out!" I yelled at him. I had nothing left with which to hurt him.

Beside his car, Samuel wrung my front door key from his chain and tossed it onto the driveway. I stood at my door, reminded of how I had seen Harry off in similar circumstances. When Samuel's car cleared the drive and whisked off, out of my life, I was once again confronted by the emptiness.

From August, I had spun out my deception, in a plan inspired by Harry's mistress, with my own finesse at the end. I planned to strip my man of everything, making him completely reliant on me. Then I would extract his seed. There I deviated from Harry's woman. I saw no point in keeping the man around after that. He could offer me nothing.

Little did I know, he had never offered me anything anyway. My plan was a failure from its inception. All I had was revenge; and that was not enough.

That was the last time I ever spoke to Samuel Baxter. He obeyed the school governors and saw out the rest of his academic year on leave, allegedly because of ill health. No doctor's certificate was ever required or produced, however. For all I know, he moved to Trentford and bought into the family business again.

In many ways, Samuel was fortunate to escape the fallout that Bakewell's guilty verdict brought. The few devout souls who had believed Satan was campaigning against Charlie fell silent. They were crushed by the volume who said they had always suspected something had been 'not quite right' about him.

Of all the people I knew closely, Joan was most deeply affected. She took a long period of sickness, and, when she was in the office, had less of her old verve. Part of her trouble may have been that Charlie continued to deny his guilt. She visited him regularly – one of the few who would – and counselled him through what had happened. Her conflict came from a realisation that her friend avoided the truth about himself, a truth with which she had struggled to reconcile herself. Joan eventually retired at the end of June 1986. She was fifty-nine and close enough to retirement to be able to afford the wait. She took a part-time job in the local library to keep herself active.

As soon as William Butler assumed his role as acting headmaster, I requested a transfer back to the General Office. I had always missed being in close contact with Joan and Betty. I had never been particularly fond of Mr Butler either. He readily granted my request. The ink was not yet dry on the memo before he had me typing the job advertisement for *The Trentford Telegraph*. I was surprised he did not offer *The Chancery Chronicle* the business, after the wonders it had done for his career.

A temporary secretary was found from an agency while the selection process was duly observed. The new headmaster's secretary, Dorothy Butler, was appointed after a rigorous interview process. She was judged to have been the best candidate at interview and she came with several years experience in a school office. At least she would not have to endure after hours dictation sessions.

Betty Trent and Jack Dawson never did connect romantically. Betty met a cardiologist one evening when she was looking her finest, and they both had the good sense to exchange phone numbers over breakfast. They married a year later. Betty handed in her notice three days after returning from her honeymoon. She was not going to live off her new husband; he would loan her the money to set up her own patisserie in Chancery. This enterprise has since flourished into a well known local chain of with shops.

Still a vice-principal, Jack Dawson is one of John Souseman's occasional drinking partners. I know little else about his private affairs except that he is unmarried and untroubled by it.

Nearly two years after my split from Samuel, John told me there was a house for sale in his village. When I thought about moving, I considered it a daunting prospect. New, unfamiliar walls have fewer echoes than old ones, but they lack the imprint of memory we associate with time and place. In my old house, I had loved and cried; the men I had loved had sheltered there with me. To move to a new house would have severed my attachments.

After a long, common sense discussion, John suggested that I move in with him. The money from the sale of my house could be put toward building an extension to his house. This was no romantic settlement. John and I had established long ago that our relationship could only be platonic. It was a pragmatic arrangement. We were at ease in each other's company and neither of us looked forward to growing old alone.

Seeing my indecision, John put his own house up for sale – an act of commitment that shamed any a man had ever made on my behalf. His house was quickly 'Sale Agreed' and he moved in with me six weeks later to occupy the second of my three bedrooms. At first, there was an inevitable awkwardness. John was most considerate, however, and we settled into a lifestyle rhythm that continues to this day.

Denied easy access to a pub up the road, John's drinking remains under control. He has one pub night a fortnight with Jack Dawson. I have no expectations of John's behaviour, except that he keeps a tidy home and lowers the toilet seat before flushing. We are cohabitants, not a couple. As I own my house outright, John does not need to pay rent or a share of the mortgage – not that it would have been a problem. We split all bills down the middle and share household tasks equally.

Honestly, I find it a relief to be in a relationship that does not require me to attend, please or perform. I do not miss the intimacy either. In many respects, John and I are like an old married couple: sexless, independent and comfortably conjoined. Living together for six years, I can honestly say I am as content as I have ever been. I admit to loving John and I expect he loves me.

Spurred on by John, I left secretarial work behind and enrolled in Trentford University to read English Literature. It was upsetting to break from my familiar old routine, but it was also invigorating. The young people with whom I shared my lectures and tutorials seemed clueless to their good fortunes, having both youth and opportunity. But I made the absolute most of my studies and secured a first class honours degree. It is reassuring that, in some things at least, effort is equal to reward.

I enjoyed university so much, that I have stayed on to study a masters degree, with a dissertation on Charles Dickens that will soon require my attention. After that, I suppose, I may continue my retreat into books and work on a doctorate. Perhaps, I will even teach.

There will never be any children or grandchildren in my future. Adoption is out of the question for an unmarried couple, especially when one of them is an alcoholic. I could blame my worthless lovers for cheating me of this life treasure but that would be too simple. I have to accept my own part in granting them a position of trust.

Eventually, I did get myself a tom cat, but I took the precaution of having him neutered.

6541455R00154

Printed in Great Britain
by Amazon.co.uk, Ltd.,
Marston Gate.